A.M. Myers

Wicked Games

A.M. Myers

Wicked Games

Bayou Devils MC
Book Eight

A.M. Myers

Wicked Games

A.M. Myers

Cover Design by Jay Aheer
Proofreading by Julie Deaton

Wicked Games

Chapter One
Rowan

"Are you guys ready for our little dark-haired beauty?" Max, Skin's resident DJ asks, his booming voice full of energy as it echoes off the walls of the club. The men scattered around the room barely look up from their drinks to give him a few seconds of unenthusiastic applause and I grit my teeth as I shake my hands out and stretch for my dance. Just like them, I wish I was anywhere else but here tonight. Max glances over at me and offers me an apologetic look but I shake my head. I don't blame him for the poor attitude in this place right now. He's a damn good DJ but I think it would take an act of God to rouse the spirits of the people in this club. Sighing, he raises the microphone to his lips again and winks in my direction. I straighten my body and suck in a breath.

Showtime.

"Welcome to the stage... Raven!" He drags my stage name out for emphasis and I roll my eyes. Mr. Alexander, my boss, thought he was so clever when he assigned that nickname to me since I'm the only girl at this club with dark hair. At first, I embraced it - making myself seem more mysterious than I really am but the more I hear it shouted through the speakers, the more it grates on my nerves. My song begins to play - "Sweet Dreams" by Marilyn Manson - and like an elastic band snapping into place, I feel myself becoming Raven as I step out onto the stage and strut toward the center in my six-inch platform heels. As I wrap my fingers around the cool metal of the pole, I look around the room and try to fight back my disgust at the disinterested expressions staring back at me. Some of them are leaning back in their chairs and sipping their drinks while others are obviously drowning their pain in booze and faceless women. In the end, though, it all boils down to the same thing. There isn't a single person that wants to spend their Thanksgiving in a seedy strip club instead of with family but some of us don't have any other option.

As much as I would love to run out of here and never look back, it's almost as if Raven has taken over my body and I find myself hooking my leg around the pole and slowly spinning as my mind drifts to the last Thanksgiving we all had as a real family... before everything fell apart. It was years ago - before Dad died, before Nora was killed, and before Lincoln ran away to escape the pain that seems to haunt us in this town, leaving Mom and me all alone. Pain swarms my chest and tears sting my eyes as I squeeze them shut, trying to fight back the memories and focus on the swing of my hips and the beat of the song but it's too late. The dam has been opened and I'm not strong enough to hold it all back tonight. Sucking in a ragged breath, I open my eyes, grab the pole again, and jump up before flipping upside down and opening my legs into a "V". On any other day, there would be cheering and men throwing money onto the stage as they looked up at me like I was some kind of goddess but as I look out at the crowd, all I can see is my own sorrow reflected back at me.

The song stretches on as I right myself and slide back down the pole, trying my damnedest not to break down in front of all these people as more memories flood my mind. I was so young when Dad's plane went down during a typical supply run but the memory is still so damn clear - the look on Lincoln's face when he came home with the police officers, Mom collapsing to her knees as she wailed and Nora and I staring at each other with wide eyes because we couldn't understand what was going on. It was like all the grownups were talking in code and no one would just come right out and say that he was gone. At least, I don't think they did but maybe I blocked it out in an act of self-preservation. Leaning back against the pole, I close my eyes again as my lip wobbles and my heart hammers in my chest.

Goddamn it.

I cannot lose it up here.

Gritting my teeth, I open my eyes, reach over my head, and grab the pole before sinking down into a crouch and arching my back so my hips lift forward. Reaching behind my back, I pull on one of the strings of my top, allowing it to come undone so I can toss it across the stage. One of the men in front of me glances up, his eyes locked onto my tits as he tosses some money on the stage before going back to his drink - whiskey, if I had to guess - and, despite the awful feeling building in my stomach, I force myself to keep going. Most nights, I can rake in a couple hundred bucks but in the four hours I've been here tonight, I've only managed to make somewhere around fifty dollars and honestly, it's not even worth the trouble. I probably wouldn't have even come in if I had any other option than sitting in my apartment alone with Ramen noodles and my overwhelming grief.

Sliding onto my belly along the stage, I pull my knees to my stomach, shoving my ass into the air as the final notes of the song ring out through the club and another man tosses a few dollar bills onto the stage as I grab the pole and stand up. Raven, the consummate professional, can't stop herself from bowing despite the lack of applause and my stomach flips as I grab the money littering the floor and my top before disappearing behind the curtain. As I descend the stairs from the stage, I glance down at the money in my hand and scoff. Fifty dollars. That brings my total to maybe a hundred for the evening, if I'm lucky. If nothing else, I guess it will pay for my groceries for the next week. With a sigh, I grab my silk robe off of the hook and slip it on, tying the belt around my waist.

"Rowan," Mr. Alexander calls from his office door just before I duck into the dressing room and I glance up, arching a brow. "How did you do tonight?"

I make a face and hold up the fifty dollars I made on my last dance and he nods.

"Why don't you head home, then? We're not even breaking even at this point and I'm just going to shut 'er down early."

Nodding, I force a smile to my face. "Sounds good, Mr. Alexander. Thanks."

"Tell the other girls to pack up as well, will you?" he asks and I nod again.

"Sure thing."

He flashes me a thankful smile before ducking back into his office and I step into the dressing room and sit down at my vanity by the door before turning to the three other girls working tonight.

"Mr. Alexander is shutting down early tonight. We can all head home."

"Thank God," Hannah sighs, shoving her heels off and they hit the floor with a clunk. "My feet are fucking killing me."

Michelle tosses her eyeliner down on the vanity in front of her and grabs a makeup wipe. "Maybe I can get home in time to tuck my kids in for bed. They were so mad when I had to leave for work earlier."

"What about you, Row?" Jen asks. "Any big plans for your suddenly free evening?"

I shake my head, trying to ignore the burning in my chest as I think about the empty apartment I'll be going home to. "Nope. Ash flew up to Juneau to see his parents for the holiday and won't be back until tomorrow so it's just me and my Netflix account tonight."

"Girl," Hannah says, shaking her head. "That's even better. Stop and grab yourself a bottle of wine and get a little "you" time."

Nodding, I turn back to my mirror and pull off my fake eyelashes with a sigh. "I might just have to do that."

It really doesn't sound all that appealing but then again, nothing does. There is nowhere in this town I want to be and very few places that I feel comfortable anymore. I guess it sounds better than sitting at home and thinking about all of the shit I've been trying to avoid all night long. And it sure as hell sounds better than being here.

As the girls start getting ready to go home, moving in a flurry of activity around me, I stare at myself in the mirror. I don't recognize the girl staring back at me or the growing darkness creeping into my eyes more and more everyday and I sigh, dropping my head as I fight back tears again.

"Ten minutes, girls!" Mr. Alexander calls and I suck in a breath, wiping away a stray tear as I stand up and walk back to my locker, grabbing my bag out of the bottom. I change clothes as quickly as possible before pulling my boots on and shoving all of my things back into my bag.

"How did you do tonight?" Jen asks with disgust in her voice and I pull the bills out of my bag before quickly counting it and sighing.

"Ninety bucks."

She sighs. "Well, you did better than me. I'm going to have to pull an extra shift this week just to make up for this shit show of a night."

"Yeah," I answer, already exhausted as I think about spending an extra night here to make up for the money I didn't make today. As it is, I already work five nights a week and I desperately need the other two away from this place to keep me sane.

"I think the girls in the bar did better than we did tonight."

I scoff. "I'm not surprised. Everyone was more interested in drowning their sorrows than watching us dance."

"Tomorrow will be better," she mutters to herself and I can't help but smile. I've known Jen for a few years now and that is always something she says whenever she has a bad night, her way of letting it all go so she doesn't take the stress of the day home with her. At first, I thought it was silly but over time, I found myself doing the same and it usually works pretty well.

"All right," I sigh, standing up and grabbing my bag off of the bench. "I'm going to head home. See you tomorrow."

She nods with a smile. "Have a good night, Rowan."

"Two minutes, girls," Mr. Alexander calls as the rest of the girls pack up and I weave my way through the dressing room toward the back door before stepping outside. Cold air smacks me in the face and I shiver, pulling my coat tighter around my body as I walk across the snow-covered lot to my car. Snowflakes whirl around me and I can't help but smile. I've always loved the snow and when I was little, I would wait all year for the first big storm so my dad and I could build a snowman or have a snowball fight. Now, every time it snows, I get this bittersweet feeling in my chest because as much as I love all of the memories I have with my dad, it still hurts like hell. My mind drifts to my most recent loss and tears sting my eyes as I try to breathe through the pain.

Glancing up, I spot my car in the back of the lot and hit the button on my key fob to unlock the car as I quicken my pace, fighting back more memories. Fuck. This past month has been absolute hell and I really don't know how much more I can take. When I reach the car, I open the door and slip behind the wheel before starting it and crossing my arms over my chest to ward off the cold. Another wave of pain washes through me as I glance over at the passenger seat and a few tears slip down my cheeks. Wiping them away, I grit my teeth and turn away as I tell myself to buck up but it's too damn late. More memories rush through my mind, reminding me of everything I've lost and I turn to the passenger seat again, my gaze falling on the urn with my mother's ashes

13

and the envelope of death certificates I picked up two days ago as a sob rips through me.

I've lost everything.

The pain only intensifies as I remember the day I got the call. It all started off so normal that it's still hard to believe that it's real three weeks later but the ashes next to me are proof that this hell is my new reality. Shaking my head, I remember waking up that morning around eleven after working late the night before and walking into the kitchen to get a cup of coffee. My boyfriend, Ash, was already gone for work and as soon as I crawled back into bed with my steaming mug of caffeine, the phone rang. My mom's picture popped up on the screen but when I answered it, I didn't recognize the voice on the other end of the line. He told me my mother was in the hospital and I needed to get there as soon as possible but he wouldn't say anything else. The entire time I was getting ready and racing across town, I just kept telling myself that she was okay but as soon as I walked through the ER doors and saw the look on everyone's face, I knew the truth.

I struggle to take a breath as the tears overwhelm me and I press a hand to my chest like I can somehow stop the onslaught of pain but it's useless. My mind flicks back to the moment I walked into the room and saw my mom lying on the table with a sheet pulled up to her chest. There was a tube in her mouth that wasn't connected to anything and her eyes were closed. She looked so peaceful, like she was sleeping, and my mind struggled to connect the dots until the doctor came in and told me he was sorry for my loss. Everything else happened in a blur. I remember hitting my knees and the loud, aching sob that ripped through me as nurses surrounded me to try and bring me some comfort.

Somehow, I got back home and I remember calling my brother to tell him but the words got stuck in my throat and I didn't know how to say that our mom was dead and we were all alone.

My gaze flicks to the mountain range where my dad's plane went down when I was a kid and I shake my head, another desperate sob swamping me. I'm an orphan and if it wasn't for my brother, Lincoln, I would have absolutely no one. Despite living in Ketchikan my entire life, I don't really have any friends here because they all either moved away or proved to not be good for me and if it wasn't for Ash holding me together these last few weeks, I don't know what I would have done. I met Ash three years ago and in a way, I think he saved me. At that point, I had been stripping for a year and I didn't recognize the girl in the mirror anymore. There was something about him that reminded me of who I truly was and grounded me again but he also never tried to force or manipulate me to quit dancing. He was everything I needed and it was so damn easy to fall in love with him. When we moved in together last year, I was certain that he was my forever but things have been off between us lately and I know that's my fault. With everything I've been going through, I haven't exactly been myself and I've leaned on him more than ever before but it seems like the more I lean, the more he pulls away. I just hope it's not too late to fix things.

Shaking my head, I suck in a breath and wipe more tears from my face as I watch the snow fall onto the windshield, each one a little different than the one before. I need to make a change, pull myself out of this funk, but I just don't know how. More than anything, I wish Lincoln was here but he lives over thirty-five hundred

15

miles away with his wife in Louisiana and it's been almost a year since the last time I saw him. Leaning my head back against the seat, I remember the phone call from him a few days ago, urging me again to move down to Baton Rouge. It's the same thing he's been saying since Mom died three weeks ago but I've been putting him off. I have to wonder, though... what the hell is even keeping me here in Alaska anymore?

Obviously, I have Ash but I can't see anything keeping him here either. Maybe we could make the move together... Ketchikan is my home, though. I've never been anywhere else and the thought of moving across the country scares the hell out of me. Shaking my head, I push the thoughts from my mind and wipe the tears from my face before clearing the snow from my windshield and pulling out of my parking space. As I pull out of the lot, I turn toward home and sigh. More than anything, what I need right now is to get to my apartment, crawl into my big comfy bed, and forget about this awful fucking day.

"Tomorrow will be better," I whisper, nodding to myself as my lip wobbles but I manage to get control of it before it dissolves into full blown tears again. Ash and I don't live too far from the club and I'm almost to my apartment when I see a gas station that's still open. Hannah's advice from earlier pops into my mind and I smile before pulling into the lot. Jumping out of my car, I run into the store, grab a bottle of wine, and pay the clerk before walking back out. As I set the bottle in the passenger seat, I glance over at the urn again and suck in a breath as I back out of my parking spot and turn out onto the road. This and the stash of chocolate I have hidden in the kitchen is exactly what I need to unwind and after the fog I've been walking around in for the last few weeks, it feels good to just do something for myself. As I pull into my usual parking spot outside of the general store, I glance up at my studio apartment on the second floor and frown.

Did I leave that light on?

God, I have been so scatter-brained lately that I probably did. Shaking my head, I grab my bottle of wine and eye the urn, contemplating grabbing it, too, before I change my mind. I know it's stupid but a part of me feels like as soon as I take my mother's ashes into my home, it all becomes real and I am not ready for that yet. At least, while she stays in the front seat of my car, there are moments when I can avoid thinking about the fact that she is gone. Sighing, I turn off the car and jump out. The sound of waves crashing against the shore greets me and I close my eyes as a feeling of calm washes through me.

When Ash and I were apartment hunting a little over a year ago, one of my favorite things about this place, besides the fact that we didn't really have any neighbors was that it is right on the water. From anywhere in the apartment, I can hear the ocean and if I want to look out across the water, all I have to do is walk into my kitchen and stand in front of the window. Even in the chaos of the past three weeks, being able to hear the waves crash against the rocks and see the water has calmed me and made me feel like maybe I'm not drowning in my pain. Opening my eyes, I glance up at the window as I turn for the stairs but stop short. Two shadows dance across the glass, coming together and wrapping their arms around each other as my heart starts to thunder in my chest.

What the fuck?

Ash is supposed to be in Juneau until tomorrow afternoon but no one else has access to our apartment.

God, he wouldn't do this to me, would he? With each breath ringing in my ears, I run up the stairs and unlock the door as quietly as possible before stepping inside and setting the bottle of wine down on the counter. A moan fills the room, echoing from behind the partition that separates our bedroom from the rest of the room and my hands start to shake as my gaze falls to the various articles of clothing littered across the floor - Ash's shirt, his sneakers, and jeans, a pair of pink lace panties, skinny jeans, and heels. My stomach rolls as the reality crashes down on me and another moan fills the room, this one deeper than before. I creep forward, careful not to make any noise but I swear my heartbeat is echoing through the room and there is no way in hell they don't hear it. Low grunts and soft gasps reach my ears as I walk toward the noise and my hands start to shake. I already know, deep down in my gut, what I'm going to find on the other side of that partition but I need to see it before it will become real. I can't have any doubt in my mind as to what is happening on the other side.

"Holly," Ash whispers, something between a plea and moan, and I suck in a breath as my thoughts screech to a halt. Holly? There is a girl I work with at the club named Holly but he wouldn't... I shake my head. Of course he would. If he is willing to cheat, why would the fact that I work with her stop him from pursuing someone? I think about the two of them, sneaking around behind my back while I've been dealing with all this stuff with my mom and it's like a blow torch has been lit inside me. Rage simmers through me as I rush forward and round the partition, holding my breath as I take in the scene in front of me. Ash is on top of her, in the middle of my bed, with the sheets pulled up around them and her pink nails are digging into his back as she moans again.

Her eyes are squeezed closed, her head thrown back in ecstasy, and I glance at the shelf next to me where the little ceramic pig Ash and I found at a flea market sits. I pick it up, staring at it before turning to the scene in front of me.

They still don't realize I'm here, too lost in each other to notice the person they've both betrayed. Their arrogance and carelessness only fuels my rage. From my spot at the end of the bed, I pull my arm back and chuck the pig at the wall above the bed. It shatters and sends little shards of clay raining down on them as Holly screams and Ash jumps off of her. She shrieks again and grabs the sheet, pulling it up to her chest as Ash stares at me with wide eyes.

"Row... I thought you were working late tonight."

I nod, grabbing another little knickknack off of the shelf and tossing it back and forth between my hands. "Clearly."

Holly sits up and scoots back along the bed before leaning back against the headboard - my headboard - and smirking up at me. What the hell? I wouldn't have called Holly and me friends but we were, at least, friendly at work but as I look at her now, all I can see is hatred shining in her eyes. Where in the hell does she get off hating me? Especially after I just caught her in bed with my man.

"Look, this isn't what it looks like," Ash says and I laugh because the whole thing is so fucking ridiculous. It is exactly what it looks like and there is no way in hell I'm buying anymore of his shit.

"Don't lie to her, baby," Holly whispers, running her hand down his back and I see red as I chuck the figurine

in my hand against the wall again. Holly screams and
Ash moves in front of her as he holds his hands up.

"Calm down, Rowan. You're acting crazy."

"Oh, baby," I whisper with a smile, grabbing the
heart sculpture he gave me on our first anniversary. "You
haven't even seen crazy yet."

My mind races through everything I've been through
in the past three weeks, everything I've lost and all of the
pain I've kept bottled up for most of my life and all of
the dreams I had for a future with him as the hurt in my
chest only intensifies.

When I was meeting with the funeral home, was Ash
screwing Holly in my bed? The thought sends my body
into motion and I chuck the figurine in my hand against
the wall again before picking up another one.

While I was in the hospital, learning that my mother
died instantly from a blood clot, was he fucking Holly in
his car? I throw the little glass figurine in my hand
against the wall and it shatters, drawing another scream
from the whore's mouth as Ash jumps out of bed and
starts walking toward me with his hands up. He's still
completely naked and I can smell the sex in the air. Plus,
he's got about five damn hickeys on his neck. My
stomach rolls and as I look over at him, I wonder how in
the hell I was ever attracted to him.

"Hey, let's just talk about this, babe."

Arching a brow, I grab a candle off of the shelf,
staring at it as I imagine chucking it at the wall, too,
before shaking my head and setting the candle back
down. "You know what? Let's not. It's not fucking worth
it. I'm leaving now and when I come back in the morning
you and your slut need to be gone or I'll call the police."

Turning away from him, I walk back over to the door
with my head held high and grab my bottle of wine as he

calls my name, begging me to come back and talk to him but I ignore his pleas and step outside, slamming the door behind me and it feels symbolic for the end of our relationship. As I descend the stairs, I expect to feel the sadness of my lost relationship or the sting of Ash's betrayal but I don't feel anything. Maybe, in the scope of all of the shit that has happened in my life lately, walking in to find Ash screwing my co-worker just doesn't rank. Or hell, maybe I'm just numb to it all now and someday soon, it will all come crashing down on me and destroy me. Either way, the only thing I want to do right now is get away from here and drink.

Jumping back in my car, I toss the bottle into the passenger seat and whip out of my parking space before turning toward the main part of town where I can find a hotel room for the night. As I drive along the coast, my gaze flicks to the mountain range where my dad's plane went down again before falling to my mom's ashes in the seat next to me. I'm sure Ash doesn't know it, yet, but he has just ended things with me and with our relationship officially over, there is nothing else keeping me here in Alaska. Everything in this place just reminds me of all that I have lost and I can't stand to be here anymore. As I pull into a parking lot of one of the hotels downtown, I put the car in park and dial Lincoln's number.

"Row?" He answers after a few rings, his voice groggy and I wince. Shit. I always forget about the time difference. "Are you okay? It's one in the morning."

I nod, releasing a breath as my big brother's voice calms me. "Yeah, I'm... okay. I've just been thinking about the last time we spoke..."

"Yeah? And?"

"Does your offer still stand? To move there, I mean." My belly flips with nerves or excitement or maybe both as I wait for his answer. He sucks in a breath.

"Of course, Row... but, are you sure you're okay? You sound off."

I let out a humorless laugh as I think about the last month of my life and shake my head. "It's been... interesting..."

"Yeah, okay. I get it," he says when I don't say anything else and I sigh, leaning my head back against the seat. "How soon do you think you'll be here?"

"I don't know. I have some things I need to wrap up here." My mind drifts over the things I need to do, like quitting my job and packing up the apartment before I realize that everything I actually care about will probably fit in the back seat of my car and take me all of an hour to pack up. "Actually, never mind. I can probably be on the road in two days."

He sighs. "What the fuck is going on, Rowan? You don't sound like yourself and you're really starting to fucking worry me."

"I promise I'm okay, Linc, and I'll tell you all about it as soon as I'm in Louisiana, okay?" I bite my lip as he lets out another heavy sigh and I wonder if he's actually going to let me get away with this. Lincoln tends to be overprotective, especially after our sister Nora was killed by her crazy ex-boyfriend eleven years ago, and I know that even if he lets me off of this phone call without telling him what is going on, he'll worry himself sick about it until I get to Baton Rouge and spill my guts. Finally, he groans.

"Fine, but you bet your ass that as soon as you step foot in Baton Rouge, you are going to tell me everything."

I roll my eyes and fight back a smile. "So fucking bossy. Hasn't your wife broken you of that nasty habit yet?"

"Girl, I fucking wish!" Tate, Lincoln's wife, hollers from the background and I laugh, feeling lighter than I have in days.

"Shut up before I shut you up myself, woman," he growls at her. I bite my lip to hold back the giggle as I shake my head. Tate is not a woman I would ever want to mess with but apparently, my brother likes playing with fire.

"You're getting stupid in your old age, Archer."

"Who in the fuck are you calling old, woman?" he yells and I can't hold back my laughter any longer.

"Okay, well, I'm going to let you go deal with that but I'll call you before I hit the road," I tell him and he hums in agreement.

"Damn right, you will. I want constant updates so I know you're safe, you hear me?"

After promising to call him with nightly updates and reassuring him that I can take care of myself at least four times, I finally manage to hang up. As I step out of my car and turn toward the hotel where I'm staying tonight, I'm surprised by how hopeful and excited I feel about this move and I can only hope that it turns out to be just the thing I need to heal all this hurt I've been carrying around.

Wicked Games

Chapter Two
Travis

"Fuck. This can't be right," I hiss, staring at the social media profile I just stumbled across on the screen in front of me before releasing a heavy breath. For months, my brothers and I have been doing everything we can think of to find the asshole that has been targeting the club and coming after women we have helped in the past but I may have just found something that rules out the only suspect we've been able to come up with. Mitch Harris was married to Dina, the first girl that was killed, and after we came to her rescue and helped her escape him, he lost his goddamn mind. When she was murdered, we all just assumed that he was the one that did it. The problem was, we didn't have any proof and when two other girls were also killed, we turned our focus away from him. But then Fuzz suggested that he was still behind it all, killing people close to us in an act of revenge for our role in his wife leaving him and since he is such a shifty character, it wasn't much of a leap. Plus, he didn't have the best alibi for the night Dina died but if what I just found is true… there is no way he is behind these deaths.

Scrolling through the profile, I shake my head. I was lost, looking for any kind of lead when I decided to go peruse Mitch's social media and noticed his new girlfriend. She likes to tag him in her check-ins every time they go somewhere together and as I was scrolling through her profile, I found a check-in for the date the latest girl, Sammy, was killed. Shaking my head and hoping like hell this is somehow wrong, I click the like for the little diner she checked in at and start flipping through photos on their page. In one photo, I spot a security camera and grin as I open a new window to hack into their system. It is surprisingly easy and I roll my eyes at how lazy and complacent some people can be. For fucks sake, it is not hard for someone like me to gain access to someone's system but they make it even easier on me when they don't change the password from the default code from the factory.

Sighing, I scroll through the dates listed until I find the one I need and click on it, selecting the camera in the dining room. The video starts at midnight so I fast forward through the entire morning until just after lunch when Eve, Mitch's girlfriend, checked in to the diner. As the video begins playing, I hold my breath and hiss a curse when Mitch walks in with Eve on his arm. Chucking my pen across the room, I lean back in my chair and it smacks against the wall, falling to the floor as I watch Mitch and Eve slip into a back booth and start making out.

"Goddamn it!"

"Problem?"

I glance over my shoulder as Storm walks into my room and arches a brow in question. Nodding, I release a breath and point to my computer screen. "Only if you count discovering an alibi for Mitch a problem."

"Fuck... seriously?"

"Afraid so." I turn back to the screen and sneer at Mitch pawing all over Eve in the corner of the booth. "This is him and his new girlfriend, Eve, making out in a diner an hour away from here while Sammy was being murdered."

"Shit." He turns away for a moment before turning back to watch the video. "What about the other two murders? Does he have an alibi for them as well?"

"He has a shaky alibi on the day Dina was murdered," I say, clicking back over to Eve's profile and scrolling down until I find the date in question and resist the urge to smash my fist into the table. "But, he was with Eve again on the day Laney was killed."

"Doing what?"

I point to the check-in. "Bowling. Apparently, they won third place."

"Can you verify that?" he asks, crossing his arms over his chest and I nod as I click the link for the bowling alley and bring up their website. I jump over to the winner's page and scroll down until their picture pops up on the screen. Turning back to him, I point to it and he sighs.

"Fuck."

I nod in agreement. "Yep."

"All right..." he says, running a hand through his hair. "We'll deal with that later. Veronica is downstairs in the war room and she might have new leads for us. You coming?"

"Absolutely," I answer, closing out of the websites and grabbing my phone off of my desk. He nods, turning to leave and I follow behind him as he walks out of my room and down the hallway to the stairs. The low murmur of multiple conversations greet us as we descend the stairs but I can't make out anything that is said since we are literally packed to the rafters in here these days.

The Bayou Devils MC wasn't always the family friendly environment it is now. In fact, it used to be a real outlaw club with its members running guns, drugs, women… anything to bring in the cash but everything changed when our President, Blaze, was shot by a rival dealer and one of our members, Henn, was sent to jail for seven years on a drug charge. Blaze started to see the error of his ways and backed away from anything illegal to open a legitimate business and when a terrified woman crashed into him in a gas station, we kind of fell into the work we do now - helping those that have nowhere else to go. Or, at least, that's the way it started. These days, we've made quite the name for ourselves and we've taken on other jobs like security and P.I. work. I didn't join the club until things had turned around and I was drawn here by their mission and I knew my computer hacking skills would come in handy but I haven't been a whole lot of help lately with this threat coming after us.

Veronica, the woman we're meeting with today, went missing almost a year ago on her way home from class and we were tasked with looking into her disappearance when Detective Rodriguez, a local cop we work with often, hit a dead end and was ordered to focus on other cases. We didn't get much farther than he did, though, and we were all shocked as hell when she stumbled into the clubhouse two weeks ago, disheveled and terrified out of her mind. She had a message for us, from the man who has been targeting the club and it set us all on edge – even more so than we already were. Blaze immediately ordered everyone and their families to come stay here, at the clubhouse, so we can keep this little family we have built safe but it hasn't been easy.

I am just getting started.

I shudder as I remember the message she delivered that day. It's haunted me day in and day out as I try my hardest to come up with answers for my brothers but I hit a wall every time. No matter where I look or what angle I try to take, I always come up empty and I can't help but feel like this fucker is toying with me. Like he knew who I was and he knew what I could do when he went about making this whole damn plan so it's tailored to drive me out of my mind. Scoffing, I shake my head.

God, how fucking narcissistic is that?

Pushing the thoughts from my mind, I follow Storm as he walks into the war room and as soon as I'm in the room, he shuts the door behind me, locking it as I slip into my seat at one end of the table. Across from me is Blaze, our president, at the head of the table and Storm takes his seat to his left with Smith, our sergeant at arms, to his right. Veronica sits in the middle of the table to my left, looking nervous as hell as we all turn our focus to her.

"You all right, darlin'?" Blaze asks her and she nods, her gaze flicking around the room like a scared animal.

"Being back here just reminds me of…"

I nod in understanding as do the rest of my brothers. The last time Veronica was here, she had just been dropped off by the man who kidnapped her and she has absolutely no idea what she was walking into.

"Just know that we're all here to help you in any way that we can," Blaze assures her and she nods, sitting up a little straighter as she sucks in a breath. "Are you ready to tell your story?"

"I am."

Pulling my phone out of my pocket, I open the voice memo app and hit record before setting it down on the table. "Just start at the beginning."

"Okay," she breathes, glancing over at me as she nods her again a little too much, almost like she's hyping herself up and I can't stand it. When I think about how many lives this guy has torn apart, messed with and used, it brings up shit that I would rather forget and makes me feel like putting my fist through a wall. All I want to do is end this but I can't help worrying that the ending won't be as pretty as I'm hoping. Veronica wraps her arms around herself as she stares down at the table and shifts in her seat, obviously uncomfortable.

"What do you remember about that day?" I ask, hoping to just get her talking. I've noticed that the hardest part for most people, after a trauma like this, is where to begin. They have so many thoughts running through their heads and so many emotions that they quickly become overwhelmed into silence. She sucks in a breath.

"It was so normal, you know? Like, shouldn't days where your life is going to change come with some kind of warning? Shouldn't there be some kind of sign from the universe that you need to pay attention?"

I scoff, fighting back memories. "I fucking wish."

"Did you go to class that day?" Smith asks and she nods.

"Yeah. I have… had English on Thursdays and it let out early that day so I decided to go home and try to relax before my next class."

Blaze scowls. "So, you deviated from your normal schedule that day?"

"Yeah."

My mind spins with scenarios and possibilities as I study her. If class let out early and she did something that she wouldn't normally do, that means he was watching her for a while, waiting for the perfect moment to strike but why pick her? She wasn't associated with us at all and there is no way he could have known Rodriguez would catch the case. It could have easily gone to a different detective and then we never would have known about it.

"What happened next?" I ask and she shudders.

"I was walking down the hallway to my apartment and all of the sudden, it felt like someone was there with me. All the hair on my arms stood on end and when I heard footsteps, I started walking faster, telling myself that I was being ridiculous because it wasn't uncommon for other people to be in the hallway but this time… it was just different."

Storm nods, leaning back in his chair with his arms crossed over his chest. "According to the police report, your apartment door was open when officers went to investigate…"

"I managed to get the door unlocked but I couldn't get inside before he grabbed me," she answers with a nod. "That's the last thing I remember from my apartment. I must have blacked out and when I woke up, I was in a cabin out in the woods."

"How did he keep you there?" I ask. She meets my gaze and the haunted look in her eyes hits me in the chest. Whoever this guy is, he held her for almost a year and she could give us vital information about who he is and what he wants but that doesn't mean it's not fucking awful to pry these answers out of her.

"There was this thick metal hook lodged in the middle of the floor and he put shackles around my wrists with a large chain connecting the two. I could go anywhere in the cabin and I could even step out onto the front porch but that was it."

Moose frowns. "He wasn't worried about alerting someone if they drove by?"

"During the entire time I was there, I never saw another person."

"What did he look like?" Chance asks softly, leaning forward and bracing his arms on the table. She shakes her head.

"I have no idea. He always wore this white mask that covered his whole face."

I narrow my eyes. "Like a Halloween mask?"

"No... it was more like a theater mask... like those ones that have happy and sad faces but this one was expressionless."

"What about his hair?" Henn asks. "Or his eyes?"

She shakes her head, picking at the edge of the table. "His hair and his eyes were both brown and kind of... unremarkable?"

"Right," I scoff. Every single description we've ever gotten of this guy always sounds exactly the same. He's perfectly average. The kind of guy that easily blends into a crowd which makes him even harder to hunt down.

"I'm so sorry I can't be more help."

Blaze shakes his head and leans forward, placing his hand on the table. "It's not you, darlin'. This guy has just been really hard to find and it doesn't help that he looks so damn average."

"Oh… yeah, that's the thing. Even if he was standing in front of me right now, I don't know that I would recognize him. Maybe if I heard him speak…"

"I'm sure that was intentional," I tell her. Why else would he wear a mask for an entire year? "How much time did he spend with you at the cabin?"

She scowls. "Quite a lot, actually. He didn't come to see me every day and there would be times when he would be gone for a couple weeks before he would come back but when he did stop by, he would stay and talk to me for hours."

"So, you got to know him, then?" Blaze asks and she shakes her head.

"I wouldn't say that. He asked me about my life and after a month or so, I was so starved for conversation that I opened up to him but mostly, he just talked about y'all."

Every chair in the room squeaks as we all jerk to attention and I suck in a breath, my heart pounding in my chest and my stomach flipping wildly.

Holy shit.
This is crucial.

"What did he say?" Fuzz asks, his gaze intense as he stares at her. Her hand shakes as she presses it against her chest, near her neck, and keeps her gaze firmly on the table.

"He talked about how much he hated you and how y'all had taken everything from him…" She looks around the room and when her eyes meet mine, I nod in encouragement. "And he told me that he has so many plans to make y'all pay. He said he wants to watch you suffer the same way he had before he tears this club apart."

The room is quiet, each of us contemplating what we've already learned and wondering how much more there is. We've already lost three girls... how much more does he have planned for us and can we really stop him?

"Do you know what he's planning?" Smith asks and she shakes her head.

"I tried to get him to talk to me about his plan but he was always very vague... I guess that makes sense now. If he was always planning on dropping me off on your doorstep, he couldn't tell me anything that would help y'all." She scowls down at the table before shaking her head. "He did tell me about a woman he met in a bar, though. I got the sense that she had something to do with you guys but when I asked about it, he told me to mind my own business and he mentioned a man he'd met that hated this club as much as he did."

My gaze snaps to her as I suck in a breath. "He has a partner?"

"I don't think so. It sounded more like this man.... was inspired by him. He told him it was always better to use pawns to do his dirty work and there was something about a brother but I don't remember that part..."

"Holy fuck," Storm breathes, falling back into his seat with wide eyes and every eye in the room turns to look at him. Blaze frowns and Storm shakes his head, looking dazed. "Ian."

Jesus fucking Christ.

If the man after us also knows Ian and was around when all that shit went down with Storm and his old lady, Ali, then this goes way fucking deeper than any of us thought.

"Was he in jail?" Henn asks and Veronica blinks up at him, shrugging.

"I don't know. He never mentioned it."

Storm turns to Henn. "What are you thinking?"

"Just that for this guy to get to Ian, he either had to be in jail or he excels at digging into our most private shit. I mean, he's got to be on Streak's level," he answers, glancing over at me and I clench my teeth. That would explain a few things, like how he's been able to hide from me so well.

"Let's not jump to any conclusions," Blaze says, his voice full of authority. He turns back to Veronica and offers her a warm smile but I can still see the stress creeping into his eyes. "Was there anything else?"

"Probably," she answers with a shrug. "I was there for so long and he talked so much but I'm trying to remember."

He nods, holding his hands up in surrender. "No one is trying to push you, darlin'. Just take your time."

"Okay," she breathes, staring down at the table again for a moment before she looks up. "The only other thing that stands out to me is that he said he's been watching from the shadows for a while and that he would step in when he felt it was necessary to maximize the pain and agony he was trying to inflict on y'all... but I don't know details."

"Christ," Moose whispers, scrubbing his hand down his face as we all look around the room, trying to wrap our minds around all this new information.

How long has he been watching us?

How many times has he intervened and fucked with us?

"What about the day you showed up here?" Fuzz asks. "What happened then?"

She sucks in a breath and her lip wobbles, tears filling her eyes as the memories play out in her head, but she manages to rein it in. "He showed up that day and took the shackles off before leading me to the front door. He was standing behind me and he had his hand clamped down on my shoulders then he lifted them off and told me to run. At first, I was shocked, frozen in place, so he nudged me forward and I took off. I didn't have any shoes on and my feet were getting all cut up but I didn't care. I was determined to get away."

"Obviously that didn't happen," Chance says and she nods.

"As I was running, I realized that he was following me, hunting me, and I thought it was the end for me. I thought he was going to kill me." A sob bubbles out of her throat and I shake my head, fighting back the growing anger in the pit of my stomach. "When he caught up to me, he threw a bag over my head and carried me back the way we came. The next thing I knew we were in a car and my hands were tied behind my back."

Blaze blows out a breath and runs a hand through his hair. "What happened when you got to the clubhouse?"

"He took me out of the car and we walked for a while... I'm not sure how far... and then when he took the blindfold off, we were standing in front of the clubhouse."

"And he instructed you to come inside?" I ask and she nods, her eyes full of pain as she glances over at me.

"Yeah. I had no idea what was going on and I thought maybe it was just another game, that y'all were in on it with him and he was just going to endlessly torment me before killing me."

Blaze shakes his head, pain filling his face as he leans forward and meets her gaze. "I'm so sorry that this happened to you, Veronica... I can't help but feel like this is our fault and if there is ever anything that you need, all you have to do is ask. This club is here for you, now and always."

"I..." she whispers, gaping at me. "I don't blame you guys. Since he released me, I've been researching the club and I know the good work you do. The only person to blame here is him but regardless, I'm thankful for your support."

"It's a really shitty induction but you're part of the family now," Storm tells her and she nods, glancing over her shoulder at the closed door.

"Based on what I saw out there, it seems like a good family to be a part of."

Chance smiles. "We appreciate you saying that."

Silence descends over the room as we all look at each other, unsure of where to go from here, and Blaze clears his throat as he stands up and motions to the door. "Okay, well, if nobody has anything else, I'll walk you out, Veronica."

"Okay," she answers, sounding more secure as she stands up and looks around the room. "If there is anything else I can help with, please let me know."

"We will, darlin'," Blaze assures her. She waves good-bye and Blaze walks her out of the room shutting the door behind him. Nobody says anything, each of us trying to process everything we've just learned. The lengths this guy has gone to in order to get back at us is extreme and I can't shake this damn feeling that I'm missing something that is staring me right in the face but I can't seem to figure out what the hell it is. It just continues to eat away at me, at all of us, but maybe that's all just part of his game and this really will end with the ruins of my club and the family we've built littered around us.

Chapter Three
Rowan

"Thank fuck," I whisper, turning down the classic rock I've been jamming to in an effort to stay awake, as the lights of Lubbock, Texas, come into view. I rub at my tired eyes and merge over into the right lane, exiting at the first exit I find with a lodging sign. I'm in desperate need of something to eat and somewhere to sleep. Hell, at this point, I don't even care if it's an actual bed or a couch or a floor somewhere as long as I get to close my eyes and drift off to dreamland. It's almost eight in the evening and I am on day five of my cross-country road trip which means I'll be in Baton Rouge tomorrow but as far as I'm concerned, it can't get here soon enough. I've been driving ten plus hours a day and I still have another ten to do tomorrow.

Yawning, I scan the buildings on the side of the road, looking for the first semi-decent looking motel I can find. Lincoln would have an absolute fit if he knew I was looking for somewhere cheap, especially after he insisted on sending me money for my trip. When I checked my bank account and saw the one thousand dollars he had deposited, I almost had a heart attack and I have been trying to avoid using it. It's too much and I fully intend on giving it back to him as soon as I get to Baton Rouge. Besides, I see no reason that I need to spend more than sixty dollars a night on somewhere to sleep. I finally spot a motel that fits the bill, sporting a sign that advertises forty-five dollar rooms and pull my car into the lot, parking in front of the small office at the front of the building before jumping out. A man with long, greasy hair looks up from behind the desk as I walk in and I smile but he doesn't return the gesture. His gaze rakes down my body before dragging back up to my face with suspicion in his eyes.

"Can I help you?"

I nod, keeping my smile in place. "Yeah. I need a room, please."

"King or two queens?" he asks, looking bored as he glances down at a notebook on the desk in front of him and I arch a brow. What the hell kind of motel doesn't have a computer? I glance down and notice a map of the entire hotel laid out in front of him with a giant "X" over some of the rooms.

"King, please."

"Smoking or non-smoking?"

"Non, please." I pull some cash out of my pocket and wait for him to tell me the price but he takes his time looking through the available rooms before picking up a pencil and puts an "X" over a room near the front of the building. He glances up at me before his gaze drops to the money in my hand.

"Sixty."

I scowl. "Your sign says forty-five."

"And I'm sayin' sixty," he answers with a shrug and I study him for a moment before nodding and turning toward the door. As much as I want to go to sleep as soon as possible, I'm not willing to let this ass take advantage of me.

"Never mind, then."

"I guess I could do fifty," he replies as I grip the door handle and I roll my eyes as I turn back to him. Sure, I could push the issue but this way we both win and I'm not willing to argue over five dollars. Nodding, I walk back to the desk and slap fifty dollars down in front of him. Sighing, he scoops it up and grabs a key off of a hook behind him before sliding it across the desk to me. "Room ten, it's the first door on the right."

"Thank you."

He nods, turning back to the magazine he was flipping through when I walked in and I shake my head as I walk back out to my car and climb behind the wheel. Maneuvering around the office, I drive to the other side of the motel and park in front of a green door with a giant ten in the middle. The parking lot is fairly empty so hopefully it will be a quiet, uneventful night and I can get enough rest to make it the rest of the way tomorrow. I am so ready to be done driving and it's highly likely that I refuse to get in a car all together for the next month, at least. As I climb out of the car, I throw my arms over my head and stretch before grabbing my bag out of the back seat before walking up to the door and unlocking it. Everything else I took from the apartment fit in the trunk so I don't have to worry about hiding it from would-be thieves. The air of the room is stale and it has a generally drab look to it but it's absolutely perfect for crashing in for the night.

As I toss my bag on the floor my stomach growls and I sigh as I glance over my shoulder at the door. I passed a couple of fast food places on my way here and there is no way in hell I'm getting back in the car so I guess I'm going to walk. Grabbing my wallet and the key to the room, I step outside again and lock the door before turning toward the little burger place I saw about a block back as my phone starts ringing. Lincoln has been obsessively checking up on me since I left Alaska and as sweet as it is, I need the man to realize I'm a grown woman and can take care of myself.

"I'm still alive," I answer.

"You'd fucking better be," he growls, annoyed, and I grin. "Where are you?"

"Lubbock, Texas. I'm stopping for the night."

He sighs. "Okay, good. I was worried about you driving in the dark."

"Lincoln…"

"Don't you even start with me, Rowan. You are the only family I have left and it's my goddamn right to worry about you."

I roll my eyes as I kick a rock across the parking lot. "I'm not your only family. What about Tate and the babies?"

"You know what I meant," he shoots back before sighing and I swear, I can feel the stress that has been weighing on him for most of his life.

"Yeah, yeah. I know but try to chill, will you? The last thing I need is you to have a stroke because you can't calm your ass down. You actually are the only family I have left."

He scoffs. "Bullshit. If I've got Tate and the babies, so do you."

"I know," I say even though I don't quite feel it. I've met Tate once and spoken to her on the phone a handful of times but the truth is, I don't really know her all that well. I can see that she makes my brother happy but also puts him in his place when he needs it so I know that she is good for him.

"So, listen, when you get here tomorrow, you will be coming to the clubhouse instead of our house," he says, interrupting my thoughts and I scowl.

"Oh... well, if you guys don't have room for me, I can just get a hotel room or stay out at your cabin."

"Absolutely not." There is no room for argument in his voice and a spike of irritation races through me. "Everyone is at the clubhouse and you need to be here, too... for your own safety."

My eyes widen as I stop outside of the restaurant and plop down on a bench next to the front door. "My safety? What the hell is going on, Lincoln?"

"Look," he sighs. "I didn't want to say anything before because I didn't want to scare you but... someone has been targeting the club and the clubhouse is the safest place for all of us right now."

"You and Tate are staying at the clubhouse right now?"

"Yes," he answers and my mind races as I watch cars race past me. What the hell is going on with all of them that they are staying at the clubhouse to keep everyone safe? "Look, Row... I'll explain everything once you're down here."

"Why didn't you tell me any of this before I left Alaska? I mean, maybe I was safer up there." Not that I have a burning desire to be back in Ketchikan but now I'm worried that I left one shitty situation for one that is even worse.

"I'm not going to let anything happen to you and with you in Baton Rouge, I can make sure of that.

Besides, not to be a dick, but what did you have up there now that Mom's gone?"

He's right but there is no way in hell I'm going to admit that. "Fuck you, Linc."

"You can be pissed at me all you want, about that comment and the fact that I kept this from you, as long as you're safe. Plus, I think this will be good for you. I don't want you to be alone."

"Shut up. I'm already almost there so you don't need to keep campaigning. I'll be in Baton Rouge tomorrow and that will be that."

He sighs again and I roll my eyes. Goddamn it, I hate how smug he gets when he knows he's right. "Good. I'll text you the address for the clubhouse and we'll see you tomorrow."

I give in and after conceding to his demands to keep him updated during my drive tomorrow, I hang up and head into the restaurant to get something to eat. They are fairly busy so while I wait for my food, I tuck myself into a quiet corner and just people watch. My phone buzzes and my stomach flips when a text from Ash pops up on the screen.

Ash:
Hey. Where you at?

I haven't spoken to him since the night I found him in bed with Holly and I guess I had naively hoped he already knew it was over but that doesn't seem to be the case. I dismiss the notification as the man behind the counter calls out my number so I shove my phone in my pocket and grab my food before slipping back outside.

There is a decent looking park with a cute little pond across the street from the motel so I walk over there before sitting down at a picnic table on the water's edge. Millions of stars dot the sky above me, shining in the surface of the pond as a duck glides across the surface and I shake my head. Back in Alaska, it's probably so damn cold that even walking to your car is miserable but here in Texas, it's perfectly cool as I pull my food out of the bag and dig in. I'm halfway through my burger when another text comes in from Ash and I ignore it without even looking at it as I continue eating. He has to have noticed that all my clothes are gone, right? Then again, maybe he hasn't. I really didn't take much else. All the furniture in the apartment is stuff we picked out together and I had no interest in taking it with me so he might still be oblivious. The only things I took, the only things I truly cared about, were mementos and photos that were already packed away in a closet.

When I finish the burger, I throw the wrapper back in the bag and munch on fries as I look out over the park. Even though it's essentially surrounded by the city of Lubbock, there is a peacefulness to it, almost like an oasis, that makes you forget for a second that you're surrounded by buildings and traffic. It's one of the things I was most worried about with this move. My favorite part about living in Alaska was being outside in nature and it is one of the things I am going to miss the most in Baton Rouge. I just hope I can find little places like this to keep me sane.

My phone vibrates again and I roll my eyes as I toss the rest of my fries in the bag and wipe my fingers on my jeans. Scooping up my phone, I open the text from Ash and roll my eyes.

Ash:
Please come home so we can talk, baby.

I stare at the message for a moment before deciding that I just need to be brutally honest with him. I hoped that after finding him in bed with my co-worker, he would realize that this isn't working but that doesn't seem to be the case. He's clearly not catching on that this is over and I don't want to drag this out anymore.

Me:
There is nothing to talk about, Ash.
I found you in bed with someone else and
I'm done. We're done.

I press send and as soon as I go to set my phone down, it starts ringing. Ash's photo pops up on the screen and I roll my eyes as I accept the call.

"Where are you?" he demands as soon as I answer. "I'll come to you and we'll work this out."

I shake my head. "No, we won't, Ash."

"Rowan," he pleads, desperation lacing his voice. "You can't just throw the last three years away, baby."

"Do you remember hearing that crash the moment you stuck your dick inside Holly? That was *you* throwing it all away, not me."

He makes a noise that sounds suspiciously like a whimper and I fight back a flash of disgust. "I made a mistake, baby. That's all it was, a stupid mistake and I want to make it up to you."

"That's not going to happen."

"Please, Rowan," he pleads and I can picture him pacing back and forth in the apartment, raking a hand through his blond hair. "Just tell me where you are, okay? I'll come meet you and we can really talk. I will do whatever it takes to fix this."

I shake my head and sigh. "Let me ask you something, Ash... was that day the first time you fucked Holly?"

His silence is answer enough and I nod to myself, feeling strangely proud that I was right. Ever since finding him with Holly, I've been looking at our relationship with a magnifying glass because there were other times that I caught him in a lie and gave him the benefit of the doubt instead of searching for more answers. Like an idiot.

"And was Holly the first girl you ever cheated on me with?"

"Rowan..."

I shake my head. "No, I've heard enough. We're done, Ash, and there is nothing else to say. Don't call me again."

I hang up as he protests loudly on the other end of the line but I don't care what he has to say. My phone starts ringing again almost immediately but I reject the call before turning back to look out at the water, feeling confident in my decision. He may have gotten away with lying to me for a long time but now that I know, there is no way in hell I would ever take him back.

My phone rings again and I roll my eyes. Part of me just wants to chuck the thing in the pond and be done with it but Lincoln would lose his shit if he couldn't contact me during the final leg of my journey tomorrow so instead, I turn my phone off and stand up to head back to my motel for the night. Knowing that our whole relationship was just one big lie, that I wasted three years of my life on a man who didn't deserve me, hurts but I also have this feeling that I'm moving on to bigger and better things without him.

Chapter Four
Rowan

The last little bit of daylight streaks across the sky as I pull into the clubhouse parking lot and I breathe a sigh of relief, happy to finally be done driving. I swear, I need some food and then I need to just be a vegetable for a while after the day that I've had. The drive was actually pretty nice and traffic was tolerable but I spent my entire day dodging call after call from Ash and I am quickly approaching my breaking point. The first call came in around eight this morning, right as I was leaving the hotel and they've been nonstop since then. Honestly, at this point, I am tempted to answer the next one to tell him to go fuck himself. When I left Alaska, I told myself that if he ever reached out, I would be civil with him but he's crossing the line into harassment now and I'm fed up.

I pull into a parking spot near the door and sigh as I lean back in my seat and turn the car off. Closing my eyes and rubbing my temples, I start to feel my stress drain away and just when I think I might be able to finally relax, my phone starts ringing and I let out a shriek of frustration, resisting the urge to start punching my steering wheel. The thought of answering it and telling him off flickers through my mind but instead, I silence it before grabbing the keys from the ignition and climbing out of the car.

"There she is!" Lincoln hollers and I turn as he jogs out of the clubhouse with Tate hot on his heels. She flashes me a smile and when Lincoln reaches me, he wraps his arms around me and lifts me off of the ground in a bear hug. His familiar scent washes over me and something inside me breaks. I fight back tears as relief and pain wash through me simultaneously. I'm finally in a place where I feel safe enough to let myself feel everything that has happened during the past month. There is no way in hell I want to cry in front of them but leave it to my big brother to turn me into a total baby.

"I missed you," I whisper and he nods, squeezing me a little tighter before setting me back on my feet.

"Ditto."

Tate joins us as Lincoln releases me and she wraps me up in another hug before pulling away just enough to drape her arm over my shoulders and drag me into her side. "Glad you're finally here. Maybe now he'll take a goddamn chill pill."

"Doubtful," I shoot back and our eyes meet before we both start laughing as Lincoln glares down at us, shaking his head.

"I should have known y'all would gang up on me."

"Oh, you poor thing," I say with a smirk, nudging his shoulder. "And y'all? When did you start talking like that?"

He shoots me a look I know all too well, a look that is supposed to be a warning but it's never really worked on me. "Don't start."

"So, where is all your stuff?" Tate asks, peeking in the back seat and eyeing my lonely duffel bag. I point to it and shrug.

"It's just that and a few small boxes in the trunk."

Lincoln scowls, inspecting the back seat as he crosses his arms over his chest. For some reason, it reminds me of Dad and I smile through the ache in my chest. "That's all you brought? Where is all your stuff?"

"I took the important stuff," I answer with a shrug, thinking back to the hour it took me to pack everything that meant anything to me and all the crap that I left behind. "The rest of it was just... stuff."

"I see," he murmurs, looking unconvinced and more worried by the second. "And your boyfriend? What's the story with him?"

Tate watches me for a second before she laughs and playfully smacks my brother's arm. "Jesus, Lincoln. Give the girl a second to breathe. Why don't you take her stuff inside and y'all can catch up later? Besides, she's got a party to get to."

"Party?" I ask, my stomach clenching as I try to hide the disappointment from my face. The very last thing I want to do right now is be thrown in the middle of a bunch of strangers. Tate squeezes my shoulder.

"Yeah, just a little get-together with the club."

I shake my head and press my lips together as I glance over at her. "Can I not? I really just want to get something to eat and crash. It's been a long day."

"Why?" Lincoln snaps, his entire body tensing as his gaze darts around the parking lot. "What happened?"

"For fucks sake, baby!" Tate exclaims, rolling her eyes. "She's been driving all damn day, that's all. Simmer the fuck down, you Neanderthal."

"Woman, don't test me," he growls, leveling a glare at her but she isn't even the least bit fazed. She releases me and stands a little taller as she meets his gaze, ready to throw down. I watch in fascination as they bicker with each other for a few seconds before my brother finally concedes and yanks the first box out of the trunk. As soon as he's gone, Tate turns to me and rolls her eyes again.

"I swear, that man has been giving himself ulcers over worrying about you."

I watch where he disappeared into the clubhouse, confused. "Yeah... he's always been protective but this is..."

"It's all this shit with the club, babe. Everyone is pretty high strung right now... which is why we all need this party to relax... before someone kills someone."

I scoff, my mind racing with questions as I grab my bag out of the back seat and sling the strap over my shoulder. "Oh, I see. Guilt tripping me into my own welcome party, are we?"

"I do what I have to," she answers with a shrug. "Now, before your brother comes back, I saw that look on your face when Linc mentioned your boyfriend. What's going on there? Are you okay?"

Anger flares through me as I remember walking into the apartment a week ago to find him and Holly together. "I got off work early and walked in on him banging my co-worker in my bed but other than that, I am just fine."

"Oh, shit," she whispers, staring at me with wide eyes before nodding. "You're better off without that ass wipe, babe, but probably best not to mention that to your brother, yeah? He would hop on a plane, like, right now."

"Who is getting on a plane?" Lincoln asks, walking up to us. Tate turns to him and flashes him a wide smile that looks fucking suspicious.

"No one."

He eyes her warily as he grabs another box out of the trunk. "Mmhmm."

"Come on, Rowan," she says, turning toward the clubhouse and starting back toward the door. "I'll introduce you to everyone. They're all excited to meet you."

"You don't have to stay long if you're really that tired," Lincoln whispers when she gets far enough away that she can't hear him and I nod before following her, my belly flipping. I've spent years taking my clothes off in front of a bunch of strangers but for some reason, walking into this clubhouse and meeting all of these people is damn near giving me palpitations. Tate waits by the door for me and when I reach her, she ushers me inside. It feels like every gaze in the room turns to look at us before Tate yells at all of them to mind their own damn business and leads me over to a group of women.

"Everyone, this is Lincoln's sister, Rowan. Rowan, this is Ali, Storm's wife," she says, pointing to a gorgeous woman with long blonde hair next to me and I smile.

"It's nice to meet you."

She flashes me a grin. "You, too, sweetie."

"And this is Carly, Chance's wife, Kady, Henn's wife, and Juliette, Moose's wife," she says, pointing to the next three women in line who all smile and nod in greeting. "And finally we have Quinn and Piper, Smith's wife and Fuzz's fiancée."

"And ex-wife," Carly quips and the other girls laugh as I look on, confused. Am I back in high school? Because it sure as hell feels like I've been transported back six years and I'm the one on the outside again. Tate pats my shoulder.

"I'll explain that one later," she whispers and I nod before turning back to the other women, forcing a smile to my face. As much as I would love to find my room and hide in there for the rest of the night, these people are important to my brother and I need to make an effort.

"Hi," I say, waving to all of them as my belly flips again. It's intimidating as hell to have everyone's attention on me and I honestly can't remember the last time I had a real friend to hang out with but maybe I could here. My mind drifts back to how nervous I was to make this move but the further away I get from Alaska, the more I'm reassured that I made the right choice.

"I know you don't really know any of us yet," Ali says. "But I promise, you're going to fit right in."

"We're really just a big, rowdy family," Kady adds and I smile through the ache in my chest as I think about the family I've already lost and how alone I've felt these past four weeks. Lincoln walks into the room and I glance over at him as he carries the urn of Mom's ashes in his arms down a hallway in the back where I assume is my room as my chest aches. It would be so easy to lose myself in the pain of her loss but I can't go down that rabbit hole right now. I push the thoughts away before scanning the rest of the room.

It's fairly large with a bar at one end and several pool tables at the other. There are several round tables scattered in the middle of the room and a couple of couches against the back wall. It's actually a pretty comfortable space which is the opposite of what I was expecting but after meeting the girls, it fits. As my gaze sweeps past the bar again, I notice one of the guys off by himself, drinking, and when he looks up and our eyes meet, my belly does a flip for a whole other reason. Even all the way across the room, I can see that he is easily the hottest man I've ever laid eyes on and a tingle races across my skin. He turns toward me, so subtly that if I hadn't been staring at him, I would have missed it and he cocks his head to the side. I'm unable to pull my gaze away for a few heavy seconds but when I finally do, I swear I can still feel his gaze burning into me.

Jesus Christ.

"Tatum, are you going to introduce the rest of us?" an older man asks as he approaches us. He is a big guy and with his medium length gray hair and the beard covering half of his weathered face, I get the feeling that people might feel intimidated by him at first but there is something about his clear blue eyes, shining with kindness and humor, that instantly puts me at ease.

"I don't know…" Tate muses, cocking her head to the side as she shoots him a look full of attitude. "Y'all are not exactly house trained and I don't want to overwhelm the poor girl."

He smirks, shaking his head as he turns his gaze to me. "Something tells me she can take care of herself."

"Well, if she can't now, I'll get her set up in no time."

"Dear God," he whispers, shaking his head in mock horror. "Please don't. The last thing I need is another taser wielding woman running around my club."

I laugh, remembering the phone call with Lincoln where he informed me of Tate's fondness for tasers. She shoots him a grin.

"You forgot about my gun."

"Oh, I haven't forgotten. In fact, I specifically remember you promising to not pull it on anymore of my boys," he says and she shrugs.

"I would say it was more of something I would take into consideration *before* I pulled a gun on any more members."

"Tate," he warns, arching a brow at her and she holds her hands up in front of her like she's completely innocent.

"Hey, just tell your boys to stop being dumb assholes and then we can avoid this whole situation in the future."

"Kodiak is a fucking saint," he mutters before shaking his head and turning to me. "I'm Blaze, by the way, president of this club."

I nod, shaking his hand. "Ah, yes. I've heard all about you."

"What have you told her?" he accuses, leveling a mock glare at Tate and she takes a step back.

"Don't look at me. I would never speak ill of my favorite member of this club."

"What was that?" Lincoln growls, sneaking up behind Tate and scooping her up in his arms as she squeals. Blaze chuckles, watching them, before turning to me.

"Don't worry. You'll get used to all of this soon enough."

I scoff, shaking my head. "If you say so."

"The truth is, Rowan, this club and everyone in this room is family and there isn't a single person here who wouldn't drop everything to be there for you at a moment's notice. And, yeah, we can be overwhelming at first but we really do mean well."

"I believe that," I tell him with a nod. "Besides, there is no way in hell my brother would have ever brought me here if he didn't trust you all whole heartedly."

Lincoln nods as he sets Tate back on her feet and pulls her into his body, wrapping his arms around her. "You're damn right I wouldn't."

"Come on. Let me introduce you to everyone else," he says, motioning for me to follow him. He leads me to a group of men before introducing me to each of them before turning to a man who flashes him a scowl as he introduces him as his son, Nix, before pointing to the woman at his side. "And this is my daughter-in-law, Emma.

I nod to them and paste what I hope is a friendly smile on my face. "It's nice to meet you guys."

"You too, sweetie," Emma says, her smile way more sincere than mine feels. Blaze and Nix hold each other's gazes for a moment before Blaze sighs and turns back to me, pointing toward the bar.

"And that's Streak. He's also good people but he's in a shitty mood tonight so maybe just wait until tomorrow to say hi."

My gaze meets Streak's across the room and I nod as a wave of warmth washes through me. It feels like his green eyes can see right through all my defenses. After all of the shit I've been through lately, I shouldn't be thinking about what it would feel like to kiss him but I am. In fact, when I'm not staring at his intense eyes, I'm looking at his full lips and wondering how they would feel against mine. There is a strange fluttering feeling in my chest and my cheeks heat as I meet his eyes again and the hint of a smile shines back at me.

God, can he tell what I'm thinking?

Can he see that every time he looks at me, all I can think about is getting closer to him?

Blowing out a breath, I force myself to look away from him and turn back to the group.

"Man, I'm just saying," Chance says, a mischievous smirk on his face as Lincoln glares at him. "Imagine if both those babies are girls. Not only are you going to have to deal with twice the amount of boys trying to get at your daughters but I have a sneaking suspicion that they'll both be just like their mama."

Blaze rolls his eyes. "Lord help us all."

I join in their laughter as I look over at my brother and his wife. When he called me a couple of months ago to tell me the news that Tate was pregnant with twins, I was so excited for them but I couldn't wrap my mind around it. I couldn't see Lincoln as a dad until I realized that he's been a dad for most of his life, ever since ours died and he stepped up to do whatever it took to take care of Nora, Mom, and me. If anyone deserves the happiness he's found now, it's my brother.

"What about you, Rowan?"

I blink and glance over at Smith, who is looking at me expectantly. "Huh?"

"You got any plans now that you're here?"

"Hell no," I answer with a laugh as I shake my head. "I'm just happy to be out of my damn car."

Moose nods, taking a sip of his beer. "See? This is why I love to ride."

They all start talking about their bikes and how much they love the feeling of being on the open road when Tate nudges me and motions for me to follow her. We slip away from the boys and she leads me across the room to a large metal door before pushing it open. A professional grade kitchen comes into view and I let out a low whistle.

"Fancy."

She scoffs as she pulls open a refrigerator. "It's necessary since we usually have a lot of people to feed. Now, what sounds good?"

"What do you have?"

"There is leftover spaghetti from lunch," she suggests and I nod. I heat up the pasta and sit down at the island in the middle of the room before digging in and she plops down next to me with a sigh.

"So, this boyfriend…" she prompts and I look up from my plate, arching a brow. "I want to hear the whole story."

I laugh. "Why?"

"Because depending on how big of a douche he was, I may just need to hop on a plane," she answers with a smile and I laugh again.

"I don't think they'll let you bring your taser or gun on board."

She sighs. "Shit. That's true… whatever, I can get creative. Tell me anyway."

I relay the whole story to her, starting with the shitty night I was having at work but careful to leave out where I was working since I'm sure if Lincoln found out I was stripping, he would lose his damn mind. When I finish, she beams at me with pride on her face.

"Well, if it had been me, things would have gotten much more violent but I am proud of you for telling him where he could stick it. It's just a shame that

59

none of those shards of pottery landed sharp side down in that whore's chest."

A startled laugh spills out of me as I look up at her and shake my head. "I didn't feel like dealing with the blood so it's probably for the best."

We laugh and as I finish my food, she fills me in on how things have been around here but remains pretty tight-lipped on this threat she mentioned when I first got here. It's annoying but if nobody fills me in soon, I'll demand answers from Linc. When I'm finished with my dinner, we wander back out into the main room. Someone has started playing music and a few of the couples are paired off, dancing together in the middle of the room like we're at some kind of middle school dance while others are lounging on the couch, talking. Tate tells me she's going to find Lincoln and I nod, turning back to look around the room as memories of Ash and his betrayal flick through my mind. It's not even that I'm all that upset about losing Ash... I mean, I am but not as much as I should be, which tells me all I need to know. I think it's mostly a pride thing combined with the fact that I lost someone else from my life so close to my mom's death. I don't wish him any ill will but I am furious that he made me look like an idiot and embarrassed that I didn't see what was really going on. And, on top of all that, to find out Holly wasn't the first girl he cheated with was just icing on the cake.

Gritting my teeth, I grab a bottle of dark liquor from the bar and sneak up the stairs when no one is watching, hoping to get just a few moments of peace and quiet. And maybe a distraction from my own thoughts. I take a sip from the bottle as I wander down the hallway, wandering aimlessly past locked doors on each side of me. The room at the very end of the hall is wide open and before I tell myself that I shouldn't do it, I step inside and look around. It's a little messy but I'm not all that surprised and there is a desk in the middle of the room with three computer monitors on it. The thing is massive and it dominates the space. In one corner are a stack of files and I barely resist the urge to snoop through them before turning to take in the rest of the room. A full-sized bed is shoved into one corner and it looks like it hasn't been made... ever. Clothes litter the floor but I wouldn't say that the room is all that messy, just... well lived in. It's obvious that someone spends a lot of time in here and I wonder whose room I just wandered into.

"Find anything interesting?"

I whirl around, my heart jumping into my throat as I come face-to-face with Streak. His hands are shoved in the pockets of his jeans and he's staring at me with curiosity mixed with something else, something intense that makes my stomach feel all fluttery. His jade green eyes bore into mine as he takes a step toward me, eliminating the space between us, waiting for an answer. I shrug.

"Not really."

He places a hand over his heart and his face crumples in mock hurt. "Are you saying I'm boring?"

"Pretty sure that never came out of my mouth," I answer and he nods as his gaze drops to my mouth and his tongue darts out to wet his bottom lip. Heat rushes through me as my body screams in protest over the fact that he's not pressing up against me right now. My thoughts jump to the bed behind us and my heart thunders in my chest.

Did someone just suck all of the air out of the room when I wasn't looking?

"So, you're in my room because?" he asks, arching a brow as he waits for my reply and I shrug as I take a step back, moving around him to look at a bookcase built into the wall by the door. Anything to stop myself from climbing him like a goddamn tree.

"Just bored, I guess…" I say, irritated by how out of breath I sound and the way my skin is zipping with need. I touch one of the knickknacks on the shelf, pretending to inspect it. "I'm Rowan, by the way."

"I know." His voice is soft but he's closed the distance between us again so I hear every word perfectly and his warm breath ruffles my hair. I spin around, backing into the bookcase as I look up at him. A few things rattle behind me but I can't pretend to care. There is something about him, something that makes me feel like he understands a part of me that most people can't even see and when our eyes meet again, all the shit I've been through in the past month fills my mind like he called it to the surface. It's hard to believe it's only been a month since my mom died when it feels like it's been years, each day dragging on as I try to wade through my grief and that's not even taking into consideration what Ash did to me.

Jesus Christ.

I need to get control of myself.

"Rowan?" he asks, snapping me out of my thoughts. I look up at him and he flashes me an expectant look.

Shit, did he say something?

"Huh?"

He takes his thumb and drags it over my knitted brow and I realize that I've been scowling at him this whole time. "What are you thinking about?"

"You don't want to know," I tell him as I turn away and lift the bottle to my lips, taking a long sip. It's a terrible idea but right now, I just want to forget and feel something other than... *this*. When I glance back at him, he tilts his head to the side and it's like he is looking right through me again. It feels like someone has zapped me with a live wire and I fight the nagging urge to tell him what he wants to know for a moment before giving into it. Sighing, I meet his gaze. "It's just been a hell of a month."

He nods, releasing a heavy breath. "Yeah, I know the feeling."

"I suppose the healthy, mature thing for us to do would be to talk about it to someone who might understand what we're going through," I reply, studying his face and I swear, the air between us crackles. He flashes me a lopsided grin as he braces his hands on the shelves next to my hips and nods.

"You're probably right... but what if I don't feel like being mature and healthy tonight?"

My breath catches in my throat and he leans in closer, almost like he is being drawn to me, like he has no control over this either and my heart hammers relentlessly as my skin aches to feel his hands on me. I've never been this attracted to someone in my life and I am so desperate to feel good. Setting the bottle down on the bookshelf behind me, I lean back on one of the shelves, placing my hands right next to his so they barely brush as I arch my back and meet his gaze. His eyes are darker and full of all sorts of dirty thoughts, commanding me with just a look to give him the green light. I'm more than happy to comply.

"Then you should probably lock the door."

"Thank fuck," he growls, one hand diving into my hair as he closes the distance between us and slams his lips to mine, his kiss so intense and demanding that I see stars. He reaches out with his other hand and shuts the door before locking it and slamming me up against the bookcase. I moan when he grinds his hips against mine, every inch of my skin on fire as he slips one hand up behind my back and starts kissing down my neck. My nipples press against the fabric of my bra, aching for some attention as I drop my head back and gasp for air. Just when I think I can't take anymore, he pulls back and a whimper of frustration slips past my lips.

His eyes meet mine, wild and needy, and his breathing matches mine as he shakes his head. "I need to say something."

"I don't want to talk." I reach up and wrap my hand around the back of his neck, pulling him back to me and he comes willingly, groaning as we connect again. His tongue flicks my bottom lip and tangles with mine as he grabs my ass with both hands and pulls me against him.

"Fuck," he gasps, pulling away again. "I have to say this before we go any further."

I roll my eyes, trying to get closer to him. "Then fucking say it."

"I just need you to know," he replies, moving closer to me like he can't stop himself before leaning in to kiss my neck again. A shudder racks my body and I close my eyes, ready to lose myself in him but he pulls away again. "This is only sex."

"Yeah, okay." I nod, urging him to kiss me again. Honestly, that's perfectly fine with me and I don't know why he felt the need to say anything in the first place.

"No, listen. We can have fun together but you need to know that this is never going to go anywhere. I'm never going to fall in love with you."

My entire body stills as my thoughts screech to a halt. I look up at him and narrow my eyes. "I see… and you felt the need to tell me this why?"

He tries to say something but I hold my hand up to stop him.

"Is it because you were going to fuck me with your "magic cock" and I would suddenly lose every single brain cell I ever had? Or did you assume that just because I have tits and a vag that sex equals love for me?"

When he tries to speak again, I place my hand over his mouth and shake my head. The more I think about all the assumptions he just made about me and whatever this thing is between us, the more fired up I get.

"You know what? Forget it. All I wanted was to forget my shit for a while and do something that felt good but if that's too much for you to handle, you can fuck right off." I try to free myself from his grasp but he refuses to release me and when I glance up at him, the look in his eyes makes me feel fucking needy all over again. Not that I'll give into it. Squaring my shoulders, I send a glare in his direction and try to wiggle out of his grasp again. "Let me go."

His answering growl hits me right in the stomach and my pussy clenches at the almost feral look on his face as he cups my cheek and forces me to turn toward him again. We lock eyes and he holds my gaze for a second before we crash together again and this time there is no stopping us. His hands are everywhere as he leaves a trail of teeth marks down my neck and when I moan, he slaps his hand over my mouth.

"You gotta be quiet, sweetheart," he admonishes with a smile that is full of promise and my heart jumps into my throat. Writhing against him, I whimper. My body is swamped with a need more intense than I've ever felt before and I don't know how much longer I can wait. He moves his hand from my mouth, replacing it with his lips as he drags my shirt up my belly and only pulls away long enough to rip it over my head. As he starts dragging his tongue down the side of my neck, I suck in a breath and reach for his belt, my hands shaking and my chest feeling like it might explode. He kisses back up to my lips and grabs a fistful of hair before pulling back to look in my eyes. "In a few minutes, you're going to feel the urge to scream my name... don't call me Streak."

I nod, frantically. He could ask for just about anything right now and I would probably agree. "What should I call you then?"

"Travis," he answers, smirking as he pops the button of my jeans and slips his hand down the front. His fingers brush over my clit and I gasp, gripping his t-shirt as my head falls back and my hips roll forward. My belly clenches as he starts flicking his fingers back and forth over the sensitive bud. The satisfied expression on his face tells me that he is just teasing me, taking his time to build me up but I don't know how much more I can take. My body is strung tight, every inch of my skin screaming for attention as my belly clenches.

"Oh my God," I breathe, my eyes rolling back in my head as he moves lower and slips two fingers inside me, massaging my inner walls with precision. The boy knows what he's doing and I swear, I couldn't be more thankful of that fact than I am in this very moment.

Leaning in, he sinks his teeth into my neck before softly kissing the same spot. He adds his thumb into the mix, circling my clit as he crooks his fingers and hits the perfect spot. My entire body tenses and I cry out as my release rolls through me, prompting him to seal his lips to mine. The fist in my hair tightens and he gives it a tug, adding another element to the already stellar orgasm. Wave after wave of pleasure roll through me, my pussy gripping his fingers tightly, and I wonder if it's ever going to end.

Jesus Christ.

Is this what it feels like when you die? Because I'm pretty sure that is what is happening to me. I've never felt anything like it but at the same time, I still want more. What kind of fucking sorcery is this and where in the hell did this boy come from?

Travis pulls back to study my face before laughing. "You want more?"

"Oh, I'm nowhere near done with you," I tell him after I catch my breath, unzipping his jeans and dropping to my knees in front of him. The hand in my hair is gentler as he watches me pull his jeans down and wrap my fingers around his thick cock. He groans and his eyes roll back in his head at the simple touch and I smile, feeling powerful. I run the tip of my tongue up the underside of his length from the base to the tip and when I see the look of bliss on his face, I vow to myself that we will be doing this again. Frequently, if I get my way. Besides, after the month I've had, I deserve all the fun and mind-blowing orgasms I can get.

Wicked Games

Chapter Five
Warren

A cold, winter breeze whips against me and I shove my hands in my coat pockets as I walk down the sidewalk, keeping an eye out for any trouble but the entire block is a ghost town tonight. Hmm… how fitting. Not only does it work to my advantage perfectly as I slip into the trees of the edge of the property but it's also how this club will look when I'm finished with them. Creeping closer to the fence that surrounds the entire perimeter of the clubhouse, I scan the parking lot and freeze when Rooster steps out to do his rounds.

"Right on time," I whisper as I crouch down and watch him walk over to the closed gate. That seems to be the one major precaution they've taken to protect themselves from me and it's actually laughable how clueless they are. There is nothing that they can do to stop me or keep me from completing my mission.

Fuck…

Maybe I haven't done a sufficient job of making them realize just how much danger they are in since their security measures are so lax but then again, that might be for the best. Let them be complacent. Let them be bewildered so when I strike and take the pound of flesh that I'm owed, it will be all the more shocking. Then again... it might make my victory even sweeter if they put up a little bit of a fight. After I mull the idea over in my head, I release a sigh. There will be time to consider it later, I tell myself, as I turn back to watch Rooster. He stands behind the gate scanning the street for a few more seconds before shaking his head and turning back toward the clubhouse.

Fucking amateurs.

If he actually took the time to walk the perimeter, he probably would have found the nice little entrance I made myself with a pair of bolt cutters long before now but I've noticed that their prospect likes to do as little as possible. Plus, on top of that, he's got the worst fucking attitude, like the entire world has fucked him over but that couldn't be further from the truth. This club took everything from me, stole every single ounce of anything good from my life. and he is just a cry baby in a cut. Maybe I'll add him to my list, make sure he knows the depths of *my* rage so he can see how insignificant his problems are because watching him walk around with this chip on his shoulder pisses me the fuck off.

Pushing the thoughts from my mind, I wait for him to step back into the clubhouse before slipping through the cut in the fence and creeping across the parking lot in the darkness. I have my ways of keeping tabs on the club at all times but when I realized they were having a party tonight, I needed to see them in person so I could witness their joy firsthand. It fuels me, knowing that I get to be the one to take it all away from them. When I get to the back wall, I flatten myself against it and move toward the window before crouching down and peeking through the glass.

Moose and Juliette, Smith and Quinn, and Henn and Kady are all slow dancing together in the middle of the room, looking far too cozy for people with their necks on the chopping block but I ignore them and scan the rest of the room. Rooster is by the bar, drowning his sorrows in a bottle of booze and I grit my teeth and my gaze flicks toward the pool tables. Kodiak and Chance are playing pool, their wives talking to each other at the table nearby and Blaze, Storm, and Ali are sitting on the couches in the corner, talking. The smiles on their face infuriate me. Fuck all of them. I am going to tear down this whole club for what they did to me but there are four people in particular that hold the heaviest blame and I'm going to do everything I can to make sure their pain matches my own before I end them. One of them is missing and I grit my teeth as I pull away from the window and look to the corner of the building. Streak is probably up in his room because that is where he spends most of his damn time and that means I won't be able to see him up on the second floor.

Hissing a curse, I push away from the building and take a deep breath before I start heading back toward the fence. My fingers twitch as I think about how happy they all looked and how I didn't get to complete the mission I came here tonight to accomplish and I fight the urge to slam my fist into the brick wall. All I wanted was to get eyes on my main targets but Streak never fucking makes it easy on me. I'm decent with computers but he's better which means I always have to be one step ahead and I can never mess up. It's the only way I've gotten away with all of this as long as I have.

I'm almost to my spot in the fence when I hear a slapping sound behind me and I whip around, scanning the lot for any sign of a threat but it's empty. My heart races as I stay motionless, waiting for something else to happen.

What the hell was that?

A low moan drifts through the air and I glance up to the second floor where Streak's room is. There is one window in his room and I sink into the shadows and watch Streak press Kodiak's kid sister, Rowan, up against it in just her pink lacy bra and nothing else. Her back arches and her lips part in a moan as he grips a chunk of her hair, tugging on it as he positions himself behind her and presses his cock into her. Her pretty little eyes squeeze shut and another moan drifts down to me. Holy fuck. She is a pretty little thing and my cock jumps at the sound of her pleasure. I can't even remember the last time I was with a woman and most of my life for so long has been devoted to making the Devils pay for what they did to me so there hasn't been time for fun of any kind.

She grips the molding on both sides of the window as Streak reaches around her front and grabs a handful of her full tits, pulling another moan from her. Shit, she is so responsive and my cock aches as it presses against my zipper. My fingers twitch and I close my eyes, imagining that it's me slamming my length into her again and again as a soft groan spills from my lips. My heart pounds in my ears and I open my eyes again as Rowan lets out a louder moan. Streak covers her mouth with his hand and pulls her back to him so he can kiss her neck as his pace quickens. I'm hard as a fucking rock watching them and I don't think I could even walk right now if I wanted to. Sinking further into the shadows, I unzip my jeans and fist my cock in my hand, pumping it slowly as I watch them. Streak releases the clasp of her bra before pulling it away and flinging it across the room.

"Yes," I hiss as her tits bounce with his thrusts and I feel a tingle at the base of my spine. Closing my eyes again, I picture her in my bed as I crawl over her and slam into her tight little pussy, using her however I want but she fucking loves it, moaning my name as my cock drives into her again and again. As the fantasy plays in my head, my entire body tenses and I release a low groan, so soft that no one will hear it, as my seed shoots all over the pavement. I drop my head back as the release rocks through me. "Fuck."

When I can finally move again, I tuck myself back into my jeans and glance back up at the window, breathing heavily. That is definitely a fantasy that I will be replaying in my head often but staying here for much longer would be stupid. Streak pulls Rowan away from the window. My ribs feel tight and I press my lips together at the loss. Before I can get too upset, they move back toward the window but stop just before it. Streak lifts Rowan off her feet and knocks a bunch of shit off his desk before setting her on the top and slipping back inside her. She clings to him as she throws her head back and moans but he doesn't let her make noise for long, pulling her back to him and slamming his lips to hers.

"Well, this is an interesting development," I murmur as I watch them kiss like they're going to die if they don't and I can't help but chuckle as I shake my head.

You know, sometimes, these fuckers make this shit *way* too easy on me.

For months, I've been trying to come up with something I can use against Streak to amplify his suffering and coming up with a whole lot of nothing but now he has just dropped the perfect thing right into my hands. The one thing Streak cares about more than anything in the world is this club and his brothers so I can only imagine that he wants to keep this little fling a secret. Grinning to myself, I pull my phone out and snap a few pictures of them in the thralls of passion and wonder how Kodiak would feel about his brother fucking his baby sister.

Would it be enough to make him cut ties?
Would it be enough to make him kill Streak?

That would be perfect, actually. Nothing would tear this club apart like one member killing another. I wouldn't even have to do anything. As I watch them, my mind begins to wander about how I could get these photos to Kodiak and another idea hits me out of nowhere, pulling a startled laugh from my lips. It's so fucking devious, so perfect that I can't believe I didn't think of it before and the best part is that while I might be pulling a few strings, I know enough about Streak to know that he will do exactly what I need him to do for this plan to work. He will play right into my hand without even knowing it.

My phone buzzes in my pocket and chuckling to myself, I slip back through the fence before answering it. "Hello?"

"This is a collect call from an inmate at the Allan B. Polunsky Unit in Livingston, Texas. Do you wish to accept the charges?" the automated voice on the other end of the line asks as I walk through the trees back toward my car.

"Yes."

"Please hold," the voice replies before silence greets me. After a few seconds, I hear a click and the sound of someone breathing.

"Warren?"

I smile. "How are you, Samson? How is prison treating you?"

"Oh, just great," he scoffs with a humorless laugh. "I was just calling to see how things were going out your way."

"Good... really good."

He sighs. "What the hell does that mean?"

"It means that things are moving along perfectly," I tell him, thinking back to the plan that just struck me. I'm not the only person Streak has messed with and Samson wants revenge on the man as much as I do. Hell, maybe even more. "Don't you worry about a thing."

"I want to know what's going on," he growls and I shake my head. I would happily keep Samson informed if he wasn't currently sitting on death row, waiting to be executed, where they record every word of every phone call he makes. Telling him everything would bring the whole plan crashing down around us and we'd both end up behind bars.

"You know why we can't."

A noise of frustration greets me before he sighs. "Just promise me you're going to get this done. I want him to suffer, Warren. I want him..."

"Okay. I think you've said enough, friend."

"Right," he mutters before sighing again and I feel for him. I can't imagine what the hell I would do if I was behind bars, unable to get justice for everything that has been done to me. I shudder as I think about sitting in a small cell every single day with only my rage to keep me company. It's enough to make you go insane.

"I'll take care of it, Sam. I promise you."

"I don't have much time left," he murmurs. "My last appeal was rejected by the court today and they're talking to me about scheduling my execution. I want to see him get what he deserves before I go."

I nod as I reach my car and slip behind the wheel. I fucking feel for the guy and wish I could do something more to make the last of his time here on this earth memorable but they're aren't exactly going to let me take a videotape of our revenge into a jail. "Don't worry. We're near the end now and you'll get your justice."

"Good. Make it hurt, Warren."

I laugh as thoughts of what I have in store for these boys plays through my head like a major motion picture. "Oh, trust me, I will."

Chapter Six
Travis

Peeling my eyes open, I blink at the bright sunlight streaming in through my bedroom window and try to stretch when I feel the warm body next to me and glance down. Rowan is curled up against me, playing little spoon as she sleeps peacefully, her lips parted and her lashes fanning out across her pink cheeks. As I watch her, my mind drifts back to last night. I was surprised as hell to find her in my room but not even the slightest bit upset since I hadn't been able to peel my eyes away from her from the moment she walked through the door. I don't know if it was the awful fucking week I've been having trying to find answers in my recording of Veronica's interview or if it was just *her* but I wanted her from just a look. I have never felt anything like it, the way she stole all of my attention without doing anything and the way I felt like I had to touch her, I had to have her. There was no other option because I wanted her more than I've ever wanted anyone else. Hell, I still do. She lets out a groan, pulling my attention to her as she stretches, rubbing her round ass against my cock and I bite back a hiss as my dick twitches. She settles again, releasing a breath.

Fuck.

I want her again despite the fact that we had more sex last night than I've ever had in a twenty-four hour period. Hell, if we could lock ourselves in this room for a fucking week without Kodiak finding out and trying to murder me with his bare hands, I might just make that happen and it still might not even be enough. Wrapping my arm around her, I blow out a breath and shake my head. It's not like I haven't been with a lot of girls because I have but usually after round one or two, my mind is drifting to other things and the girl I'm with isn't able to hold my attention. I don't see that being a problem with Rowan. At all. There is something about her that I can see myself getting totally lost in and maybe that's exactly what I need right now. But I meant what I said to her last night - there is no way in hell this is ever going any further than that. She and I are hella attracted to each other, the sexual chemistry is fucking insane, and we have earth shifting sex but I don't do love. I won't be the next in the long line of Devils to fall in love, get married, and start popping out babies.

"No…it's too early," Rowan mumbles to herself before throwing her arms over her head in a stretch and my eyes fall to her tits, appreciating the way her back arches and her ass presses into me again. I lean down and press my lips to her neck as a soft moan slips past her lips.

"Princess, if you keep doing that, you're gonna make me hard."

She grins and wiggles her ass against my cock without opening her eyes. "I like the sound of that."

"So do I," I groan, gripping her hip and kissing her neck again before biting at her earlobe. "But I don't think you want to wake up the whole house with your screaming."

"Fuck," she hisses, her eyes snapping open as she throws the covers off of her legs and jumps out of bed. I watch her run around the room, grabbing her clothes and throwing them on as I laugh.

"What are you doing?"

She shoots me a glare. "I have to get back down to my room before anyone wakes up. If Lincoln realizes I spent the night up here, he's going to lose his shit."

"You're a grown woman and you can sleep with whoever you want to," I tell her and she stops in the middle of my room, arching a brow.

"Okay. You go tell him you fucked his little sister eight times last night."

The thought makes my balls crawl back up inside my body. "Uh... better get going, then."

"That's what I thought," she says with a laugh as she continues getting dressed and when she's got everything back on, she walks across the room and leans over me, pressing her lips to mine. I'm sure it was supposed to be a quick kiss but our bodies have other ideas and I can't stop myself from pulling her down on top of me with a groan. She straddles my hips and rocks against my cock, moaning before she pulls away and shakes her head. "We can't."

"I know."

She flashes me a devilish grin. "My brother might actually kill you if he finds out about this."

"That's why we're going to keep it on the down low."

"Do you regret it?" she asks, chewing nervously on her bottom lip. It's so goddamn cute that I can't help but smile as I reach up and cup her cheek.

"Not a fucking chance."

"Good. Me either," she whispers before leaning down and pressing another quick kiss against my lips, pulling away just enough to let her mouth brush against mine as she smiles and meets my gaze. "Can't wait to do this again."

Shit.

"Me either," I agree, kissing her again but she stops it before it can go too far. God, I want to pull her back to me and spend the whole fucking day in this bed. She jumps off the bed and winks over her shoulder at me as she walks to my bedroom door. I watch her as she cracks it open and peeks into the hallway, checking that the coast is clear, before slipping out and shutting it behind her.

Sitting up in bed, I turn and lean back against the wall, sighing as I run a hand through my hair. I glance over at the bedside table littered with condom wrappers and I shake my head.

Eight times in one night?

Really?

It's hard to believe but at this point, the entire evening is just a blur of naked skin, kissing, biting, and moaning so who fucking knows. Maybe her and I hooking up was an awful idea and I'm pretty sure that if Kodiak finds out, I'll have to go on the run but I can't deny that it was exactly what I needed. This weight I've been feeling for weeks now is a little lighter this morning and if the look in Rowan's eyes last night was any indication, she needed it just as much as I did. Besides, like I said, she is a grown ass woman and she can do whatever she wants with her body so what the hell is wrong with the two of us using each other to deal with our shit if we both are clear that it will never go any farther? Then again, if I use the words "using" and "your sister" in the same sentence when talking to Kodiak, I'm a dead man either way.

Pushing those thoughts from my mind, I throw the covers off of my legs and climb out of bed, sweeping the wrappers into the trash before grabbing my jeans off of the floor and getting dressed. I shuffle over to my desk and sink into my chair, scrubbing my hand over my face and yawning. As I pull up Veronica's interview, I shake my head. I've listened to the thing close to fifty times and at this point, I could probably recite it for anyone else but I just keep hoping that I'll hear something new, something that will break this whole case wide open even if I know that's stupid. Just as I'm about to push play and listen to it again, I remember her comment about the woman her abductor met in a bar and I lean back in my chair, scowling. There is only one person he could be talking about and she is also just about the last person I want to go speak to.

But we need answers.

Groaning, I grab my phone off of the desk as I stand up before heading for the door as I slip it into my pocket. Goddamn it. I would rather do just about anything than meet with this girl but I know it's my best bet. Every other leads we've managed to track down has been a dead end and we need a new angle – even if that angle is someone I can't stand. I yank the door open with more force than necessary and Moose turns to look at me with wide eyes as he stops in front of his and Juliette's room with a cup of coffee in each hand.

"Everything okay?"

I nod. "Yeah. I just realized I need to talk to Tawny, though."

"Shit," he whispers with a wince and I can't say that I blame him. If anyone knows exactly what Tawny is capable of, it's Moose. "Take back up."

"You volunteering?" I ask and laugh when some of the color drains from his face. He shakes his head.

"Absolutely fucking not."

Moose and Tawny were hooking up for a while before he met his wife, Juliette, but she got it in her head that they were getting serious when they couldn't have been further from the truth and when he ended things with her, she fucking lost it. Blaze had to kick her out of the clubhouse and the next thing we knew, the police were talking to Moose because she had filed assault charges against him. In the end, the charges were dropped due to lack of evidence and we thought that was the end of it until Tawny showed up at the clubhouse a few weeks back. She told us about the guy she met in a bar who had encouraged her to let him punch her in the face so she could press charges against Moose and mess up the club's image. There is no way in hell this isn't the same guy and if she's had an up close interaction with him, I need to speak to her.

"I'm serious, Streak," Moose says, snapping me out of my thoughts. "I won't get anywhere near her but you need someone with you. The last thing any of us needs is her claiming some shit again."

I nod. "I hear you. I'll go see who's up."

Nodding in approval, he turns and slips back into his room as I head downstairs to see who is awake and willing to go along with me. I can't believe I was really about to go talk to her, all alone, when I know what she's like. If you're going to be around Tawny, you need fucking witnesses. The bar is quiet when I walk in and I sigh, glancing back toward the stairs.

Shit.

People usually give me a hard time about sleeping until noon but lately I've been up before everyone else, my mind constantly working over the case as I try to find some answers, even in my sleep. Not that it's done a damn bit of good. A door opens from down the hallway and I turn my head as Rowan steps into the room in fresh clothes, a jean miniskirt and t-shirt, with her dark hair piled into a bun on top of her head.

"Hey," she says, flashing me a loaded smile that has me thinking about taking her back up to my room.

She's going to be the death of me.

"Anyone else up?"

She shakes her head, her gaze dropping to the keys in my hand. "I don't think so. You going somewhere?"

"Yeah…" I sigh, looking over at the door before turning back to her. "Actually, you want to go with me?"

"Where are we going?"

I laugh as she comes out from behind the bar and stops next to me. "Is that a yes then?"

"Obviously," she shoots back, rolling her eyes and I shake my head as we start walking toward the clubhouse door. "You didn't answer my question."

"Uh… we're going on a little mission and I need backup."

She studies me as we step outside. The chilly early morning air wraps us up and she crosses her arms over her chest to keep herself warm. "I hate to tell you this now that you've chosen me to go with you but I'm not good in a fight. Like, if someone comes after you, I'm no Tate."

"Thank God," I answer, laughing, and she grins at me. "And it's not like that. I need to go talk to someone and it's best to have witnesses when around this particular person."

"Why?"

We reach my car and I open the passenger door for her as I reach into the back seat and grab one of my hoodies before handing it to her. "It's kind of a long story but I'll fill you in as we drive over there."

"Okay." She takes the hoodie with a smile and pulls it over her head. She's swimming in it and it covers her skirt, too, making her look like she's not wearing anything else, but she doesn't seem to care as she sinks into the bucket seat of my sixty-nine Impala. Once she's in the car, I shut the door and jog around to the other side, sliding behind the wheel. The rumble of the engine makes me smile and as I pull out of my parking space, she turns to look at me. "Start talking."

I arch a brow. "You're a bossy little thing."

"I seem to recall you liking it last night."

Well, she's got me there. Shaking my head, I ignore her comment and begin telling her the Tawny saga as we drive through Baton Rouge to her apartment, starting with the way she worked her way through several of the guys, trying to get one of them to make her their old lady before settling on Moose and then framing him for assault. When I'm done, she falls back in her seat and releases a breath.

"Okay… well, now I see why you needed backup. Who the hell lets a stranger hit them so they can blame it on someone else?"

I shrug. "Someone not right in the head."

"Clearly," she agrees before turning to look at me. "You said she worked her way through several of the guys, right?"

"Yeah... why?"

She scowls. "Did you sleep with her?"

"Oh, hell no." I fight back a shudder of disgust. "I told all of them to stay the hell away from her but do you think they listened to me?"

"Obviously not."

I nod as we pull up in front of Tawny's apartment. We haven't even made it out of the car yet and I already want to leave. Sighing, I turn off the engine and climb out, waiting for Rowan on the sidewalk as she rounds the hood and when she reaches me, she slips her hand into mine. I peek over at her as we approach Tawny's door, wondering why the hell this feels so natural but before I can delve too deeply into it, she knocks on the door. We wait for a few seconds before the door squeaks open and Tawny glances out at us through the crack.

"Why are you here?" she asks, her voice shaky and her eyes darting between Rowan and me. "I haven't been back to the club or bothered any of you."

I nod. "I know, Tawny. We're here because we need to talk to you."

"Why?" she asks, opening the door a little wider but not enough to let us into her place. Rowan takes a step forward and offers her a warm smile. It's actually impressive given how disgusted she was by Tawny's behavior on the way over here.

"Hi, Tawny. I'm Rowan, Kodiak's sister, and we really need your help with something. Do you think we could come in and talk for a little bit?"

Tawny eyes her skeptically before glancing at me. "You really need my help?"

"We do," I answer with a nod and she pulls the door open, allowing us to step into her apartment as she takes a deep breath. Rowan releases my hand as we walk into Tawny's living room and I miss it more than I should. As Rowan and I sit next to each other on the couch, Tawny perches on the edge of a bar stool.

"I don't know how I can help you..."

"I need to know about the guy you met in the bar... the one who punched you and tried to get you to blame it on the club."

She sighs. "I've already told you everything I know about him."

"Actually," I say, trying to keep my voice soft and understanding so she'll open up to me. "I wasn't there when you showed up and I'd like to hear everything in your words."

After studying me for a second, she sighs and nods. "Okay. Where would you like me to start?"

I pull my phone out of my pocket, pulling up the voice memo app and starting a new recording before I set it down on the coffee table. When I look up at her again, I notice that her hands are shaking but I can't understand why. When she showed up at the clubhouse and got into it with Moose, Blaze threatened to take evidence of her drug use to the cops but none of us have ever done anything to make her feel like we would hurt her. At least, I don't think we have...

"How about his name?" Rowan asks, pulling me out of my thoughts and I glance up at Tawny. She sighs.

She sighs. "Shit, I don't know... I was so drunk... oh, wait. I remember. He said his name was Warren because his dad loved the book, *War and Peace*."

"Okay," I reply, ignoring her commentary. Warren can't be all that common of a name and maybe if I search through the receipts at the bar, I might have a chance of finding him. Would he really be that careless, though? Turning back to her, I ask the one question that I'm pretty sure I already know the answer to. "What about what he looked like?"

She shrugs. "Average? I don't know... he has brown hair and brown eyes. He was a little taller than me and slim but kind of unmemorable if he hadn't socked me in the face."

Her description matches every other one we've ever gotten from anyone who had an interaction with him and I nod in irritation. "What about what happened that night?"

"What about it?"

Gritting my teeth, I fight back my irritation and Rowan lays her hand on my leg, forcing me to take a deep breath before turning back to Tawny. "Like did he approach you or did you approach him?"

"Oh, it was all him. I went to the bar to drown my sorrows after Moose dumped me. I was already a couple drinks in when he came up to me and offered to buy me the next one. We started talking and I told him all about you guys and that I had just been dumped."

I nod, remembering the way Moose told the story after she had stopped by the clubhouse to explain herself. "And framing Moose was all his idea?"

"Yeah. He said you guys weren't as clean cut as you like to pretend you were and he wanted to expose you. When I said I didn't want anything to do with y'all anymore, he brought up how funny it would be if a member got arrested for hitting a woman."

87

"Right, and then he lured you out behind the bar and punched you?"

She nods. "That part gets a little fuzzy. He was plying me with drinks for most of the night and I was *very* drunk by then. He took advantage of that."

"Do you remember anything else?" Rowan asks. "Anything that might help us find out who this guy is?"

"Well…"

I arch a brow. "What is it?"

"I don't really know if it will help but I clearly remember thinking that right before he hit me, his face changed and he hit me way harder than he needed to…"

Rowan scowls. "What do you mean?"

"I mean, he hit me so fucking hard that he fractured my cheekbone and he seemed so angry in that moment but the rest of the night, he was perfectly charming and nice… I don't know… It was like he became a different person," she sighs and shakes her head. "I'm sorry I can't be more help."

I stand up and grab my phone off of the coffee table as I shake my head. "No, it's okay. We're all kind of spinning our wheels here but I knew this was a long shot. I appreciate you taking the time to talk to me, though."

"If I think of anything else, I'll let you know. I want to help."

"That would be great," I tell her, pulling one of the club's business cards out of my back pocket and writing my cell number on the back before handing it to her. "You can reach me at that number."

She takes it and nods, before frowning. "I am sorry about all of this… and I'm sorry again that I couldn't be more help. If I could fix what I did, I would."

"Look," I say, sighing. "What you did was fucked up but you were also a pawn in this guy's game and I don't really think you would have done this if he hadn't been buying you alcohol all night and coercing you into it."

"Thank you for saying that," she whispers and I nod as Rowan stands. Tawny hops off of the bar stool and walks us to the door, promising again to call if she thinks of anything before we leave. As soon as we're outside, Rowan slips her hand into mine again and I glance down at her.

"You okay?"

I nod. "Yeah... just fucking frustrated."

"Let's go get some food. I always think better after I eat something," she says and there is no room for argument in her tone but oddly, I don't give a shit.

"Yes, ma'am." I laugh as I release her hand and throw my arm over her shoulders, pulling her into my body. My stomach growls, as if on cue, but even if I wasn't starving, there is no way in hell I would turn down an opportunity to spend a little more time with her. Not when she makes me feel like maybe I actually have a chance of solving this and saving my club.

Wicked Games

Chapter Seven
Rowan

"Here are your pancakes and bacon," the waitress says as she sets a heaping plate of food in front of me with a smile. After she's pulled a container of syrup out of her apron and set it on the table next to my plate, she turns to Travis and sets his plate in front of him. "And the hash brown scrambler with sausage and gravy for you. Is there anything else y'all need right now?"

Her gaze flicks between the two of us as I inspect the table for a moment and when I look up at her, I shake my head. She glances over at Travis as he does the same, flashing her a friendly smile. "Naw, I think we're good. Thanks, Mia."

"No problem, Streak. Just holler if you need anything else." She returns his smile before walking away from the table and after she disappears into the kitchen, I turn to back to Travis.

"You come here often?"

He smirks. "Is that your best line?"

"Shut up," I shoot back, rolling my eyes as I resist the urge to pick up one of the jelly packets and throw it at him. "I just meant because you two obviously know each other."

"We don't *really* know each other, if that's what you mean, but Tate used to work here before she married your brother and Mia is a friend of hers."

"Oh, I see."

"But, listen," he whispers, lowering his voice as he leans in and flashes me a devilish grin. "If you want to fuck again, all you gotta do is ask, sweetheart."

I arch a brow. "I thought we had already agreed that it definitely would be happening again. And again and again…"

"Maybe I just want to hear you beg for it," he answers with a grin that makes my belly do a little flip and my mind jumps back to last night when he had me pressed up against the window… and on all fours on the bed… and pressed up against the wall. Jesus Christ, how the hell am I even walking this morning? Lifting my chin in an act of defiance, I cross my arms over my chest and meet his gaze.

"And what if I want to hear *you* beg for it?"

He laughs. "Never going to happen."

"Don't underestimate me, Travis. I have tricks you haven't seen yet," I tell him and his eyes snap up to meet mine as a slow smile stretches across his face and he shakes his head.

"Fuck. That turns me on."

Smiling, I grab my fork and cut into my pancakes, feeling pretty damn pleased with myself as Travis subtly tries to adjust himself under the table. My breath hitches as I remember what it felt like when he slid inside me last night and my skin tingles with need.

How in the hell am I still ready for more?

"So," I whisper before clearing my throat and glancing up at him. We definitely need a new subject before we end up slipping into the bathroom for a quickie or fucking in his sexy car. He arches a brow, watching me with a knowing look in his eye.

"So?"

"Why don't you tell me what's been going on with the club and this threat that everyone keeps talking about?"

His mood darkens in an instant and he shakes his head. "Sorry, can't. It's club business."

"I see…"

I don't see.

Not at all.

"But shouldn't I know since I'm technically involved now? I mean, I'm living there with you all and my brother is one of this guy's targets, right? I have a right to know what's going on."

He shakes his head. "Nope."

"Fine," I answer with a huff but my mind is still spinning, trying to find an angle to use against him that he can't argue with. Another idea hits me and I brace my elbows on the table. "But what if me not knowing gets someone hurt? Or it gets me hurt? Isn't it better that I have all the information so I can make smart, informed decisions?"

"You're not going to let this go, are you?" he asks, studying me and I shake my head. His gaze narrows and he glares at me for a second before he sighs. "All right but if Blaze asks, I didn't tell you shit."

"Deal."

Scowling, he stares down at the table, deep in thought, and I watch him for a second before clearing my throat.

"Uh, Travis?"

He shakes his head. "Sorry… it's just hard to know where to even start."

"The beginning sounds like a good place," I offer, half sarcastically, and he scoffs, shaking his head.

"This is going to sound stupid but I'm not really sure when it all really began. It's hard to keep track of everything now and remember when shit went down. Plus, each time I learn something new, I've got to figure out how it fits into everything."

"Have you ever watched those true crime shows or CSI?" I ask and he shakes his head as he leans back in his seat and takes a sip of coffee.

"No. I don't watch a lot of TV."

"Okay, well, in those shows, you always see a big fucking board with all the evidence laid out in a timeline and I think maybe that's what you need. Besides, if you can see it in front of you, all at once, maybe you'll notice something you didn't notice before."

He studies me for a second. "Huh… I can't believe I never thought of that before."

"So, I only did like two semesters in college before I dropped out but I was super interested in psychology and took a class on it where we learned that when people are too close to a problem, like you are, it's like being in the middle of a thick forest. You can see what's right in front of you but you can't see very far into the distance or anticipate what is up ahead."

His scowl is etched into his face as he crosses his arms over his chest and I can practically see the wheels in his head turning. "I need to step back, then?"

"Or just get an outside perspective," I reply, motioning to myself and he laughs, staring at me for a second before he nods.

"Okay, I'll give it a shot."

I smile. "For now, just give me the CliffsNotes."

"Has your brother told you anything? Or Tate?" he asks and I shake my head, my mind drifting back to the party last night. They mentioned talking to me about it later but I don't know if they meant it or if they were just stalling in the hope that I would forget about it. If that's the case, I'm sure they think they're protecting me by not telling me but I fully believe what I said to Travis. There is no way I could possibly make the right decisions and keep myself safe without knowing the facts. He sighs. "Right, okay... For the last two or so years, someone has been targeting the club but at first, we didn't know anything was going on..."

"What do you mean?"

He runs a hand through his hair. "Well, in the work we do, sometimes the women we rescue go back to their abusers so when the first girl was killed, that's what we thought happened."

"Oh," I whisper, staring at him with wide eyes. When people kept mentioning this threat, never in my wildest dreams did I think that people had died and that things were this serious. Now it makes perfect sense why Lincoln wanted me at the clubhouse instead of at his cabin.

"I'm sorry," he says, reaching across the table and grabbing my hand. "You said you wanted to know."

I nod. "I do... I just never..."

"It's bad, Rowan. Really, really bad and that's why we're all so fucking stressed and at each other's throats."

Squeezing his hand, I nod. "Keep going."

"The first girl that was killed, her name was Dina and we all assumed her piece of shit ex had been the one to kill her."

I nod. It makes sense with the work the club does and it probably would have been my first assumption as well. "So what changed?"

"For a long time, nothing. We lost another girl but the case was so different that we didn't even connect them until later and then we lost someone that made us all wake up."

"In what way?" I ask, my food abandoned as I soak up every word he says.

"The man we rescued her from was dead so he couldn't have come back to kill her and when someone found her, our business card was right on top of her body like someone placed it there."

I blink as my mind races. "Jesus."

"Yeah," he breathes with a nod. "And then just a few weeks ago, this girl walked into the club. The thing was, though, it was a girl that had been missing for close to a year and we had been investigating her case."

"I'm guessing it wasn't a coincidence, then."

He shakes his head. "The man who had abducted her dropped her off at our front door and he had a message for us."

"What was the message?" My heart is pounding in my chest and I am hanging on his every damn word, somewhere between fascinated and terrified.

"I am just getting started…"

Christ.

I pull my hand from his and we both fall back into our seats as silence descends over our table and my mind races. Travis is right, this is so much bigger than anything I ever imagined and just thinking about the planning and patience it must have taken this person to put all of this together is astounding. Shaking my head, I meet his eyes across the table.

"Do you know anything else?"

He shakes his head. "Nothing concrete. That's why we were going to talk to Tawny today."

"Right," I whisper. God, that feels like it was days ago and we literally just left her apartment. "So did she tell you anything that you didn't already know?"

"Yes and no… She gave me a name which is something but that doesn't mean I'll find any information on him and she said the thing about how angry he was but that's one of the things that doesn't really help my investigation."

Sighing, I nod. "True, but I guess it's good to know who you're dealing with because there is a difference between someone who is in control of their rage and someone who isn't."

"And what would that be?"

"Someone who isn't in control of their anger makes mistakes."

He nods, turning to look out of the large window next to our table as he sighs, stress lining his face, and my heart breaks for him. "Then I'd say this guy is very much in control of his rage."

I want to tell him it's going to be okay but I don't know that it will and there is no part of me that wants to lie to him so instead, I turn back to my food and take a bite of pancakes. It's tasteless now and my mind can't stop going over everything he told me. Maybe I should have stayed in Alaska. It would have been lonely but at least I'd be safe. Then again, I'm glad I'm here with my brother... even if we're technically in the trenches right now.

"You regretting that move from Alaska right about now?" Travis asks and my head whips up, my gaze meeting his as I shake my head.

"How in the hell do you do that?"

He arches a brow. "Do what?"

"Read my fucking mind," I answer, pushing the food around on my plate aimlessly with my fork and he laughs.

"Well, in this particular instance, it was all over your face."

I sigh. "Oh... well, just so you know, I'm not sure if I regret it yet. I love Alaska and it's where I grew up but it was quickly becoming hell so in that sense, I'm happy to be here."

"What made you leave?"

"What didn't?" I shoot back with a dry laugh as tears sting my eyes. God, how is it that even just the mention of my home state can bring back all of the awful memories I've been trying so hard to forget since I got here? "My mom died a month ago and I didn't have any family left there..."

"So you came to Baton Rouge for Kodiak?"

I shake my head. "No, I came for me. I needed something... different and new. Plus, after I walked in on my ex-boyfriend banging this girl I worked with, there was nothing keeping me there."

"Shit," he mutters, making a face of pity and I shake my head.

"No, it's okay. I wasn't actually that hurt by it all which means it was past time to end things anyway. I was just pissed and embarrassed and the fact that he did all that while I was dealing with my mom's death was a kick in the teeth."

"Yeah, that's fucked up," he agrees with a nod and I shrug.

"Better to find out now than after I wasted anymore of my life on him," I say. He narrows his eyes and cocks his head to the side as he studies me. Fuck, I hate it when he does that... but I also kind of like it. I squirm in my seat, uncomfortable with his scrutiny but he doesn't seem to care as he continues watching me. Finally, I slap my hand down on the table and sigh. "What?"

He shakes his head. "I was just trying to decide if you really meant all that or if you were just putting on a brave face."

"How about both?"

"Fair enough," he answers with a nod. Grabbing my mug of coffee, I take a sip and do the same to him, studying him closely as he arches a brow and fights back a smile. "What?"

"Oh, now I'm just waiting for you to tell me something about you."

He laughs, shaking his head. "That's not going to happen."

"Why not?"

"This is supposed to be casual, remember?" he asks, motioning between the two of us and I roll my eyes.

"So? Does that mean that all I get to know about you is your name? Besides, you only told me that so I could scream it later."

He grins. "And what a glorious sound it was."

"Shut the fuck up." I laugh, grabbing a jelly packet and lobbing it across the table at him. He catches it and grins as he drops it on the table next to him. "Just tell me something… anything. Fuck, I don't even know how old you are."

"Twenty-eight."

I clamp my hand over my heart with a dramatic gasp. "Oh my god, you're so old! See, this is something I should have been made aware of before I slept with you."

"Watch it."

Arching a brow, I meet his stare. "Or what?"

"Princess, if you think for one second that I give a shit about the other people in this diner," he says, his voice low and full of a growl that makes goose bumps creep along my flesh. "You've got another thing coming."

"Oh, yeah, what will you do?"

"Push me and find out," he answers and I watch him for a second before smiling sweetly. My heart thunders in my chest and my belly flips with excitement because a part of me is scared but more than anything I want to find out what he'll do. Leaning forward, I level a glare at him.

"Do you honestly think I'm going to be scared of someone so… geriatric?"

His green eyes flare with heat and my belly flips again as my pussy clenches with need. With a casual smile that betrays the intense look he's firing in my direction, he stands up and pulls his wallet out of his back pocket. Taking one last sip of my coffee, I stand up, every cell in my body humming as I struggle to catch my breath.

Shit.

The anticipation is killing me.

He tosses a few twenties down on the table before slipping his wallet back in his pocket and stepping back so I can start walking toward the door. I shoot him a confused look as my thoughts screech to a halt and my heart sinks. Goddamn it, I was really looking forward to…

I let out a squeal as he scoops me up and throws me over his shoulder before casually strolling out of the diner with every other customer staring at is. My cheeks heat and I cover my face as a giggle bubbles out of my lips. God, I don't even care that he embarrassed me in front of all these people because between last night and this morning, I've thought about my mom and Ash a total of two times instead of the constant mental anguish that I was going through before and it feels so good to laugh again. And it feels even better that it's genuine. Around Travis, I'm not forcing smiles to my face or laughing because I know that's the appropriate reaction and it just reaffirms again that moving here was the right choice for me. Plus, this is only day two and despite the threat to the club and the danger we're all in right now, I'm really looking forward to finding out what else Baton Rouge has in store for me.

Chapter Eight
Travis

I pull the Impala into the clubhouse parking lot, thanking God that it seems quiet as I glance over at Rowan in the passenger seat and slip into the last space in the lot, the one furthest away from the clubhouse door. My mind has been running crazy on me since I hauled Rowan out of the diner over my shoulder and the quick kiss she pressed against my lips once I set her down next to the car only made me want more. If it hadn't been for the little old lady giving us some serious side-eye as she climbed out of her car, I might have just pressed her up against the Impala and fulfilled my need right there but instead, I held her door open for her and tried to come up with anything to calm myself down. It didn't work. Since we got in the car, I haven't been able to stop thinking about all the things I want to do to her and the idea I had this morning about locking us both in my room for a week is becoming more and more appealing. Just the thought makes my cock ache and I shake my head. She's fucking addicting and like any good addict, I need my next fix. Throwing the car in park, I turn it off and turn to her as she pulls my hoodie over her head. Her tits come into view, pressing against her thin t-shirt and I have to bite back a groan. Once it's off, she balls it up and hands it to me with a smile on her face. I take it from her and toss it in the back seat as my gaze falls to her lips, remembering how fucking perfect they looked wrapped around my cock last night.

I need her again.

Before I can even think about what I'm doing, I reach across the car and grab her, pulling her into my lap as she lets out a squeal of surprise but she doesn't fight me. Giggling, she straddles my lap in the cramped space as her skirt rides up around her waist and our eyes meet. Her breath hitches and in an instant, we collide. Neither one of us made the first move but it was more like we were pulled together by an unstoppable force, like there was no other option. We're almost feral as we go at it like animals, all rough, desperate touches, and the sound of our heavy breaths filling the car. Her lips sear themselves into my memory and I groan as her tongue darts out to tease mine as she grinds down on my lap.

Fuck. Yes.

"We should stop," she whispers in between frantic kisses as her hands creep up under my shirt and I nod as I grip the back of her neck to pull her closer.

"Mm-hmm." Yeah, we should definitely stop this… just as soon as I get my fill… or hell freezes over. Whatever happens first.

Reaching down between the door and my seat, I find the recline lever and pull it, sending us backward but it barely even slows us down as she slowly rocks her hips against mine and sinks her teeth into my bottom lip. My cock swells, pressing against my jeans and I groan loudly as I fight the urge to flip us over and fuck her like my life depends on it. Instead, I grab a chunk of her hair and pull it, forcing her head back as I leave a trail of kisses down her neck. She arches her back, pushing her chest out as her nipples press into the fabric of her t-shirt and my cock jerks, desperate to get inside her again.

"My brother could come out here," she says, panting for air as her hips continue moving on top of me, making me hard as a goddamn rock, and I'm not sure who exactly she is trying to convince - me or her. Either way, it's not working. I glance down and have to fight off another groan when I see the white lacy panties covering her perfect little pussy and an image of pulling them to the side and slipping inside her fills my mind.

"Let him," I growl, grabbing the front of her shirt and lifting it above her chest before sinking my teeth into her tit. She gasps and rocks her hips against me again and again, faster now, as she plants her hands on my chest. Is she...? Her fingers dig into my skin and she picks up the pace, rubbing against my hard length to get herself off and my eyes widen in disbelief.

Holy shit.

It's so, *so* hot but I'm fucking torn.

On the one hand, I would love to watch her use my body to make herself come and I'm pretty sure the memory would be primo spank bank material for the rest of my goddamn life. But I also can't wait to get inside her again. I fucking want her like I've never wanted another girl, fucking ever, and my body is strung tight, in a constant state of need and I don't want to pass up any opportunity to get another taste of her. My mind rages, warring between the two options, and I honestly can't make up my mind.

"Oh, God," she moans, her cheeks heating and her eyes squeezing shut as she rocks a little faster and my decision is made for me. All I can do is stare at her and try not to blow my load in my pants like a fucking fourteen-year-old as her moans get louder and louder. Grabbing her hips, I help her rock against me as I thrust up and she starts to shake as she gets closer, desperately clinging to me as the pleasure mounts.

"That's it, Princess, use me. I want to see you come."

"Travis," she cries out, lowering her head and meeting my eyes as she reaches forward and wraps her fingers around my throat. Fuck me, that's the hottest shit I've ever seen in my life and if she's not careful, I'm going to fuck her right in the middle of this parking lot. I don't give one single shit who sees us. Her mouth hangs open as moan after moan echoes through the car, her eyes burning into mine and my cock throbs. She holds me captive with her gaze, fire burning in their depths and I couldn't look away even if I wanted to. Digging my fingers into her hips, I press her down harder into my lap as I thrust up into her, eager to watch her shatter on top of me. She rocks back and forth and her eyes widen, giving me the warning I need to pull her lips to mine so the entire clubhouse doesn't hear her screams. She cries into the kiss as her entire body shudders in my arms and her release ignites my own, sending me spiraling through the haze of an orgasm so intense I almost black out.

Jesus fucking Christ.

"Rowan," I groan, burying my face in the crook of her neck as my cock throbs and she continues shaking in my arms, trying to catch her breath. We lie in silence for a few seconds before her body melts into mine and she releases a breath.

"That was fucking insane."

I nod. "Fuck yes, it was. What the hell was that choking thing?"

"I don't know," she answers, turning just enough that she can meet my eyes. "I just did what felt right in the moment. Did you not like it?"

"I didn't say that," I shoot back with a grin and she smiles, her eyes twinkling and just like that, I'm thinking about going again. This fucking girl, man… she's dangerous to my health because I'm pretty sure I would forgo any other bodily need as long as I was inside her.

"I'll remember that for next time."

Groaning, I lay my head back and close my eyes. Fuck, I swear I can still feel her fingers around my throat and I can't wait to do it again. She sighs, laying her head on my shoulder and I wrap my arms around her, enjoying this one perfect, peaceful moment before we have to go back in the clubhouse and pretend like none of this happened. I don't know how the hell I'm going to stay away from her, though.

"We should probably go inside," she whispers and I nod. She's right. If they haven't noticed that we're out here yet, someone will soon and the last thing I want to do today is get into it with Kodiak.

I nod. "Yeah… dunno how I'm going to get up to my room without people seeing the wet spot on my fucking jeans, though."

"Tell 'em I spilled a soda on you." She laughs and I scoff as I dig my fingers into her hips. She squeals and wiggles in my arms, trying to bat my fingers away from her.

"Stop. I hate being tickled!"

Smiling, I smack her ass. "Come on. Let's go but you better come up with another story besides you spilled a soda on my goddamn pants."

Laughing, she opens my door and slips outside, straightening her clothes while I put the seat back up and climb out next to her. The parking lot is still empty and I breathe a sigh of relief as I give her a little nudge toward the clubhouse.

"You go first and I'll follow behind you in a few minutes."

She nods, pressing a quick kiss to my lips before she walks over to the door. I lean back against my car and pull out my phone to waste time. Once I get inside, I need to investigate the name Tawny gave me and I might even take Rowan's advice and get the entire case set up on the giant white board we have in the war room but I can't do any of that until I get up to my room. As I waste time, I run through scenarios in my head of what I'm going to walk into and blow out a breath. Overthinking and running through every single possibility has always been something I've done and I honestly hate it but I can't stop. My brain just won't ever shut the hell up and I'm always fucking thinking about something. It's annoying as hell and one of the reasons I like being around Rowan so much because when I'm with her, it's easier to just be in the moment instead of a million miles away.

I wait a few more minutes before tucking my phone in my pocket and walking across the lot. As I step inside, I hold my breath but it's surprisingly quiet. In fact, the bar area is completely empty and I run up to my room before anyone can stop me or ask me why the hell my crotch is wet. Upstairs, I slip into the bathroom attached to my room and take a quick shower before throwing on some clean clothes. Once I'm presentable again, I sit down in front of the computer and start looking through bar receipts for anyone named Warren around the time Tawny made her accusations. Only one name pops up - Warren Ehlye.

"What in the fuck kind of name is that?" I whisper to myself as I quickly look it up. My search doesn't give me any answers but as I study the name, I realize it could be pronounced "Eli" so I run a quick search on that and begin reading to myself. "In the Old Testament, Eli was the high priest and last judge of Israel..."

Does that mean something?

Is it supposed to be a message to us?

Shaking my head, I file the thought away for later and search the full name. I can't help but smile when a property record pops up for one Warren Ehlye. It's a little cabin way out in the woods and I resist the urge to jump up and let out a whoop.

This is our fucking guy.

I print off the property records before digging a little more into Warren but it doesn't take very long for me to run into a problem.

Fuck.

I should have known it was too good to be true.

Sighing, I scrub my hand over my face and grab the files off of the desk as I stand up. First, I need to get these all laid out in order on the white board and then I'll tell everyone what I found, not that it's much. With the folders under my arm, I head back downstairs, ignoring Moose, Blaze, and Chance as they sit at one of the tables talking. I can feel their eyes on me as I slip into the war room, shut the door, and lock it behind me. Working quickly, I lay all of the files out on the table and put them in order, double-checking the dates, before taping them to the white board and putting a date by them. When I'm finished with the main cases, I put up other things that have happened like the break-in at the clubhouse and when Tawny accused Moose before stepping back and looking at it all in front of me. Nothing jumps out at me right away but I hope something will stand out to the rest of the guys or at the very least, it helps us keep the story straight in our heads.

"Streak," Storm calls from the other side of the door and I walk over, yanking it open. He arches a brow and glances into the room. "You all right?"

I nod. "Yeah. You want to round everyone up though? I have things to show you."

"Sure," he answers, eyeing me skeptically as he turns and walks out of the room to get the rest of the guys. Blaze, Chance, and Moose get up from their table and nod to me as they walk into the room and when I glance up, I meet Rowan's eyes. She peeks at the white board behind me before her gaze flicks back to me and she smiles.

Shit.

I really can't wait to get more time alone with her later.

"Did you find something?" Kodiak asks as he walks up to the war room and when I glance back over at Rowan, she has turned away from me. Sighing, I nod.

"Yeah, I'll explain in a minute."

Everyone else files into the room and takes their usual seats before all turning to look at me. Blaze arches a brow as he crosses his arms over his chest and leans back in his chair.

"All right, Streak. You have the floor."

I nod. "Right. So, I've been going over the interview with Veronica for the past week and something stood out to me."

"What?" Chance asks, leaning forward and bracing his elbows on the table.

"Veronica said that the man who took her talked about a woman who he met in a bar..."

Blaze nods, scowling at me from across the room. "Right. And?"

"And I had a suspicion that it was Tawny. We knew that she met some guy in a bar and he convinced her to try and frame Moose so it just made sense. I went to talk to her this morning to see if she had any other information to give me."

"Okay," Fuzz says, studying the board. "And did she?"

I nod and point to the name written at the top of the white board. "She gave me a name."

"How in the hell do you even say that?" Smith asks.

"It's pronounced Eli."

Blaze tilts his head to the side as he studies the board. "Did you find anything on this Warren Ehlye?"

"One thing," I answer with a smile. It's not the resounding victory I'd hoped it would be but it's still something. "Warren Ehlye owns a little cabin deep in the woods."

"Are you saying you found him, Streak?" Moose asks and I shake my head.

"No. Warren didn't even exist before two years ago but then that leads me to the rest of this." I motion to the white board. "I've laid out the entire case, in order, starting with Dina's. She was killed in early two thousand seventeen and there was nothing else until Laney was killed in early two thousand eighteen."

"And then nothing again until Veronica went missing in early two thousand nineteen?" Blaze asks and I nod.

"At least, nothing that we know about yet. Veronica did mention that Warren might have had a role to play or influenced shit with Ali back then," I say, pointing to the date in two thousand seventeen. "But until it's confirmed, I don't want to put it up on the board."

Fuzz sighs. "Everything picked up this year."

"Yeah, I realized that, too," I tell him, turning back to the board. For the first two years, there was only one death a year but this year, we've had a girl go missing, another die, Tawny trying to frame Moose for assault, the break-in at the clubhouse, and Veronica showing up on our doorstep. Sighing, I turn back to him. "It makes me think we're nearing the end of his little game."

"I don't like the fucking sound of that," Storm growls, raking a hand through his hair and a ripple of unease works its way through the room. Blaze sighs and sits forward.

"Okay, we need to look into the cabin… Fuzz and Storm, I want you to do that but be discreet. We can't afford to piss this guy off anymore and I want to remind you *all* that we may be dealing with a lot but Fuzz and Piper's vow renewal is coming up soon and we're not going to let this asshole steal even a moment of their happiness. Is that clear?"

I look at each of my brothers as they all nod in agreement and all the changes that have happened in the last two years. I've built a real family with all of the people in this room and I have to wonder if we'll all be standing here when this thing is finally over or if we'll be burying more people that we love. Or if we'll even have a club to come home to.

Wicked Games

Chapter Nine
Warren

Big, fat rain droplets splatter against my windshield as I climb out of the car and I cast an annoyed glance at the dark gray sky hanging over me before grabbing the box of supplies I brought along out of the passenger seat and slam the door. I've got a long walk ahead of me since I like to park so far away to avoid detection from anyone who may be passing by and I would prefer to do it in dry conditions. Not to mention that this weather will only make it harder to do what I came here to do. I will have to be extra careful and it will take time, time I don't have. Shoving my free hand in the pocket of my jeans, I start walking toward the cabin, eager to get there as soon as possible so I can finally put this place behind me and move on to the next stage of my plan. It's hard to believe it's been two years since this all started, since I managed to find this little cabin out in the woods and finally put all of this into motion. Especially since there were times when I wasn't sure it would work, that I would actually make it here, but now that we're nearing the end, I cannot wait to watch the destruction.

After everything I've lost… everything they took from me… this is *justice*.

The forest is quiet as I walk along with the box tucked securely under my arm and I spot a few landmarks that are familiar to me. Seeing them gives me this weird sense of peace and it's hard to believe that this is the last time I'm going to be out here. Over the last year, I've spent so much time at this cabin that it started to feel a little like home. I scoff at the word. I don't have a home, not really, and it would be monumentally stupid of me to forget that fact. This place is nothing to me and once it's all over, I doubt I'll ever think of it again. It was a tool and it's been incredibly useful, in more ways than one, but it's served its purpose and when I finally end this, I'll be walking away from everything here in Baton Rouge. Not that there is much left for me here anyway. Memories of my life before it collided with the Devils floods my mind and I grit my teeth as the pain in my chest swells. I can't ever forget what they took from me or why I've put in the insane amount of work it's taken to make all of this come together.

The cabin comes into view and I stop, moving behind a tree as I scan the area until I'm certain that no one else has been here since I left the last time. As I move closer to the little log structure, I smile. I know Streak went to go see Tawny this morning and hopefully the dumb bitch remembered just enough information to lead him here but first, I need to get the place ready. We can't have company coming over before each room is looking its best. As I step up onto the back porch, I set the box down next to the stairs and shake off my boots as I grab the white crime scene booties from the box and slip them on. The hair net comes next and after I snap it over my head, I grab the latex gloves and pull them on.

Once I'm all decked out in my gear, I grab the bottle of cleaner and sponge I brought along and step inside. The place is still pretty clean since I scrubbed it down right after I released Veronica but I need to go through it with a fine tooth comb and make sure there isn't a single shred of evidence left for them to find.

Except for the things I want them to find, that is.

Laughing to myself, I get to work, starting in the tiny bathroom at the back of the cabin and scrubbing every surface once before I go back and do it again for good measure. When I'm finished, I go out to the main room and look around. It was supposed to be a living room slash bedroom when I bought the place but the only things I needed in here were the twin bed in the corner and the shackles in the middle of the floor where I kept Veronica secure for so many months. She is the one thing in all of this that I actually felt a little bit bad about. I mean, she didn't really have anything to do with the club until I brought her into this whole mess and after talking to her, I realized that she was exactly the kind of girl I would have gone for before the Devils stole my life from me. But it doesn't matter. I can never go back and now, neither can she. Shaking my head, I push away the memories of all our talks in this room and get back to work, scrubbing the shackles and the hook embedded in the floor before moving on to the windowsills and the walls. The mattress was replaced after Veronica was released so I don't have to worry about them finding anything there either. Once I'm done in the main room, I duck into the small kitchen and scrub everything there before going back to my box on the back porch and grabbing the photos I brought along.

It's been so goddamn easy to mess with these guys and this is just going to be another level on top of all of that. They have no fucking idea how deep this goes and how many situations I've had my fingers in, influencing others when I needed to and keeping the Devils distracted with dumb bullshit when I was making big moves. It's actually comical how clueless they are.

Or maybe I'm just that good.

Back in the main room, I tape the photos to the wall and hang the white mask I always wore around Veronica on a nail before taking a step back and looking at it with a smile. The best part of all this is that while they may have suspicions about my involvement in things, they'll never find any concrete proof and that will drive them crazy - Streak especially. My mind drifts to the night I snuck up to the clubhouse and my smile grows when I think about Rowan. I've learned quite a lot about her since that night and the more I learn, the more intrigued I am. I've honestly been toying with the idea of adding her to the plan but things have been working so well that I don't want to mess anything up.

God, I want her, though.

The sound of gravel crunching grabs my attention and I walk over to the window, pulling the curtain back just enough to peek outside. A smile stretches across my face as Storm's truck rolls up the narrow driveway to the front door. "Perfect."

I watch them park and climb out of the cab before I slip out onto the back porch and quietly close the door behind me with my heart hammering in my chest and adrenaline pumping through my veins. Fuck, this is everything. One of my favorite things about this whole chase has been that they have no clue who they are looking for and it's been so easy for me to blend into a crowd and watch them. But this, this fear and excitement about the small possibility that I could get caught is even sweeter than I imagined.

"Let's check out inside," Storm says and I nod eagerly. A part of me can't wait for them to find the present I left inside but there is another part of me that wishes I could take them out, here and now. Storm is one of the names on my list and I can't tell you how many nights I've laid awake, imagining wrapping my hands around his throat and watching the life drain from his eyes but deep down, I know it's not enough. He needs to bleed, metaphorically and physically, before I take his life. But how convenient would it be if they were to find me out here and I had no other choice but to kill them? Then again, it wouldn't be too hard to attach another set of shackles to the hook in the floor and take my time exacting my revenge on them.

"We should do a perimeter check."

"No," I hiss, shaking my head at Fuzz's suggestion as I turn to look at the forest around me. There really is nowhere for me to hide right now and this can't end yet. It's too fucking soon and they haven't hurt enough yet.

"Dude, look around," Storm shoots back with a sigh. "No one is here and we haven't even seen another car for the last twenty minutes. This place is fucking remote."

"And what if he's here?"

He is, I think to myself, smiling.

God, they don't have a fucking clue.

"This place is abandoned. He's gotten all he can from it so let's stop wasting our time and just see if there is anything inside."

119

"Fine, whatever," Fuzz growls and I turn, peeking in the window as they open the front door and step inside. Their gazes are immediately drawn to the artwork on the wall and I feel damn near giddy as I watch their matching scowls.

"What the fuck is this?" Storm murmurs, walking up to the photo of Clay, Smith's brother… or should I say, late brother. He rips it off the wall and stares at the image, a range of emotions flicking across his face, before he passes it to Fuzz. "What the fuck is this supposed to mean?"

"Your guess is as good as mine," Fuzz answers, his eyes snapping up to the other photos on the wall. There is a photo from each of their relationships on the wall, something that they each went through with their old ladies like the charity ball Carly attended with Chance where her mother sold her to Damian Griggs or the day Biche shot up Henn and Kady's wedding. The fun part will be watching them try to figure out which events I had a part in and which ones I didn't. Or maybe they'll just assume I was involved in all of them and go crazy trying to protect the ones they love from the big bad wolf. Either way works for me. I glance down at the photo in my hand, the only one I saved from the wall and smile at the sight of Rowan propped up on Streak's desk with her head thrown back and her eyes closed.

This one is just for me.

"It's the mask Veronica talked about," Storm says, drawing my attention back to them as he flicks the mask with his fingers in irritation. I can't stop smiling as I move away from the window and quietly slip off of the porch. They don't have much more to look through and I want to be well hidden by the time they come back out so I grab my box and jog into the trees. There is a particularly thick section of brush far enough away from the back door to avoid detection and I slip behind it. It's quiet for a few moments and I grit my teeth, wondering what the hell they're doing in there and wishing I had stayed on the back porch when Storm yanks open the back door. My breath catches in my throat as I watch him scan the forest around me and my heart hammers in my chest. Finally, he shakes his head.

"There is nothing here," he calls to Fuzz before shutting the door and I laugh to myself quietly. Stupid. Just fucking stupid. Although watching him struggle to figure this out makes me realize I'm glad I didn't act impulsively and just murder both of them right here because seeing their frustration is so much more fun for me. And shouldn't I have a little fun with this? Besides, they deserve any and all pain I can dish out to them.

I wait a few more minutes before I hear the truck doors slam and I watch them drive away from the cabin, thinking of the next step in the plan. The action is about to ramp up and I am so going to enjoy ripping apart *everything* they hold dear.

Chapter Ten
Rowan

My phone buzzes in my pocket and I sigh as I set the knife down on the counter and pull it out as I glance at the chaos around me. Shaking my head, I turn back to my phone and roll my eyes when I see Ash's name on the screen along with his dumb smiling face. Silencing it, I shove it back in my pocket as I try to brush off my irritation but I'm not very successful. This is the third time he has called me today, which is less than the five times he called yesterday, but it's still three times too many. I haven't answered a single call since I spoke to him in Texas but he just keeps trying, leaving me increasingly agitated and rude messages. They started out innocent enough, with him saying that he hoped I was ready to talk and that he missed me but the last couple have been endless rants about me leaving him and what a cold-hearted bitch I am for leaving him and throwing us away.

Whatever.

You wanna know what I don't give a single fuck about? Ash's opinion of me. Besides, he doesn't have a single goddamn leg to stand on after I found him, dick deep, in Holly, the skank.

"Who was that?" Tate asks, nudging me with her shoulder and I sigh as I glance over at her, rolling my eyes to emphasis my annoyance.

"Ash, douchebag ex-boyfriend extraordinaire."

She makes a face as she looks up from her cutting board. "Are you still speaking to him? After what he did to you?"

"Absolutely not. The last time I talked to him was when I was in Texas and that was just to tell him that we were done and he needed to move on with his life but he's not getting the hint."

"How many times has he called?"

I arch a brow. "Today? Three times."

"Do we need to be worried about him?" she asks and warmth spreads through my chest. When she says "we", she's not just talking about her and Lincoln. She's talking about this club as a whole and every single one of its members. I haven't been here all that long but that doesn't seem to matter because as soon as I walked through the front door, I found myself a new little family. It doesn't diminish the pain of the ones I've lost but it is nice to feel like I belong somewhere and that I've got people who have my back. After feeling so alone in Alaska, it's absolutely incredible and this place already feels like home.

"No, Ash isn't like that, at all. It's just annoying that he can't get a fucking clue. Besides, you would think Holly would be keeping him so busy that he wouldn't even have time to worry about little old me."

"Is that the girl he cheated on you with?" she asks and I nod. She makes a stabbing motion with her knife and I can't help but laugh. "Were you direct with him?"

124

"Like a fucking lightning bolt."

"Well," she muses as she starts chopping again. "You could always just hand the phone to your brother and let him deal with this loser."

"Ah, yes, but then I would have to tell him what this loser did and I thought we were trying to keep him from jumping on a plane."

She purses her lips before her smile turns devious. "You're right… but *I* could always have a little chat with him."

"Are you even scary over the phone? Without your gun or taser?"

"Oh, don't you dare underestimate me," she warns with a heated look and I hold my hands up in surrender. Truthfully, I'm just giving her a hard time. I have no doubt that Tate could make Ash piss himself with her words alone and if it comes to it, I'm not above letting her do just that. I want to be done with the whole damn thing.

"Okay, I won't and if he doesn't leave me alone, I promise to let you loose on him."

She grins and does a little shimmy next to me. "Christmas has come early this year."

"Speaking of, is anyone planning on doing anything for Christmas? I mean, I realize everyone is feeling the stress of this threat against the club right now but we should at least put up a tree, right?"

"Maybe we'll bring it up at dinner," she says, motioning to the chaos around us. I look around the room and sigh. All of the girls have been running around this kitchen for the last two and a half hours, working their asses off to make some big family dinner for all of us and I know the guys have been super stressed the past few days but I don't know that this will help. Actually, I'm not even sure exactly what happened but I did hear something about a cabin, some photos, and the threat to the club. The whole thing has every single member on edge and their paranoia has been getting to all of us. The tension has been almost unbearable and on top of all that, Travis has been locked in his room almost twenty-four-seven since yesterday morning and I haven't gotten a chance to be alone with him since our little rendezvous in his car two days ago. My cheeks heat as I think about that morning. Honestly, I don't know what came over me but I couldn't stop myself.

Neither one of us could.

"You know what I really need?" I ask and she arches a brow as she glances over at me. "Everyone to take a damn chill pill. I mean, have they ever considered that they all are playing right into his hand?"

"Just give it a rest, girl. I tried the same speech with Lincoln and he damn near tore my head off. They're all worried and us being so flippant about it isn't helping."

I sigh. "I'm not being flippant but there is no way that any of them are thinking clearly right now and it just seems like they are letting this guy get the best of them."

"Has anyone explained the whole situation to you?"

"Yeah," I whisper, my mind drifting back to the diner with Travis two days ago. "Streak did."

"Then you know how serious it is."

I nod. "I do. But I also think they need to be smart about how they handle all of this. Whoever this guy is keeps winning because they are all wound so damn tight and scared of the next thing that is going to happen."

"You're preaching to the choir, girl, but all we can do is try to help them chill out and think clearly. Which is why this dinner is so important… well, and we have an ulterior motive…"

"You do? What is it?"

She smiles. "The girls all want to be able to go out and celebrate Piper's bachelorette party but we need to butter the guys up and convince them of that."

"Good fucking luck," I shoot back with a laugh. I'm new here but even I know this is a damn long shot and that's putting it mildly. Hell, when Tate, Emma, and I ran to the store earlier for supplies, Blaze insisted on driving there so he could protect us. I considered protesting but, after the mood in the clubhouse over the past two days, I decided against it. She shakes her head.

"No, listen…we have a plan."

"Well, I hope it's something at the clubhouse because that is all the guys are going to agree to," I tell her and she shakes her head as a smile stretches across her face.

"That's why we're going to suggest that we all go, even the guys. How can they say no when they will all be there to protect us?"

I roll my eyes. "Like this, 'absolutely fucking not'."

"That was actually pretty good. If I didn't know better, I might start looking around for Lincoln." She laughs and I join her, nodding.

"It better be. I've been practicing my Lincoln impression since I was old enough to speak."

"Rowan, are those vegetables ready?" Ali calls and I nod, grabbing my cutting board and holding it up. Tate and I are apparently "useless" in the kitchen so we

127

were both assigned chopping duties which hasn't been all that bad considering the craziness on the other side of the kitchen. "Throw them all in that bowl there and then y'all can go relax until dinner."

I carry my cutting board over to the bowl she pointed out, scraping them all inside before I turn back to her. "Are you sure you don't need help with anything else?"

"Um... maybe if you get the tables put together and set. I think this will all be ready in about fifteen to twenty minutes."

Tate nods and loops her arm through mine. "We're on it."

We walk out of the kitchen and stop when we see the tables all laid out in one long line with plates and silverware already set up. Blaze looks up from the bar and follows our gaze before nodding. "Figured if y'all were doing the cooking, the least we could do is set up and clean up."

"Aw, Blaze," Tate coos, smacking his arm. "You shouldn't have."

He laughs. "I didn't. I made the boys do it."

"Well, in that case, you definitely should have," I tell him and he laughs again before nodding toward the stairs, where all the guys are presumably holed up in their rooms.

"Y'all go relax until dinner and I'll deal with anything else that needs to be taken care of."

As Tate and I nod and start walking toward the stairs, I lean in and whisper, "You think he's on to our plan?"

"No," she whispers back before glancing over her shoulder again. Blaze smiles at us and there is something about the look in his eyes that makes me think he knows exactly what is going on. But, let's just hope that he doesn't ruin it by saying anything to the rest of the guys. I don't think he will, though. He's been trying to keep this club together just as much as anyone else and he knows that besides our little plot, this dinner will be good for everyone. Tate and I walk up the stairs before she releases my arm. "I'm gonna go hunt down my husband."

I nod. "Yeah, have fun with that."

"I will," she answers with a grin before her expression turns serious and she points a finger at me. "You let me know if that fucker calls you again."

"Yes, ma'am."

She smiles before ducking into the room she shares with my brother and when the door closes, I look down the hallway, wondering where I should go even as my feet start carrying me forward toward Travis's door. I don't know if he wants to see me since he's been locked away up here for so long but the truth is, I miss him. Sucking in a breath, I stop in front of his door and knock.

"What?" he snarls from the other side and I arch a brow as my lips part in a silent gasp. Opening the door, I step inside and cross my arms over my chest.

"Wow. Rude, much?"

"Row," he breathes as he glances up at me and sighs, his body deflating in his office chair before he holds his hand out to me. "Come here."

I narrow my eyes and shake my head. "After you just snapped at me like that? I don't think so."

"I didn't know it was you…"

"And?" I ask, closing the door behind me before leaning back against it. His gaze drags down my body and I've never felt sexier in a pair of jeans and a t-shirt.

129

He licks his lips and it takes every ounce of my strength to stay where I am.

"So you're not going to come over here?" he asks, his tone a mixture of playfulness and seriousness as he turns his chair to face me. My belly does a little flip and I shake my head.

"Nope."

"You've seen what I'm willing to do to get what I want in public so are you really going to push me when we're all alone?"

I shrug, trying like hell to look unaffected but my entire body is humming. "Maybe I want to see what you'll do. Did you ever think of that?"

His eyes flare in response and a shiver twists down my spine as my heart hammers in my chest. Every fiber of my being is strung tight, on a hair trigger, as I wait for him to make his move.

Fuck.

I missed this.

Our eyes meet from across the room and he grins just before he lunges out of his chair, straight for me. I squeal and try to get away but he's on me in the blink of an eye, caging me in against the door as he presses his body up against mine. I look up at him and move up onto my toes as he swoops down, slamming his lips to mine in a scorching kiss. The feel of him against me, the feel of his kiss... it all makes me want to melt on the spot and every cell in my body is singing with relief as I wrap my arms around his neck and thread my fingers through his hair. He groans, wrapping an arm around my waist as he presses me up against the door and grinds his hips into mine.

"Do we have time before dinner?" he asks, dragging his lips down the side of my neck and I shake my head. Honestly, I have no fucking clue how much time before dinner is ready but I don't really care. I'll happily skip it. Giving his hair a little tug, I reach down between us and grab his jean covered cock.

"Screw dinner."

He groans, pulling us away from the door. His lips find mine again as he guides us over to the bed and falls back onto it, dragging me on top of him. I straddle his hips and he cups the back of my head as he nips at my bottom lip.

"Fuck," he whispers as he grabs a handful of my ass and thrusts up off the bed. "I want you so fucking bad but we can't skip dinner."

I pull back. "Why not?"

"Because then your brother would come looking for you and find us like this... and because I want to show you something."

"What?" I ask as he sits up and wraps his arms around me with a grin. Before I can ask him anything else, he stands up with me in his arms and I let out a shriek as I cling to him. He just laughs. The sound is incredibly infectious and I find myself smiling despite the fact that I'm certain he is going to drop me on my ass. With his arms securely wrapped around me, he carries me over to the desk and sits in his office chair with me still straddling his hips as he scoops a stack of photos off of the desk and hands them to me.

"What are these?" I ask, staring down at the first image. It's in front of this cute little house that I don't recognize. Storm, Ali, and a big brown dog are sitting on the sidewalk in front of some house and I turn to Travis with a scowl. He sighs.

"Warren... the name Tawny gave us when we went to visit her?"

I nod. "Yeah..."

"He owns a cabin way out in the woods and Storm and Fuzz went to check it out two days ago. They found all those photos inside and they insinuate that Warren has been watching us for two years now."

Glancing down at the photo again, I shake my head, confused. "Okay... And? I mean, you already knew he was watching you, right?"

"Yeah," he answers with a sigh. "But this combined with the things Veronica, the girl who was kidnapped, said in her interview makes us think that he had a hand in way more things than we realized, like the shit that went down when Storm met Ali."

"Oh..."

He nods. "The thing is it's impossible to prove and there is still a possibility that he's just messing with us, trying to drive us all crazy... and it's fucking working. I've been going out of my goddamn mind and..."

Grabbing his face, I press my lips to his and his arms wrap around my waist almost instantly as he groans into my kiss, his entire body relaxing beneath me. When I pull away, he presses his forehead to mine and releases a breath.

"Thanks. I fucking needed that."

I nod, cradling his face in my hands. "I could tell."

"You make everything better," he whispers so quietly that I almost don't hear him and despite the fact that I really want to say something, I remain silent. After a moment, he pulls back and sighs. "Dinner is probably going to be ready soon, huh?"

132

"Yeah, probably."

He leans in and presses another quick kiss against my lips before pulling back. "You'd better head downstairs now, then. We don't need people seeing you come out of my room."

"Okay," I agree, imagining the hell that would ensue if my brother caught me sneaking out of Travis's room. It would be a nightmare and the clubhouse doesn't need anymore stress right now. Leaning in, I steal one more kiss before I climb off his lap and turn toward the door.

"Wait."

I glance back at him as he stands. "Come see me tonight once everyone is in bed?"

"Maybe," I answer with a grin even though we both know I will absolutely be up here just as soon as the clubhouse is quiet. He grabs my hand and pulls me back into his arms, spinning us so he's closest to the door as he presses his lips to mine. "You know, in order for me to leave, you have to stop kissing me."

"I'm fucking trying," he growls as he steals another one and I smile against his lips. Finally, he pulls away. "Let me check the hallway before you go."

"Okay." I watch him walk toward the door, pulling it open just enough to peek into the hallway before he turns back to me and nods.

"You're good." He smacks my ass as I walk by him. "See you later, Princess."

I shoot him a look as I slip out into the hallway and as I walk away from his room, I hear the door click closed behind me. Grinning to myself, I practically run down the stairs and slip down the hallway to the movie theater where I'm staying without being noticed. Just as I walk into the room, I hear a banging sound coming from the bar area.

"Soup's on!" Blaze yells as the banging stops, his voice echoing through the entire building and my belly does a little flip as I think about getting this dinner over with so I can be alone with Travis again. It is going to be torture to sit at the same table as him but act like I'm not thinking about him ripping my clothes off. The anticipation is only going to make tonight that much sweeter, though. Or, at least, that is what I'm telling myself to make it through the next few hours.

Chapter Eleven
Rowan

"You headed to bed?" I ask Lincoln as he stumbles off of his bar stool with Tate trying her best to support his large body against her own. He has been posted up there since dinner ended and it's just been the three of us for the past hour as I read my book on the couch and waited for him to decide that he was done. It felt like a damn eternity, especially when I couldn't stop thinking about the lingering looks Travis shot me all night long when no one was looking or the way he pressed me up against the wall and kissed me senseless when we both ended up in the back hallway alone. I shiver as I remember the way his hand slid up under my shirt as his lips consumed mine.

"Yeah, you should, too," Lincoln slurs and I nod as I look back down at my book. Yeah, that's not going to happen for a while. I have plans. My mind drifts back to dinner and I can't help but smile. At first, the guys were outraged that we would even suggest something like going out to a club for Piper's bachelorette party when Warren was on the loose and actively coming after the club but after some convincing and a tiny bit of ass kissing, they came around. They agreed to let us go out as long as we all stayed together and we listened to everything they said. I'm pretty sure that last part has nothing to do with Warren but whatever. We're all excited for the chance to get out and have some fun.

"Night," Tate calls as they head for the stairs. I smile at her as she glances back at me and winks. What the hell? "Don't stay up too late."

Oh, shit, does she know?

"Night," I tell her, proud of how steady my voice sounds when internally I'm freaking out. Whatever, it's a problem for another day. Besides, I'm fairly certain that Tate would protect my secret. I motion to my brother as he leans into her more. "And good luck."

She scoffs. "Yeah, thanks."

As they start up the stairs, I pretend to read the page in front of me but the entire time, I'm very aware of their progress and as soon as I hear their door close, I throw the blanket off of my legs and climb off the couch. With my book in my hand, I practically run across the room to the theater, eager to see Travis. Once I'm inside, I close the door behind me and lock it before walking over to my suitcase. During dinner, I had the best idea to surprise him and I can't wait to see his face when he sees it. Riffling through the clothes, I find the one I'm looking for and hold it up with a grin. The top is a little black strappy leather thing from my stripping days that frames my tits rather than covering them and the matching panties are crotchless, which is going to make Travis lose his damn mind.

When it's on and properly situated, I stand in front of the full length mirror one of the guys put up for me and turn to the side to examine how it looks from the back. Back in Alaska, I bought this and wore it often but it never felt like this. I never had butterflies in my stomach and my heart was never racing when I thought about baring it all for someone. My nipples pebble at the thought of Travis seeing me like this and I bite back a moan as I grab a t-shirt and a pair of shorts out of my bag, throwing them on. Once I'm covered, I take one last look in the mirror before walking out of the theater.

God, I'm so fucking nervous.. and excited... and turned on.

"Evening," Blaze says as I walk into the bar area and I jump so high I nearly hit the ceiling before turning to look at him as he pours some dark liquor into a glass and I press my hand to my chest.

"Jesus, you scared the hell out of me."

He smirks and nods. "Yeah, I caught that. You headed somewhere?"

"Uh…"

Arching a brow, he stares at me over the rim of his cup and just waits.

"I was…uh…" I mutter, looking toward the stairs before realizing what an epically dumb idea it was.

"That's what I thought," he sighs, taking another sip of his drink. "I know we just met but can I give you some advice?"

I nod, hesitant. "Sure."

"Be careful with Streak. I love that boy like my own son but he's been through some shit and I honestly don't know if he's the settling down type. I would hate to see you get hurt."

I consider protesting, telling him I have no idea what he's talking about but from the look on his face, it's clear he knows what's been going on between Travis and me. For fucks sake, does the whole damn club know? Is it the secret that everybody is in on but no one will talk about? One thing is for sure - my brother still has no idea because if he did, I would know. Travis would know. Hell, all of Baton Rouge would fucking know.

"I know what I'm doing," I tell him and he shakes his head.

"No, darlin'," he says, shaking his head. "You really don't. I don't want to see this club fall apart because you two couldn't keep your hands to yourself. Everyone else may be clueless but I see what's going on."

Taking a step toward the bar, I lean forward on my elbows and meet his gaze. "We agreed to keep things casual. This is just fun and nothing more."

"Yeah.. where have I heard that before?"

I open my mouth to assure him again that both Travis and I know what we're doing but he stops me, holding his hand up as he shakes his head.

"You both are adults and I'm not here to tell you what to do with your lives but think about what I said. There will be consequences for what y'all are doing." He leaves with his drink in his hand without another word and I watch him go back to his room before releasing a sigh.

Is he right?

Should Travis and I stay away from each other for the good of our ourselves and this entire club?

Could we even if we tried?

As I mull those questions over in my mind, I wander up the stairs but the entire time, I'm considering going back to the theater and just going to sleep but it's like some invisible force is pulling me toward Travis's room and I'm powerless against it. I stop right outside his door and raise my hand to knock but something stops me.

Is this a mistake?

I think about the time Travis and I have spent together over the last few days but despite what Blaze says, I can't see anything wrong with it. Sure, my brother won't be happy but one, it's none of his business who I sleep with and two, Travis and I are just having fun. No one is going to get their heart broken here. Shaking my head, I push all those thoughts aside and softly knock on the door. Before I can even pull my hand away, it flings open. Travis grins at me as he reaches out and wraps his arm around my waist, pulling me into the room as he shuts the door behind us and locks it.

"Finally," he breathes, leaning in to kiss me but I place my hand in the middle of his chest to stop him as my heart skips a beat. His answering scowl is adorable and I can't help but laugh.

"I have a surprise for you."

He frowns, looking down the length of my body. "Give it to me later."

"I can't." I laugh as he tries to peel my shirt over my head and I stop him. "I have to *show* you now."

"Is it under here?" he asks, grinning and his eyes shining with mischief as he tries to take my shirt off again. Giggling, I bat his hands away before pushing him back toward his chair.

"Yes. Now, take your clothes off."

His brows shoot up in surprise but he grins as he takes a few steps backward before pulling his shirt over his head and tossing it to the floor. His eyes never leave mine as he reaches for his jeans, unbuttoning them and shoving them to the floor with his briefs. I drop my gaze as he wraps his hand around his already hard cock and my pussy throbs as heat rushes through my body. I look up and arch a brow. He shrugs.

"I might have been getting a little impatient," he answers, all nonchalant as he continues pumping his shaft. His eyes burn into mine as I nod in reply and try to catch my breath. Watching him stroke himself is sexy enough but when you add in the fact that I already know how amazing he can make me feel with that cock, it's almost too much to bear. "Now what?"

Smiling, I nod to his office chair. "Sit down."

He sinks into his office chair, slowly stroking his length as his gaze roams over my body and a devilish grin lights up his face. "Your turn."

"You have to close your eyes first," I instruct him and he happily complies, still pumping his cock slowly. Inside, my belly is doing flips and my heart is pounding with excitement and nerves as I reach down and grab the bottom of my shirt, pulling it over my head. I toss it to the floor next to his and shimmy out of my shorts before spreading my legs a little wider than normal and leaning back against the bookcase.

Shit.

I wish I would have brought some heels with me.

"Okay," I whisper, each breath ringing in my ears and his eyes snap open before widening.

"Where in the fuck..." he breathes, his gaze locked onto my bare tits as my nipples tighten with need. Oh, God, I love it when he looks at me like that. "...did you get that?"

I push off of the bookcase and take slow, deliberate steps toward him but it doesn't feel quite the same without my heels and my nerves kick in again. God, what the hell is wrong with me? This is tame compared to the stuff I usually do on the stage but I feel like a goddamn virgin right now. "Can I tell you a secret?"

"Absolutely," he vows. I bite back a nervous giggle at how eager he is and wonder what else I could get him to agree to right now. I'm pretty sure he would say yes to just about anything I asked.

"Do you promise not to tell anyone?" I ask, stepping up beside him and trailing the tips of my fingers up his arm as I move behind him. He shudders, goose bumps popping up behind my touch, and nods, dropping his head back just enough to watch me.

"Yeah. Cross my heart and everything, Princess."

Smiling at the nickname he has given me, I strut back around to stand in front of him before leaning in and bracing my hands on his knees. His gaze falls to my tits again and his Adam's apple bobs as he licks his lips and strokes his cock a little faster. "I was stripping in Alaska."

His eyes flick to mine and I can see the surprise shining back at me as my stomach churns and my heart stalls in my chest. Oh, God, please don't think the worst of me...

"Oh, yeah? You gonna show me some of your moves, baby?" he asks and it's exactly what I needed to hear to embolden me to do just that. I nod, standing up and slowly turning to give him a chance to get his fill before I sit back in his lap, rocking my hips and rubbing against his cock. Warm breath hits my neck as he leans forward with a groan and his fingers dig into my hip. I slap his hand away, despite every cell in my body screaming at me to let him touch me.

"No touching the dancers."

He arches a brow as I lay back against him, rolling my body against every hard muscle as I hook my arm around his neck. Turning into me, his lips brush my throat and I fight to keep my eyes open as my belly clenches and a shudder rocks through me.

"Oh, it's like that, is it?"

"For now," I whisper as I brush my fingers over my nipple, teasing him with what he can't have just yet as I release a heavy breath. My breasts ache and I imagine him pinching one between his fingers while he leans down and sucks the other into his mouth. A moan slips between my lips and his body tenses underneath me.

"And what if I don't want to follow your rules?" He nips at my earlobe, pulling another moan from my lips and I move away as I shake my head and ignore his question. Bracing my hands on his knees again, I begin rocking against him, rubbing my ass against his erection at an excruciating slow pace and drawing out the pleasure and pain before leaning back again.

"Tell me what you like."

"You," he groans in my ear, his cock jerking against me and I can feel his fingers twitching against my sides, desperate to reach out. My nipples ache fiercely, begging to be touched, and every inch of my skin is on fire, desperate for him. Wetness coats the insides of my thighs and my pussy is throbbing with need as I think about him putting his hands on me. Turns out, I'm torturing myself just as much as him.

"Do you want to touch me?" I ask.

He sneaks a light caress against my leg before pulling his hand back, almost like he couldn't stop himself any longer and it's sexier than I imagined. "Fuck yes."

A.M. Myers

I grab his hand and place it on my belly before slowly lowering it toward my pussy as his breathing grows rough behind me. "I'll let you touch one thing only and when I say stop, you have to stop."

"You're playing a dangerous game, Rowan," he whispers, his voice full of grit, and it sends a shiver up my spine but I don't stop. I open my legs and slide his hand in between them.

"Jesus fucking Christ, they're crotchless?" he hisses in my ear as his fingers find my clit and massage the little bundle of nerves. He sinks his teeth into my neck and I jerk against him, goose bumps covering my entire body as I reach behind me and grip his hair.

He growls, "Come here."

Before I even have a chance to stop him, he pushes me out of his lap and spins me around before pulling me back to him as he stands. His lips slam against mine, his kiss fierce, as he pulls my hair and I cry out. He swallows up the sound as he walks us backward toward the bed. Just before we reach the mattress, he lifts me off the floor and I wrap my legs around his waist as he presses my back against the wall. Moaning into his kiss, I roll my hips against him, rubbing up the length of his cock and when the head hits my clit, my eyes roll back in my head. He rips his lips from mine before wrapping his hand around my throat, his eyes blazing. My heart jumps into my throat and my pussy clenches at the feeling of his fingers around my neck.

"You like that, Princess?"

My eyes almost roll back in my head as I nod. "Yes."

"Fuck," he growls, releasing his hand and pulling me away from the wall before tossing me on the mattress like I weigh nothing at all. He looks predatory as he stares down at me and I swear I can see all the things he wants to do to me playing out in his gaze. God, I want that, too. I need him on top of me, inside me, all around me but he just watches me, amplifying my desperation for him, before he bends down and scoops something up off of the floor. I drag my gaze away from his face and my eyes widen when I see the belt in his hand. My belly flips and my pussy clenches again as warmth floods my body.

What in the hell is he going to do with that?
And why does it excite me so damn much?

I don't get long to think of possibilities as he moves on top of me and throws one of my legs over his shoulder before dragging my hands above my head and wrapping the belt around my wrists, tightening it. With the belt still in his hand, he slams his fist into the mattress, keeping me secure and completely at his mercy. My clit throbs for relief and I swear to God, I'm fucking dripping but he's barely done anything to me yet.

He meets my gaze again and holds it as he drops a hand between my thighs and slips two fingers inside me. Gasping, I arch off the bed and he presses his lips against mine to silence me. My entire body trembles beneath him, pleading for the release that is just below the surface and as he takes his time building me up with slow strokes of his fingers, my body screams for more. I writhe underneath him, begging with everything but my words to give me what I need. He doesn't and each time I try to urge him to go faster by rocking my hips up into his hand, he pulls away, kissing my body instead to draw out the torture before slipping back between my thighs. Sweat rolls down the side of my face and my legs are shaking but he won't let me come and just when I think

144

I'm about to lose my mind, his hand disappears and the head of his cock presses against my entrance.

"Yes," I say, something between a hiss and a plea, and he pulls back to look in my eyes. I nod, desperate for him to move. To emphasize my point, I lift my hips off the bed, rubbing against him and he groans, his eyes closing. "Please. I need you, Travis."

His eyes spring open and I watch as the final thread of his restraint snaps. He surges forward, filling me completely and I turn my head into my arm to mask my scream as he releases a low groan that makes me shudder around him.

"Fuck, Rowan," he hisses as he pulls back and thrusts forward again, dragging another moan out of me. I know I need to be quiet but I really can't help it. Not when he's doing this to me. Not when it feels this damn good. Grinning, he leans in closer and clamps his hand over my mouth as he increases his pace, fucking me so hard that I am pretty sure the earth moves beneath us. "What have I told you about being quiet, Princess?"

"Please," I whisper, my voice muffled by his hand and he pulls it away. "Please, Travis. I need to come.... I'll do anything."

He releases the belt holding my hands and I quickly wiggle out of it before he hands me a pillow and winks. "Scream into this."

That's all the warning I get before he pins my legs back against the mattress and begins fucking me with such ferocity that I lose all track of time. The only things that matter are him and the way he is wringing every drop of pleasure from my body. I cling to the pillow and scream his name into it more times than I can count, my body building to impossible heights before I explode, crying out as my release tears through my body and my legs shake but even that doesn't slow him down. He continues driving into me again and again as he groans and his heavy breaths fill the room. He pulls the pillow from my face and leans down to kiss me, releasing my legs as his lips meet mine. I wrap them around his hips and throw my arms over his shoulders as I feel myself teetering on the edge of another orgasm.

"Travis," I breathe against his kiss. "I'm going to come again."

"Do it," he demands as he reaches between us and flicks his thumb over my clit before circling it. It's all the encouragement I need. My back arches off the bed as my pussy clenches around him with my second release, this one stronger than the first and he grits his teeth. His muscles tense and he thrusts into me one last time, releasing a long, drawn out groan before dropping his head to my chest and blowing out a breath. "Holy shit."

I nod because I honestly don't think I have the strength to do anything else right now and he rolls to my side, lying on his back as he pulls me to his chest and rests his hand on my back. It feels so damn comfortable and easy to be here with him and we just lie in the silence for a while, catching our breath as he drags his fingers across my skin.

"So, I have a question about this whole stripper thing," he says after a while and I pull back to look at him, arching a brow. I knew this was coming.

"Oh, yeah? What's that?"

He pulls away just enough to roll to his side so he can face me and I do the same. "Can you actually dance on a pole? Like all those crazy moves and stuff?"

"Yeah," I answer with a laugh. "I started taking lessons just so I didn't look like an idiot on stage but then I started to really like it so I kept doing it."

He makes a face. "Hmm…"

"What?"

He shakes his head. "Nothing. I'm just thinking about how I could sneak a stripper pole into my room 'cause that is something I definitely want to see."

"Not going to happen," I say, laughing as I settle back into his arms and he lets out a little huff of annoyance as he pulls me closer.

"Why not? I want to see all your tricks."

"Baby, even with what just happened, you still haven't even seen a fraction of my tricks. Why don't you learn all those first before you worry about the pole?"

He grins and presses his lips to my forehead. "I can't fucking wait."

Wicked Games

Chapter Twelve
Travis

"Come on, you son of a bitch," I hiss, gritting my teeth as my fingers fly across my keyboard and I lean in closer to the monitor like it's going to somehow help me crack this whole thing wide open. "Fucking show me something."

I've been up here all goddamn day, digging into every aspect of Warren Ehlye's life only to hit dead end after dead end and my patience is gone at this point, fucking non-existent. Hours ago, I thought, maybe, I had finally found something when I stumbled across a bank account in Warren's name but after further digging, I realized he only uses the damn thing to pull money out of ATMs so it's not like I can even track his fucking spending. In the end, it was zero help. When I hit another dead end, I ball my fists up with a yell, resigning the urge to fling the keyboard across the room, and fall back into my chair.

Fuck, I need a break.
Just one goddamn break.

Oh, and also, fuck this sadistic asshole and his stupid fucking mind games.

God, I want to put my fist through a wall.

Turning to look out of the window, I blow out a breath and try to calm myself down as I unclench my shaking hands and lay them flat against my thighs. There is a pounding in my ears and lights flash in my vision as memories bombard me.

Of course.

As if this wasn't hard enough on me already but now Warren's little game is reminding me of shit I've worked too fucking hard to keep buried.

I'm sure that's what he wants, though.

He wants me to lose control.

"Breathe, asshole," I whisper to myself, closing my eyes and taking a deep breath through my nose as I attempt to push the memories away. "Think of something happy."

Rowan's face pops into my mind and I smile as I feel some of the tension seep out of me. I focus on her, remembering the little show she put on for me last night and how fucking sexy she looked before my mind drifts to the day before that when she kissed me as I was spiraling out of control. I don't know what it is about her but she calms everything and makes me feel like it's not an impossible task to find this jackass. Opening my eyes, I release a breath and look at the screen, my mind clearer than a moment ago. When I searched for other properties in Warren's name, there were none which means he's got to be renting something. The problem is that it's not hard to find a landlord that will let you pay in cash and there is no way to track it if you want to stay off the radar, which he clearly does. His bank account flickers through my mind and I remember a charge of four hundred dollars on the first of every month from an ATM and I turn back to the computer. Maybe if I look up the address of the ATM he pulled the money from each month, I could find out the general area he's living in.

Yeah, the smart thing for him to do would be to pull cash away from home but then that would leave a radius where he never gets cash which would also give away his location. Warren has proven how smart he is in the past though, so he is probably pulling cash out all over the city, changing when and where he does it so it can't be tracked by me. Honestly, I'm not expecting to find anything because he would never be this careless but I still have to check. Just like I thought, his ATM transactions are completely sporadic and they don't give me a clue as to where he's staying. Leaning back in my chair, I stare at the screen as I try to come up with another way to track him.

"Four hundred dollars," I mutter, shaking my head as I lean forward again. It's not a lot to live on so he's either renting an absolute shit hole or he has roommates.

Holy fuck... what if he has a partner?

I haven't been able to find any evidence to suggest that it's true but he hasn't been above using other people to do his dirty work in the past so it's possible. Jesus, it makes perfect sense. That's why we can't track him or get anywhere on this case because not only is he probably using an alias but he has someone he's working with, someone that can do things like own property or rent cars. Fuck me. He's buried under so many layers that I don't stand a chance. Warren is a fucking ghost and that is exactly the way he wants it. It gives him all the freedom he needs to tear this club apart one little piece at a time but who in the fuck would agree to partner with him?

Someone who hates us as much as he does?
Someone he manipulated?

Fuck, I don't even know where to start and there are just too many possibilities to figure it out. It frustrates me more than anything else. I like having the answer. I like being the guy that my brothers can call on when they need help but, in this, I'm fucking useless. And my uselessness is going to get someone I care about hurt… or worse. Turning to look at the door to my room, I think about everyone that is in this clubhouse right now and how much they mean to me. It's more than they even realize. When I joined this club, I was so fucking lost and angry but they gave me a purpose and a family when I thought I would never have either. Losing them, any of them… it would kill me.

My phone rings on the desk, snapping me out of my thoughts and I shake my head as I scoop it up and glance down at the screen as Storm's name stares back at me.

"Hey, what's up?" I answer and he sighs.

"Man, we've been sitting on the damn cabin for three fucking days and there is nothing."

I nod. When Blaze told them to sit on the cabin and watch for Warren, I told him it was stupid but no one listened to me. "Yeah, I figured. It was clear by the shit he left on the walls for us that he was done with the place."

"I suppose you're right. How's shit there?"

"Fine, I think," I answer with a shrug. Honestly, I don't have a fucking clue since I haven't ventured out of my room much today. "The girls are all in your room getting ready for Piper's bachelorette party."

He sighs. "Fuck me. I forgot about that shit…. Well, we're on our way back now."

"Okay. We'll be here."

"Hey, make sure my wife isn't wearing anything too short… or too low cut… or fucking backless," he growls and I laugh, shaking my head.

"Fuck no, dude. I am not going into the middle of that war zone and telling your old lady what she can or can't wear. If she didn't kill me, Tate definitely would."

He scoffs. "Pussy."

"Asshole."

"You planning on packing tonight? Just in case?" he asks and I glance up at the sign on the wall that doubles as a gun safe. I usually don't have a reason to carry but there is no way in hell I'm letting us all go out without bringing my piece along.

"Yeah. I think we all are."

"Well," he mutters. "I guess it will be interesting. See y'all soon."

After we say good-bye, I set my phone back down on the desk and lean back in my chair as I scrub a hand over my face. Honestly, going out tonight is a terrible fucking idea, like we're waving a red flag at an angry bull, but it also feels like exactly what I need. I'm so goddamn stressed out by all of this and I deserve a few hours to let loose, a few hours to not think about Warren and his plan for us.

"Knock, knock."

I glance up as Rowan walks into my room, shutting the door behind her and when she turns back to me, I swallow back a groan. Fuck, why the hell does she always have to look so fucking good? Dragging my gaze down her body, I take in the tight gold dress she has on

153

that hits her mid-thigh and I think about how easy it would be to pull it up over her ass and slip inside her. It has cutouts all the way up her body on both sides, revealing tanned skin and my hands ache to touch her.

"Are you trying to give me a coronary?"

She smiles and it lights up her whole face. Jesus, she's gorgeous and I don't just mean her body, although that is spectacular but it's deeper than that. It's the way her eyes sparkle with this playfulness that makes you want to dive in, consequences be damned, and the way she has the nerves of a virgin and the confidence of a bombshell at the same time, this perfect mixture of contradictions that I can't quite figure out.

"Is it that good?" she asks and I drag my thoughts back to her dress. Is it that good? Hell fucking yes, it is but she looks just as good in a t-shirt and a pair of jeans.

"Definitely." I hold my hand out to her and she walks over to me before climbing on my lap and straddling my legs. I drag my hands up her thighs and take a deep, cleansing breath. Fuck. She is magic. "Have you gotten this approved by your brother yet?"

Scowling, she smacks my chest and I can't help but laugh. "Fuck you. I'm a grown woman and I can wear whatever the hell I want."

"I think Kodiak would disagree."

"Lincoln can shove it right up his ass. He doesn't tell me what to do," she snaps and I laugh again at her cute little scowl as she glares at my door like Kodiak is standing on the other side. She turns, staring daggers at me but it only makes me laugh harder and her lips twitch. "Stop it. Let me be mad at you."

I shake my head. "Can't. Now, come here and kiss me."

Sighing, she practically melts on my lap, despite the furrow of her brow, and leans in to press her lips to mine as she presses her hands to my chest. I grab her ass, pulling her closer with one hand as I cup her cheek with the other and flick my tongue against her bottom lip. They part in an instant and she moans into the kiss as her fingers grip my t-shirt. All of my stress, all of the shit I work so hard to forget but never really do just melts away with her touch and I'm just a guy, kissing a girl that sets his world on fire. For the first time in a long time, I feel like myself. There is no hiding, there is no mask, there is just us and it's all because of her.

"You should start getting ready," she whispers before stealing a few more kisses and when she pulls away, I groan.

"Come back."

She shakes her head, her smile bright. "I'm serious. We're all almost ready. You need to get dressed."

"What's wrong with what I'm wearing?" I ask, glancing down at my jeans and t-shirt and she rolls her eyes as she climbs off of my lap.

"You're really going to go out with me, looking like this," she replies, motioning to her body. "Dressed like that."

I arch a brow. "Am I going out with you? What about your brother?"

"I don't give a fuck tonight. We've been under a shit ton of stress and I want to have fun with you... so you can't be dressed like that."

"Fine," I shoot back with a laugh as I stand up and walk over to my closet. Honestly, I don't really care

155

what I wear but if it will make her happy, I'll change. "Are you going to pick it out for me?"

"Absolutely not. You're a big boy."

"Nice of you to notice," I say, wagging my eyebrows before winking at her and she scoffs as she rolls her eyes, fighting back a smile.

"Oh my God, men," she groans playfully, giving me a little shove before walking over to the bed and sitting on the edge as I start riffling through the closet. "The black one."

I turn back to her as I pull the black button up shirt out of the closet. "Thought you weren't gonna pick it out for me."

"Do whatever you want. I just thought it would look hot on you and I couldn't help thinking about taking it off of you when we get back," she says, shrugging like she didn't just throw down the gauntlet. Fuck me. All night, I'm going to be thinking about getting her back up to my room and peeling that little gold dress off of her with my teeth.

"You got more tricks to show me, Princess?"

She grins. "Maybe. You'll just have to wait and see."

"Anyone ever tell you that you're a tease?" I ask, my gaze flicking down her long, tan legs as she crosses them and leans back on the bed.

Jesus Christ, I want her.

I pull my eyes back up her body and when I meet her eyes, she smiles. "Don't pretend like you don't like it, Travis."

"I don't know what you're talking about," I protest, turning away from her as I pull my t-shirt over my head and toss it to the floor before slipping into the button up. She lets out a little laugh and I glance back at her as she stands up, arching a brow in challenge. Oh, that look fucking kills me. It's the look she gets when she wants to play and that usually only leads to one thing.

"Is that right?"

I suck in a breath as my cock twitches. "Yep."

"Hmm," she hums to herself as she struts across my room in her black heels but I turn away like I'm not interested. Also, so she can't see that I'm fucking hard as a rock now, just from one look. She stops next to me and places her hand on my bare chest before slowly dragging it down the front of my body. Jesus Christ, if she doesn't stop, we won't make it to the club. Continuing down over my stomach, she inches lower and lower, torturing me with possibilities as my breath sticks in my throat. Her hand drags down the front of my jeans, brushing over my dick and I bite back a hiss as I turn to look at her. Meeting my eyes, she smiles before leaning in and pressing a kiss to my cheek. "Challenge accepted."

Fuck. Me.

Chapter Thirteen
Rowan

The door to the club opens and "Shameless" by Camila Cabello rushes out to greet us as I turn to look at Tate and the other girls with a smile. A few of the guys make a noise of annoyance behind us as we all walk into the club but we ignore them, too excited to be bothered by their irritation. My giddiness with going out and having a good time tonight is also the reason I was easily able to brush off my brother's bitch fit when he saw the little gold dress I have on. The boy really should have learned by now that he can't tell me what to do. Butterflies flutter around in my belly as we stop just inside the door and my gaze is drawn to the middle of the room where people are dancing together, moving to the beat as it pulses through the club. I'm eager to get out there and let loose.

Something brushes against the back of my hand and I glance to my other side as Travis drags his knuckles across my skin and peeks down at me with a grin, forcing one to my lips as our eyes meet. A shiver races down my spine at the heat in his eyes and my mind flips to the next time I can get him alone. God, there is something so damn exciting about our little secret but there are times, like tonight, where I just want to hold his hand or dance with him without the rest of the world breathing down on us. It would be amazing if he and I could just be out in the open about our casual, no strings attached relationship without the rest of the club lobbing their expectations at the two of us and ruining it.

"Come with me," Tate instructs, hooking her arm through mine as she starts dragging me away from the group. "I'm buying you a drink."

"Goddamn it, Tate!" Lincoln yells and she turns back to him with a look that I can only imagine makes him think twice about saying anything. Or maybe not. I'm halfway convinced that the thing my brother loves most is riling his wife up.

"What?"

He sighs. "Y'all promised to stay together."

"Look," she shoots back, grabbing my hand with hers and holding it in the air. "I have my buddy, my taser, and my gun. Are we allowed to go to the bar?"

Stepping toward us, he nods. "If I come with you."

"Fine, but stay the hell back. We need to have girl talk," she hisses, turning before he has a chance to reply and dragging me through the crowd. Lincoln makes a noise of frustration as he trails after us and I shake my head. I know we promised the boys we would all stay with them but if anyone can protect me from Warren or whoever the hell is after us, it's Tate. She'd probably grab him by the balls and eviscerate him right in the middle of this club without a second thought.

"What can I get you, ladies?" the bartender asks, a flirty smile on his face before his gaze flicks to the behemoth behind us. Glancing back at my big brother, I roll my eyes and laugh. He has his large arms crossed over his chest and he's glaring daggers at the bartender, who has taken a step back.

"I'll just get a water," Tate says before turning to look at me. "What do you want? It's my treat tonight."

I look up at the bartender and smile, hoping to make him feel a little more at ease. "A whiskey, please. Neat."

Nodding, he walks down the bar to begin making our drinks and Tate turns to look at her husband with a sigh.

"I thought I told you to stay back so we could have girl talk."

He scowls. "What the hell do you need to talk about that you can't say in front of me?"

"Lincoln... baby," she says, patting his arm as she shakes her head and fights back a smile. "There are literally not enough hours in a day to answer that question."

"What the fuck ever," he growls, stomping a few feet away from us and slipping onto a bar stool. Tate rolls her eyes and nudges me before pointing to a couple of open stools a few feet in the opposite direction. I nod, fighting back a giggle at how much she likes to antagonize him. Some people might see it as mean but it's exactly what he needs because Tate forces him out of that provider slash protector mode he fell into when our dad died. Granted, that was exactly what my mom, Nora, and I needed at the time but for so long, I watched my brother live for everyone around him. He never did anything to make himself happy until the day he left Alaska and he was miserable. Not that he would ever admit it but I could see it and now that Tate has come into his life, I can see the weight it has lifted off of his shoulders. And like I said, he gives as good as he gets with her.

"So," Tate muses as we sit down and the bartender sets our drinks in front of us. "What's going on with you?"

I shake my head. "Nothing."

"What about Ash? Has he called again?"

"Yeah, he calls at least once a day still," I tell her, taking a sip of my drink and enjoying the burn as it blazes a path down my throat. It's irritating as hell that Ash still hasn't gotten a clue but I have to believe that he'll figure out that it really is over soon enough and then the calls will stop.

"That offer to go up to Alaska is still on the table."

I laugh. "Thanks, but I don't think anything that drastic is required. He'll figure it out soon enough."

"Okay. If you say so," she muses, turning to me with narrowed eyes and my belly does a little flip. "Anything new to report?"

Her look says it all. She knows something and she's trying to get me to tell her about it before she has to tell me she knows. I can only think of one secret she could be hinting at but Travis and I swore we would keep our little fling under wraps so I shake my head and look away as I take another sip of my drink.

"Nope."

"Hmm… so then, when I saw Streak press you up against a wall in the hallway and kiss you like he was about to take his last breath, that was… nothing?"

I shrug, my cheeks burning as I think about the kiss she witnessed. "It's casual."

"Right. That didn't look like a casual kiss. You know what else didn't look casual? The grin on your face when you stumbled out of his room the other night."

Fuck.

I thought we were being so careful to sneak around but clearly, we need to be more diligent.

"Look, the truth is, I don't care what you do with Streak. You're a grown woman and from what I can see, the boy is fucking smitten but just know," she says, pointing down the bar to my brother, "he, however, is going to flip his fucking lid if he finds out about this. Especially if he thinks Streak is screwing you around."

Turning, I meet her gaze. "It really is just casual, Tate. We both needed a distraction from…"

"Yeah. That's how it always starts, girl, and the next thing you know…" Her voice trails off as she points to her wedding ring and her little baby bump. I shake my head.

"We're just having fun."

Sighing, she nods and takes a sip of her water. "If you say so. What do you think he thinks we're talking about right now?"

"Huh?" I ask and she points down the bar to Lincoln, who is staring at us with a scowl. I imagine everything he just saw and laugh.

"He probably thinks you're trashing him."

"You're probably right. Don't tell him this but I'm fucking crazy about that man. I know you don't know me all that well yet, Rowan, and I'm sure you've heard some crazy ass shit about me from the other guys but I really want you to know how much I love your brother. That man has saved me more times than I can…" Her voice breaks as her words trail off and she sniffles, dabbing at her eyes. "Fuck. These dumb ass pregnancy hormones. I don't cry, okay?"

Nodding, I laugh. "I got that."

"But I do mean everything I just said. Lincoln and these babies mean fucking everything to me and you're a part of that. You've been through so much lately and lost so much but you still have family and people that love you."

"Jesus," I whisper, tears stinging my eyes as her words smack me right in the chest. "What in the hell are you trying to do to me? Look at us, crying in a damn club when we're supposed to be celebrating."

She shakes her head. "For fuck sake. Let's go dance before I have to murder all these guys for seeing that I possess the ability to cry."

"Let's do it." I nod as I throw back the rest of my drink, twisting my face as it burns down my throat. We stand up and Lincoln is by our side in an instant, looking intense as he scans the crowd. I nudge him with my elbow and roll my eyes when he turns his glare on me. "Simmer down, big brother. Tonight is supposed to be fun."

"Maybe for you but for the guys, it's fucking stressful. Where are y'all planning on going now?"

Tate points to the dance floor where the rest of our group is, some of them out on the floor dancing and others sitting at the tables on the edge of the crowd, and he releases a sigh.

"Thank God."

As we weave our way through the crowd, Lincoln wraps his arm around Tate's shoulder, pulling her close and she grabs my hand, making sure I don't get lost which I find amusing. As much as she gives my brother a hard time about his overbearing nature and protectiveness, she is almost as bad. Almost. "Body Party" by Ciara starts playing as we reach the edge of the dance floor and Tate squeezes my hand before leaning in closer.

"Go dance with your boy," she whispers before motioning to Lincoln. "I'll distract the bear."

I grin. "Best sister-in-law ever."

She releases my hand with a laugh and shoves me toward the dance floor as Lincoln guides her toward the tables. When he realizes that I'm gone, he spins around but I shimmy closer to our group and give him a little wave to let him know I'm okay. Tate whispers something in his ear and he sighs before nodding and leaving me to dance. Once the coast is clear, I search the room for Travis, excited to dance with him, out in public, and turned on from our little game earlier. My teeth sink into my bottom lip as I remember the way I skimmed my hand over his cock and the sound he made when I pressed my lips against his throat as I trail my fingers down toward my cleavage.

"Looking for something?"

A grin stretches across my face at the whispered question and my eyes close as I lean back into Travis's body, his scent surrounding me as a shiver works its way up my spine. His hands grip my hips as he presses a quick kiss against my neck before dragging his nose up to my ear.

"Dance with me?" I ask and he shakes his head. He navigates us to the corner of the dance floor, away from our group as he kisses my neck again. I spin in his arms. Looking up, he scans the crowd for a second before glancing back down at me with a grin.

"You gonna show me some of those tricks you talked about?"

I shake my head. "Baby, those moves are best reserved for somewhere more… private."

"Great idea," he says, wrapping his arms around my waist and pulling me farther away from the dance floor as I shake my head, laughing.

"No. Come dance with me."

He looks out at everyone dancing around us before meeting my eyes and shaking his head as he drops his arms from my body. "Princess, I can't dance."

"I refuse to believe that," I tell him, arching a brow and he laughs, his hands going back to my hips as he pulls me closer.

"And why is that?"

I meet his eyes and wrap my arms around his neck as I lean in close and let my lips brush over his. "'Cause you know how to fuck."

"Rowan," he groans before sealing his lips to mine and pulling us further into the shadows, away from prying eyes. I lean up on my toes, trying to get closer to him and his hands slip down to my ass before he lifts me up and I wrap my legs around his waist. Well, shit. It's a damn good thing that no one can see us over here because if they didn't know what we were up to before, they sure as hell would after seeing this.

But do I even care?

I don't know that I do. Travis and I are having fun with each other and I don't see why the hell I have to keep making excuses for that or apologizing for it. Why can't we just be out in the open around the club without everyone watching us and waiting for the moment when it all explodes?

"Fuck, baby," he breathes, kissing down my neck as his grip on me tightens. "I've wanted you so bad since you walked into my room in that dress."

I smile as I run my fingers through the hair at the base of his neck. "Yeah? Have you been thinking about taking it off of me all night?"

"Yes."

"And have you been thinking about what I might be wearing underneath it?" I ask as warmth rushes through me and I fight back a shudder. He nods, his teeth nipping at my neck.

"Hell yes."

Giggling, I pull back to meet his eyes. "Any ideas?"

"Don't get me started, Rowan. I'm this close," he whispers, his voice gravelly, as he sets me back on the floor and holds up his thumb and pointer finger before pinching them together until they almost touch. "To hauling you into a bathroom and fucking you until we both can't stand."

The thought makes moisture pool between my thighs and I close my eyes as my back arches against him. "Travis."

"Jesus Christ," he hisses, slipping a hand into my hair and slamming his lips to mine as his other arm holds me firm against his body. His cock presses into my belly, through our clothing, and I desperately wish we were back at the clubhouse right now. We stumble into a wall and I gasp. He takes full advantage, slipping his tongue past my lips and tangling it with mine as he thrusts his hips into me with a growl. "You turn me on so fucking much. You know that?"

I nod. "Yeah, I do."

"You love it, don't you?" It's halfway between a question and an accusation but I can't even deny it. I adore the way one touch from me can make his eyes flare with need and the way, whenever he's near me, he has to be touching me. Nodding, I rub my tits against his chest, desperate for friction.

"I love it."

"Fuck, baby," he whispers, shaking his head as he pulls back just enough to separate us and plants his hands on the wall next to me as he struggles to catch his breath. "We have to stop."

My bottom lip pokes out and I scowl. "Why?"

"Because, I'm about to fuck you up against this wall in the back of a crowded club and you deserve better than that," he answers, his eyes on mine and his need shining back at me like a beacon but my heart stutters at his thoughtfulness. Even knowing the things I've done in my past and knowing that I was willing to let him do just that right here and right now, he still has enough respect for me to stop us. Reaching up, I cup his cheek and press a soft kiss to his lips as I fight back tears. When I pull away, he studies my face and his brow furrows. "What was that for?"

I shake my head. "For just being you, Travis."

"Oh," he whispers as a shy smile stretches across his face and he sighs as pushes off of the wall, takes my hand and lacing our fingers. "Want a drink?"

"Desperately."

He laughs and we walk back out into the main area as the song changes to something darker that I don't recognize. It's kind of a weird choice to play in a club but whatever. I'm not a DJ so what the hell do I know?

"Hey, just so you know," he says as we reach the bar and I turn to face him. "As soon as we get back to the clubhouse and I get you alone, we're picking this right back up."

I grin. "I was really hoping you would say that."

Before he can say anything else, the lights go out, throwing the entire club into darkness and Travis's arms wrap around me, making me jump as he pulls me closer and panicked voices sound out around us. The music swells and my heart thrashes in my ears as I try to catch my breath.

What the hell is happening?

A single spotlight flashes on, illuminating a spot on the far corner of the dance floor where a man stands, in all black with a white mask covering his whole face. A white mask just like the one the boys found in the cabin…

"Holy fuck," Travis whispers. "We have to go."

The light goes out before we can move and one of his hands falls away. Crying out, I cling to his shirt and he presses his lips to my head.

"Shh. I'm right here, baby. Just getting my gun."

My hands shake and my heart is racing as I try to see through the darkness but to no avail. "Did you see anyone else when the light came on?"

"No. Last I saw, everyone was on the dance floor. If a light comes on again, we need to move, you hear me? Head straight for the door and don't look back."

I shake my head. "I need to get my brother and Tate."

"Kodiak will take care of Tate and I don't think the light will stay on long enough for us to find everyone." Just as his words stop, the light flicks on again, this time all the way across the club, closer to us, and the man is standing there again. It feels like he's staring right at Travis and me but I don't have time to dwell on it as he begins pulling me through the mass of terrified people, toward the door. I try to search the crowd for the rest of our group but the lights go out again. We freeze, right in the middle of a large group of club patrons. Terrified whispers and random names fill the air around us as everyone tries to figure out what is going on and my entire body shakes. Where will he pop up next? Travis keeps his grip on me firm, probably too firm, but it feels good in this moment as we both try to catch our breaths and wait for the next light to flick on.

"Are you okay?" he asks, pressing another kiss to my head and I nod but I'm not okay. Not a single part of this is okay and the thought hits me that we may not make it out of this club tonight. My chest aches and my thoughts slow to a crawl as I try to wade through the utter terror wreaking havoc on my body in the darkness. "Get ready to move again, I think."

My breath sticks in my throat and my heart races as we wait and after a few seconds, a light flicks on. This one is by the bar this time, right where we were standing before, and the man stares at us in the crowd. The black holes of the mask where the eyes are supposed to be feel like they're burning into me and I can't move. My entire body is shaking so badly that I don't think I can make my legs work and all I want to do is cry.

"Move, Rowan," Travis barks in my ear and it spurs me into motion, somehow, as we take off for the door again, shoving our way through the crowd. I spot the door to the club up ahead and see Storm and Ali moving toward it from our right as we close in on it. The lights go out again but this time, Travis doesn't stop. He's like a bulldozer, shoving other people out of his way as he drags me along with him and despite my fear, I know he would do anything to protect me from the man seemingly stalking us through this club.

The light comes on again, this time by the dance floor and I scream when I see him standing right next to my brother and Tate. Tate spots him first and delivers a swift kick to his chest that sends him flying backward onto his ass and in the next moment, Lincoln has her in his arms and they are running toward the door and us. We reach the door just as the light goes out again and Travis yanks it open, flooding the room with light from the streetlamp outside, drawing the attention of everyone else in the club.

"Fuck," he hisses. "Keep moving. Don't stop, you hear me?"

I nod as we slip outside and the next second, a steady stream of bodies pile out of the club, spilling out onto the sidewalk as some people fall to the ground but everyone else just tramples over them. It's complete fucking chaos and my heart jumps into my throat as I think about the people that were still in there, all of the people we could lose tonight. Once we get halfway down the block, Travis finally stops but he doesn't release me and he doesn't put his gun away as his gaze flicks over the surrounding area.

"Oh, thank God," someone cries and we spin around as Emma and Nix come running up to us. Emma throws her arms around me, pulling me out of Travis's arms and into a hug as tears roll down her face. Jerking back, she meets my eyes. "Have you seen anyone else?"

"Storm and Ali were near the door when we were and my brother and Tate were still by the dance floor… I don't know about anyone else," I whisper, struggling to hold back my tears as my body shakes.

171

"There!" she shouts, pointing into the crowd as Storm and Ali burst out of the mob of bodies and I breathe a small sigh of relief before my gaze goes back to the crowd, searching for everyone else. Travis pulls me back into his body, securing his arm around my waist, and I feel his body relax slightly against me.

"There they are," a voice calls from across the street and we turn as Henn, Kady, Chance, Carly, Moose, Juliette, Fuzz, Piper, Smith, and Quinn come running up to us. Everyone starts hugging but I turn back to the crowd, searching for Lincoln and Tate. Pain radiates from my chest and my heart hammers out of control as tears sting my eyes.

This can't be happening.

I can't lose them.

"I have to go back," I whisper, shaking my head as I try to free myself from Travis's grip. There is no way I'm leaving here without Lincoln and Tate so I have to go back and find them.

"Are you fucking insane?" Travis asks, his grip on me tightening as I turn to look at him. Tears slip down my cheeks and I plead with my eyes as we stare at each other.

"It's my brother, Travis. I have to go get him. I have to go back."

He shakes his head. "There is no way in hell I'm letting you go in there again. It's a fucking madhouse but if anyone can get through it, it's your giant of a brother. Just wait here."

"I can't lose him, Travis," I whisper, my heart shattering in my chest at the thought. If they don't make it out of that club, I'll truly have no one. His face crumples and he shoves his gun into the waistband of his jeans before cupping my cheek and pressing his forehead to mine.

"You're not going to lose them, okay? They are going to be fine. Both Tate and your brother are more than capable of taking care of themselves, Princess. I promise."

I shake my head. "You don't know that. Lincoln and Tate are the only family I have left. I have to go back for them."

"No," he growls, shaking his head before he presses a kiss to my lips. "I'm not going to let you put your life in danger, too. They'll be fine."

"So…" someone says and we pull apart, looking up as Chance arches a brow. "This is a thing?"

Carly smacks him in the chest and shoots him a glare. "Not the time."

"Right," he answers with a nod and shoves his hands in his pockets but as I look at everyone else's face, I know our secret is out. There is no putting this genie back in the bottle.

"Rowan!"

I gasp, turning at the sound of my brother's booming voice coming through the crowd but Travis still won't release me so I throw my hand in the air.

"Over here, Lincoln."

A moment later, he steps out of the crowd with a very angry Tate thrown over his shoulder and as soon as he sees me, he rushes over. Travis releases me just before Lincoln wraps me up in a hug, crushing me to his body.

"Thank God," he breathes, his body shaking and his breathing heavy.

"For fucks sake, Lincoln," Tate seethes, pounding her fists against his back. "Put me the fuck down so I don't kick your poor sister in the face."

He sets her back on her feet before pulling us both back into a group hug and she huffs in annoyance, fighting against it for a second before giving in. Lincoln looks up, making sure everyone else is here before he sighs.

"Everyone okay?"

The rest of the group nods but they all look anything but okay after what just happened. Although, I'm sure I don't look much better. One thing I do know, for sure, is that after tonight, it's clear that things are getting infinitely more dangerous and I'm terrified of what Warren has planned for us.

Chapter Fourteen
Travis

I scrub my hand down my face as the footage from the club last night plays on the screen in front of me but there is nothing to see. Literally, it's just pitch black staring back at me as soon as the lights go out and it doesn't matter that I've watched the damn thing five times, trying to see anything through the darkness or before the lights go out or after they come back on. As always, Warren had this stunt planned out perfectly. My thoughts drift back to when the lights went out last night and I shake my head as my heart starts to beat a little faster. I've never been so fucking scared in my life and I held onto Rowan like she was a life raft because nothing else was more important to me than getting her out of there safely. She was my one and only priority, which probably sounds awful as hell considering all of my brothers and their wives were also in the club but I knew they were all packing, just like me, and they would do whatever it took to get out of there. I didn't need to worry about them. For as long as I live though, I'll never forget the way Rowan's body shook in my arms and the terror in her eyes. I'll also never fucking forget the way Warren stared at us when he popped up the second and third time.

The look fucking chilled me to the bone.

Once we got back to the clubhouse, we all sat down with Blaze, who stayed back to babysit the kids while we went out, and told him what happened. He was furious, of course, and we all are desperate to take action but there is nothing we can do. Until we find concrete evidence on who Warren is or who he is working with, if he's working with someone, we can't exactly start firing shots. Maybe that is the worst part of all of this - we just have to sit here and take his attack without being able to fight back because he is always in control of the game. He has planned this thing down to the very last detail and, so far, everything has gone his way. It's infuriating. Each day, it feels like my rage grows more and more and the longer it takes me to find him, the more I can't stop thinking about what I'll do to him when I do finally track him down.

Fuck…

I can't let my thoughts go there. I've worked so fucking hard to not be that person, that monster, and I can't let this situation pull me into the darkness I've been running from my whole life.

Shaking my head, I cross my arms over my chest and sigh as the video starts playing again. I watch as Rowan and I walk out of the back hallway and smile, remembering our stolen moments in the club before everything went to shit. After we got back last night and we had our little talk with Blaze, I hauled her up to my room because there was no way in hell I was going to let her go. We spent hours lost in each other, fucking all over this room like it was our last night on earth because it honestly felt like it almost was, before we passed out and even then, I didn't let her go until we spent some more time tangled together this morning. It will be interesting to see what happens now that the whole club knows about us, apart from Kodiak. Maybe someone will tell him the truth... Hell, maybe someone already has but I suspect that's not true since I'm still in one piece.

"Streak," someone calls from the other side of the door as they knock and I turn away from my computer as Storm walks in, stress lining his face. He and Ali were close to the door when the final light came on last night but not as close as Rowan and me. They ended up fighting through the crowd as it surged out of the club and Storm said he was pretty sure he broke a couple noses in his mission to get his wife to safety. I nod in greeting as he shuts the door behind him.

"What's up?"

He sighs and throws himself into the other chair in my room. "Just got off the phone with Rodriguez. He looked into the report from the club last night and the owner said that he was approached by someone who wanted to put on a little show in the club."

"So he just let him?" I ask, arching a brow, as I wonder how fucking stupid this guy is. Last I checked, no one has died but there were some serious injuries caused when people fell by the door and everyone else just ran over them. At least three people are in the ICU this morning after that circus last night. He shakes his head.

"No, he told him to get fucked. At first..."

"What changed then?"

Storm grimaces. "He said the man offered him a thousand dollars to allow the performance."

"So, of course he took it," I scoff, shaking my head. Can't say that I really blame the guy but it begs the question, where the hell did Warren get a thousand dollars? When I checked his account yesterday, he didn't have that kind of money and there were never any transactions that large made in the last two years. My idea about him working with a partner springs to mind and I blow out a breath, shaking my head.

"He might be working with someone else."

Storm sighs. "I've been having the same thought lately but it doesn't help us much."

"I know," I agree, turning back to the video playing on a loop on my monitor. "It just makes him even harder to find. I'm almost afraid to ask but did the owner give a good description of the guy?"

"Uh, no," he scoffs and I turn back to him. "Why?"

"Because he never actually saw his face. Apparently, he communicated through email only and when he showed up at the club to do his performance, he was wearing the mask. He claimed it was part of his "process"."

Gritting my teeth, I grab the pen holder off of my desk and chuck it at the wall. "I'm so fucking sick of this douchebag!"

"We should make a club," he quips, nodding in agreement and I scoff, some of my anger melting away as I shake my head at his shitty joke.

"Thanks, asshole."

He shrugs as he stands up. "Got you to stop throwing shit, didn't it? I got to go check in on my wife and kid."

"How is Ali after last night?"

178

"Fucking traumatized," he answers with a sigh, pain on his face, and I shake my head, thinking about the effect last night is going to have on all of us. "Speaking of which, though... you and Rowan?"

I shrug. "Yeah. It's just..."

"Casual," he cuts in, nodding as he arches his brow. "Yeah, I heard but you know that's dumb as hell, right? The way y'all were with each other last night was anything but casual."

"Okay, cupid. Why don't you mind your own damn business? Just 'cause all of you think marriage and babies are the best things ever doesn't mean everyone else does. Rowan and I are just having fun."

He purses his lips and nods as he turns toward the door, not buying a single word I'm saying. "Make sure you really emphasize that part when Kodiak finds out. I wanna see what happens to the human body when you drop it off the roof."

"Fuck you." I laugh as he opens the door. Kodiak won't like it, for sure, but he wouldn't murder me over this... I don't think. He flips me off as he walks out of my room and shuts the door behind him as I turn back to my computer and sigh. Closing out of the video, I lean back in my chair and try to think of a new angle, any other way I could look at this, that might give us the lead we need but I'm drawing a giant fucking blank. My phone rings on the desk and I grab it, scowling at the unfamiliar number on the screen before I answer it.

"Hello?"

"Travis, long time no talk. How are you, my friend?" a voice asks and I scowl as I pull the phone away from my ear before shaking my head and pulling it back.

179

"Uh… who is this?"

The voice on the other end of the line scoffs. "You don't remember me? And here I thought we had such a special relationship."

"Okay, who the fuck is this?" I demand and he laughs.

"It's your old friend, Warren."

No…

An ice cold wave of dread washes over me as I sit forward in my chair and try to think of something to say. Why in the fuck is he calling me? His laughter greets me and the dread is quickly replaced by anger.

"Oh, that got your attention, didn't it? Let me ask you, how did you like my little show last night?"

I grit my teeth, shoving out of my chair. "Oh, yeah. It was really something."

"I'm so glad you enjoyed it. What about Rowan? Was she entertained, too?"

My heart pounds in my ears at the mention of her name and I clench my fists as I pace back and forth through my room, trying to calm myself.

"Don't fucking talk about her."

He laughs again. "Touchy touchy. I thought you didn't do relationships, Travis."

"I don't," I snap, my hands shaking out of control as I think about all of the awful things I want to do to this fuck for the hell he's put us through over the last two years. And how in the hell does he know that I don't do relationships?

"So, then you have no say when it comes to her, do you? If I wanted to get to know her, too, it would be well within my rights. I have to admit, I've watched all of your brothers meet their wives and lose their damn minds as they tripped over their own two feet in their

180

attempts to woo them. It's always bored me before but there is just something about our little Rowan, isn't there? She's special."

"You listen to me, you son of a bitch. You stay the hell away from her or I'll…"

"You'll what?" he growls, cutting me off. "You gonna start taking after your daddy?"

All of my thoughts screech to a halt and I freeze in the middle of my room. "What the hell do you know about that?"

"Oh." He laughs and the sound grates on my nerves. "I know everything, Travis Hornback."

"Don't fucking call me that." I roar as I smash my fist into the wall but it does nothing to quell the rage pumping through every inch of my body. My anger only seems to delight him though because he laughs again.

"Why not? It's your name. I mean, sure, you can get it legally changed to your mother's maiden name but we both know the truth. Don't we, Travis?"

I shake my head. "You don't know shit and when we find you…"

"Oh, speaking of your little club, there is something I need you to do for me," he interrupts and I shake my head as I spin toward the door, clenching and unclenching my fist.

"Not happening."

A noise of disapproval greets me. "I wouldn't be so quick to say that, Travis, or I might have to start showing you what I can really do."

"What is that supposed to mean?"

"Oh, just that if you tell anyone about this little conversation, I'll have to start coming after people you care about. Maybe I'll even start with… ooh, Tate.

Wouldn't that just destroy your pretty little girlfriend and her brother? And then after that, I could send him the photo I have of you fucking his sweet little baby sister on your desk. Trauma like that, back to back, is enough to make anyone snap, don't you think?"

My heart pounds in my chest and pain swarms my body at the thought of losing any of the people in this club. I fucking hate the idea of keeping this from everyone but what other choice do I have? Until we know who Warren truly is, I have to keep my mouth shut.

"Travis?" he asks and I grit my teeth and I nod. "Fine."

"Excellent!" he exclaims and I can hear the triumph in his voice. It tears through me as my anger flares out of control and I vow that I'll do whatever it takes to find this asshole and put an end to him. "Well, I've got to get going. Plans to put into motion and all that but I'll talk to you soon, Travis."

He hangs up before I can say anything else and I throw the phone against the wall as I let out another scream, rage spiraling through me like a tornado and consuming everything else in its path. The door to my room opens and Rowan steps in with a shocked expression as she shuts the door behind her.

"What the hell is going on in here?"

I shake my head, holding my arms out to her and she eliminates the distance between us without a second of hesitation. Pulling her into my body, I bury my face in her hair and my body sags in relief.

"I'm sorry, Princess. I… was just frustrated that I couldn't find anything from the surveillance videos," I lie, the deceit seeping through my system like poison as she pulls back to meet my eyes. The concern on her face fucking kills me and my entire body aches to tell her the truth about what just happened but I think about Warren coming after her and it stops me. She presses her hand to my cheek and I lean into the touch.

"I know last night was…"

"Hell," I supply and she nods.

"But we're going to figure this out, okay? Don't give up hope, Travis."

I close my eyes as my name rolls off of her tongue, almost like her voice is erasing Warren's from my mind, and nod. "I won't, baby. I promise."

"Good." She leans up and presses a soft kiss to my lips as I tighten my arms around her waist. "Now, Storm sent me up here to get you. Blaze just called everyone into church."

I nod and kiss her again. "Thanks. I'll come find you afterward, okay?"

"You'd better," she quips as I release her and when I turn to walk away, she smacks my ass. I turn back to her with a grin.

"Watch it, woman. You're going to start something you can't finish."

She cocks her head to the side and smiles. "Actually, I think you're the one who can't finish it and besides, I still have tricks, remember? Now, go."

"Yes, ma'am," I tell her and her grin widens.

"Ooh, dirty talk, I like it."

Laughing, I walk out of the room with her trailing behind me and I marvel at her ability to make me relax even after the most stressful, rage inducing situation I've ever been in. When we get to the bottom of the stairs, she shoots me a wink and joins Ali, Tate, Emma, and Nix at the bar and I slip into the war room, flinging myself into my usual seat across from Blaze, who walks in and shuts the door right after me.

"Okay, so we're not going to be long today but we've got a job to do in four days that we need to go over," Blaze says as he sits down in his seat and slaps a folder on the table. Kodiak shakes his head.

"I'm sorry but what? After what fucking happened last night, you really think it's a good idea to take a job?"

Blaze sighs. "I don't know but this mother and her children need our help and we only have a limited window to get them out."

"Why?" Chance asks, scowling and on edge like the rest of us.

"Because they will be traveling through Baton Rouge in four days, on their way to relatives in Arizona and we're going to get them out when they stop at a gas station right outside of town."

Everyone starts talking, all at once, arguing with Blaze about why this is a terrible idea and while I agree with them, my mind jumps back to my phone call from Warren and the threats he made. Listening to them bicker about this seems so fucking stupid when I think about the things he vowed to do if I said a word about our conversation and I wish that his promise of violence made it easier to keep it to myself but it doesn't. These are my brothers and every cell in my body is screaming at me to open my mouth and tell them what is going on. How would he even know if I did say something? He mentioned having a photo of Rowan and me together and I clench my fists as I think about him, standing outside the clubhouse and watching us together.

Fuck.

We need more security and we need tighter patrols around the clubhouse but, of course, I can't say any of this to my brothers without telling them about the phone call.

"Okay," Blaze barks, dragging my attention to him once again. "I understand y'all are concerned about us going out to do this job but one thing we are not going to do is let this animal control us. This club has always helped people and that is what we're going to do now, Warren be damned. He doesn't get to control our lives and that includes Fuzz and Piper's wedding in two days. We are going to fucking party and celebrate them without looking over our shoulder and being scared. Do I make myself clear?"

Everyone nods and he turns to me.

"Streak, did you find anything on the surveillance videos?"

I shake my head. "Only if you're into complete and total darkness."

"Fuck," he sighs and scrubs his hand down his face, the stress of this whole situation shining in his eyes as he turns to Storm. "And what about you? Did Rodriguez have any information for us?"

Storm begins recounting everything he told me upstairs about Warren and the club's owner and I lean back in my chair, wondering how much hell we're in for from Warren before this whole thing ends and the one thought that dogs me more than any other is wondering who will be left standing after the smoke clears.

Chapter Fifteen
Warren

I take a drag of my cigarette, the smoke burning my lungs, as I scan the clubhouse parking lot but it is nothing compared to the rage burning through my chest as I watch them all gather to celebrate Fuzz and Piper renewing their vows. All day I've sat here, watching them as they set things up, laughing and having fun as they talked about what a special day it is for the happy couple.

How fucking sweet.
So sweet I want to hurl.

When I first heard of this wedding, a part of me hated the idea of letting them take a break from the panic and paranoia I've instilled in all of their hearts and minds, especially after how well my stunt at the nightclub went, but after taking some time to think about it, I decided this was better. It's my little gift to them, the only small instance of charity they'll see from me in this game we've been playing. So, let them celebrate and be happy for this one moment. Let them live and remember what their lives were like before I came to get my

Wicked Games

revenge and let them get a glimpse of a normal life before I rip it all away.

Brutally.

Violently.

In a pool of blood.

It's what they deserve. No, actually. Now that I think about it, it's not anywhere close to what they deserve but it will have to do because if I had my way, I would lock them all away and make them live the rest of their lives in slow, agonizing pain but it's just not practical. I clench my teeth so hard that my jaw aches as I watch Fuzz step up to the end of the aisle in his cut with Streak and Smith by his side. He rubs his hands together, waiting for his bride to join him as all of his brothers and their wives look on with smiles on their faces.

Not for long, though.

God, what I wouldn't give to carve those grins from their faces.

It won't be the same but I'm certain that the wedding gift I got for the happy couple will do a good job of erasing the joy from every face in the room. Except mine, of course. I grin as I think about them opening it. Fuck, I wish I could be there to watch it all go down but sadly, I can't. That's okay, though. Just knowing the horror they'll feel when they see what I've given them gives me a little piece of happiness, one that will sustain me for a little while until I can launch my next attack.

I am so close to ending this, so close to getting the one thing I have wanted more than anything else in the world for as long as I can remember - vengeance... justice. There is a pounding in my ears and my hands shake, rage coursing through my veins as I think about what they did to me, everything they took from me. I used to fucking be somebody and then they came into my life, tearing it all apart. My thoughts drift to the plans I still have in store for them and my smile grows. It's taken me a hell of a long time to put all of this together and most days, I hate how long I had to draw this out. I want action and I want it now but my drive to inflict the most pain, the most suffering possible, keeps me going. Now, this is almost over and when I'm done, they'll be left with the same thing I have.

Nothing.

The music swells and the clubhouse doors open to reveal Piper in her wedding dress with Blaze by her side, beaming out at the rest of the crowd and I grip the steering wheel in front of me as my smile matches his. They are all happy now but they have no idea what I have in store for them and all I can think is, *let the games begin.*

Chapter Sixteen
Rowan

"Wyatt," Piper says, her voice cracking and tears shining in her eyes as she peeks up from the little notecard in her hand at her husband. "The first time we stood up at an altar like this and vowed to love each other for the rest of our lives, we had no idea what we were getting ourselves into or just how hard it would be to fulfill those vows. We couldn't have predicted the trials in store for us or the pain that would follow but, as cliché as it sounds, I would do it all again to wind up here with you now. I've loved you with the innocence of a girl and as I stand before you as the woman I am now, that love has only gotten stronger. Now that we're back together and beginning our life as husband and wife again, I can't wait to see everything the future has in store for us. I'm certain that it won't always be easy but I know we'll always face the storm together, with your hand in mine."

Blaze, who is officiating this little shindig, clears his throat, dabbing at his eyes and I can't help but smile at what a softie he is. He nods to Fuzz, who turns to his wife.

"Pip, I think it's fair to say that we've been through hell in the last ten years and I've spent a lot of time hating you for the part you played in it all but as soon as you walked back into my life, I finally understood that old saying about there being a thin line between love and hate because even when I hated you, even when I couldn't stand to hear someone say your name, I still loved you with every single piece of my heart. When you left, you took a part of me and I wasn't whole again until you sat down across from me in that restaurant and said "Hi, Wyatt"."

Color rushes to her cheeks as a few chuckles ring out and I can't help but smile at how adorable they are. There is something so special about their story, which I was informed of last night when us girls snuck out to the roof and polished off two bottles of wine, and I'm honestly in awe of the kind of love survives through everything they've thrown at it. Piper drops her gaze to the floor but Fuzz nudges under her chin with his fingers, guiding her eyes back to his before he goes on.

"I know, beyond a shadow of a doubt, that there isn't anything that can come between us or pull us apart again. Whether you like it or not, you're stuck with me, Pip, and I'm going to spend the rest of my life loving you and the family we're building together... including all of these hooligans," he adds, smirking as he tilts his head toward the crowd. The guys stand up and cheer loudly before Blaze shoots them all a stern look. They sink back into their seats as Blaze begins his portion of the ceremony and my gaze flicks to Travis as he stands at Fuzz's side. Our eyes meet and his lips twitch with the hint of a smile that makes my belly flip and my heart skip a beat.

When he turns back to watch the happy couple, I drop my gaze to my lap and take a deep breath to calm myself before glancing up again. The girls and I spent all morning getting this portion of the parking lot set up for the wedding and honestly, after we were done, it was almost unrecognizable. This is the second Devils wedding I've attended and just like Lincoln and Tate's beach nuptials last year, Fuzz and Piper's wedding is a perfect contradiction, completely unexpected and one of the sweetest things I've ever seen in my life. It has all the tradition and class of any other wedding I've been to but with the added element of the guys decked out in leather and the Harleys parked on either side of the altar. It's the perfect mix of Fuzz and Piper and honestly, after the incident at the club a few days ago, I think we're all a little more appreciative of how special this is.

My thoughts flash back to that night in the club and a shiver runs down my spine as I remember the spotlight coming on and illuminating the man in the mask. I've honestly never felt fear like that in my entire life and Warren has haunted my dreams every night since. It's not even like I'm running from him or he's chasing me as I sleep but I'll just be going about my business in the dream when he pops up out of nowhere, staring at me with dark pits of nothingness where his eyes should be and I've woken up in a cold sweat more than once. Of course, Travis has been insisting that I sleep in his bed with him and sneak down in the morning before anyone else wakes up but I'm not complaining. The feeling of his arms wrapped around me is the one thing that has kept me from losing my mind.

"By the power granted to me by the internet," Blaze says, his voice proud as he looks between Fuzz and Piper. "I now pronounce you husband and wife... again."

Laughing, we all stand, clapping and cheering as Fuzz wraps his arms around his wife and claims her in front of all of us with a possessive kiss that forces my gaze to Travis but he's already watching me. His intense eyes and signature smirk greets me and he winks before breaking out into a full smile that takes my breath away. God, the boy is too damn attractive for his own good. I shake my head as heat rushes to my cheeks and butterflies flutter around in my belly. Since most of the girls and I got so drunk last night, Travis refused to fuck me no matter how much I begged him and I'm definitely feeling it today. As soon as we get a chance, I'm stealing him away for myself because needy is not a good look on me. Grinning to myself, I remember the lingerie I slipped on underneath the green satin dress I'm wearing and wonder what his reaction will be when he finally gets a chance to see it. I'm going to pray for worshipping my body until the wee hours of the morning but at this point, I might just take anything.

Blaze hollers out over the crowd, telling us to get inside for the after party and we break off into three groups - some of the girls running into the kitchen to check on the food while some of the guys hang back to put decorations away and the rest of us follow the bride and groom into the clubhouse. Streamers are stretched across the entire room and someone moved all of the tables out of the middle of the room so people can dance without bumping into anything. Flutes of champagne are set up on the bar top but I slip behind it, grabbing the whiskey and pouring myself a glass as music begins pumping out of the speakers. As I look around the room and all the happy smiling faces in every direction, it's hard to believe just four days ago, we were all huddled outside a mob and shaking in fear after being stalked by a faceless man. Maybe that's the hardest part for me. No one knows what Warren even looks like... the man could walk into this club and we would have no clue and yet, he seems to have his fingers in every aspect of our lives.

Like, how did he know we were going to be at that club that night?

"Enjoying the wedding, Princess?"

I smile as I feel Travis step up behind me and press his front to my back. His breath washes over my skin and I shiver as I raise my glass to my lips and nod.

"I did. You?"

He shrugs. "It was all right."

"Not a fan of weddings?" I ask, watching as some of the couples begin pairing off and dancing in the middle of the room. Emma's twin boys, Grady and Corbin, dance with their little sisters, Harper and Charlie, and I can't wipe the smile off of my face as I watch them gently pulling them around the dance floor. Travis's hand skates up my side, pulling my attention back to him and I suck in a breath as my nipples tighten.

"It's just not my thing."

Arching a brow, I glance back at him over my shoulder. "And why is that?"

"Weddings are kind of the polar opposite of casual, sweetheart," he answers and I turn, leaning against the bar as I search his face. I suppose I didn't realize he took this whole "casual" thing so seriously.

"Are you telling me that you *only* do casual relationships?"

He nods. "Yeah."

"Have you ever had a relationship?" I ask, my curiosity getting the better of me as something I can't quite name nags at me, demanding my attention. He sighs and shakes his head.

"Nope."

"Huh," I whisper, surprised by his admission as my stomach drops. What the hell is that? "And you never want anything more than casual?"

He shakes his head again, peeking up at me as his tongue darts out and traces along his bottom lip. "No… what's with all the questions tonight?"

"Just curious," I answer, turning to look out at the dance floor as I take another sip of my drink. "Trying to get to know you a little better and all that."

Silence stretches out between us and I shift back and forth as I try to think of something else to say but my mind is blank. What happened and why the hell is this suddenly awkward between us? We've always been able to be open with each other and we've always been on the same page when it came to our relationship so why do I feel let down right now? God, this wedding is messing with my head - that has to be it. He clears his throat and lightly touches my arm, pulling my gaze back to him as he lifts his chin toward the middle of the room.

"Dance with me."

I arch a brow. "Are you asking me or demanding?"

"Asking you," he answers before a devilish grin stretches across his face. "Knowing that you'll say yes."

"Oh, you think I'm that easy, do you?"

He laughs, trailing the tips of his fingers up my arm as goose bumps pop up in his wake. "Only for me, Princess. Come dance with me."

"I thought you couldn't dance?"

196

"Yeah, I'm pretty sure I can manage that," he answers, pointing to Fuzz and Piper as they sway back and forth to the song. Crossing my arms over my chest, I peek up at him.

"Are you sure? People will see."

"Let 'em," he answers, shrugging with that cocky grin on his face that gets me every single fucking time when it comes to him. Unable to say no to him any longer, I set my drink down on the bar and he takes my hand, leading me a little ways into the room as a few people turn to look at us. Lincoln and Tate are on the other side of the room, talking and laughing with each other but as soon as Travis wraps his arm around my waist and pulls me into his body, I swear I can feel my brother's gaze on us.

"Kodiak is staring daggers at me right now," he whispers in my ear, confirming my suspicions and I fight back a giggle. "Fuck. I think he's thinking about killing me."

I shake my head. "Don't worry. Tate will run interference."

"I suppose if there is one person you want on your side in a fight," he replies, looking down at me with a grin. "It's Tate."

Laughing, I nod. "She'll be happy to hear you think so."

"Yeah, make sure you tell her. I'll take all the brownie points I can get with that woman," he says before giving me a mock shudder of fear and I laugh, feeling us both relax a little from our earlier conversation.

"You do realize that Tate is the kind of person that doesn't give a shit about brownie points if you hurt someone she cares about, right?"

He arches a brow. "Is that a warning?"

"No," I answer with a laugh, shaking my head. "Just an observation."

"Mmhmm," he hums, pulling me closer into his body as we drift across the floor. I smile up at him before narrowing my eyes.

"You claimed you couldn't dance."

Laughing, he shakes his head. "I promise you, this is the extent of my abilities. Although, I wouldn't say no to private lessons, up in my room in oh, ten minutes."

"Wow… with a proposition like that, I can't possibly say no. I'm so in the mood that you're lucky I don't jump you right here," I reply dryly and he laughs, leaning in closer as he moves us away from the group.

"Princess, it's not like I can really do the things I want to do to you in front of everyone. Give a guy a chance."

I pull back and peek up at him. "What kinds of things would you do if everyone in this room knew about us?"

"Nothing," he answers, his eyes heating as he stares down at me. "There is no way in hell I want anyone in this room seeing the look on your face when you lose control. That's mine."

"Yours?" I breathe, my heart hammering in my chest as I search his face. The possessiveness staring back at me takes my breath away and I lick my lips, trying to force my mind to work when my body is in overdrive. He nods, leaning in like he might just kiss me before his gaze flicks over my shoulder and he pulls back with a sigh.

"Kodiak is really cramping my style."

I scoff, patting his shoulder as I tell myself to relax. "You poor thing."

He nods in agreement before pulling me closer and guiding me around the floor as my mind spins. What the hell is happening between us tonight? Every statement seems to be loaded with meaning and I don't know if it's just the emotions of the day or something else but our relationship feels different. Then again, we've all had a roller coaster of a week but once everything calms down again, things will go back to normal for Travis and me, I'm sure of it.

The door to the clubhouse opens and we all turn to look as a man in a delivery uniform steps inside with a medium-sized package in his hands. Travis releases me as he cocks his head to the side, studying the man. The delivery guy freezes, his gaze flicking over every pair of eyes staring back at him before he clears his throat.

"Uh, I have a package for Wyatt and Piper."

Fuzz raises his hand. "Over here."

"Right," the delivery man says, walking across the room and setting the package down on the closest table before handing Fuzz a clipboard to sign. He scribbles his name then hands it back with a nod of thanks. Clutching his clipboard to his chest, the delivery man practically runs out of the clubhouse as we all turn to the box. The outside is stamped with the labels "perishable" and "open immediately" but those are the only clues available to us.

"Is there a note?" Blaze asks from the back of the room and Piper nods as she plucks a little card off of the top, opening it.

"To Wyatt and Piper, congratulations on your special day."

Travis scowls, wrapping his arm around my waist and pulling me into his side. "It doesn't say who it's from?"

"Nope," she answers before looking around at all of us. "Did one of you send it?"

Everyone shakes their head and she shrugs before grabbing the pocket knife Fuzz holds out to her and flicking it open. She drags it along the top seam of the box where it's taped together before handing the knife back to her husband and popping open the top. A horrified scream fills the room and she stumbles backward almost tripping over her dress but Fuzz catches her before she can hit the floor, pulling her into his arms as he whispers something to her but her eyes remain wide in fear and her hands shake. Curiosity getting the best of us, we all surge forward almost like we're being pulled in by the box itself and when I get close enough to peek inside, I gasp and clamp my hand over my mouth as I stare down at the contents. My breath catches in my throat and tears sting my eyes.

It isn't real...

This can't be real. I tell myself to relax as spots dance in my vision and I focus on each breath entering and leaving my lungs, putting all of my attention on the act itself so I don't have to think about what is in front of me.

In.
Out.
In.

Out.
In.
Out.
Just fucking breathe, Rowan.

"Jesus fucking Christ," Storm whispers, his voice as haunted as I feel as I stare down at the box's contents, trying to make my brain form even a single thought but the only thing that registers is the fear pumping through my veins. My hands shake and my body feels on edge as my heart hammers in my chest. Tears streak down the sides of my face as I wrap my arms around my body and shiver.

When in the hell did I start crying?

"Is that Tawny?" Carly asks, horror in her voice. Horror that I feel down to my very core as I try to pull my gaze away from the contents of the box but I can't.

She just keeps looking at me...

Tawny's severed head stares back at me as my hands shake and my stomach churns violently. It's terrifying, hard to look at, and I desperately want to turn away but, no matter how hard I try, I can't force my eyes from her face, my heart pounding and my entire body rigid. My ribs feel tight and Travis wraps me up in his arms, pulling me firmly against his body as he buries his face in my hair and presses his lips to my head. His body is impossibly tense and he's shaking, too, pulling on every last one of my heart strings as I turn into him and wrap my arms around his waist. We back away from the group a little, needing a private moment as we both try to wrap our heads around everything that has just happened but as far as I can tell, it's senseless.

Who could do something like this?

201

As soon as the thought pops into my head, I want to roll my eyes at my own idiocy. Every person in this room knows who did this. The question is why? But as I run it through it in my mind, it doesn't take long to come up with an answer. Tawny told us everything she knew so she was no longer of any use to Warren and with her able to identify him, she had to go. It's as simple and sick as that and as an added bonus, he could send us this part of her to one, ruin what was supposed to be a happy day but two, let us know exactly what he's capable of.

"This is my fault," Travis whispers and I jerk back, looking up at him but he won't meet my eyes, his face contorted into a grimace.

"What are you talking about? This isn't your fault. This could never be your fault."

He shakes his head and his eyes finally find mine before he closes them and takes a deep breath. "I went to talk to her about Warren and now she's dead. How is this not my fault?"

"No," I whisper, cupping his face as pain floods my chest. His eyes pop open and his pain filled gaze meets mine, stealing the air from my lungs. "This is all Warren and you're reacting exactly the way he wants you to. You couldn't have known he would do this."

"I should have," he hisses, gritting his teeth as his gaze goes back to Tawny. He blows out a breath again but it doesn't seem to calm him in the slightest as he drags his eyes back to mine. The pain shining back at me feels like a knife to my chest and my heart cracks wide open as I try to think of anything I can say or do to ease his suffering right now. "I should have fucking known, Rowan. I should have known."

I lean up on my toes and press a kiss to his lips, feeling every ounce of his pain as he holds me tighter and kisses me like I am the air he breathes. I don't know if it's doing any good but any other time he's been too stressed to function with all this Warren stuff, distracting him with a kiss has helped. And more than anything, I just want to help him release this guilt he feels right now. When we finally part, I meet his eyes again and hope he can see my sincerity. "You've done everything you could think of to find this monster and his actions do not reflect on you, do you hear me? He is the only one responsible for this and I will not listen to you talk about yourself like that when you are one of the most sincere, genuine men I've ever met."

"Rowan," he whispers, his voice cracking as he shakes his head.

"Is that another note?" Carly asks before he can say anything else and we turn back to the group as she points inside the box where a little envelope is tucked on the side. Storm takes a deep breath as he reaches in and grabs it. We all stare at him, the air in the room thick with fear, as he pulls out the little card and hisses a curse.

"What does it say?" Tate asks, her expression fierce and her gun in her hand as my brother wraps an arm around her, pulling her into his side. Storm scrubs his hand down his face and shakes his head.

"One down, four to go."

Wicked Games

Chapter Seventeen
Travis

"Mmm," Rowan groans as she throws her arms above her head in a stretch and I glance down at her. She arches her back, pressing her body against mine before she relaxes and opens her eyes, blinking up at me. Flashing me a sleepy smile, she snuggles closer and shuts her eyes again. "Morning."

I pull her closer and release a sigh. "Morning."

She pulls back, scowling up at me as she cups my cheeks and inspects my face. "Did you get any sleep last night, Travis?"

"I'm fine," I tell her, pulling her back into my body. I'm fucking not fine but I would have been a hell of a lot worse if she hadn't been here by my side. Fuck. I don't even want to imagine the spiral I would have fallen into if I didn't have her grounding me all night long.

"That's not what I asked you," she shoots back, arching a brow and I sigh. From the moment Piper opened that box and we all realized what was inside, Rowan has been my fucking rock and she spent hours last night, just lying in bed with me and telling me that what happened to Tawny wasn't my fault. It was sweet of her to try and take the blame from where it belongs, firmly on my shoulders, but I know the truth and, according to the package we received last night, so does Warren.

After we read the second note from Warren, the one that made it clear he was gunning for certain members of the club, Blaze called Rodriguez. As soon as he showed up and took one look inside the box, he called in a whole damn team of people, including the medical examiner who took the head away to inspect it. If I didn't know her death was my fault before, I sure as hell did after Rodriguez told us that Tawny's tongue had been removed and in its place was the business card I had given her the morning Rowan and I stopped by her apartment.

I just don't know what I'm supposed to do about all of this.

A part of me feels like Warren wants me looking for him. It feels like he has singled me out for some reason and he enjoys the game we're playing as well as my growing frustration but sending Tawny's head the way he did, feels like a clear fucking warning to stop looking into him and I would be stupid to ignore it. But how can I just abandon my club like that?

"Travis," Rowan sighs, pulling my attention back to her and I shake my head.

"I'm fine."

She lets out a huff of annoyance. "Again, not what I asked."

"Sorry, Princess," I tell her, sighing as I stare up at the ceiling and pull her into my body again and sigh, her presence once again comforting me. "My head is just all messed up."

"Yeah, that tends to happen when you don't get any sleep and can't think clearly."

I shake my head. "I'm fine, Rowan."

"I swear to God," she growls, swinging her leg over my body and climbing on top of me as she plants her hands on my chest and pins me with a glare. "If you tell me you're fine when you're so clearly not one more time, I'm going to kick your ass."

"Yeah? What are you going to do?" I ask, fighting back a grin despite my somber mood. She scoffs.

"Like I'm gonna tell you my game plan."

I grip her hips, loving the feeling of her skin underneath my fingers. "That sounds like the talk of someone who most definitely doesn't have a plan."

"Just try me, Broussard. I have to imagine that some of my pole moves would work just as well to take down a person."

Well, fuck me.

"Now I'm intrigued."

She grins. "You know what else you are?"

"What?" I ask, arching a brow as I search her face. She grins and leans down, letting her lips hover above mine and every cell in my body is screaming at me to close the distance between us. So I do. Thrusting my hand into her long, dark hair, I pull her down to me and seal my lips to hers. Sighing, she melts into my body and I resist the urge to fist pump in victory as my chest puffs out with pride. In my head, I'm the only fucking man who has ever made her feel like this and I'm a goddamn king as she wiggles her hips, rubbing against my cock. When she pulls away, her eyes meet mine, gray pools of desire, and she flashes me an indulgent little smile. "You were saying?"

Shaking her head, she crawls off of me and stands up next to the bed. "I think I made my point."

"And what point is that?" I reach out and play with the bottom of her t-shirt, trying to lift it up to get a peek of the black lace panties she's wearing and she swats my hand away.

"Don't start something you can't finish."

My gaze snaps to hers and I narrow my eyes. "I always finish, Princess, and so do you... multiple times."

"Oh, I know," she whispers, color staining her cheeks as she grabs her jeans off of the floor. "But we don't have time right now. People will be waking up soon."

"Who cares? Everyone already knows so just stay."

She shakes her head. "Not everyone knows. You ready to tell my brother about us?"

"Are you?" I ask, arching a brow and she shrugs.

"Look, he won't like it but he'll just have to get over it. I'm tired of sneaking around like we're doing something wrong."

I nod, toying with the idea. "I agree... but then again, I like my body in one piece."

"Oh, stop it." She laughs as she sits on the edge of the bed. "Lincoln is just a big teddy bear."

"Only if a teddy bear could rip you apart with his bare fucking hands and has an inclination to do just that," I shoot back, my eyes widening as she laughs again.

"You're being ridiculous."

I shake my head. "I'm not and I can promise you that if we tell Kodiak about us, he will probably rip off your favorite part of my body."

"I think you're thinking of your favorite part."

"All right, woman," I growl, grabbing her and pinning her to the mattress as I climb over her. "Do you need a reminder?"

She arches a brow in challenge. "Of what?"

"Of how much you love it, too," I answer, thrusting into her and her breath catches in her throat, her eyes fluttering closed for a second before she opens them again. Downstairs, a door slams and I sigh as I turn toward the door.

"Told ya."

"Fine," I grumble, kissing her again before flopping down onto the bed next to her with all of the pent-up sexual frustration I feel. "But come find me later so we can continue this."

Climbing out of the bed, she shakes her head. "So bossy."

"Sweetheart, if you meant that to be a bad thing, you have to get that "fuck me" look out of your eyes first," I tell her and she rolls her eyes, fighting back a smile as she backs away toward the door. "I'm serious about later, by the way."

She shrugs. "We'll see."

"Don't tease me, Princess."

"Why not?" she asks as she opens the door and stops to pin me to the bed with a look full of defiance. "What are you going to do about it?"

She winks and walks out before I can say anything else and I stare at the door, the thought of going after her consuming me. I jump up to do just that, grabbing my jeans off the floor and slipping them on before I walk to the door, yanking it open. Piper blinks up at me from the other side, her hand raised like she was just about to knock and I arch a brow.

"Something I can do for you, darlin'?"

She nods. "Yeah, I need your help with something. If you have time…"

"Sure," I answer, my gaze flicking over her shoulder to where Rowan stands at the other end of the hallway, smirking at me. I shoot her a look that lets her know it's fucking on as soon as I wrap up whatever this is and she shrugs before starting down the stairs. Stepping aside, I let Piper into my room and leave the door open as I go over to my desk and sink into my chair, pointing the other one for her. She sits down and takes a deep breath, wringing her hands together in her lap. "You doing okay this morning?"

"Um… I don't know…"

I nod because I'm sure her head is just as scrabbled as mine. "I get that. What is it that you need from me?"

"Well," she answers, taking a deep breath before looking up at me. "I'm not even really sure that I want to know the answer to this but it's been bugging me for days so I just thought…"

"Okay, what is it?"

"My therapist, Dr. Brewer, made a comment to me that I haven't been able to stop thinking about… it was about Lillian," she whispers and I lean back in my chair, scowling as I watch her. Lillian was a friend of hers who thought they could be more but I have no clue where she could be going with this. "She said that shortly before everything went down, Lillian had met someone who was encouraging her to go after what she wanted. At the time, Dr. Brewer didn't know what they meant but in light of everything that has been going on… do you think it's possible that this person she met was Warren?"

Her question suck punches me and the events of last night come flooding back into my mind as I blow out a breath and shake my head.

"Piper, I think where Warren is concerned, anything is possible."

She nods like she already knew the answer. "That's what I thought. Do you… think you could look into it for me?"

The last fucking thing I want to do today is anything to do with Warren but how can I say no to her? She clearly needs this and who fucking knows, maybe I'll actually find something this time. Sucking in a breath, I nod.

"Sure. I'll look into it."

She releases a breath. "Oh, thank you. I… um, I actually got a call from the man who managed her apartment building. She didn't have any family and all of her stuff was sold or given away except for this box that he didn't feel right throwing out. Apparently, there were some of her diaries in there and I thought they might give us some insight but I haven't been brave enough to read them by myself. Will you help me?"

"You already have them?"

"Yeah," she answers, nodding, and I study her for a second before sighing. I don't want to even fucking think of Warren at this point but I can't deny her the help she needs. I'm not expecting anything, though. If Warren did have something to do with her friend going all psycho, I'm sure he hid all his tracks very well. It's been the same damn story since this investigation started and I don't expect it to change anytime soon. "Still down to help?"

I nod. "Yeah. Go get 'em."

She thanks me before practically running out of my room and as soon as she's gone, I lean back in my chair, running my hand down my face as my mind drifts to Warren's note last night.

One down, four to go.

Honestly, it scares the shit out of me and maybe it's me just being fucking full of myself but I can't help but think this is just another way to torture me. I'll go down the rabbit hole trying to figure out which four of us he's specifically targeting and it will, undoubtedly, make me lose my mind. Which is what he wants.

Fuck.

Am I on his list?

Piper walks back in with a box of stuff before plopping it down at my feet and I arch a brow as she sits back down and I push the thoughts of Warren's threat from my mind. Glancing down, I sigh. The box is full of personal stuff, little trinkets and several thick notebooks that I can only assume are Lillian's diaries.

"First, I gotta ask, does your husband know about this?"

Shaking her head, she leans over and starts digging through the box. "No. He doesn't want me thinking about her or what she did anymore... he thinks it's not good for me but I need to know."

Shit.

Why are all these damn women asking me to do shit that will most definitely end up with me getting my ass kicked by one of my brothers?

"Okay," I sigh before nodding. "I'll do this but you gotta tell Fuzz right after. Deal?"

"Deal."

She grabs one of the notebooks and hands it to me before grabbing another for herself and we start flipping through them. Most of the entries are bland, talking about her day and shit like that but occasionally, one pops up that makes my eyebrows shoot up. Not that they have anything to do with Warren but Lillian was cuckoo for Cocoa Puffs and it fucking shows on these pages.

"Wait," Piper says, her eyes scanning the page in front of her. "I think I found something."

She hands the notebook to me and I read the entry on the page.

Dear Diary,

I went down to the coffee shop today and met this wonderful man who listened to me for almost an hour as I told him all about my Pip. He said she sounded like a really great girl and that if I loved her as much as I claimed then I should do whatever it takes to get her. I left there feeling so confident and he's going to meet with me again tomorrow to go over a plan. I haven't felt this hopeful in a long time and I can't help but think that this is all going to work out. Piper and I are fated to be together, I just know it. The way she looks at me, I can feel the power of our connection...

I drop the notebook on the desk and shake my head as I blow out a breath. God, I feel fucking crazy just from reading that.

"What do you think? Could the guy be Warren?" Piper asks and I shrug.

"It's possible but I'll have to keep digging to know for sure and even then, we probably won't find anything concrete."

She shakes her head. "I don't need anything concrete."

"Can I ask why you want to know?" I can't see any way that knowing Warren had a part in this is going to help her and it might even make it all worse but that's just my opinion. She chews on her bottom lip as she stares at the notebook and finally, she looks up and sighs.

"I know what Lillian did was insane and that her obsession with me can't be blamed on anyone else but…"

I nod, leaning back in my chair. "You want someone else to blame."

"A little bit," she admits with a nod. "It's just hard to reconcile these two people that were Lillian… like my friend is a completely different person than the one who did all these crazy things."

"Can I be honest with you, Piper?"

She nods, sucking in a breath. "Of course."

"I think you need to let this go. It can't be healthy," I tell her, hoping my voice doesn't sound too harsh and she sighs before nodding.

"I know I should just let it go but maybe these notebooks will help you somehow with Warren as well as giving me closure so I have to pursue this."

Sighing, I nod. "Okay, well, I'll keep looking into them and if I find anything, I'll let you know but please don't get your hopes up."

"Thank you," she says, her voice full of emotion as she stands up and walks over to me before leaning down and hugging me. "I really appreciate your help, Streak."

I nod, patting her back. "Don't mention it and don't let your husband kill me."

"Don't be stupid." She laughs as she pulls back and turns toward the door. "You're way too important to this club for any of these guys to kill you. I can't promise there will be no maiming, though."

"Oh, excellent," I answer, rolling my eyes and she laughs again as she walks out of the room. As soon as she's gone, I turn back to the notebook laying open on my desk and sigh before grabbing it to dive right back into the rabbit hole I desperately want to escape.

Chapter Eighteen
Rowan

"They're pulling into the gas station now," Travis says into his phone laying on the desk, his fingers flying over the keyboard as he leans closer to the monitor, his complete focus on helping Blaze, Storm, and Chance complete the rescue they are doing right now. Apparently, the wife contacted the club and asked for their help but the issue is that they are only passing through Baton Rouge on their way to visit family so the club has to step in and rescue the wife and their two kids at a gas station along the interstate while this woman's husband is in the bathroom. It honestly sounded insane when he told me about it earlier but this is what they do. As I watch him work, I can't help but smile at the tiny little crease between his eyebrows and the way he bites his lip in concentration. Shaking my head, I turn back to the newspaper laid out on the bed in front of me, open to the help wanted pages.

Yesterday, Lincoln, Tate, and I drove the three hours to Grand Isle to sprinkle Mom's ashes in the ocean just like she wanted and it was intense. We went to the same beach where Lincoln and Tate were married last year, the last place we were all together as a family because it seemed like the perfect spot to scatter her ashes and even though she has been gone for over a month now, actually watching her ashes sink below the water felt like I was truly letting her go. All of the pain I've been running from smacked right into me and I spent the night, sobbing into Travis's chest while he rubbed my back and pressed kisses against the top of my head. When I woke up this morning, I was still sad but I also knew it was time to move on with my life and finally put some roots down here in Louisiana, starting with a job.

"Dad just went into the bathroom," Travis says, distracting me from the paper and I lean back against the wall and cross my arms over my chest as I watch him. "Move now."

"We're fucking going," Storm answers.

"Asshole," Travis mutters, making a face at the phone that makes me laugh. It's nice to see him like this since the last two days have been hard on all of us. After the wedding, the mood in the clubhouse was even darker before and it's uncomfortable to be stuck here. Everyone wants to be jumping into action, doing something to find Warren and stop whatever evil plans he has but there is just nothing to do. But that doesn't stop any of them from trying and when they can't find answers, they come harass Travis. It weighs down on him so much and I'm just about ready to tell them to take a fucking hike the next time they barge in here demanding answers that no one has. Which I can freely do now since I told my brother all about Travis and me yesterday. To say he wasn't pleased would be an understatement but after Tate and I talked him down a little, he agreed to let me run my

218

own love life. He hated every second of it but I think it
went as well as could be expected. I mean, Travis is still
in one piece and there isn't a single bruise or broken
bone on his body so I consider it a win. Lincoln did make
it very clear, though, that if he saw me crying even once
and Travis was the cause, he would break every single
one of his fingers. So, like I said, it went as well as
expected.

"He's on his way back to the van. Where are
you?"

"Pulling out of the lot now," Storm answers. "Let
me know when he steps outside."

Travis types a few things and I see the screen
change from one security camera before he flicks back to
another one. "You're good. He can't decide what fucking
snack to get."

"Priorities, man." Chance laughs.

"Pulling onto the interstate now," Blaze calls and
Travis flicks through a few cameras again before
nodding to himself.

"He's paying now. I'll keep an eye on him for a
bit."

They hang up but Travis remains focused on the
screen and I climb out of bed before walking over to him
and leaning on his shoulders as the man walks out of the
gas station and sees his empty van.

"Is he going to call the cops?" I ask, wondering if
they made it look like a kidnapping and Travis shakes his
head.

"Naw. She left him a note that tells him not to
come looking for her."

I purse my lips as he stands outside his vehicle,
raking his hands through his hair. "But the kids…

wouldn't that make y'all accessories to kidnapping the kids?"

"They aren't his kids. He married Anne eighteen months ago and immediately started beating her so she never let him adopt them. She said she had to get out before he turned on her kids."

"What happened to their real dad?"

He shrugs. "He's dead but I don't know what happened to him."

"That's so sad."

"Yeah," he answers with a nod. "But you can go back to whatever you were doing over there. I'll just be another few minutes with this."

I hold my hands up in surrender and back away from him. "Kicking me out, huh?"

"Never." His gaze flicks to mine and the sincerity shining in his eyes almost knocks me off my feet. I wouldn't say that we've both been clingy lately but we have definitely been leaning on each other to get through all of the shit going on around us and honestly, I don't know what I would do without him. Somehow, he keeps me sane despite the chaos and I think I do the same for him. Or, at least, I hope I do. "What are you working on over there?"

"I'm looking for a job," I say as I crawl back into bed with a sigh and scoop up my newspaper, scanning the help wanted section again. There are quite a few jobs listed but none of them have really caught my eye yet. Although, I suppose it would help if I had any idea what I wanted to do but for so long, I've been just surviving instead of living so I don't even know where to start. Hell, I don't even know what I like.

"I don't like it."

I glance up at him. "You don't like what?"

"The idea of you getting a job right now. Until we catch Warren, I don't really want you leaving the clubhouse alone," he says, his gaze flicking between me and the computer screen with the same concern on his face. Sighing, I shake my head and set the newspaper in my lap.

"Are you really trying to tell me I can't work?"

He nods. "For now."

"You know," I muse, cocking my head to the side as I flash him a look of defiance. "I don't think you get a say."

"Sure I do," he shoots back, standing up and stalking across the room to me before planting his fists on the bed and leaning in for a kiss. When I won't give him one, he growls and grabs the paper, tossing it to the floor behind him. Before I can object, he grabs my leg and pulls me down to my back on the bed as he looms over me with a grin. "You're so fucking cute when you're mad."

I narrow my eyes at him. "Don't give me that shit. I'm getting a job and you can't stop me."

"Whatever you want to believe, Princess," he answers before sealing his lips over mine and I sigh. My biggest weakness is my need for him and it doesn't matter how mad I am when he kisses me because I can't resist him. Pulling back, he flashes me a triumphant grin. "Hey, what do you say we get out of here?"

"And go where?"

He shrugs, leaning down and stealing another kiss. "Anywhere. I'm fucking tired of being cooped up in this place."

"Wasn't it you who just said I shouldn't leave the clubhouse until Warren is found?" I ask, arching a brow but he is unfazed, shooting me a cocky grin.

"I said you shouldn't leave alone and you're not. You'll have me there to protect you." That damn grin on his face only gets wider as he stares down at me with fire in his eyes and there is no way in hell I'm backing down from this challenge. Pasting a coy little smile on my face, I drag my fingertips down his arm as I sink my teeth into my bottom lip and meet his gaze again.

"Wow, baby," I breathe, arching my back so my tits press up against his chest. "That really turns me on."

His gaze searches mine, hungry and ready to pounce, and as he leans down to kiss me again, I press my hand against his face and shove it away from me.

"Not."

"Oh, you're gonna pay for that one, Princess," he growls as my belly does a little flip as I wiggle out of his arms and slip off of the bed, evading his grasp. We square up on opposite sides of the room, Travis ready to close the distance between us and me ready to bolt in the other direction to get away from him, and he flashes me a predatory smile as he takes a small step forward. My belly flips and I fight back peals of giggles as I watch him stalk toward me. He springs into action and I shriek as I try to get away from him before he hooks his arm around my waist before I can get away and pulls me into his body. Breathing heavily, his eyes meet mine for just a moment before we slam together, kissing like we're drowning in our desire and we stumble backward until we run into the wall.

"Travis," I breathe when he moves down my neck, pressing hot, needy kisses against my skin and he growls, moving back up to nip at my ear.

"I had a whole plan, you know," he whispers as his hand slips under my t-shirt and he cups my breast, giving it a squeeze.

"What was it?"

He shakes his head, moving back to my lips before pulling back enough to meet my eyes. "I had a whole little... thing planned for us."

"Like a date?" I ask, my heart skipping a beat and butterflies flapping around in my belly as I search his gaze. He looks away and nods, a look of nerves flicking across his face.

"I wanted to do something normal with you. Something that didn't involve shit like stalkers in nightclubs and severed heads showing up at weddings."

I can't wipe the grin off of my face as I lean in and press a kiss to his lips. "Okay. Do I need to go change or will this work for what you have planned?"

"You look amazing, Rowan," he replies, his gaze dropping down my body and I laugh. I'm just wearing jeans and a t-shirt but with the way he looks at me, it feels like it could be a ball gown. Meeting my eyes again, his teeth sink into his bottom lip. "You really want to go?"

I nod, my smile so wide it feels like it's going to crack my face. "I do. Now, how do we sneak out of here?"

"You go downstairs like you're going to your room and then sneak out of the back door. I'll storm out of the front like I'm pissed about something and we'll meet at the Impala."

Leaning forward, I plant another quick kiss on his lips before pulling away. "Okay."

Wicked Games

"Go and I'll meet you down there." He smacks my ass as I turn to leave and I shoot him a look over my shoulder before slipping out of his room and practically running down the hallway to the stairs. A few people are milling around in the bar area but they barely give me a second glance as I walk down the hallway to my room. Stopping outside of the door, I grab the handle like I'm going to open it before peeking behind me. Everyone has moved onto something else so I release the handle and sneak over to the back door, squeezing my eyes shut as I press on the bar to open it. It makes a little squeak but I slip outside without glancing back to see if anyone else heard before softly closing the door and booking it across the parking lot to Travis's Impala. My heart races and I can't wipe the grin off of my face. I swear, it's like I'm sixteen and sneaking out of the house to meet up with a boy all over again. Although, I'm not sure if Lincoln would be any less pissed this time around as he was when I was a kid.

Stopping next to the car, I turn toward the front door just in time to see Travis shove it open and stomp outside but as soon as he sees me, a big grin stretches across his face, breaking his cover. No one really seems to notice though and once he reaches the car, he jumps behind the wheel, while I wait for him to unlock my door. Instead, he rolls down the window, leaning across the seat to talk to me.

"Will you get the gate? The code is zero, five, two, zero."

I glance up at the lock on the gate and nod before running over to the gate and punching in the code. It unlocks with a click and as soon as it swings open, Travis drives the Impala out onto the street before stopping to wait for me. I close the gate behind me and

224

double check that it's locked. The last fucking thing we need is Warren getting into the clubhouse… not that it's not already easy enough for him to get to us. Sighing, I walk over to the Impala and sink into the passenger seat before turning to Travis. He flashes me a blinding smile and grabs my hand as he takes off down the street.

"So, where are we headed to?"

He glances over at me and winks. "It's a surprise."

Shaking my head, I watch him as we drive, wondering what is going through his head right now. Maybe this is just what he said, an excuse for us to get out of the clubhouse and seize a little bit of normal but it feels an awful lot like more than the casual relationship we agreed to and I don't know what to do with that.

"What are you thinking so hard about over there?" he asks, pulling me out of my thoughts and I blink at him before leaning my head back against the seat and flashing him a smile.

"Just trying to figure out where we are going."

He laughs. "You're not good with surprises, are you?"

"I guess not," I answer and his brows knit together as his gaze flicks between me and the road repeatedly.

"What do you mean, you guess not?"

I shrug. "I've never really had anyone do something like this for me."

"Come on, you've had boyfriends before," he replies. I arch a brow at the word boyfriend and he releases a nervous chuckle. "Not that we… I mean, I'm not…"

I scoff. "Don't worry, Travis. I know what this is and even though I've had boyfriends before, none of them ever did anything like this. I've never even really been on a proper first date."

"What's a proper first date?" he asks and I have to laugh at how clueless and inexperienced we both are when it comes to relationships.

"You know, like when you meet someone and you like them so you ask them out. For me, it's always just been I start hanging out with someone and we like each other so we become a couple before we ever even have a date."

He shakes his head. "That's a fucking shame. A gorgeous girl like you deserves shit like this."

"Oh, how romantic." I laugh, crinkling my nose at his statement as butterflies flutter around in my belly. When I'm with him, the rest of the damn world just fades away and here in this car, on our way to a date, nothing else exists but I wish I knew more about him. There is this glaring contradiction when I look into his eyes and I can tell he's experienced real pain in his life. I want to hear about it and if possible, ease just a little bit of his suffering. Leaning on the arm rest between us, I flash him a smile. "Tell me something about yourself."

"And why would I do that?"

"Because," I say, batting my lashes at him as he fights back a grin. "I asked you very, very nicely."

He arches a brow. "Did you? It sounded more like a demand to me."

"Will you, Travis Broussard, pretty please tell me something about yourself?" I ask, laying it on thick as I stare up at him and wait for his answer. He laughs, shaking his head.

"Jesus… like I could say no to you. What do you want to know?"

For fucks sake.

I wanna know everything but I need to ease him into this or he will shut down on me in a second. I run through a list of questions in my mind before landing on one and peeking up at him. This is the most softball question I've ever fucking heard in my life so there is no way he won't answer it.

"Are you from Baton Rouge?"

He shakes his head. "No."

"Where are you from?" I ask and he scowls as we pull to a stop at a light, searching my face. Jeez, I thought it was a softball question but I guess not. Or maybe he's locked down so tightly that he finds any question at all probing.

"I thought it was just one question."

I shrug. "I never said that. Come on, Travis. It's an easy question."

"Fine," he sighs, his gaze locked on mine for a moment before he shakes his head and blows out a breath. "I'm from Texas."

"What brought you here?"

He fidgets in his seat as he turns to look up at the stoplight. "My mom was from this area."

"Was?" I ask, my heart sinking for him. Pain splashes across his face and he scrubs one hand down his thigh while the other grips mine tighter and he nods.

"She died."

Looking up at the clear agony on his handsome face, my heart breaks for him but I don't say the obligatory "I'm sorry" because it was one of the things I hated the most when my mom died. Instead, I raise his hand to my lips and press a kiss to it in a silent show of support. Something that tells him I know I can't make it any better but I'm here for him and the look he shoots me almost makes me melt in my seat. It's full of appreciation, relief, and something else I can't quite name but it makes me feel all kind of gooey inside as I give him a soft smile.

"Thank you, Rowan," he whispers, his voice cracking in a rare show of emotion and I nod because I know that more than anything, he just needs me to be here for him right now and that's what I'm going to do for as long as he lets me.

Chapter Nineteen
Rowan

"Hey," Travis whispers in my ear, sneaking up behind me and gripping my hips as I startle and my heart jumps into my throat. I peek over my shoulder at him and he flashes me a smirk, wiggling his eyebrows that has me fighting back a smile of my own. "Having fun?"

I turn back to the main room where Emma, Ali, Storm, Tate, and Blaze are decorating the nine-foot Christmas tree Blaze hauled into the clubhouse an hour ago in an effort to lift everyone's spirits. They were all excited to get a little piece of normal but for me, it only reminded me that this is the first Christmas without my mom so I run upstairs and started spying on them from the top landing. Sighing, I shrug. "I guess."

"Feel like sneaking away for a bit? I have a surprise for you," he says, pressing a kiss to my neck, just below my ear and a shiver runs down my spine as I struggle to keep my eyes open. My gaze flicks to the couches in the corner of the room where my brother, Chance, Carly, Smith, Henn, and Kady are all sitting around, talking and Lincoln glances up before leveling a glare at the man standing behind me. Travis's grip on my hips tightens as he presses another kiss against my skin.

"What is it?" I ask, ignoring Lincoln's murderous look as I turn to face Travis. His arms wrap around me as he flashes me a playful smile and presses his body to mine, his gaze heating. I arch a brow and twirl my arms around his neck, fighting back a smile at his terrible poker face. "Oh, it's like that, is it?"

"Only one way to find out."

"Lead the way, then," I tell him and he takes my hand. His answering grin is so adorable that I would have done just about anything to see it but he doesn't need to know that. As he drags me down the hallway, my mind drifts to our date last night. It was simple but also kind of perfect and exactly what we both needed after the stress of the last couple of days. Travis took me to this line of food trucks parked near a cute little park and we got something to eat before walking around for a bit. When we got back to the car, things got steamy and we ended up re-enacting what happened in the clubhouse parking lot the morning we got back from Tawny's apartment except this time, I wasn't just getting myself off. Smiling at the memory, I glance up as Travis opens the door to get up to the roof and looks back at me with a twinkle in his eye. If I didn't already know he had a surprise planned for me, one look at his face would give it away in an instant but I kind of love how he can't keep a secret to save his life. And the way he's so excited to do something like this for me just melts my heart every single freaking time.

"Close your eyes, Princess," he instructs when we get to the top of the stairs and I arch a brow as I shoot him a look but he doesn't back down. Finally, I sigh and close my eyes. He gives my hand a squeeze and opens the door at the top of the stairs before leading me out onto the roof. A cool breeze caresses my skin and I shiver, prompting him to pull me into his arms as he presses his lips to the top of my head. "Okay, open."

Opening my eyes, I blink a couple of times before taking in the scene in front of me. He has set up an air mattress with pillows and two large, fluffy comforters right in the middle of the roof and I turn to him with a scowl. "What's this?"

"I was thinking about last night and you said one of your favorite things was to look at the stars so... ta-da."

"Travis," I breathe, smiling as I drop my head back to look up at the sky. Millions of stars stare back at me and warmth rushes through me at his thoughtfulness as my heart beats a little faster. Turning into him, I throw my arms around his neck and press up on my toes to seal my lips to his. As his arms wrap around my waist and pull me closer, he makes a noise somewhere between a sigh and groan before the tip of his tongue teases my lips, demanding more and I give it to him without a second thought. One hand slips into my hair, cradling the back of my head as his tongue explores and teases my mouth but my entire body begs for more contact. Just when I think he might give me what I want, he pulls away, breathing heavily, and meets my eyes before shaking his head.

"I really didn't bring you up here for that..."

I shoot him a look and he chuckles.

"Well, not just for that." He pulls away and takes my hand again. "Come on. Let's look at some stars."

Peeking over at him as he leads me to the air mattress, I can't help but smile. "This is very cute."

"I'm a cute guy," he answers, shrugging, as he shoves me back onto the mattress and I laugh, bouncing a few times before settling into one spot in the middle of the bed. When I'm comfortable, he lies down next to me and pulls me closer, wrapping his arm around me as I lay my head on his chest. Silence descends over us but it's comfortable as we both look up at the sky, dotted with millions of tiny little lights and as I stare up at them, I feel more at home here in Baton Rouge than I ever have before.

"Thank you for this, Travis," I whisper, turning my head to look at him as he does the same. He smiles and butterflies flutter around in my belly.

"Anytime, Princess." He leans down and steals a quick kiss before pulling back and meeting my eyes. "I have a question for you."

I nod. "Shoot."

"I've noticed the tattoo on your ribs and I've been trying to figure out what it is since the first time I saw it but I'm at a loss," he says with a laugh and I smile, despite the pain in my chest, as I cuddle into him. I toy with a loose thread on the sleeve of his t-shirt as I think about the ink embedded on the side of my body and tears sting my eyes.

"It's the mountain range where my dad died."

He sucks in a breath and places his hand on my cheek, directing my gaze back to his as his brows knit together and pain flashes through his eyes. Just like last night when he shared his loss with me, he doesn't anything. Instead he just presses his lips to mine again in a soft kiss that says everything that sounds so trivial when spoken out loud.

He's sorry.

He knows what I'm going through.

232

He's here for me.

Somehow, when he utters all those things with a kiss instead of words, they mean so much more and my chest constricts as I squeeze my eyes shut, a few tears trickling down the sides of my face. When he finally pulls away, the emotion staring back at me in his green gaze steals the air from my lungs and I can't cope. He shakes his head before pressing his lips to my forehead and I fucking melt.

"You have got to be one of the strongest people I've ever met, Rowan."

I shake my head. "I'm not any different from anyone else. I've lost a lot but there are people who have lost more or they were born with no one in their corner fighting for them. I think that would be worse than loving someone only to lose them."

He leans in to kiss me again and just as his lips brush mine, a clinking sound echoes through the air, breaking us apart as we look at each other with wide eyes.

"What the hell was that?"

He shakes his head before jumping up and creeping over to the edge of the building. When he gets to the edge, he peeks out into the parking lot before hissing a curse and running back over to me. He grabs my hand, his mouth pressed into a thin line, and his eyes hard as he meets my gaze. "We have to go."

"What's going on?" I ask and he sighs, running his hand through his hair.

"The cops are about to bust in downstairs."

My eyes widen. "The cops?"

"Yeah," he answers, his gaze flicking everywhere like he's searching for a threat. "They've got fucking

S.W.A.T and everything. This is bad, Row… really fucking bad."

My heart hammers in my chest as he pulls me off of the mattress before tucking me into his side. We walk back over to the door and duck inside. Once in the stairwell, we hear the front door of the clubhouse slam open and several people yelling and my hands start to shake. He stops halfway down the stairs and presses me against the wall, slamming his lips to mine. It gives me something to focus on, something to distract me from the fear running rampant through my body and when he pulls away, he meets my eyes.

"I've got you, baby, you hear me? You have nothing to be scared of. Okay?"

I nod even though I have my doubts. "Okay."

He kisses me one last time before he laces his fingers with mine and we walk the rest of the way down the stairs, stepping into the hallway. Before we can move in either direction, three police officers charge up the stairs decked out in tactical gear with their guns drawn.

"Get down!" the first one screams but I'm frozen in place, shaking as I stare at the large weapon pointed at my chest. Travis gives my hand a squeeze, tugging on my arm as he sinks to the floor and I follow his lead as everything swirls around us in slow motion. I can hear yelling in the main area of the clubhouse and someone is crying… "Get on your fucking stomach!"

I try to catch my breath as I sink to my belly and Travis grabs my hand as two of the officers move on down the hallway, searching for more people, while the one who screamed at me stands over us, his gun still trained on my body. Laying my head flat on the floor, I look at Travis as tears streak down my face. Fury lights up his eyes and his gaze flicks to our babysitter but I give his hand another squeeze to stop him from doing anything stupid.

"I'm okay," I whisper, soft enough that the cop standing over us won't hear me and he searches my face for a moment, desperation and anger shining in his eyes, before nodding.

"I got you."

I nod. "I know."

"Shut the fuck up," the cop hisses, nudging my arm with his boot and Travis's gaze flicks up toward him as his nostrils flare and his lip curls back in a snarl. My heart hammers in my chest at the thought of him getting hurt because of me and I squeeze his hand again. When he looks back at me, I shake my head and it stops him but it doesn't do much to quell his rage.

The other two officers step back into the hallway with Moose, Juliette, Fuzz, Piper, and Nix walking in a single file line in front of them as they train their guns at their backs.

"Up," the officer guarding us orders and Travis stands up before helping me to my feet and wrapping his arm around me as I glance at the officer's last name printed on his name tag.

Riley.

He grabs my arm, his fingers digging into my skin as he jerks me out of Travis's grip and I let out a squeak of pain as tears sting my eyes. Holy shit. That really fucking hurt.

Travis steps forward, his hands balled into fists at his sides and that snarl on his face again. He looks ready to murder someone and I get the feeling that he doesn't give a single shit if he goes to jail or gets shot. The thought sends a powerful wave of pain crashing into me and I shake my head as his gaze meets mine.

"Please, no," I whisper, still shaking my head. His gaze flicks to mine and he searches my eyes for a moment before he nods but his muscles don't relax one bit as he falls in line behind me. The three officers lead us down the stairs and into the bar area before instructing us to line up along one wall, opposite from everyone else, and press our backs against it.

"Keep your hands where I can fucking see them," Officer Riley orders so I splay my hands flat against the wall as my heart climbs into my throat. Another officer leads Quinn and all of the kids out of the movie theater. Her eyes are wide with fear as she holds baby Magnolia in her arms and the kids are all terrified, some of them screaming as tears run down their chubby little cheeks and others trying to pull away from the group in an attempt to escape. It all breaks my fucking heart.

"Get your hands off of me," Emma snarls, pulling the attention of everyone in the room as she and Ali try to step forward to get their children but an officer has a hand on both of them, pushing them back. Nix and Storm both look ready to tear someone's head off but two other officers have a gun trained on each of them, daring them to make a move. Emma tries to shove the hand away but it's no use. "I am going to get my children."

The officer trying to restrain them glances back at Riley, who nods in approval so he releases them. They march across the room, their heads held high like they are daring one of them to take a shot. When they reach their kids, Ali takes Magnolia from Quinn and gives her arm a reassuring squeeze before walking back over to the wall. Emma crouches down and all four of her kids rush her, throwing themselves into her arms. Her boys, Grady and Corbin, cast very pissed off glances at the officer who tried to stop her and despite the situation, a small smile stretches across my face at their fierce protective streak. No doubt something they learned from their daddy and grandpa.

"Listen up," a severe looking woman calls as she walks into the room in a tailored pantsuit and I instantly dislike her. Maybe it's the blatant arrogance rolling off of her in waves or her smug face as she looks down at all of us but I can't stand the bitch and I don't even know her name yet. She stops in the middle of the room, crosses her arms over her chest, and flashes us a cold smile as her gaze flicks over the faces around her. "My name is Sergeant Williams. I'm looking for Logan Chambers."

Storm steps forward and raises his hand. "That's me."

"Excellent. Come with me, Mr. Chambers, and the rest of you, wait here." She snaps her fingers, expecting him to follow her like a dog as she starts walking toward the war room with all the swagger of someone who knows they are in complete control. Storm fights back a snarl as he walks behind her and once they step inside, she shuts and locks the door but it feels like a jail cell slamming shut.

"Are you okay?" Travis asks as he inches closer to me along the wall, concern in his eyes as he hooks his pinky finger with mine. I nod but despite that, he still scowls and glances down my body before he gaze flicks to my arm where Riley grabbed me. "Did he hurt you? 'Cause I swear to God, I'll fucking…"

"Travis," I snap and his gaze meets mine again. "Don't do anything stupid. I'm okay."

He nods, his body sagging with relief. "Good."

"What do you think this is all about?" I ask and he shakes his head before scanning the room.

"I don't know but you don't bring this much fire power for something small."

Uncomfortable silence descends over all of us as we wait for Storm to come back out of the war room and my belly flips as my mind screams for relief.

I want out of this room.

I want to get away from these damn cops.

Oh, and also, I hope to never see Officer fucking Riley again.

Yelling reaches us through the door of the war room but it's not Storm losing his temper in there and as I listen to Sergeant Williams demand answers from him, I rack my brain for what any of us could have done that would have brought this level of persecution down on us but I've honestly got nothing. These people, despite the biker club reputation they get saddled with, are some of the kindest, most down to earth people I've ever met and every single one of them has accepted me into their family, as I am, with no reservations or conditions. They don't seem like the kind of people who would ever do anything to warrant a fucking S.W.A.T. raid let alone a police investigation.

The door to the war room swings open and Storm marches out, a scowl on his face and rage in his eyes, followed by Sergeant Williams looking smug as shit as she glances around the room. "Malcolm West, you're up next. Everyone else can have a seat somewhere and I'll get to you eventually."

As soon as Blaze walks into the room and the door closes, we all congregate around the tables in the middle of the room. Lincoln walks up to me and pulls me into his arms as he releases a sigh.

"Are you okay?"

I nod, glancing behind him as Tate walks up. "I'm fine. What about you guys?"

"We're good, little sis," he assures me before we all sit down together. Travis pulls his chair closer to mine before sinking into it and grabbing my hand. Storm sits in the middle of the group before scrubbing a hand down his face and sighs.

"I'm not going to lie, y'all. This is… fucking bad."

Ali grabs his hand in between both of hers and gives it a squeeze. "What is it, baby? Why are they here?"

"They have a video of a man… a man who looks and sounds exactly like me but he's saying shit I didn't say, shit I wouldn't ever say…"

"Like what?" Travis asks as he grips my hand tightly. Storm blows out a breath and shakes his head, the stress of the situation showing in every movement of his body.

"He talked about how hard the club had worked to be an asset to the community but that, despite everything we've done, we were still treated like second-class citizens. Then he started talking about if the people of Baton Rouge wanted to be afraid of us then we were going to give them something to be afraid of. He said we were going to start attacking the city for their neglect and carelessness…"

"Jesus," Chance hisses, leaning back in his chair. My heart races as my mind struggles to wrap itself around everything he's saying.

"How did they get this video?"

Storm scoffs. "A concerned citizen brought it to their attention after it was posted on the internet."

"This is so fucking bad," Travis groans, dropping his head back and closing his eyes as he grits his teeth. "Fucking Warren. It's got to be."

"How, Streak? How in the fuck does this person in the video look like me and how the hell am I ever going to clear my name when they have what looks like concrete evidence? I'm totally fucked and if this is Warren, this club is fucked, too. He just fucking won."

A.M. Myers

Chapter Twenty
Travis

Sighing, I scrub my hand down my face and lean back in my chair as the computer screen in front of me blurs but it doesn't matter because the moment I close my eyes, the video of Storm threatening the city of Baton Rouge plays in my mind. I've probably watched it close to twenty times since last night and I know the whole damn thing backward and forward. Not that it helps us any because as it turns out, the video is exactly what I thought it was – a deep fake. Albeit a very good one and if I didn't know Storm personally, I might not have even noticed that it wasn't real. Which is why my newfound knowledge will be no use to us in clearing Storm's name.

Last night, Sergeant Williams and her merry little band of psychos spent hours in the clubhouse, first interviewing each and every one of us, including Rowan who has only been here for like two weeks, before having her team execute the search warrant they obtained while they were questioning us like terrorists. They tore the place apart, looking for any evidence of the attacks she is convinced we have planned or weapons to bring those plans to fruition but in the end, they found jack shit. But that's just because all of our guns are very well hidden. Finally, after four hours of dogging us, Williams breezed out of here but not before promising us that this was far from over and that she would be keeping her eye on us.

As soon as she was gone, Blaze called Rodriguez to see if he knew anything or had heard anything but he's almost as much in the dark as we are when it comes to this case. He did say that Williams has been sniffing around the club for about a week but he couldn't ask any questions or dig into it for us since the top brass knows about his involvement with the club and they've been watching him. It's nice to know that with as much good as we've done and all the people we've helped, we're still looked at like criminals in this town.

Fuck.

Maybe fake Storm has a goddamn point.

"You got anything for me?"

I open my eyes as Blaze marches into my room and sinks into the chair next to my desk and I shrug, pointing to the video paused on my screen. "It's a deep fake but that's not going to help us."

"What the fuck does that mean?" he asks, his brows furrowed as he studies the screen. Sighing, I sit forward again and press play. The video begins playing but I've slowed it down significantly and when we get to the right spot, I pause it, pointing to fake Storm's blurry face in the frame.

"See this?"

He nods. "Yeah."

"It happens so quick in the real time version that you wouldn't even notice it or you would think it was a camera malfunction but it's not. This is proof that this video is a deep fake..."

"Yeah," he sighs, cutting me off. "You keep saying that but what does it mean? What the fuck is a deep fake?"

"Basically, someone took a shit ton of pictures of Storm and then ran it through a program that used artificial intelligence to analyze his face and make a copy of him."

He scowls at the screen. "So this video is… what?"

"This video is someone, who is not Storm, standing in front of a camera and mimicking his voice to say all this shit and then on the computer, they swap the other face for Storm's to make it look like he is the one threatening the city and promising violence when really, it's someone else."

"Okay," he murmurs, scrubbing his jaw as he stares at the screen. "And how hard is this to do?"

I shrug. "Just depends on the person."

"How hard would it be for you to do?"

"Fucking cake," I tell him, shaking my head. "This video is really well done, so well done that in order to get it dismissed as evidence, we would need to bring in fucking experts and shit."

Sighing, he turns to me. "You think it's Warren?"

"I do. He's shown before that he is skilled at computers or working with someone who is and he's had the time to watch us and get more than enough photos of Storm to make a deep fake this good. From there, he just finds someone with the same body type as Storm and he's fucking golden."

"But what about the voice?" he asks. "And his tattoos. How did they get all of this put together?"

"With enough time, anything is possible and he's had two fucking years, boss. I mean, have you seen the shit they can do in movies now? This is nothing," I tell him, pointing to the screen and he blows out a breath as he drops his head into his hands.

"And there is no way to dispute it?"

I shake my head. "Like I said, you're gonna need an expert. I noticed some things that didn't fit Storm but I know him very well and I see him almost every fucking day. To Williams, this looks like a perfect copy of him. Plus, people don't really know about deep fakes and the harm they can do. When someone sees a video of something, they believe it as fact and that's going to be fucking hard to fight."

"Fucking Christ," he breathes, falling back in his seat as he closes his eyes and massages his temples with his fingers. I can see the stress of the past month weighing down on him and I wish I could do something to help. It's my fucking job to find answers for this club and I can't even fucking do that anymore. Finally, he opens his eyes again and sighs. "Keep digging, okay? Anything you can think of, go after it. There has to be answers or clues somewhere."

I nod. "I will."

He stands up and slaps my shoulder before walking out of the room like he has the weight of the world on his shoulders and I whisper a curse as I turn back to my computer and turn the screen off. I'll keep digging into everything, just like he asked, as soon as I get some goddamn sleep. Grabbing my phone off of the desk, I unlock it to text Rowan and see if she wants to come take a nap with me when it starts ringing. A familiar number pops up on the screen and I grit my teeth as I press the green button.

"Warren."

"You remembered me this time," he answers, the sound of the smile in his voice grating on my nerves. God, what a cocky motherfucker. "I'm so honored, Travis."

I scoff. "Don't be."

"Don't be like that. I just wanted to call to catch up... and I heard you guys had an unexpected visitor last night," he prompts and I press my lips into a thin line, my blood boiling. It's all the confirmation I need that I was right - Warren was behind the police raid and the video but knowing that doesn't really do me any good since I can't prove it. "But then again, I suppose you're used to late night police raids, aren't you?"

"Shut the fuck up," I snarl. There is a pounding in my ears and just like the last time Warren called, all I can think about is putting my fist through a fucking wall. He knows what he's doing and his words hit the exact bullseye he wanted them to but knowing that doesn't lessen my anger. In fact, it only amplifies it. The memories that have been haunting me all damn night, the memories I've been shoving back down, rise to the surface, resurrected by his words and I'm drowning in pain I've been ignoring for as long as I can remember.

"Or what? Face it... you don't have a fucking leg to stand on. Tell me, how does it feel to know that you can't stop me? To know that all you can do is sit back and watch as I tear this club apart?"

"I'm not going to let that happen, you fucking monster," I shoot back but it only makes him laugh. It's fucking condescending and infuriating. Raking my shaking hand through my hair, I blow out a breath as lights flash in my vision and the room spins. I fucking hate this. I'm never out of control, never this unstable, and all I want is to go back to the way things were before Warren ever walked into our lives, whenever that was.

"Funny thing about monsters, Travis, is that they are made, not born but then you already knew that, too, didn't you? Your momma made your daddy what he was and your club has created me. You have no one to blame but yourselves for the pain and destruction that is coming."

My heart hammers in my chest and it's hard to breathe as the memories flood my mind again, pulling me down with the current and there is only one person in the world that can help me right now. Rowan's face pops into my mind and just her memory soothes a part of me like the princess taming the dragon in all those stupid books my mom used to read me but it's not enough. I need *her*. Opening my desk drawer, I grab my burner phone and punch in Rowan's number, saving it in my contacts before I start typing out a text to her to ask her to come up to my room.

"I wouldn't do that if I were you," Warren says, the warning clear in his voice and I pause halfway through typing my message, the hair on the back of my neck standing on end.

"What the fuck are you talking about?"

He scoffs. "How dumb do you think I am? I'm talking about the second phone in your fucking hand that you're trying to text someone on. Put it away... or I will take some of this anger I've been keeping a tight lid on and let it out. Didn't I promise to pay a little visit to Rowan?"

"Don't you even fucking mention her, you son of a bitch," I growl, every single muscle in my body tightening as I think about him coming near my girl and he laughs, overjoyed by my outburst.

Fucking cool it, asshole.

You're giving him what he wants.

"Again, I have to ask… or what? Are you going to stop me, Travis?" He scoffs. "I don't think so. I've got you chasing your fucking tail and when I don't… Rowan certainly does."

I grit my teeth at the mention of her again as I imagine plunging a knife into this fucker's chest, anything to keep him away from her, to keep her safe. My hands shake as other images enter my mind, images I thought I'd burned from my memory but this time, it's Rowan in the center of it all – bruised, broken, and bloody.

No.

No.

No.

Squeezing my eyes shut, I try to force the horrific scene from my thoughts but the more I try to make it leave, the more prominent it seems to become, looming over me and taunting me with a collision of my past and my future and looking a whole lot like destiny

"I must say, it's been entertaining to watch the two of you together," he muses but his voice is just background noise now as the pictures in my head taunt me with the possibilities. Possibilities that make me want to throw up and rage all at the same time. "She certainly is talented, isn't she? Think she'll show me some of those moves she's always promising you?"

Fuck no.

Those are our thing, you fucker.

Taking a deep breath, I shove the images back enough to gain a little bit of control but my knee still bounces as I look around the room, wondering how the hell he has been keeping tabs on me, how he knows so much about Rowan and me. I would have noticed new cameras around the clubhouse and there is no way in hell he got into my system so how the fuck is he doing it?

"No thoughts on us sharing sweet little Rowan, Travis?" Warren asks, his voice full of a sick glee that makes my stomach turn and a wave of heat rushes over me as I clench my fists again.

"Over my dead body."

"Oh, that can be arranged, my friend," he answers, laughing to himself. "In fact, I like that idea a whole lot. Want to know what I'll do to her once you're out of the picture? I've put a great deal of thought into it…"

Shoving myself out of my chair, I kick it and it skates across the floor as Warren laughs in my ear.

"Well, that made you mad, didn't it?"

"Go fuck yourself, Warren," I growl and the silence on the other end of the line is heavy as I wait for his response. Finally, he takes a deep breath.

"No, Travis. I'm not going to fuck myself but as soon as you're out of the picture, I'll be helping myself to your little firecracker as much as I damn well please and there won't be a single thing you can do about it. I've spent most nights dreaming about the first time I'll slide inside her sweet little pussy since the moment she got to town. Tell me, is it even better than I imagine it is?"

My chest aches as the pictures try to worm their way back into my thoughts and his words burrow underneath my skin. "I will fucking kill you myself before I ever let…"

"Enough," he snarls, his mask slipping for just a second before he calms himself again. "We both know you don't have what it takes, Travis. Now, I've got to get going but remember what I said last time, you tell anyone about our little chats and next time, you'll have a whole body to deal with instead of just a head."

Wicked Games

Chapter Twenty-One
Rowan

"This is a terrible fucking idea," Blaze grumbles, crossing his arms over his chest as he scans the mall's parking lot. Tate hooks her arm through mine and flashes him a look of annoyance along with a heavy sigh.

"We have to keep living our lives, Blaze."

He shoots her a glare. "We fucking won't if we get killed by a madman."

"We're not getting killed. You have your gun and I have mine, too. Plus, Rowan's got my taser so you need to take a chill pill. We're prepared for anything. Besides, how upset would your sweet grand babies be if they woke up on Christmas morning and there were no presents? They have no idea what's going on with the club and they shouldn't."

"Those kids are the only fucking reason I agreed to this little shopping trip but we still need to be quick. In and out within an hour."

She scoffs. "Yeah, okay. Good luck with that."

"Goddamn it, Tate. Why don't you take this more seriously?" he snaps as we make our way across the parking lot to the mall doors and she sighs again. When Tate first ran the idea of doing a little Christmas shopping past me this morning, I was in agreement with Blaze but the more I thought about it, the more a little piece of normal in the chaos of everything else sounded like just what we needed. If I thought people were on edge before the raid of the clubhouse, it has nothing on the mood hanging over all of us now. And it's not that we're not taking this threat seriously but we all desperately need a break from it.

"I do take the threat seriously but Warren didn't put in all this work just to take some of us down in a fucking mall. Also, how would he be able to achieve that? It's five fucking days before Christmas, this place is packed to the fucking rafters and it would so insanely stupid to come after us with this many witnesses."

He rakes his hand through his hair. "That's just it, Tate. In a crowd this size, he could easily get lost in the chaos and I'm not even sure he wouldn't do something as drastic as taking out innocent civilians to get to us."

"Blaze, I know we haven't always has an easy relationship but I say this with love... you *need* to relax. The way all of you are going, you'll keel over from strokes or heart attacks before Warren ever gets to you and then what is it all for? We'll be as quick as we can and we'll be careful if you promise to just fucking take a breath."

He meets her eyes as we reach the mall doors and after a tense moment, he sighs and nods. "Okay, but keep an eye on our surroundings, you hear?"

"We will," she assures him before pulling open the door. Christmas music and the smell of cinnamon and nutmeg smacks me in the face and as we step inside, it's like stepping into another world. Tate was right, this place is packed and there is a little twinge in my chest as Tate starts pulling me along with her. Right inside the doors is a large food court, bustling with more people than I've ever seen in one place, and as we pass various vendors, new scents greet me and my stomach growls. Tate stops in front of a large mall map in the center of six different hallways and she turns to look at us. "Where to first?"

"I need to find a toy store," Blaze says, scanning the mall. "As you mentioned, my grand kids will riot without toys on Christmas morning."

She nods, pointing to a store down the hallway to my right. "Let's save that one for last since it's right here. Anyone else have somewhere they need to go?"

"Nope," I answer, shaking my head when she glances at me. I'm just along for the ride and if I happen to find something that I think someone will like, I'll grab it. Otherwise, I'll just order something online for my brother and Tate.

Shit...

Do I need to get something for Travis?

"Piper?" Tate asks and she blushes as she glances back at Blaze before turning and pointing to a store on the sign. I look up the number and bite my lip to keep from laughing. Tate isn't as successful as she flashes Blaze a smile.

"You might want to hang out here while we go to the first store."

He scoffs. "If you think I'm going to leave you girls alone, you're out of your damn mind. Where are we going?"

"Suit yourself," Tate whispers, her smile wide as she points to the lingerie store Piper asked to go to. Staring at it for a second, his cheeks redden before he pulls back and clears his throat.

"I think I'll stand guard outside the store."

The three of us burst out laughing as Tate nudges him and winks. "Sounds like a good plan, old man."

"You're a pain in my goddamn ass, you know that?" he grumbles as we all walk toward the hallway straight in front of us. The lingerie store is in the second space on the left and Blaze posts up outside the door, crossing his arms over his chest and scanning the crowd, as we step inside. Tate turns to Piper.

"So, what are we looking for?"

Color rushes to Piper's cheeks as she looks around the room. "Truthfully, I don't know. I… kind of wanted to just do something for Wyatt to take his mind off of all this shit."

"You could do a sexy little dance for him," I tell her, toying with the lace of a little red number next to me and she shifts uncomfortably, shaking her head.

"Uh, no. I can't dance… especially not like that."

I glance back at her. "It's really not that hard and I could show you a few things… if you want."

"I'm sorry," Tate interrupts, staring at me with raised brows. "How do you know "a few things"?"

Shit…

I didn't really think that all the way through.

Tate has been a close ally since I got here, keeping my secrets and trying to smooth things over with my brother when it comes to Travis and me but I have no idea how she will react to my former job. Sucking in a breath, I meet her gaze as my belly does a little flip.

"If I tell you, you can't tell my brother."

She nods. "Deal… unless you're like in danger or something."

"Wouldn't you just come rescue me then?" I ask and she laughs, nodding.

"Maybe but Lincoln would be pissed." She nudges me. "Now, come on, tell me all about your experience doing sexy dances?"

Taking a deep breath, I nod. "Back in Alaska, I was… stripping."

"Oh," she whispers and my breath catches in my throat but she scoffs and swipes her hand through the air like she's dismissing it altogether. "Is that it?"

I nod, studying her. "Um… yeah…"

"Hell, that's not what I was expecting but I can honestly say I've done worse. Though, we should definitely keep that between ourselves because your brother would shit a brick."

"Right," I answer, laughing as I turn back to the racks as I imagine what my brother's reaction would be if he ever found out. My stomach rolls at the thought and I don't have to dive into my imagination too much to realize it would be a disaster. I turn back to Tate as she picks up a pair of panties. "What do you mean you've done worse though?"

She sighs, tossing the underwear back onto the rack before glancing over her shoulder at Piper, who is flicking through another rack as she chews on her bottom lip. Grabbing my arm, she pulls me away in the other direction. "So, this isn't really public knowledge but before I met your brother, I did whatever it took to survive and for a while, that included escorting."

My eyes widen in shock and she shakes her head.

"I never had sex with any of them or anything but there were some girls who did."

255

I nod, trying to wrap my mind around this new information. "So, what did you do then?"

"Basically… I was arm candy," she answers with a shrug as she begins browsing through one of the racks and I watch her, seeing her in a whole new light. At first, I thought maybe she was just being nice to me and keeping my secrets to try and build a relationship between the two of us but the more I get to know her, the more it's clear to me that this is who she truly is - kind, funny as hell, open minded, and the least judgmental person I've ever met.

"Ooh, want to get this for Streak?" she asks, holding up a black lace bodysuit with baby pink frill around the edges and I fight back a smile as I shake my head.

"I already have one like that."

She laughs as she puts it back on the rack and nods in approval. "All right, girl, get it. You are going to get something for him though, right?"

"Uh… I don't know. I thought about it but I don't think you're supposed to get the guy you're casually fucking a Christmas present."

The sales lady's head whips in our direction and I realize how loudly I was talking as blood rushes to my cheeks and Tate laughs again, moving closer to me to continue our conversation.

"First of all, that was amazing. Second, y'all are *not* casual."

I scowl at her as I grab a sheer baby doll off of the rack. "What are you talking about? We are casual."

"Okay," she shoots back, clearly not buying it and I prop my hand on my hip as I narrow my eyes at her. She sighs. "You can look at me like that all you want but it still won't change the fact that you and Streak are so far from casual that I can hear wedding bells."

"That's ridiculous."

She shakes her head. "No, what's ridiculous is y'all pretending like there is nothing there when anyone with eyes can see the connection you share."

Before I can respond, my phone starts ringing and I sigh, putting the hanger back on the rack before pulling it out of my bag. Ash's name stares back at me and I roll my eyes as I silence it.

"Who was that?"

Sighing, I slip the phone back into my bag. "Ash."

"Still?" she snaps, her eyes widening as she studies me. "I thought that he had stopped."

"Nope. He still calls every couple of days and leaves me a voice mail begging me to just talk to him and saying how much he misses me. On the last one, he talked about how empty the house was and how miserable he was without me until my voice mail cut him off."

She shakes her head. "Jesus Christ. I was joking the first couple of times I talked about jumping on a plane but the boy is clearly not getting the message."

"Whatever. Maybe I'll just go get a new number and he can call this phone to his heart's content."

Laughing, she wraps her arm around my shoulders and nods. "We should. There's a cell phone store in the mall we could swing by."

"Let see how much shopping Blaze actually lets us get away with first," I answer, grinning as I turn to check on the old man at his post. His arms are still crossed over his chest but he seems to have relaxed a little bit so maybe he won't be rushing us out of here anytime soon. As I turn back toward Tate, my gaze sweeps over the crowd and I freeze, my heart jumping into my throat as I grip the closest rack to keep myself from collapsing. The man in the white mask, the same one from the nightclub, stands in the middle of the crowd – mothers, daughters, teenagers, fathers – all milling around him without a care in the world. It's like he's invisible because none of them even spare the strange man in a white mask a second glance.

Fuck.

Am I hallucinating this?

He's standing at such an angle that I don't think Blaze can see him from his post and my heart races as my gaze flicks from Piper to Blaze before finally turning to Tate. She takes one look at my face and grips my arm as her brows knit together and she searches my face.

"Rowan, what is it?"

I try to swallow my fear but I swear, I can feel his gaze in the side of my head and I'm thrust right back into that nightclub as he stalked closer and closer to Travis and me. "It's him… the man from the club… the one in the mask…"

"Blaze," she calls out as she turns to search the crowd. Blaze rushes into the store and walks over with Piper on his heels and when he stops in front of us, Tate sucks in a breath, pointing to the man. "There."

Blaze follows her gaze, his entire body tensing. "We need to go."

"Fuck no," she hisses, releasing my arm to reach behind her back and grab her gun. "Let's end this now."

He shakes his head. "Absolutely not."

"Why? I'm so fucking tired of this asshole and his shit. I know you are, too."

"Tate, put your gun away," he growls, the command in his voice clear as he levels a glare at her. Her gaze flicks between him and the man in the hall.

"We have the chance to put an end to all of this right now. Same way I could have ended it at the nightclub if Lincoln hadn't stopped me."

Blaze shakes his head. "There are far too many people here to start shooting and you could just as easily get killed. Not to mention, the police raid and investigation. We. need. to. go."

"Fine," she snarls, shoving her gun back in its holster as I glance back out at the hallway. The man is still there, completely unbothered by the fact that we know he's there and my heart races as I think about all the things he's done to the club over the past two weeks and questions bombard me.

What is he doing here?
Why is he just watching us?
What is his plan?

"Rowan, let's move," Blaze says, snapping me out of my thoughts and my belly does a little flip as I nod, unable to take my eyes off of the man. I remember the utter sense of dread I felt the night we all went out to the club and the certainty I had that we weren't going to make it out unscathed. But we did...

Blaze goes first, putting a protective arm around Piper andTate does the same with me as we follow them out of the store. I can feel every ounce of tension in the air but it's such a contrast from all of the normal people around us just finishing up their holiday shopping without even realizing the threat that is right next to them. In the hallway, I glance to where he was standing but my heart stops when I can't find him.

"Where did he go?"

Tate shakes her head as her hand slips behind her back, ready to grab her gun at a moment's notice. "Just keep moving, Row… and maybe get that taser out now."

"Okay," I whisper, nodding as I pull the taser out of my bag and turn it on. My hand shakes as I grip it tightly, my gaze flicking around the mall and my heart pounding in my ears.

Where is he?

"We're almost there," Tate tells me when the front door comes into view and I nod, glancing behind us and sucking in a breath. He's there, walking calmly in the same direction we are and I barely resist the urge to sob as my mind drowns in fear. I nudge Tate.

"Behind us."

She glances over her shoulder and gives me a curt nod before stepping closer to Blaze and Piper. "Pick up the pace. He's behind us."

I swear I can feel his fingertips brushing against the back of my shirt as we all walk a little faster toward the exit but I refuse to look back again. My stomach flips and tears sting my eyes as my heart hammers out of control in my chest. The memory of the way Travis held me in the nightclub, the last time we were in this situation, pops into my mind and I can't help but wish he was here now.

"Keep moving," Blaze calls back to us as we step outside and cold air blasts us in the face. Glancing up at the gray sky looming over us, I can't help but think it's indicative of our situation as one single thought echoes through my mind.

I'm going to die here.

Sucking in a breath, I can't stop myself from glancing back again but when I peek over my shoulder, he is gone. It should calm me, reassure me that I'm safe now but the only thing worse than seeing Warren is not seeing him because if I've learned one thing since moving here, it's that he is always working behind the scenes, plotting his next move and it usually proves disastrous for us. Turning back to face Blaze and Piper as we near the SUV, I take another deep breath, desperately trying to calm myself but my hands won't stop shaking and my heart is about to beat right out of my chest. When we finally reach the vehicle, Tate opens the back door for us and ushers me inside first before forcing Piper in next to me. Once we're inside, she jumps in and Blaze slips behind the wheel and starts the engine, refusing to take his eyes off the parking lot. He locks the door and puts the SUV in reverse as the sound of a motorcycle engine rips through the air. I turn to look out of the window as one races up our aisle and pulls to a stop behind us, blocking us in.

Oh, God, this is it.

"Fuck," Blaze hisses, his eyes hard as steel in the rearview mirror. He backs up as far as he can without hitting the bike and Warren doesn't even flinch as the bumper of the SUV inches closer and closer to him. When Blaze can't back up anymore, he puts the vehicle in drive. The spots on either side of us are open as well as the space next to the small truck parked in front of us, allowing him to crank the wheel to the left and slip through the maze of cars without incident. His knuckles are white on the steering wheel as he races down the aisle, toward the exit, and he periodically glances in the mirror to monitor Warren. The sound of the bike's engine revving fills the air again as lights dance across my vision as I reach down and grab Tate's hand off of the seat. Her eyes meet mine and despite the bravado she usually walks around with, I can see her fear as she squeezes my hand.

"Tate, call Kodiak. I want him, Chance, Streak, Henn, and Moose to meet us on their bikes and surround the SUV," Blaze orders and she nods, releasing my hand to make her phone call. As soon as my brother answers, she fills him in on what is going on and his shouted demands for more information fill the car even though she doesn't have him on speakerphone.

"Later, Lincoln," she snaps, her knee bouncing next to me as she turns to look out of the window. "Just get here now."

He says something else to her but it's too quiet to hear and as she ends the call, I turn to glance behind us. The bike is probably about five car lengths back now but I can tell it's creeping closer and I just hope the boys get here before he catches us.

What would he do if he actually caught us?

The thought sends me into a tailspin and I press my hand against my chest as I turn forward again and flop into my seat as an awful idea about what he could have planned for us flicks through my mind and I struggle to breathe. If everything he's done so far has just been a warm up to his main event, how bad will it get and will any of us survive? My mind drifts to the note that came with Piper and Wyatt's wedding present as I shake my head.

One down, four to go.

Does that mean he's only coming after a certain four people and he has no intention of hurting anyone else or are we all just collateral damage in his quest to get to those people? Will he sacrifice everyone and everything to complete his mission?

"There they are," Blaze says, pointing to a line of bikes as they roar past us going the opposite way. Flipping in my seat, I stare out of the back of the SUV as they cut across the median and start gaining on us, weaving through the other cars on the road with what looks like reckless abandon but I know each and every one of them is hyper-focused on reaching us before anyone else does. Warren glances over his shoulder as they race up behind him and he falls back, blending into the other traffic as the boys reach the SUV and surround it with their bikes.

"Only a few more minutes to the clubhouse," Tate whispers and I'm honestly not sure if she's reassuring me or herself but either way, it's nice to hear. Settling back into my seat, I turn to the other side and watch Travis as he rides along next to the SUV and I can almost imagine his furrowed brow as he focuses on the road in front of him. A wave of peace washes over me as I stare at him, fighting back the fear and panic so I throw all of my focus on him, remembering the way he held me last night while we slept, like he never wanted to let me go. Shaking my head, I dismiss that thought. This is a high pressure situation and it's making me overthink things and imagine things that aren't really there. Travis and I are casual, despite what everyone else says, and it would be monumentally stupid of me to forget that.

Finally, after what feels like an eternity, we pull to a stop in front of the gate to the clubhouse and Lincoln jumps off his bike before punching in the code and standing back to let us all in. As soon as Blaze has the SUV parked in its usual spot, Tate opens the door and we all spill out of the vehicle. Before I can even get two steps from the door, Travis runs up to me and scoops me up in his arms, lifting me off of my feet as he crushes me to his body and buries his face in my neck. His entire body is shaking and his chest heaves as he struggles to catch his breath but he still doesn't release me until both of our heart rates have slowed.

When he finally sets me back on my feet, his eyes meet mine before scanning my body methodically, checking for injuries as his hands smooth over my skin. "Are you okay?"

"Yeah," I whisper, my voice still shaky as I nod and he releases a breath before pulling me back into his arms and presses his lips to my forehead.

"Fuck, baby. I was so scared…"

I nod because he doesn't need to explain. Just like the other night when we laid under the stars, I can see and feel everything he is trying to say in his eyes and in his touch. His hand slips into my hair and he begins massaging my head as he shakes his own and presses another kiss to my forehead. Our connection wraps us up, cocooning the two of us in our own little world as he releases another sigh - one that tells me how happy he is that I'm safe and just how worried he was that he was going to lose me.

"I'm never going to let anything happen to you, Rowan," he whispers and I nod because I already knew that. When I'm with him, I'm safe. He blows out a breath and kisses my forehead again. "I'd rather die."

Me, too.

Chapter Twenty-Two
Rowan

Rain pelts against the windows of the clubhouse as thunder rumbles in the distance. It's totally indicative of my mood these past few days. Sighing, I cup my hands together in front of me and let the water from the showerhead fill them up before releasing it and watching it fall to my feet. Turning, I step back into the spray and let the water trickle down my body. It's Christmas Eve and almost everyone else is gathered here in the main room, wrapping presents for all of the kids to open tomorrow morning but I haven't really been able to get into a festive mood this year and I'm terrible at trying to fake it. Especially with what happened at the mall four days ago. I'm not sure how they can all sit around drinking eggnog, wrapping presents, and acting like Piper, Tate, Blaze, and I weren't just stalked through a mall by a madman. Travis has barely left my side since we got back to the clubhouse four days ago and we've spent the last few days lying in bed and watching movies in an effort to distract ourselves from how terrified we are of everything that is going down around us. I haven't even really been down to my room except to grab a clean set of clothes every day and at this point, Travis might as well clear out a drawer for me.

Sighing again, I turn and rinse my hair, closing my eyes as the warm water cascades down my back and I yawn, desperate to crawl into bed with Travis and pass out. Nightmares have been plaguing me every night since seeing Warren in the mask again, seriously limiting how much sleep I get, which is one of the reasons Travis was so insistent about me spending every night with him in his bed. He wanted me to feel safe enough to get a full eight hours but that hasn't happened yet.

The shower door opens, startling me, and I jump as my eyes snap open and my heart climbs into my throat. Travis steps inside before closing the door behind him and pulling me into his arms.

"Sorry, Princess. Didn't mean to scare you."

"I'm okay," I tell him as I shake my head but the words sound hollow. "Something I can do for you?"

"Nope. I'm here for you," he answers, pressing a quick kiss to my lips before he turns me to face the showerhead and I scowl, glancing back at him.

"What does that mean?"

He moves behind me and grips my hips as he leans down and presses a soft kiss to my neck. Goose bumps race across my skin and I sigh as my eyes flutter closed. I lean my head back against his shoulder and he nuzzles into my neck, kissing me a few more times.

How in the hell did he know this was just what I needed?

I swear, I'm beginning to wonder if the boy is telepathic.

"I've got something for you," he says as he plants a few more kisses against my skin, leaving a trail of heat in his wake as he molds his body to mine and wraps his arms around my waist. His cock jerks against my lower back and I wiggle, grinning to myself as he groans in my ear.

"Is it that?"

His lips stretch into a grin against my neck. "Maybe later."

"Maybe," I scoff because he and I both know he's a sure bet every single day of the week. Turning in his arms, I lay my head against his chest. His large arms wrap around my body, holding me close as the water trickles down my back, and he presses his lips to my forehead. This is the only damn place I feel completely safe since the incident at the mall and if I could get away with it, I don't know that I would ever leave his arms. Right here, right now, is my happy place. As he presses another kiss to my forehead, he drags one hand up my back and cups the back of my head before massaging my scalp with his fingers. Moaning, I lean into his body as my eyes close and a shiver runs down my spine.

Oh, hell, that feels so good.

"Oh my God, Travis," I breathe, every muscle in my body relaxing with his touch while goose bumps simultaneously race across my flesh. He groans, spins me back toward the showerhead, and slips his hand between my legs as he nips at my neck.

"Is this what you need, baby? Want me to take your mind off of everything else?"

I nod, arching my body against him. "Yes."

His fingers find my clit and he circles it slowly, again and again as he reaches up with his other hand and wraps his fingers around my neck. My head falls back against his shoulder and I moan, slapping my hand against the shower wall to keep myself from falling as my legs shake.

"You gonna come all over my fingers?" he asks, his voice full of gravel as he nips at my earlobe and my nipples tighten as my back arches more and I nod. He strums over my clit and I gasp as I rock my hips with him, pressure building in my belly. The hand around my throat releases as he grabs my tit, his fingers digging into my skin as he growls into my neck but the bite of pain only adds to the pleasure. Grinning, he presses a kiss to my skin and pulls his fingers away from my pussy but before I can protest, his slips them inside me.

"Travis," I cry out as his fingers thrust in and out of me and the heel of his hand rubs against my clit. My body trembles against him as I reach up and thread my fingers into his hair. His hard cock presses against my back and I reach back with my other hand, wrapping my fingers around his length and he groans in my ear. His cock jerks in my hand and I moan again, remembering how it feels when he thrusts inside me as my pussy clenches around his fingers.

"There it is," he growls, curling his fingers inside me and hitting the perfect spot to send me flying. I grip his hair and give it a tug as an orgasm rocks through me, wringing pleasure from my body as my entire body shakes but before I can come back down, he spins me into his arms and slams his lips to mine. He grips my jaw in his hand as we stumble back into the shower wall and it doesn't matter that I've already come because in an instant, I want him again. His kiss is fierce, demanding, and everything I need right now and I am putty in his very capable hands. His tongue tangles with mine, teases and exploring my mouth with the promise of more as I hook my leg over his hip and grind into him, desperate

A.M. Myers

for some friction. One of his hand slips down my body, stopping to grab my tit before he pinches my nipple between his fingers and his other hand grips my ass, pulling me into his body.

"Oh, God," I whisper, dropping my head back as he thrusts his hips, rubbing his cock along my slit as he drags his lips down my neck. My nipples ache for attention and I cry out when he leans down and sucks one into his mouth. His tongue toys with the sensitive little bud and I slip my fingers into his hair as I lean back against the shower wall and reach down to wrap my fingers around his cock. He groans, scraping his teeth over my nipple and my body jerks as everything south of my belly clenches. "Travis."

"Fuck,' he groans softly, straightening to his full height and thrusting into my hand as his lips find mine again. He reaches behind my head and grabs my hair in his fist, forcing my head back as he gives it a tug and bites at my neck. I wiggle against him, my entire body tingling with a need so fierce that it's stealing the air from my lungs and wiping every thought from my mind - every thought except him. His hands glide over my body, giving me just a tiny taste of what I need, before he grabs my hips and spins me around to face the wall.

Yes.

Planting my hands on the wall in front of me, I arch my back and glance back at him as he presses his cock against my entrance and meets my gaze, sinking into me slowly. My lips part in a silent gasp as he stretches me, filling me completely with his length and his eyes hold me captive as he grips my hips and his fingers dig into my skin. The bite of pain sends a shiver down my spine and my heart hammers in my chest as he slowly pulls back before sinking into me again.

I'm hypnotized, entranced, and completely his.

He glances down to watch his cock sink into me again and his teeth sink into his lip as his grip tightens. Leaning over me, he presses a kiss to my shoulder before biting me in the same spot and I cry out, turning to the wall as I close my eyes and revel in the feeling of his push and pull.

"God, Rowan," he whispers, pressing his forehead between my shoulder blades as he keeps the same pace but it's not quite enough. I need more but he doesn't care. Releasing my hip, he moves his hand up to my breasts and grabs it as he drives into me with a little more force and I moan, hoping it encourages him to give me more. It doesn't. Instead, he pulls me upright until our bodies are almost one and reaches down between my legs to toy with my clit as he continues casually thrusting into me.

"Travis," I beg, tears of desperation stinging my eyes and I reach over my head and thread my fingers through his hair. He groans in my ear, kissing my neck before he grabs my leg and lifts it up until my foot settles on the bench next to us. Gripping my hips again, he picks up the pace and the sound of slapping fills the bathroom as pleasure explodes through my body. I lean over and press my hands to the wall again as his ragged breath rushes over my skin, sending a shiver down my spine.

God, I love hearing how turned on he is and I absolutely love knowing that he's just as desperate for me as I am for him. I love the fire in his eyes when he looks at me and the way he grabs me like he owns me but most of all, I love that I can let go with him. When we're together, there is nothing else on my mind and I don't worry about a single goddamn thing because I know, with more certainty than I've ever felt before, that Travis has got me.

"Where did you go, baby?" he asks, leaning over me and wrapping his fingers around my throat again. I shake my head as my eyes roll back into my head.

"Nowhere."

He uses the hand around my throat to pull me back onto his cock as he surges forward and his other hand slips into my hair as he bites the top of my shoulder. "You going to come for me?"

"Yes," I whisper, my pussy clenching at the thought and he groans again.

"Reach down between your legs, Princess," he orders, his voice full of gravel as he releases a ragged breath in my ear. "I want to watch you play with your pretty little clit when you come."

My skin aches everywhere, every inch of me begging to be touched as the delicious, frustrating pressure continues to build in my body. My legs shake and I do as I'm told, slipping my hand between my legs and pressing my fingers to my clit and he groans in my ear again.

"Hard?" he asks and I can't nod "yes" fast enough. His dark chuckle is the only warning I get before he sets a merciless pace, pounding into me harder than ever before as I scream, struggling to stay on my feet. The hand around my throat disappears before clamping over my mouth and he nips at my ear lobe but doesn't slow down or back off.

"Travis," I cry into his hand as my body jerks with each thrust of his hips and just when I think I can't take anymore, that I'm going to die from the pain and pleasure of it all, my body lets go. Spiraling into the abyss of my orgasm, my knees give out but Travis doesn't let me fall as he wraps his arms around my body and holds me up as he continues driving into me until he stills and releases a loud, rumbling groan. He pours himself into me and I close my eyes, leaning back into his hold as I struggle to catch my breath. My entire body tingles with the aftermath of my release and I'm almost certain that there is no way I'll be able to walk out of this shower.

"Baby," he whispers into my hair, his chest heaving with heavy breaths as he nuzzles into me and warmth rushes through my chest at the gesture.

"I don't think I can walk."

He laughs. "Don't worry. I got you."

"I know you do," I whisper, my thoughts from a moment ago rushing back to me as he sets me on my feet. He keeps his arm wrapped around me and lets me lean back against his body as he turns off the shower before guiding me out onto the mat. Grabbing a towel off of the rack, he wraps it around my body before turning me to face him.

"Still can't walk?"

I shrug, peeking up at him with a smile. "I guess I can manage now."

"Good," he answers, pulling me into his arms. "Because I really do have a present for you but it's in the bedroom."

"You mean to tell me that wasn't my present?" I ask with a laugh, pointing to the shower and he grins, wrapping his arms around me.

"You think my cock is a gift?"

I roll my eyes. "I didn't say that."

272

"Mmm, I think you did but no, that is not what I was talking about," he answers and I pull back, narrowing my eyes at him.

"You got me a Christmas present?"

"Maybe. Guess you'll have to get your ass in the room to find out," he shoots back and before I can protest, he spins me toward the door and smacks my ass, urging me forward. My head spins as we walk back into the room and I throw my hair up in the towel before pulling one of his t-shirts over my head and plopping down on the bed. Once he has a pair of mesh shorts on, he walks over to me with a little red box in his hand and sits down next to me. I eye the gift in his hand.

"I didn't know we were… I didn't get you anything," I tell him, my cheeks heating as I mentally kick myself for not picking up a little something for him. He shakes his head, his eyes melting me as he stares at me with something I can't quite name. It makes my belly do a little flip. "You don't need to get me anything."

"I really should…"

"Here. Open it," he says, interrupting me as he drops his gaze from mine and thrusts the box into my hand before I can protest any further.

Sucking in a breath, I nod and lift the lid off of the box, gasping. The necklace inside has a delicate chain and the most unique star pendant I've ever seen in my entire life. The main star has four points and the entire thing has what look like diamonds embedded in it while the second star in the back is pure metal and shifted to the left so it's four points fill in the gaps left by the other star. It's absolutely gorgeous and makes me think of the time my dad took us all camping and taught us about the

North Star and how to use it to find our way home. Tears sting my eyes and I look up Travis.

"You like it?" he asks, chewing on his bottom lip. "It popped up in an ad when I was online and it just made me think of you…"

I flash him a wide smile despite my tears and lean forward, pressing my hand to his cheek as I seal my lips to his. His hand half slips into my hair and relief pours off of him as the kiss grows into something more. When he pulls away, my heart is racing and butterflies flutter around in my belly as he flashes me a silly grin.

"Thank you, Travis. This is…" I look down at the necklace and attempt to swallow the lump in my throat. "You have no idea how much this means to me and I'm so sorry I didn't get you anything."

He brushes his thumb over my cheek and his eyes hold me captive once again. "Believe me, Rowan. You've already given me so much."

Chapter Twenty-Three
Travis

Running my hands through my hair, I blow out a breath before grabbing my beer off of the picnic table I'm sitting on and taking a sip as I watch the sun sink toward the horizon. I spent most of the day digging into anything Warren related I could think of but every lead I found only took me to another dead end, as usual, and now my head aches and I desperately want to put my fist through something... or someone. My chest feels tight as I shake my head and tell myself to calm down but it's easier said than done when I have this asshole taunting me every minute of every day. I swear, it's like I'm eighteen all over again, diving into a world I don't really want to be a part of and hunting down a monster. The only difference is that this time, it doesn't hit quite so close to home.

Fuck.

Ever since the day Warren followed the girls and Blaze through the mall, I've been single-minded in my determination to find him and end all of this. I spend my days with Rowan and then I stay up all night, searching even the deepest, darkest corners of the internet but none of it does me any good because he already planned for every move I would make. Somehow, he knows me and he knows how I think. He's put every contingency in place to make sure I don't figure out who he is before he completes his mission and rips this club apart. Scrubbing my hand down my face, I take another sip of my beer as I remember the way my heart stopped when Tate called Kodiak from the mall and told us what was going down. During the entire drive to them, all I could think about was the threats Warren had made against her and the images I've been fighting so hard to keep buried pushed their way into my mind in an instant. Thankfully, we got there in time but I'll never fucking forget that feeling.

It's been a week since the incident at the mall but I still hate letting Rowan out of my sight for long and I can't even imagine how much of a goddamn nutcase I would be if she left the clubhouse without me. I can't stop thinking about what could happen to her if I'm not there to protect her and it's part of the reason I'm not sleeping much. Rowan has enough nightmares for the both of us and I don't want to burden her with all of my shit. My jaw aches as I grit my teeth, thoughts of my darkness tainting her making my stomach turn. She is perfect, just as she is, and the only thing that brings me any kind of peace these days so I'll do whatever it takes to preserve that, even if it means never sleeping again.

"You pouting?"

I glance over my shoulder as Storm walks out of the clubhouse with a beer in his hand and I shake my head, sliding down the picnic table to give him room to sit. "Nope. You?"

"Naw," he answers, rolling his eyes. "I just had to get out of there. The girls are all taking photos of Mags in her new dresses."

I laugh, taking a sip of my beer as I turn to watch the sunset again. I guess all the guys went a little crazy or got super bored leading up to Christmas and bought Storm's daughter, Magnolia, a shit ton of frilly dresses and toys. In fact, all of the kids made out pretty well this year so they've definitely been more entertained for the last two days.

"I noticed Rowan sporting some new jewelry. You get that for her?"

I arch a brow as I turn to look at him. "You noticed that, huh?"

"No," he scoffs, laughing before he takes another sip of beer. "Ali did and mentioned it to me and then Tate pointed it out to Kodiak when I was there."

Shaking my head, I glance back at the clubhouse door. "I don't know whether that woman is trying to help me or get me killed."

"When it comes to Tate, it's probably a good bet to just assume both. Plus, with pregnancy hormones, it could change every hour."

"Don't let her hear you say that," I warn him and he shoots me a look that calls me a moron in eight different languages before shaking his head.

"Yeah, no shit," he fires back before sighing. "How are things going with Warren?"

I scoff. "They're not."

"Blaze mentioned that you found something about that video," he prompts and I nod, breaking down the whole deep fake thing for him just like I did for Blaze and he stares off into the distance, quiet for a moment before whispering a curse.

"So, I'm really fucked then?"

I shake my head. "Naw, man. I'm not giving up and I'll find answers for you, okay? You can't think like that."

"I can't seem to stop thinking like that," he replies, scrubbing his jaw. "Ever since the raid, all of my thoughts revolve around what Ali and Mags are going to do when I get sent to prison."

I clap my hand on his shoulder and he glances over at me. "None of us are going to let that happen, man. I don't care what I have to do…"

"Appreciate it," he murmurs, nodding, before he stares off into the distance again and silence falls over us. We sip our beers, both of us lost in our thoughts and I run through all the information I've looked up on deep fakes, trying to find a way to prove that the man in the video isn't Storm but like I said to Blaze, whoever made it is really fucking good. I've even considered making a replica of the video using the real Storm to show the subtle differences I noticed but it's a slippery slope and I don't want to make the problem any worse.

Storm nudges me, pulling me out of my thoughts as he points to a big white van pulling up outside of the fence. "What the fuck is that?"

"Your guess is as good as mine," I tell him, cocking my head to the side as a well dressed woman steps out of the passenger side and fluffs her hair as she looks around. The side door opens and three men step out and one of them turns back to the van to pull out a giant camera as one of the others points to the clubhouse. "What the fuck?"

"What do you say we go see what's going on?" Storm asks and I nod as we both stand up and set our beers down on the table.

"Sounds good."

We start off across the parking lot and when they notice us walking over to them, they all start rushing around to set up the camera and start rolling, The woman pastes a professional smile on her face that looks as fake as her tits before bringing a microphone to her mouth as the cameraman points to her. She launches into her intro and Storm nudges me with his shoulder.

"Be charming."

I scoff. "I'm always charming."

"Then be extra charming today," he growls under his breath as we reach the fence and we overhear snippets of her report. She's here to investigate the video of Storm and why the club wants to hurt the city of Baton Rouge and my stomach drops.

"Can we help you?" Storm calls when we reach the fence and she ushers the cameraman to follow her as she struts over to us and flashes us that smile. It's honestly a little terrifying.

"I'm Christina Hill with Channel Eight news and I'm here to investigate the video that was posted to the internet two weeks ago. You're Logan Chambers, aren't you?"

He nods, his body tense and his hands fidgeting at his sides before he shoves them in his pockets. "I am."

"Care to tell the people of Baton Rouge what your club has against them and why you're threatening to hurt people?"

"We're not," he answers. "That video isn't real."

279

She frowns, glancing back at the camera with a worried expression before facing us again. "I see... and what about the other videos? Are you saying they're all fake?"

"What videos?" Storm asks, glancing over at me but I have no fucking clue what he's talking about. Her gaze flicks between the two of us as she takes a fraction of a step back. It's a subtle tell but one we both notice.

That's it.

Our fates are sealed.

"There are eight other videos that were posted to the Bayou Devils website. Do you really expect people to believe that you don't know what I'm talking about?" she asks and Storm nudges me before tilting his head to the clubhouse and I nod as he turns back to Christina Hill.

"Ma'am, the Bayou Devils don't have a website so yes, we have no idea what you're talking about."

I turn and start walking back to the clubhouse as she asks him another question and when I'm far enough away from them to not draw a ton of attention to myself, I pick up the pace, running across the pavement as my mind races. Storm is right. The club doesn't have a website or any social media and though I've thought about making one in the past, we all decided as a group that it was best if we did our work through word of mouth instead. Most of the time, it allows us the privacy we need to protect the people we rescue as well as ourselves.

When I get inside, I run over to the stairs and race up them, drawing looks from Kodiak, Chance, and Blaze as they sit around on the couches talking, but I don't have time to stop to explain what is going on. Once I'm in my room, I sink into my chair and wiggle the mouse to wake up my computer. The screen springs to life and I fire up the internet before navigating to the search engine and typing the club's name into the search bar. As soon as I hit enter, a page of results pop up and the first website claims to be the official site for the Bayou Devils MC. I click on it and hold my breath as the page loads.

The home screen doesn't have much on it, except the video of Storm and my heart hammers in my chest when I see the little arrow on the side of the screen. I click it. Another video slides into the same place, this one of Chance and I press play as my stomach rolls.

"For far too long, the city of Baton Rouge has looked down on us, casting us as villains without any proof and we've taken it. We live with it every day despite the work we do to protect our neighbors. I've been glared at, mothers have moved across the street with their children when they see me coming, and I've even been spit on. For what? The way I look? The tattoos on my arms? The cut I wear? We've had enough..."

I pause the video and shove away from the desk as I lean back in my chair and run my hand through my hair as I struggle to form a single thought. Time seems to slow as I stare at the screen and every cell in my body aches to take action, do something about this but I can't come up with anything. Shaking my head, I roll forward and click the arrow again, revealing a video of Moose but I can't stand to watch it yet so I keep clicking through video after video until I get back to Storm's. There is one for each of us and no doubt, each one promises pain, violence, and bloodshed to the citizens of Baton Rouge - our home, our city.

Ringing echoes around the room and I blink at the screen a few times, unable to process what it is, before it finally registers. Sucking in a breath, I dig my phone out of my pocket. "Hello?"

"Hi, Travis," Warren says, his voice sickeningly cheerful and I turn away from the computer as I grit my teeth and glare out of my window where Christina is still interviewing Storm. Blaze has joined him but I'm not sure that will help anything. It seems like she has already found us guilty and with the evidence she has, I can't blame her.

"What the fuck do you want?"

"Gosh." He chuckles. "So hostile. I was just calling to chat. I noticed that you got my little present and before you say anything, I know Christmas was two days ago but I've been so busy, you know?"

Scanning my room, I wonder how in the hell he's watching me - something else I haven't been able to figure out despite my relentless digging but nothing has turned up.

"Travis, you still there?"

"You enjoying yourself?" I snarl before shaking my head. My head is still so fucking fuzzy and it's making me ask him dumb questions. Shaking my head in an attempt to clear it, I suck in a breath and turn back to the computer.

Jesus, get it together, Broussard.

He laughs again. "Oh, immensely. So... do you like my present? I know it's not as nice the one you gave Rowan on Christmas Eve but I really tried."

"Go fuck yourself."

He tsks before releasing a heavy sigh into the phone. "Are you okay, Travis? You don't quite sound like yourself. Have you been getting enough sleep?"

"Shut up," I snap, that all too familiar feeling of wanting to put my fist through a wall flooding my body as I grip the arm of my office chair until my hands ache.

"That's no way to talk to the man who holds all of your friends' lives in his hand," he murmurs, sounding disappointed and my stomach rolls at his ability to sound completely sincere no matter what emotion he's portraying. "You do remember what will happen if you reveal any of this information to your brothers, right?"

I nod. "I remember."

"Excellent. I'm glad we're on the same page... although, I would love any excuse to finally get my hands on our little Rowan. I've been dreaming about her every night, you know, and the anticipation is just killing me."

I want to fucking rage at him, scream and tell him to stay the hell away from her but that hasn't worked in the past and as I think about him actually laying his hands on her, I struggle to take a breath. I need to find something else, a way to discourage him from going after her but what can I do? As I rake my hand through my hair, I wonder if he is only focused on her because of me and if I reacted with disinterest, he would lose interest. Sucking in a breath, I try to calm my frazzled nerves as I shrug.

"Go ahead. She is just another in a long line of women I've fucked and honestly, I'll get bored with her soon enough."

He roars with laughter and my chest feels like it's going to explode. "Did you really think that would work? My infatuation with Rowan has absolutely nothing to do with you, Travis. I want *her*. I have from the moment I watched you press her perky tits up against your window, putting her on display for me. Torturing you with it all is just an added bonus."

There is a pounding in my ears and spots flash in my vision as I think about him watching us that first night we were together. He would have had to been outside the clubhouse to see what we did and knowing he was right there makes my blood boil. How many other signs have we missed?

"Nothing to say to that, old friend?" he asks and I shake my head. "Fine, then. I'd better get going anyway. There is so much work left to do before we end this but I'll talk to you soon."

He hangs up before I can say anything - not that I had anything else to say to him - and I toss my phone on the desk before dropping my head into my hands and releasing a breath.

Dread.

Rage.

Pain.

And fear.

It all swirls around inside me, each emotion pulling the life from my veins and feeding another as I desperately try to stay afloat and I don't know how much longer I can hold all of this together. Sooner or later - and I'm leaning toward sooner more with each day that passes - I'm going to break and the thought terrifies me more than anything else.

Chapter Twenty-Four
Rowan

"Go ahead. She is just another in a long line of women I've fucked," Travis says, stopping me in my tracks just outside his room. The door is wide open and he's in his office chair, facing away from me with his phone pressed to his ear. "And honestly, I'll get bored with her soon enough."

Pain blooms in my chest and I blink, frozen in place as I try to wrap my mind around the words he just said but it's like trying to wade through mud.

She is just another in a long line...

I'll get bored with her soon enough...

Tears sting my eyes as the pain only intensifies, spreading through my body like poison, and I take a step back as my lip wobbles. I shake my head. The words repeat themselves over and over again in my mind, tainting me, tormenting me, and on each trip around, they lash out, inflicting another wound as the ache in my chest continues to grow until it's so intense that it's difficult to even take a breath. Turning away from his room, I lift my chin and press my lips into a thin line, trying to look strong and put together as I hurry down the hallway, desperate to get somewhere private. The only upside of this situation is that everyone else is outside, watching the news crew that pulled up awhile ago, so there will be no one to see me totally lose my mind over this boy.

I descend the stairs as quietly as possible before breathing a sigh of relief at the empty bar. A smashing sound echoes through the clubhouse, coming from upstairs, and I flinch as I slip down the hallway, running now as the tears threaten to fall. As soon as I'm in my room, I shut the door behind me and make sure it's locked before turning and pressing my back against it. Hot tears fall down my cheeks and something between a gasp and sob escapes me as I sink to my ass and clamp my hand over my mouth. The pain in my chest is so overpowering that I want to claw at my own chest, like I'm trying to physically rip my heart out so there is a valid reason for this pain I'm feeling and I reach over to my bed, grabbing my pillow and burying my face into it as I cry.

Memories from the last three weeks rush through my mind on a loop - that first night Travis and I had together, our breakfast at the cafe the morning after, the way he hauled me out of the diner over his shoulder, the night I danced for him, our food truck date, the night he took me up on the roof to look at the stars, the night in when he told me I was worth more than a quick fuck in the back...

Did it all mean absolutely nothing?

God, I'm so fucking stupid. From the very beginning, he told me it would never be anything more and I was happy with that arrangement. I never wanted or expected anything more but somewhere along the way things obviously changed. The problem is, I didn't realize just how much our relationship had changed until two minutes ago when I overheard him calling me "another in a long line". The idea of him with another woman pops into my mind, unbidden and completely unwelcome but my subconscious doesn't seem to care and I drop my head back against the door as the tears continue to fall.

I love him.

There is no other explanation. Somewhere along the way, while he and I were "just having fun", I fell head over heels in love with Travis Broussard. It should be a happy revelation or maybe a scary one but all I can feel is the pain of his words as they rip through me again, like I can't resist punishing myself with my own stupidity.

How could I fall in love with him?

He made things so clear to me and not once, did I ever think that there could be more for us so how did I let this happen? I remember what I said to him that first night, that sex didn't equal love to me but what I never planned for was the fact that our physical connection would pale in comparison to the emotional one we've built in the last twenty-one days. Travis is my person, the one I always look for in a crowd and the one who makes me feel safe when I'm feeling out of control and chaotic. He makes me feel seen and cherished.

My body shakes with my sobs as I grab the star pendant hanging around my neck and squeeze until the points of the star dig into my skin. It distracts me from my shattered heart but only for a fraction of a second before I remember the way he held me after Warren chased us through the mall and on the night of Fuzz and Piper's wedding. I felt something different then, something new but I dismissed it as stress. It wasn't and I should have known then. Travis has always been my sanctuary and despite the chaos raging around us, when we're together, nothing else exists. It's been that way from the beginning and I ball my fist before slamming it against the wall next to me.

So, so stupid.

For as long as I can remember, I've had walls up around my heart and as I look back, I don't think anyone has ever been able to scale them… not fully. Not even Travis but that's because he smashed them down with that first look and I didn't even notice. All of my hang-ups in my previous relationships didn't matter with him and I should have seen that it was more than just the "casual" nature of our relationship. Scoffing, I shake my head. We were never casual… or, at least, I wasn't. I just wish I would have realized that before I got my heart broken into a million pieces. Thinking back to my attitude when I first got here, I hit the wall again.

I didn't want this.

I wasn't looking for it and yet, here I am, sitting on the floor of my room, crying my eyes out over a man who makes me feel wanted and needed and seen, a man who stole my heart with his intense eyes and crooked grin, a man who ravaged me at every opportunity but also, somehow still made me feel cherished and a man who will never love me back. His words flicker through my mind again as anger and pain creep through me, twisting together so tightly that I can't even tell where one ends and the other begins but I'm not mad at Travis. He hasn't done a single thing wrong so I can't be mad at him. I wish I could be but the blame lies on me. I let myself fall for him even knowing that there could never be more than this.

My breathing stutters and I close my eyes again, taking a deep breath as I run through my options. On the one hand, I could completely cut things off with him and end it all right here and now but as I try to imagine that conversation, I don't think I can bring myself to do it. I could tell him I love him but there is no doubt in my mind where that would lead and then I would be back to option number one. Or… I could just keep going. But could I keep my feelings to myself while he and I continue our relationship? Could I really be the same with him knowing that a time will come when he will end it with me? It will suck but will it hurt any worse than breaking up now? Will my heart be anymore broken?

My tears slow as I open my eyes and stare up at the ceiling again as my mind races but the more I think about it, the more I know there is only one thing I can't do and that is walk away from him. I love him and there is a big part of me that feels like I might just love him for the rest of my life and I would rather spend every moment I can with him than walk away now and wonder how many moments I could have had. Plus, my heart just can't take it. I'm going into this knowing full well that it will end, that someday he will tell me that it's time to let go and move on but I can't be the one to do it.

Wiping the tears from my face, I suck in a breath and my body shudders with the aftermath of my meltdown as I turn to look at my bed. I have barely spent any time in this room but tonight, I think I need to sleep here. It's still too raw but maybe after a good night's sleep, I'll feel more equipped to face the reality of my situation tomorrow. Dragging myself off of the floor, I wipe my eyes again and take a deep breath as I sink into the mattress and lie back. As I pull the blanket up over my head, I turn on my side and snuggle into my pillow, my mind still going over everything that has happened with Travis over the past three weeks as tears threaten to fall again.

"Hell no, you need to go!"

Jerking up in bed, I scowl as the angry chanting pierces through the clubhouse walls, growing louder and louder with each second. What the hell is that? I throw the blanket off of my legs and sit up in bed before turning to look at the exterior wall. The chanting remains consistent, nagging at me to look for answers but there are no windows in the theater so to sate my curiosity, I will have to go out and interact with people. Turning, I glance at my face in the mirror before groaning and desperately trying to wipe the tears from my face. Not only do I not want Travis to see me crying and have to have that awful conversation but if Lincoln sees my tears, he'll rip Travis's throat out and ask questions later.

"Shit," I whisper as I stare at my red, puffy eyes in the mirror. This is a lost fucking cause. Looking around the room, I spot my giant sunglasses and decide "fuck it" as I grab them and slip them on before grabbing a hoodie and pulling it over my head. I put the hood up and open the door before shoving my hands in my pockets as I walk out. The clubhouse is empty and the chanting is louder out here so I peek out through the window at the bottom of the stairs. Protestors line the street out front, signs in their hands that tell us to leave Baton Rouge and that we're all going to jail and my brow furrows.

What the fuck is going on?

Turning away from the window, I cross the clubhouse to the front door and step outside. Everyone is congregated by the bikes, watching the people in the street scream with a mixture of fear, sadness, and anger flashing across their faces. Joining them, I step up next to

Tate and she glances over at me, frowning at my sunglasses before she sighs and wraps her arm around my shoulders.

"What's going on?"

She shakes her head. "Your guess is as good as mine. What's with the sunglasses?"

"Sun's bright," I answer, refusing to look at her as I point to the setting sun. It's barely peeking over the horizon now and there is no way in hell she bought that but I don't care. The clubhouse door opens and we all turn as Travis walks out. At first glance, his green eyes appear hard and cold but beyond that, there is fear and more pain than I've ever seen in him before. He stops when he sees us all huddled together and searches the group until his gaze lands on me and one corner of his mouth kicks up in a half smile. It's my smile - the one he always gives me when we're in a room full of people and pain ripples through my chest at the gesture. My heart pounds and tears sting my eyes. Even though I know he can't see it because of the sunglasses, I still feel like he's looking right through me and I turn away before he sees the one thing I'm desperately trying to hide from him.

"Streak," Blaze calls, turning to watch Streak as he tilts his head toward the crowd. "You got any fucking idea what's going on here? Or what the hell that reporter was talking about?"

I sneak a peek over at him as he drops his gaze to the ground and runs a hand through his hair, nodding. When he glances up again, a range of emotions flicker through his eyes.

"Yeah... I went upstairs and did some research after she showed up and asked us about our website..."

"We don't have a website," Chance says and Travis nods, shifting from one foot to the other before crossing his arms over his chest. I've never seen him so out of sorts and despite the ache I feel, I want to comfort him.

"That's the thing," he replies, shaking his head. "We do now and it's a pretty safe bet that Warren made it for us."

Moose scowls, cocking his head to the side. "Okay, but how does that explain this?"

"Storm's fake video is on there… as well as seven others, one from each of us. We're all spewing the same hate the fake Storm did and saying that we're going to come after the city of Baton Rouge."

Oh, shit.

This is bad.

"Fuck," Blaze whispers, horror in his voice as he turns back to the crowd and shakes his head. The white news van is still out front with a professional looking woman interviewing protestors as the rest of the crowd screams their hate at us. The thing is, I can't blame them. If I was in their position and I saw videos like the one of Storm that was posted, I can see how easily it would be to get enraged and demand justice or take matters into your own hands.

"How could you have missed this?" Storm asks and I glance over at him as he shoots a glare at Travis and my muscles tighten. Every part of me wants to surge forward, get in his face, and defend my man but if I get too close to Travis, if he touches me, I'll break. I will fall apart right here in front of everyone and I can't have that so instead, I cross my arms over my chest and rock back on my heels as I drop my gaze to the ground.

"I…"

"You were looking into my video so why didn't you think to look for others, Streak?" Storm rages, cutting him off and I blow out a breath and keep my gaze fixed on the ground. When silence blankets the group, I peek up. Travis sighs and grabs the back of his neck with a grimace.

"I didn't think of it."

Storm clenches his fist. "Goddamn it, Streak!"

"Hey," Blaze barks, turning back to all of us and commanding our attention as his gaze flicks over all of us. "We are not going to do this. This is a family and we have all been working our asses off to figure this out, including Streak, so knock it the fuck off. That's an order."

His words leave no room for argument and we all nod before turning to Storm. He stares at Travis with disappointment in his eyes but eventually, he nods also.

"I'm sorry, guys," Travis whispers and the pain in his voice breaks my fucking heart. The weight of the world is resting on his shoulder and most of the time he carries the burden without complaint but tonight, he looks like he's going to break. My chest hurts, this time for the man I love with every fiber of my being and tears fill my eyes as my body aches to close the distance between us and wrap him up in a hug. When he glances up and looks right at me, our connection sparks through the air like electricity and I can't stop myself any longer.

It will hurt.

It might even kill me but I won't leave him standing out in the cold.

Chapter Twenty-Five
Travis

Something has changed.

I scoff as the thought runs through my mind because it seems like our whole lives have been turned upside down in the two days since the protestors first showed up but in this instance, I'm talking about Rowan and me. As I stare out at the protestors lining the street, I lean back in my chair and think over the past two days since they first showed up, trying to find the moment that it all changed but I can't make any sense of it. She left my room that morning and we were good, better than ever and the way she smiled and pressed her lips to mine is burned into my memory but by the time people started gathering outside of the clubhouse, she was different. Her big ass sunglasses may have hidden her eyes from me but it didn't matter because it was evident in the way she avoided looking at me and the way her body slumped like she was in pain. But, why? Even when she hugged me after Storm went off, I could feel this distance between us that was never there before and it hasn't gotten any better since. Every single touch, every single kiss reveals the fracture in our relationship but I don't know what to do to fix it.

Sighing, I shake my head, unable to pull my eyes from the street where the protestors are still going strong as I take a sip of my beer and my stomach turns. Yesterday, the size of the crowd doubled from the day before and the same thing happened today. It's gotten so bad that Rodriguez sent officers over to make sure everyone remained civil… or as civil as you can be when an entire mob thinks you are monsters and wants to run you out of town. He also informed us that Sergeant Williams wouldn't be giving up on her investigation anytime soon and it's a safe bet that she's got guys watching us right now. With everything going on, it's not fucking ideal but, despite what the city of Baton Rouge thinks now, we're not monsters and we haven't done anything wrong.

"Don't you wish you could just march over there and yell at them that we're innocent and being set up by a psycho?" Fuzz asks, leaning back in his chair with a sigh before taking a sip of his own beer. I nod.

"Every fucking minute of every fucking day."

Storm sighs. "It probably doesn't look great that we're all sitting out here, drinking beer and watching them like we find this amusing or something."

Amusing is the last word I would use to describe this shit show. Our city has turned on us in an epic way and I honestly don't know how we can come back from this, how we ever get back to business as usual.

"What are we supposed to do?" I ask, resisting the urge to ball up my fist. The last thing we need is for any of us to look angry or aggressive out in the open, where the crowd can see us. It would only reinforce their beliefs if we showed the same rage they saw in the videos. "Are we supposed to hide inside until this is all over?"

"I'm sure that is what Warren would like us to do," Fuzz quips, his lip pulling back into a snarl for a brief second before he collects himself. "He wants us trapped and acting irrationally."

Blaze nods, his brows furrowed as he watches the people in the street scream at us and takes a sip of his own beer before sighing. "Makes all of us easier to slaughter."

"You all right, boss?" I ask, glancing over at him. He's been unusually quiet since last night when he called all of the guys into the war room to go over a game plan. We didn't come up with much of anything, though. Turning back to the crowd, I sigh. "Besides the obvious, I mean."

"Yeah… no… I don't know. I've just had a lot on my mind."

Storm frowns. "Like what?"

"My legacy," he answers, a deep, haunting sadness creeping into his eyes as he turns to look at the clubhouse. "This place, the club… it was never meant to be the mess it became before we made the decision to turn things around and when I got shot eight years ago, I thought that was it. I thought my legacy was going to be a piece of shit that sold guns and drugs to selfishly make himself as much money as possible. And then, I got a second chance. I've worked so hard to turn things around since then…"

"And you have, Blaze," I tell him, my brows furrowed as I glance over at my brothers. They look as bewildered as I feel. Blaze shakes his head.

"It won't matter. After all the work we've done to turn things around and all the good we've done for the people of this community, this is what we're going to be remembered for."

"You can't think like that, boss."

Blaze sighs and shakes his head again. "We have to be realistic, boys. Even if the protestors go away, even if we manage to prove our innocence and Williams drops her case against us, the name Bayou Devils MC will always have people in this city whispering. There is no way back and, in that sense, Warren has succeeded in his mission to tear this club apart."

"No... Blaze..."

"I don't like it anymore than you do, Streak, but it is what it is. All we can do now is adapt, forge ahead, wade through the mud and hopefully, when we get to the other side, we'll have enough pieces to rebuild."

"What are you really saying?" I ask him and he stares off into the crowd for a moment before shaking his head and dropping his gaze to the pavement in front of him as he takes a long pull of his beer before tossing the empty bottle in the trash can next to us.

"I don't know, Streak. I don't have anymore answers than you do but I just can't shake this feeling..."

Storm frowns. "What feeling?"

"Nothing," he says as he stands up and sighs. "I'm just a sad old man and not good company tonight. I'll see y'all tomorrow."

Without another word, he walks back toward the clubhouse and I turn back to Fuzz and Storm as they both shake their heads, their eyes haunted with Blaze's comments. Not that I can blame them. It was heavy shit and it has me so concerned for the future of my club.

"You know," Storm whispers. "I think I'm gonna head to my room, too."

Fuzz nods. "Yeah, I need to go find my wife."

They both stand up and tell me good night before walking back to the clubhouse and I sigh, my chest aching as I sink further into my seat and take a sip of my beer as I stare at the protestors. The sun is starting to set and soon, they'll start getting lanterns out and continue yelling into the night before finally crawling into their tents to get some sleep only to start all over again tomorrow. Now that the officers are here, we've been able to leave the clubhouse to run errands like grocery shopping which Tate, Blaze, and Emma did today so we're set to withstand the onslaught for a while but I hope it ends soon. The people in the street, they unknowingly taunt me with my inability to catch Warren or even figure out who he really is and each moment I have to listen to their chants, the more I feel like I'm going crazy.

I need Rowan.

"What the fuck did you do to my sister?!"

I turn as Kodiak charges out of the clubhouse with Tate right on his heels, desperately trying to grab him and stop him but he just brushes her off each time, his eyes blazing as he charges right for me. The ache in my chest is deeper when I think about the distance between us these past two days and the spark that has been missing from her eyes as I shake my head at him.

"Uh… nothing."

His lip curls back. "Bullshit. You did something to her."

"Lincoln," Tate urges, grabbing his arm as he stops in front of me and I peek a glance over at the crowd, which has grown suspiciously quiet.

"This is not a good place to do this, brother."

"Don't fucking call me that right now, you little fuck," he snaps, balling his fists at his sides. "The only reason I'm not snapping every single one of your fingers right now is because I promised Rowan I wouldn't unless I saw her crying because of you, which I haven't, but she hasn't been acting normal so whatever the fuck you did, fix it. And if you break her heart or hurt her in any way, so help me God, I will fucking end you. Are we clear?"

My gaze flicks back to Tate and she chews on her bottom lip as she flashes me a wide-eyed look. I consider telling him that our relationship is casual before Storm's comment about him dropping me off of the roof pops into my mind. Instead, I nod. "I got it."

"Good. I saw her going up to the roof ten minutes ago to read."

"You're ordering me around now?" I ask, arching a brow and he takes a menacing step toward me. I hold my hands up in surrender before I set my bottle of beer down and stand up. "Fine. I'm fucking going."

"Not one goddamn tear, Streak," he calls after me as I walk toward the clubhouse and I raise my hand to let him know I heard him. Emma and Quinn are lounging on the couch when I slip inside, watching their kids play around them and I nod to them before walking over to the stairs and taking them two at a time. I have no fucking clue what I'm going to say to Rowan or how I'm going to get her to open up and tell me what is bothering her but I know I have to. The distance between us is killing me and it has to be doing to same to her so I'll do whatever it takes.

Opening the door to the roof, I step outside and she glances over her shoulder at me from the air mattress that has been up here since the night I surprised her with star gazing. A range of emotions flicker through her eyes before her brows knit together and pain swarms her gray depths. It only lasts a second, a fraction of one even, before she regains her composure and turns away from me. It doesn't matter though because it was enough to confirm for me that this isn't all in my head.

But what the fuck is going on?

"Hey," I say, rubbing my sweating palms on the side of my jeans as I close the distance between us and sink onto the mattress next to her. "What are you doing?"

She holds her book up. "Reading."

Fuck.

Now what the hell do I say to her?

I try to come up with something to say, something witty that will make her say more than a couple of words to me or hell, at this point, I would settle for something that will make her angry enough to start talking but my mind is completely blank. Peeking over at her, I watch her read her book and remember her doing the same thing in my bed as I worked. Each time she would feel me looking at her and glance up, offering me a smile before she turned back to the page in front of her but now, she won't even give me even a sliver of attention.

"You want to go back to my room and watch a movie?"

She shakes her head. "Maybe later."

"Well," I muse, nudging her with my shoulder. "Can I get a kiss?"

Looking up, she turns to me and searches my eyes for a second before leaning forward and pressing her lips to

301

mine but there is no feeling behind it. All of the fire and connection that was there two days ago is gone and when she turns back to her book, I rake my hands through my hair before turning to look out at the horizon.

You know what?

Fuck this.

I'm not this fucking pathetic and I'm crazy about this girl so we're going to hash everything out right now. As I glance over at her again, I decide to go with the angry option since she always reveals more than she means to when she's all fired up, and swipe her book out of her hand. Her head snaps up and she levels a glare at me.

"What the fuck do you think you're doing?"

Closing the book and tucking it under my arm, I shrug. "Getting your attention."

"Congrats, you got it. Now give me the book back," she snaps, holding her hand out expectantly and I search her gaze. She's mad but not mad enough to spill the beans so I flash her a grin and shake my head.

"No."

Pain flashes through her eyes again and she turns away from me as she stands up. "Fine. I think I'm going to go to bed."

"Hell no," I growl, shooting to my feet and grabbing her arm as she tries to walk away from me. I spin her around to face me but she stares at the floor and shifts her weight from one foot to the other before going back again. My throat constricts, feeling painfully tight, as my thoughts spin.

Why is she doing this to me?

"Rowan," I whisper, cupping her cheek and she grips my hand with both of hers as they tremble. I force her head up but her eyes are closed, blocking me from her thoughts. "What is going on, baby?"

"I can't do this." Freeing herself from my grip, she turns to go back inside and gasps, stopping in her tracks as she looks out at the street. I scowl, taking a tentative step toward her.

"What's wrong?"

She points out to the street and I follow her hand. There, in the middle of the crowd, stands Warren in his white mask and dressed in all black. The other protestors mill around him like he doesn't even exist and he has his head tipped back, staring straight at Rowan and me. Eliminating the distance between us, I wrap my arms around her and press a kiss to the side of her head.

"Time to go inside, Princess."

She shakes her head and turns back to me. "Don't tell me what to do."

"This isn't a negotiation," I argue, arching a brow as I dare her to defy me with a look. Unfortunately, she does. Crossing her arms over her chest, she mimics my expression and shifts her weight to one foot as she pops her hip out. God, I love this side of her but I'm not backing down. I don't want her out here with Warren down there, even if there is a fence, a crowd of people, a building, and the entire club between them. The thought of him even looking at her makes me want to put my fist through a wall and all his taunts about making her his come rushing back to me.

I need to get her somewhere safe.

When she still won't back down, I shrug and grab her, tossing her over my shoulder before turning and heading for the stairs.

"Put me down!" she yells, pounding her fists against my ass but I don't give a shit. I'll do whatever it takes to protect her and she can be mad at me all she wants.

Ignoring her tantrum, I carry her down the stairs and turn toward my room before ducking inside, shutting the door and locking it. Once we're safely inside, I let her go, sliding her body down mine and when she lands on her feet, her breath catches in her throat as our eyes meet.

There it is.

Our spark, our connection is back, and it swirls through the air around us as my heart pounds in my chest and everything that has been off for the past two days clicks into place. Our breaths tangle together in the space between us and we inch closer, neither one of us able to stop it or pull our gazes away and when she places her hand on my chest, the feeling radiates throughout my entire body.

"Rowan," I whisper, brushing my thumb over her cheek as her eyes flutter closed like she's savoring every second of it and I lean in, letting my lips brush over hers. She gasps, jerking back and shaking her head as she grips my shirt in her fist.

"I… can't. I'm so sorry."

"Why?" I ask, struggling to take a breath over the ache throbbing through me at her rejection. When she doesn't answer me, I reach for her but she releases my shirt and pulls away, her eyes shut tight as she continues shaking her head. "What's going on, Rowan? What is happening between us? I need to know because I fucking hate this and… I miss you, Princess."

Her eyes snap open and the tears in her eyes steal the air from my lungs. "I can't do this."

"Rowan," I repeat as she turns toward the door and unlocks it. My feet are glued to the floor and as much as I want to go after her as she pulls the door open and slips into the hallway, I can't move, too stunned to do anything but gape at her retreating form as everything inside me crumbles.

Chapter Twenty-Six
Rowan

"This is hell," I whisper to myself as I pull my knees to my chest and wrap my arms around them. The sky is clear today and the sun beats down on me as the protestors on the street below continue their screaming for the fourth day in a row but in a weird way, I'm kind of getting used to their constant berating. My gaze travels over the crowd before landing on the real source of my unease – Warren.

He's not chanting.

He's not screaming.

He's not holding up a sign that tells us all to leave town immediately.

He's just standing there in the middle of the protestors and staring up at me.

Apparently, after Travis and I first saw him last night, he informed the others and Blaze called Rodriguez to go grab him but by the time he made it through the mass of people, our mystery stalker was gone. When he showed up again this morning, we called again and Rodriguez went after him but somehow, he managed to slip away before Diego could get to him and at this point, he has told us that he'll keep an eye out but we need to stop calling him. I think the guys would be mad except there isn't really anything Rodriguez could do if he did catch Warren. As far as anyone outside of this building is concerned, he's just a man protesting in a mask and there is nothing illegal about that.

It would be nice to finally know who he really is, though.

Sighing, I turn away from the crowd but Warren's eyes seem to burn straight through me still and it makes my skin fucking crawl. A part of me wants to go back inside but the other part doesn't want to leave this spot when going inside means being cooped up with Travis. And I can't do anything around him without feeling like my heart is being smashed into a thousand pieces. Avoiding him takes every ounce of willpower I possess but it hurts. Every second that I spend across the room from him, telling myself not to glance in his direction is hell but being in his arms again, kissing him when I know the end is coming for us is pure agony. My mind drifts to the moment we shared in his room last night and tears sting my eyes. I can't be with him and it kills me to be without him so I'll just keep hiding up here on the roof, avoiding everyone, until I get a handle on my emotions.

Or hell freezes over.

I'm not sure which one will come first.

The door to the roof opens and my heart jumps into my throat as I glance over my shoulder before releasing a breath as Tate steps outside. She flashes me a smile and I do my best to return it but I know it looks forced. There is a gleam of determination in her eyes as she marches over to me and plops down next to me on the air mattress. My belly flips.

"How are you?" she asks, propping her elbows on her knees and cocking her head to the side as she studies me. I nod before turning back to the protestors.

"Good."

She hums. "You know not a single person believes that, right? Oh, and also, I'm having a hard time keeping your brother from murdering Streak so maybe y'all could work things out already?"

"There's nothing to work out, Tate," I whisper, peeking over at her as she scowls.

"What do you mean?"

I take a deep breath and meet her eyes. "If I tell you, you're sworn to the sister code… it's like girl code but even more intense and you can't tell a fucking soul."

"Okay," she agrees, nodding. Turning back to watch the people filling the street below us, I take another deep breath and try to ignore the relentless ache in my chest.

"I love him…"

"Streak?" she asks. I nod and she scoffs in return. "Well, obviously."

Glancing back at her, I shake my head. "We agreed to casual. On the first night I was here, he told me we would never be anything other than sex and then I was stupid enough to fall in love with him."

"And? Look, people say dumb ass shit all the time and then things change. Besides, I'm ninety-nine percent sure that boy loves the hell out of you, so what's the problem?"

"He's never had a girlfriend, Tate," I tell her, tears gathering in my eyes as I turn back to the crowd and Travis's words run through my mind. "He straight out told me that he was never going to fall in love with me and that he never wanted anything more than casual relationships. You don't see this as a problem?"

She sighs. "It's an annoyance, for sure, but he can't control how he feels anymore than you can. And I'm telling you, he's head over heels."

"Stop saying that," I plead, my heart breaking at the mere suggestion that he could love me back because I already know it's not true. One of the things I love about him is that he's completely upfront about everything. He's honest, to a fault, so if he felt something more, he would have said something.

"Girl…"

I shake my head. "No. I can't, okay? You really think someone that made such a big deal about never having anything more than casual relationships is suddenly going to decide he loves me and wants a real one? I'm not that naive and I know you aren't either."

"People are stupid, Row. I mean, you should have seen me before I met your brother… I was a fucking mess and then in walked Lincoln and I had no control over how he made me feel and it sure as hell wasn't an easy road to get to where we are now but we did it and I've never been happier. You just have to take a chance."

"And what if he says no?" I ask, my bottom lip wobbling at the thought. Pain pierces through me and I turn to the crowd as a tear slips down my cheek. Reaching over, she rubs her hand down my back and I peek back at her as she grins.

"Then your brother and I will make him regret that he was ever born."

Laughing through my tears, I shake my head. "I don't want him to get hurt."

A.M. Myers

"Oh, Lord," she whispers, pulling me into a half-hug as more tears fall down my cheeks. "You're so far gone, sweetie."

"I know."

Sighing, she just holds me as more tears fall down my face and even though I don't want it to, the idea of telling him how I feel pops into my mind. I picture sitting him down in his room and saying the words and then I imagine the horror on his face afterward. My heart shatters at the thought and I bite my lip to hold back the sob as I push it all to the back of my mind and cry. After a moment of my little pity party, I order myself to get it together before sitting up and taking deep breaths as I wipe my eyes.

"How long has he been down there?" she asks and I look over as she points to Warren before rolling my eyes.

"Awhile. He's just been watching me."

She does a dramatic little shiver next to me. "Fucking creepy ass son of a bitch."

"I know. Maybe it's the mask but when I see him... I get this hollow feeling in my chest like I'll never be happy again."

"Hell no. You can't think like that," she barks and I glance over at her as she narrows her eyes at him. "We'll figure this out and beat him and then things can go back to normal."

I arch a brow. "You really think that will happen?"

"I have to believe it will."

Nodding, I turn to look out at the crowd as the past month races through my mind. So much has happened and I have no idea what normal will look like for me since I was thrust into the middle of this but I'm looking forward to a bit of calm when this is all over.

"Who the hell is that?" Tate asks and I glance over to where she's pointing. At the front gate, the guys have gathered on one side, looking intimidating as hell as they stare at a man on the other side of the fence with a police escort and I squint, trying to see him better as the gate slides open.

"Holy shit…"

Tate turns to me. "What?"

"It's fucking Ash."

"What?" she whispers, turning back to Ash as he walks into the parking lot with all of the guys around him. "Cheating, piece of shit, scum-bag ex-boyfriend Ash?"

I nod. "Yep."

"Come on," she says as she jumps up and grabs my hand, pulling me up with her. "You go see what he wants and I'll go get my gun and taser."

Despite the situation, I laugh. "Is that necessary?"

"Is breathing?" she calls over her shoulder as she practically skips toward the door and I laugh as I follow behind her, trying to figure out what the hell Ash is doing here in Baton Rouge. Did I ever even tell him where I was going? Thinking back to the last time I spoke to him when I was in Texas, I shake my head. I don't think I did but I guess it wouldn't have been that hard for him to figure out since Lincoln is the only family I have left. That still doesn't explain why he's here, though.

The clubhouse is quiet when I step into the bar and I groan. Everyone is going to be outside to witness whatever the hell this is but I can't really say that I blame them. We've been practically climbing the walls for the past four days so at this point, anything is entertainment.

But that doesn't mean I want it to be at my expense. The sun blinds me as I step outside and I blink at the harsh light but I still can't see Ash because everyone has their back to me as they crowd around him.

"I'm here to see Rowan." His voice drifts over the crowd and I hear my brother's answering grunt. Oh, boy, that's not good.

"Yeah, you said that but you still haven't told me who the hell you are." Lincoln is in full-on protective brother mode and Ash should probably be happy that he doesn't already have his balls in a vise grip. The clubhouse door opens and Tate steps out, a huge grin on her face and her taser in her hand.

"No gun?" I whisper and she winks at me as she pulls up her shirt, revealing the holstered gun at her waist before she shakes her head at me.

"Of course I brought the gun."

"I'm Ash." His voice is shaky, pulling my attention back to the hidden confrontation, and I release a sigh.

Shit.

I need to get over there.

After nodding to Tate, I work my way through the crowd, hoping to reach them before any guns or tasers are pulled out.

"Is that supposed to mean something to me?" Lincoln asks, his voice unwavering and if I was Ash, this might be the point where I pissed my pants. My brother is an intimidating man even when he's not trying but when he wants to be scary, I don't know why anyone would challenge him.

"Y-Yeah," Ash answers. "I'm Rowan's boyfriend…"

"Ex-boyfriend," I snap as I finally get to the front of the group and step up next to Lincoln. He flashes me a look of annoyance and arches a brow but I glance over my shoulder, meeting Travis's gaze as he stands a few feet behind us. A hint of a smile tugs at his lips and color rushes to my cheeks before pain swarms my body and I turn away from him, training my gaze on Ash again.

"Row," he whispers. Relief splashes across his face as he takes a step forward and reaches for me. Lincoln shifts his body in front of mine, acting as a barrier as he crosses his arms over his chest.

"Hold up. You mean to tell me that my sister broke up with you and you followed her thirty-six hundred miles to Louisiana? Give me one good reason why I shouldn't kick your ass into next week, you little fuck."

Ash holds his hands up like that is somehow going to calm my brother down and I bite back a laugh. Honestly, after what he did to me, it's not even close to what he deserves but Lincoln doesn't know about that. Ash should probably thank his lucky stars for that small miracle.

"I just want to talk to her."

Lincoln takes a menacing step forward. "So you stalked her?"

"No!" he shouts, his voice cracking as he takes a step back and looks at all the other people around us like they're going to help him. "It's not like that."

Sighing, I loop my finger through Lincoln's belt loop and pull him back as I move to his side again and he flicks an annoyed glance down at me. Oh, well, he can just get over it.

"What do you want, Ash?"

His gaze snaps to mine and he smiles. "Hey, baby… can we go somewhere to talk?"

"Right here seems fine."

"You…" he murmurs, glancing between my brother and me before he looks at all of the guys standing behind us. "You want to talk right here? In front of everyone?"

I nod, mimicking my brother's pose as I arch a brow. I may not want Lincoln to kill him but that doesn't mean I forgive him for what he did or trust him. "Sure. Why not?"

"It's just that we need to talk… about what happened…" he says, running his hand through his hair as his gaze continues to bounce around the group. Tate steps up on the other side of Lincoln and he glances over at her, studying her for a moment, before turning back to glare at Ash.

"What happened?" he asks, his voice booming and full of threat as he turns and stares down at me with questions in his eyes. Shit. Maybe I should have been honest with Lincoln and told him what happened with Ash as soon as I got here but it seemed like the best move at the time. Then again, I'm not the one who brought it up so what do I have to feel guilty about? "Rowan. Don't fucking test me. What happened?"

"I walked in on him banging my co-worker," I admit, leveling a glare in Ash's direction as he drops his gaze to the concrete before turning back to my brother. "But I don't need you defending me, Lincoln. I can handle this."

"Bull fucking shit. This little pissant is not going to disrespect my baby sister like that and then show up here like he has any fucking right to you. I'm done with this whole fucking conversation."

"Jesus fucking Christ," someone whispers and I turn back to Ash as he sinks down to one knee and pulls a ring out of his pocket. His hand shakes violently as he holds it up to me and meets my eyes.

Oh, you've got to be kidding me.

"Rowan Grace Archer," Ash says as he wipes his free hand on his jeans. He honestly looks like he's about to throw up and I take a tiny step back. "I think I've loved you since the first day I met you and I know I made a huge mistake but you're my world..."

"You've got to be fucking kidding me," Lincoln growls and I peek back at all of the people behind us, searching the group for the one person I want to see more than anyone else but he's gone. Frowning, I turn back to Ash as he continues his proposal but my mind spins with thoughts of Travis.

"Everything since you left has been awful and I realized just how much I need you in my life. I want to spend forever with you, baby, and I'll do anything to make you happy. Will you marry me?"

He can't be serious.

Right?

I mean, not once since I walked out of the apartment that night have I given him the impression that there was ever a chance between us so it makes no sense that he's here, down on one knee and asking me to marry him. And if I didn't know I was in love with Travis before, I sure as hell would now since I can't seem to push thoughts of him from my mind. Shaking my head, I take a step forward and cover his hand with mine before pushing it down. "Ash... no."

"No?" he asks, bewildered, and I shake my head again as his gaze bounces around the group. There's no way he's surprised by my answer.... Right? He jumps to his feet and stares at me like I've lost my mind. "No?!"

"Hey, she gave you an answer," Lincoln snaps. "Which seems like more than you deserve and now it's time for you to leave."

"Whatever. I should have known better than to try and make a whore into a house wife," he snarls, his eyes burning a hole through me with their hatred before he turns his glare to my brother and smiles. "You know she was a stripper, right?"

My stomach drops and I gasp, taking a step back as Lincoln lunges at Ash, grabbing him by the collar and dragging him toward the gate with no regard for the protestors out front. My heart races as I watch them. Ash knew damn well that my brother had no idea what I was doing for work in Alaska and as I think about what Lincoln is going to say when he gets back, my stomach rolls.

"Hey, it's going to be okay," Tate whispers, wrapping her arm around my shoulders, and I notice that everyone else has moved away from us, pretending that they're minding their own business when clearly, they're not. Glancing over at Tate, I shake my head.

"I never wanted him to know."

She nods. "I know but he'll get over it, sweetie. He loves you way too much not to."

We watch Lincoln stop in front of the gate and punch in the code before sliding it open and tossing Ash out into the protestors as their screaming gets louder. After shutting the gate again and making sure it's locked, he marches back over to us and I take a step forward as my heart pounds so fiercely it feels like it's going to smash into my rib cage.

"Lincoln…"

He holds a hand up to stop me but doesn't say a word as he turns and stomps into the clubhouse. The door slams and Tate follows after him, flashing me a reassuring look as tears sting my eyes. I turn to look at Ash as he stands on the other side of the fence, smirking at me like he's enjoying watching my whole life fall apart around me. Turning away, my gaze lands on Warren in the middle of the crowd and just like on the roof, it seems like he's looking right at me and I glance over to where Travis was standing before he disappeared as a tear slips down my cheek. I've never felt more alone in my life and for the first time in a month, I wonder if coming to Baton Rouge was a mistake.

A.M. Myers

Chapter Twenty-Seven
Travis

Pressing the bottle of bourbon to my lips, I tip it back
and let the liquor pool in my mouth before swallowing it
down with a wince as I slam the bottle back on the bar.
The bourbon leaves a burn in its wake, blazing down my
throat before settling into a comforting warmth in my
stomach but no matter how many times I repeat the
process, I don't feel any of the relief I'm desperately
searching for. If it was going to drown out my pain, it
should have by now since I'm halfway through the
fucker. I arch a brow and lift up the bottle, swishing the
liquid around on the inside before setting it back down
with a sigh. The image of that loser getting down on one
knee in front of Rowan plays through my mind, the same
way it has since the moment I walked away from them
and my chest burns at the thought of his ring on her
finger. It's hard to imagine that she actually said yes to
him but I didn't stick around to find out and I spent most
of the day in my room, avoiding everyone.

I picture her in a white dress, walking down the aisle
to that asshole and grab the bottle, taking another swig of

bourbon before shaking my head. She wouldn't say yes…Then again, how in the hell did he know she was here in Baton Rouge? My mind flashes back to the morning we went to go see Tawny and our breakfast afterward. She told me that it was better to find out about his cheating now and that she hadn't been that upset by finding him with another girl but she also admitted to putting on a brave face at the time. Could she have started talking to him again? Is that why there has been this distance between us lately? Is she going back to him?

But if that were the truth, why wouldn't she just tell me?

We've always agreed that things between us were casual and had an expiration date so if she wanted to get back with this douche bag, she would have just said something. Right? Fuck, why does that bother me just as much, though? Sighing, I grab the bottle and take another swig of bourbon before slamming it back onto the bar. An image of her with that little shit pops into my head and I grit my teeth, remembering the way her skin felt beneath my fingertips and the way she moaned my name. It's been four days since the last time I was with her and each one feels like an eternity. I'm losing my fucking mind over here and the one thing that can make me feel better, the one person I need can't even stand to be in the same room as me.

What did I do?

My eyes burn and my chest aches as the morning the protestors showed up plays through my mind. We woke up in bed together and her smile was so damn bright and happy, making me believe that everything was going to work out, that we all stood a chance. I remember pressing my lips to her neck and inhaling her scent -

hazelnut and something else that I can't quite put my finger on but it always makes me think of warmth and comfort - and I slipped inside her, kissing her and making love to her until we were both shaking. And then everything fell apart. Pain splinters through me and I grab the bottle, flinging it at the wall and watching it shatter into a hundred pieces but even that doesn't relieve the ache in my chest.

Fuck.

I miss her.

"Are you okay?"

I spin around and meet her eyes as she stands at the entrance of the hallway, her arms crossed over her chest as she leans against the wall in her sleep shorts and tank top, watching me with a cautious gaze.

I wish she would look at me the way she used to.

Every part of me wants to close the distance between us, pull her into my arms, and tell her we're done with the bullshit but instead, I scoff and turn back to the bar. "Yeah, I'm fine."

"Clearly," she whispers and I peek back at her as she walks across the room. She goes to step behind the bar and I jump up.

"Stop!" I yell, making her jump as she looks up at me with wide eyes. "You don't have shoes on and I don't want you to get hurt."

She glances down at the broken glass on the floor before nodding and climbing onto one of the bar stools as I walk behind the bar and grab a broom. When I peek over at her again, she's staring down at the bar top and picking at it, refusing to meet my eyes but I can't look away from her and my mind wills her to glance up. Just one look from her – that's all I need right now to know that there's a little bit of hope for us but she refuses to meet my gaze and my throat feels tight as I turn and start sweeping up the glass.

"Did you say yes?" I hiss, clenching the broomstick as my stomach rolls at the thought.

Jesus Christ.

What the hell is wrong with me and what am I going to do with myself if she did agree to marry that fucker?

She sucks in a breath and I look up, unable to stop myself. Our eyes meet and the pain in her eyes shocks me to my core. I stumble back a few steps, glass crunching under my boots, but I still can't pull my gaze from hers. God, I've missed those eyes and even when she looks like she's about to cry, she's still the prettiest girl I've ever fucking seen. Her brows furrow as she studies me before slowly shaking her head and glancing down at the bar top again.

"Do you even fucking care, Travis?"

"What the fuck is that supposed to mean?"

She shakes her head and her breathing stutters, a sure sign that she is going to cry and I scowl as my grip on the broomstick tightens and it creaks under the strain. "Nothing."

None of this makes any goddamn sense and I have no idea what I can do to get her to open up to me but I know we can't keep going like this. We're both clearly miserable and one of us needs to put an end to it. She releases a heavy breath and slips off of the bar stool before turning and walking away from me. My heart jumps into my throat and I drop the broom, jumping over the bar before I even have time to register the move and closing the distance between us. She gets halfway across the room before I catch her, pulling her into my arms.

"What do you mean, Princess? Why would you ask me if I care?"

Silence descends over us but I wait, dead set on just holding her in my arms until she tells me what's wrong or it fixes itself. Either way works for me and I'll never say no when it comes to having her here, like this. She presses her hands and her forehead to my chest and I close my eyes as I pull her closer, feeling like myself again for the first time in four days.

"Come on, Row. Please talk to me," I plead and she shakes her head, slipping out of my grasp before I can stop her.

"I can't. I'm sorry."

I watch her for a second as she takes off for her room before going after her. This, whatever it is, ends now and we're not leaving a bedroom until she and I are back to normal. She gets all the way into her room before I'm able to grab her hand and spin her back to face me. Closing the door behind me, we stumble back into the wall and I cup her cheek in my hand, forcing her gaze to mine.

"No. Fuck that. I'm not letting you go. You're mine, Rowan."

Tears gather in her eyes and her bottom lip trembles as she tries to look away from me but I won't let her. "Please don't do this, Travis."

"Why?" I whisper, pressing my forehead to hers and closing my eyes. "Why can't I do this? Why can't I kiss you anymore?"

"Please."

I shake my head. "No, I'm not letting you go this time. Why have you been avoiding me? I miss you so much, baby, and I... I need you."

"Travis," she pleads, planting her hand on my chest and trying to push me away but I won't budge. Instead, I lean in and let my lips brush against hers as she closes her hand into a fist, gripping my t-shirt. "You don't understand."

"What don't I understand? Talk to me about it because I meant what I said, I'm not letting you go… unless you really did say yes to that asshole's proposal today?"

She shakes her head. "I didn't."

"Then you're mine. Say you're mine, Princess," I urge, desperate to hear her say the words but she shakes her head again as my throat tightens and I clench my teeth.

"I can't."

Come on, baby.

Give me what I want.

The last time we were this close pops into my mind and I remember how distant she was until I threw her over my shoulder and she got pissed off at me. I don't particularly want to make her mad but at this point, I'll do whatever it takes to get her to open up. Sucking in a breath, I grip her jaw in my hand and her eyes pop open like I just pressed the magic button. She stares up at me with wide eyes filled with surprise and there's a little spark of something else, something I recognize and I can't help but smile.

"There you are."

She narrows her eyes and tries to jerk out of my hold but she's not going anywhere. "Let me go."

"Not until you say you're mine."

"Fuck you," she seethes, gritting her teeth, but there is still an incredible amount of pain in her eyes that I just can't make sense of no matter how hard I try. Leaning in closer, I press my body to hers as she leans back against the wall.

"Gladly, but first, tell me what happened between us. What am I missing, Rowan?"

She lifts her chin in an act of defiance and locks gazes with me as my heart stalls at the walls she's built to keep me out. I can see them shining in her eyes, so strong but I don't back down. I can't. Our breaths tangle in the space between us and I shift my body, pressing into her as I demand her surrender with just a look. Little by little and brick by brick, I see her defenses start to crumble and I resist the urge to grin as I brush my thumb over her cheek to encourage her to open up to me. Just when I think she's exactly where I want her, she drops her gaze to the floor.

"Look at me."

She shakes her head. "No."

"Look at me," I urge, brushing my thumb over her cheek again and she tips her head back but her eyes are squeezed together, shutting me out. I stare down at her beautiful face for a moment, trying to think of something I can do to get her to open her eyes but when a tear slips down her cheek, I can't take it anymore. I can't stand to see her cry and she may hate me right now but I know this is what she needs. Blowing out a breath, I lean in and claim her lips, commanding her body to relent to me. It's stiff at first and she pushes on my chest but not enough to make me think she actually wants me to stop so I flick my tongue against the seam, demanding entrance. She sighs as her lips part and she melts into me just like every other time and every cell in my body sings at the small victory. This is always where we're meant to be, just like this in each other's arms, and she knows it as much as I do. Gripping my t-shirt in her hands, she makes a pleading sound in the back of her throat as she pulls me closer like she can't stand to be away from me anymore and I smile into her kiss.

Fucking finally.

Bending down, I pick her up and press her back against the wall again as she wraps her legs around my waist and throws her arms over my shoulders, her kiss growing hungry and desperate. I can't fucking blame her though. These past four days have been hell and I've missed her so damn much that this feels like a dream.

"Say you're mine, Rowan," I command, pulling my torso away from her as she leans back into the wall with her shoulder and shakes her head. Reaching down, she tugs on my shirt before pulling it up over my head. As soon as it hits the floor behind me, I pull her back to me and seal her lips to mine again, pulling her away from the wall and walking over to the couch. I sink into it with her straddling my thighs and she plants her hands on my chest, her hips rocking against me as she whimpers into the kiss. She drags her lips to my neck and kisses a line down to my shoulder as my head falls back and my hands slip under her shirt.

"Take my clothes off, Travis," she whispers, working her way back up to my lips and I groan when we connect, dragging her shirt up her body before only pulling away long enough to rip it over her head. Her bra comes next, hitting the floor behind her, and I cup her tit in my hand before sucking her nipple into my mouth. Gasping, she arches her back, pushing her chest closer to me and I flick the sensitive little bud with my tongue, pulling a breathy moan out of her before I release her with a pop.

"Give me what I want, baby."

She shakes her head, rocking her hips against my cock and I thrust up into her as I grit my teeth but it's not enough. I fucking need her and I'm desperate to feel her skin on mine. With a growl, I grip a chunk of her hair and pull her lips back down to mine as I grab her hip with my other hand and help her grind on my lap. She pulls away and stumbles off my lap with ragged breaths. My heart jumps into my throat as I glance at the door, wondering if she's going to make a run for it but when I turn back to her, she's unbuttoning her jeans and nodding to mine.

"Off."

I resist the urge to smile as I pop the button of my jeans. Fire lights up her eyes for the first time in days and like an addict, I can't get enough. After shoving my jeans down my legs and kicking them off, I sit back down on the sofa and wrap my hand around my cock as I watch her slide her red lace panties down her legs. As she kicks them across the room, she looks up and her eyes lock with mine, all of that attitude and sass I love so much shining back at me and my chest feels like it's going to explode. There she is. These little moments of the way things were between us before a few days ago keep giving me hope that this isn't truly over and as soon as one ends, I'm impatiently waiting for the next one.

"Come here," I tell her, holding out my hand and color stains her cheeks as she walks back to me and climbs onto my lap. Reaching up, I press my hand to her cheek and search her eyes as she stares down at me but she's not giving anything away. Those fucking walls are back up in full force, completely blocking me from her thoughts.

I fucking hate it.

"Touch me, Travis," she whispers, the look in her eyes shifting to a plea as she rocks her hips on my lap and I groan, pulling her down to kiss her as I drag my other hand up her thigh.

"You're so fucking beautiful, baby."

She moans and reaches between us, wrapping her fingers around my cock. "Please."

"You want me to touch you?" I ask, peppering her lips with quick kisses that just tease and she nods frantically, pumping my length in her hand. Fuck, it feels so good that I just want to lose myself in her but I'm on a mission tonight. I go in for another kiss but this one is different, softer, lingering, and when she starts to melt into me, just when she thinks I'm going to give her what she wants, I pull back. "Tell me you're mine."

She blinks at me before narrowing her eyes into a glare. "Fuck you."

"Just as soon as you give me what I want," I tell her. She studies my face before releasing my cock and letting out a huff of annoyance as she tries to climb off of me. I don't let her. Holding her hip firm in one hand, I reach between us with the other and just let my thumb graze her clit. Her eyes widen and her hips buck. Her expression changes, flashing me begging eyes as she rocks her hips, trying to get the sensation back but I keep it just out of reach

"Travis," she whispers, the ache in her voice going straight to my balls and I fight the urge to give her exactly what she wants, only grazing her clit again. She moans.

"You want more?"

Nodding, she braces her hands on my shoulders and rocks her hips again. "Yes."

"Tell me you're mine."

"Fuck me first," she whispers, closing her eyes and letting her head fall back as I brush my thumb over her little bud again. "And I will. Please, Travis… please."

Shit.

How am I supposed to deny her when she looks like a fucking goddess and she's begging me for more? This doesn't mean I'm giving up but I'll just have to use something else. Rowan isn't the only one with moves. Pressing my thumb to her clit, I begin circling it and her head snaps up, her eyes lock with mine, and her lips part as she gasps for air, her fingers digging into my shoulders. I slip my fingers down to her pussy and groan as I drag them back up, covered in her arousal. Her hips rock, getting herself off on my fingers as I watch and I hiss a curse as I stare down at her, enraptured.

How in the fuck did I lose the upper hand here?

"Tell me you're mine," I tell her, pulling my fingers away and she cries out, turning hate filled eyes on me as she shakes her head.

"No." Before I can say anything else, she climbs out of my lap and drops to her knees in front of me, flashing me a devious smile as she wraps her fingers around my cock and closes her lips over the tip.

Fuck me.

"Rowan," I breathe, threading my fingers through her hair as she takes my length into her mouth and sucks, her tongue massaging the underside of my shaft as it pulses with need. She slowly pulls back, dragging her lips over every inch of me and I struggle to catch my breath as my eyes roll back. When she drags her teeth gently over the head, I growl, reaching down and grabbing her arm before hauling her back onto my lap.

Fuck, I need inside her.

Nothing else matters.

"Oh," she whispers as I rub my cock along her slit before pressing against her entrance. Looking up, I meet her eyes and she grabs my shoulders again, nodding for me to push inside her.

"Tell me," I urge, gritting my teeth as every cell in my body screams at me to slip into her pussy. She shakes her head as she starts sinking down on me and I'm a fucking goner. Relief rushes through me as she takes me deep, her body gripping me and pleasure floods my body. Groaning, I grip her hips as she starts to move, slowly rising up on her knees before dropping down again in a torturous pace that sends a wave of painful bliss rushing through my body.

Damn it.

This is never going to get me what I want.

Eyeing the other end of the couch, I wrap my arms around her waist and pick her up as she clings to me and shrieks with surprise as I carry her over there and lay her down on her back. One leg gets thrown over my shoulder as I perch on the edge of couch and slip inside her again. This time I hold nothing back, slamming into her aggressively as she writhes and moans beneath me, gasping for air as her tits bounce with each thrust of my hips. Just when I'm about to lose control, I stop and pull out of her but keep her pinned beneath me.

"Tell me you're mine, Rowan." My voice is hard this time, commanding, but she still flashes me a look of defiance before shaking her head and lifting her hips off of the couch.

"Fuck me."

Growling, I drive into her again and resume my pace, pounding her sweet little pussy as I reach up and wrap a hand around her throat. Her eyes widen but a smile tugs at her lips as she cups her tits in her hands, toying with her nipples.

Jesus Christ, she's trying to kill me.

The pressure builds and one look at her tells me she's just as close as I am so I slow down, keeping it just fast enough to keep her orgasm alive.

"You want to come, baby?"

She nods. "Yes."

"Then tell me what I want to hear."

She flashes me a look that screams "fuck off" as she reaches down between us and circles her clit with her fingers and I can't help but smile as I pull her hand away and pin it over her head.

"I don't think so, sweetheart. You want to come, you have to give me what I want."

Growling, she tries to rock her hips in an attempt to urge me to give in to her but it's not happening. Flashing her a grin, I increase my speed but not enough to get the job done and she groans loudly as she squirms beneath me.

"I fucking hate you."

I shake my head. "No, you don't."

"Yes, I do. I fucking hate you, Travis," she snaps but her eyes betray her as she stares up at me with what is supposed to be a glare. Even knowing that she's lying her ass off, I hate hearing those words roll off her tongue and I grit my teeth for a moment before leaning down and slamming my lips against hers as I give her what she wants. My pace is merciless as I grip her jaw and kiss her with all of the anger I feel over her comment and she screams into the kiss as her pussy clenches around me with her release. It steals the breath from my lungs and I groan as I rip my mouth from hers and thrust into her three more times before my body lets go with such fierceness that I swear I see stars.

"Travis," she whispers, clawing at my back and I groan again, my cock throbbing with my release as I bury my face in the crook of her neck and try to catch my breath. Rowan has other ideas. She pushes me off of her just enough that she can guide my lips to hers and clings to me as she kisses me like never before. My cock jerks inside her, ready to go again, and I groan as I pull back and meet her eyes.

"Say it, baby. Tell me you're mine."

She sighs, her eyes softening as she shakes her head. "Of course I'm yours, Travis. Always."

Chapter Twenty-Eight
Rowan

"Incoming," Travis whispers as the clubhouse door opens and I peek over my shoulder as my brother steps out into the setting sunlight, scanning the lot before his gaze lands on me. My belly flips. He hasn't said a single word to me since throwing Ash out of the parking lot yesterday and I've barely even seen him as I've spent the day moping around the clubhouse, waiting for this moment. Travis drags his hand down my back and my body relaxes slightly as I turn back to him. He smiles and presses his lips to mine before standing up. "I'll be at the bar. Come find me when you're done."

A smile tugs at my lips despite my shaking hands and I nod. "I will."

"One more," he murmurs before leaning in to steal one last kiss before turning and walking back to the clubhouse. Travis and Lincoln pass each other and nod in greeting but tension fills the air around them and I sigh at just how ridiculous they are. My brother closes the distance between us, his hands shoved in his pockets and his gaze glued to the ground in front of him as my heart thrums in my chest.

Oh, God, I'm so nervous.

"You two work things out?" he asks as he sits next to me on the picnic table and I sigh as my mind drifts back to last night. Heat rushes to my cheeks as I think about everything we got up to in my room and butterflies flap around in my belly. I can't help but grin. After what happened, I know I can't stay away from him anymore but I'm not naive enough to think that he's suddenly going to decide he wants more. This will end and it will hurt but I don't want to focus on that anymore. I want to be happy and enjoy the time I do get with him instead of ruining it all by obsessing over the end. Maybe it's reckless and stupid but all I can do at this point is jump back in with both feet and deal with the aftermath when the time comes.

"Yeah, I guess we did."

He glances over at me, his expression hard. "Did he apologize for whatever asshole thing he did to upset you?"

"It wasn't like that, Linc. Travis has been amazing to me."

"If that were true," he growls, crossing his arms over his chest and turning back to the crowd. "He wouldn't have hurt you."

I lay my hand on his bicep and he meets my eyes. "Please believe me, big brother. Travis has been nothing but kind, respectful, and honest with me since the beginning."

"Then why have y'all been avoiding each other for four fucking days?"

"It was my issue," I whisper and he sighs as his gaze flicks to the crowd. There is a current of tension swirling in the air around us and my belly flips again as I try to figure out what he's going to say about the information Ash revealed. If I know my brother, and I do, he's going to rip me a new one and spend the next hour chewing me out about how I'm better than that. The silence stretches between us and the longer it takes him to kick off the conversation, the more anxious I feel. Dropping my gaze to the ground, I shove my hands in the pockets of my hoodie and my knee shakes, bouncing up and down as I try to telepathically will him to say something. Finally, he clears his throat.

"I owe you an apology, Rowan."

My head snaps up. "What?"

"Look," he sighs, running a hand through his hair. "I've tried my damndest to be the best big brother I could be but clearly, somewhere along the way I failed you. I made you feel like you couldn't come to me and tell me absolutely anything because I would judge you. That's on me and it fucking kills me…"

"Lincoln, please… stop. It wasn't like that, at all. Stripping wasn't something I was proud of. I didn't tell anyone about it except Ash and we can all see how that turned out for me. This isn't on you."

"Yeah, it is and I know I've been too protective at times but I've only ever wanted you to be happy and safe. That's it and I'm so fucking sorry if I made you feel like there were things about yourself that you couldn't tell me."

I shake my head and tug on his arm, forcing him to look at me and the pain in his eyes hurts worse than anything else I have ever felt. Tears sting my eyes and I shake my head again. His face crumples and he pulls me into a hug, crushing me to his massive body as a wave of comfort washes over me.

"All I ever wanted was to make sure you didn't feel like you were missing out on anything because Dad was gone and here I fucked it all up."

"Lincoln," I whisper, a tear trekking down my cheek as I pull back to look at him. "Please don't ever think that. You are amazing and I've always thought that. The way you stepped up after Dad died and became the man of the house even though you were still a kid yourself… I've always admired you and if anything, I didn't tell you about the stripping because I just wanted you to be proud of me."

He smiles. "I am proud of you, kid. Fucking always… but can I ask you a question?"

I nod.

"Why stripping?"

Sucking in a breath, I turn to look out at the protestors as the question runs through my mind but the more I ask myself why I did it, the more stumped I feel. Turning back to him, I shrug and force a smile to my face.

"Would it be too cliche to say daddy issues?"

He winces and I immediately regret my terrible joke. "I'm sorry… I didn't mean that…"

"No," he whispers, nodding his head. "You did and I even understand. As hard as I worked, as much as I tried, I couldn't be Dad and his absence left a hole in all of us."

I sigh in agreement as I lay my head on his shoulder. "Honestly, after you left Alaska, I just felt so numb and… empty. I don't know that I was thinking about much of anything those days… I was just going through the motions and surviving each and every day as it came at me."

"I guess I have another thing to apologize for then," he says and I scrunch up my nose in confusion as I lift my head off of his shoulder and look at him.

"Huh?"

"For leaving Alaska. I shouldn't have bailed on you and Mom like that."

I scoff and lie back down. "Don't be fucking ridiculous. You couldn't live your whole life for us, Lincoln. It's not right and neither Mom or Dad would have been okay with that. My issues do not need to be shouldered by you, as much as I appreciate your mushy, soft heart."

"Shut the hell up with that shit." He laughs, shaking his head as he peeks down at me. I grin at him and he rolls his eyes. "Can I ask you something else?"

"Always."

He lifts his shoulder, prompting me to lift my head up and glance at him. He searches my face for a moment and my belly flips.

"Are you in love with him?"

I blink. "Travis?"

"Yeah," he answers, still trying to read me and my heart hammers in my chest as my hands shake. "Do you love him, Rowan?"

I nod. "Yes… but you can't… you can't tell anyone or say anything to him…"

"So this is what the past four days have been about? You love him and he doesn't love you back? I swear to God, I'll kick his ass until he has enough fucking sense in his head to realize you're the goddamn best he's ever going to get. That little motherfucker isn't going to mess my little sister around…"

"Lincoln," I cut in, laughing at his rant and furious expression as I lay my hand on his arm again. "Please, don't. I know what I'm doing."

He shakes his head. "You're going to get your heart broken."

"I know," I murmur, the ache in my chest so fierce that I struggle to breathe through it as I try to put on a brave act. Lincoln's gaze flicks over my face, studying me, before he scoffs and rips his arm from me.

"What's so special about this dick hole that he thinks he can do better than you? He would be the luckiest son of a bitch alive to call you his and he's rejecting you?" The disgust on his face as he glances over at the clubhouse has me grabbing his arm all over again, hoping he doesn't decide to march in there and confront Travis.

"Please, Linc... the whole thing is complicated. Just let me handle this. Please."

He shakes his head, looking at me like I'm insane. "I'm not going to let him hurt you."

"I'm already in too deep and I can't go back now. Whether we end today or months from now, it'll hurt and I've accepted that."

"Well, I fucking haven't," he huffs as his gaze snaps to the clubhouse door and I pull on his arm, making sure he stays here with me and hears me out.

"You can't make him love me, Lincoln... and I wouldn't want you to."

He huffs in annoyance again as he glances back at me and I can see him thinking through everything I've just said. Finally, he sighs.

"Do I, at least, get to kick the shit out of him when it all goes down?"

Laughing, I shrug. "Maybe. Talk to me then and we'll see."

"It's fucking something, I suppose," he growls, crossing his arms over his chest again and brooding as he stares out at the protestors. His jaw ticks and I would bet good money that he's planning exactly what he is going to do to Travis if I ever give him the green light. I can't see myself doing that but I guess we'll see. "Hey... one more thing..."

"What?"

He sighs. "I'm sorry that I pulled you here to Baton Rouge in the middle of this mess. If I had known it was going to get this bad... I would have made you stay in Alaska."

"There is no way in hell I was staying there after what Ash did."

"Oh, yeah," he mutters, turning to me with a look of disgust. "What did happen with all of that? I hope you made him pay."

I shrug. "He lost me so I'd say he's hurting pretty bad... even if he doesn't know it yet. Oh, and I hurled breakable things at the wall in an attempt to impale the two of them with clay."

"Good." He laughs before glancing at me with an evil grin. "Speaking of which... maybe I'll just let Tate loose on Streak when..."

His words are interrupted by the sound of glass shattering and we both jerk toward the protestors as one of them lights a rag on fire before hurling a mason jar filled with liquid over the fence. It lands on Chance's truck and flames roar up from the impact.

"Holy shit..."

Lincoln wraps his arm around me and we stand up as another protestor lights another Molotov cocktail and flashes us a grin. He hurls it over the fence and I watch in horror as it sails toward us with remarkable accuracy before landing on the pavement a few feet in front of us.

"Fuck. Get inside now," Lincoln orders, shoving me toward the clubhouse door as he follows behind me and another cocktail flies over the fence.

Oh, shit.

This is so bad.

The street is full of people and we're trapped in here like rats.

"Blaze!" Lincoln roars as soon as we step inside and everything in the room screeches to a halt before Storm turns the music down, a look of concern on his face.

"What's going on?"

Lincoln releases me and they huddle together, whispering about the situation before they march off toward Blaze's office and everyone else turns to me. My heart climbs into my throat and I point to the window.

"Look outside."

They all rush to the closest window and gasps fill the room followed by angry hisses and whispered curses but I turn away from them, desperate for only one person and before I can even fully turn around, his arms wrap around me and he buries his nose in my hair.

"What's happening, Princess?"

I pull back and meet his eyes. "The protestors... they're throwing Molotov cocktails over the fence... one hit Chance's truck and one almost hit me."

"Fuck," he snarls, his face the picture of rage as he pulls me tighter into his body. He's shaking and his heart is racing against my ear and I grip his t-shirt, clinging to him with everything I have. Storm, Blaze, and Lincoln step out of Blaze's office and Blaze whistles to get everyone's attention.

"We can't stay here anymore."

Murmurs of agreement ripple through the room.

"I'm going to call Rodriguez and get us an escort out of here but y'all need to go pack and we need to be quick. Understand?"

My mind is blank as his words slip in one ear and race out of the other. A chill descends over me as I turn to look out of the window, trying to put all of the pieces together but it's like someone dumped a hundred different puzzles in a bag and I can't find any that fit. Travis grabs my arms and gives me a little shake, forcing me to focus on him as he meets my eyes.

"Go pack your stuff, baby, and I'll be down in just a minute, okay?"

I nod on autopilot and when he releases me to go to his own bedroom, I walk across the bar as chaos rages around me. Flames dance in the window as I pass by it and it feels like something out of a dream. I lean my shoulder against the wall in the hallway and close my eyes, remembering the cocktail hitting the ground right in front of me and tears sting my eyes. When I open them again, I lightly slap my face and suck in a breath.

"Get it together, Rowan."

I take a few seconds to take a couple of deep breaths to calm myself down and when I feel more in control, I push off of the wall and slip into my room. Moving through the room like a tornado, I throw things into my bags haphazardly, not even checking if things are clean before I shove them into my luggage and when it seems like I have everything, I zip my bags closed and carry them out into the main room. Travis is back at the bar, two bags at his feet as he chugs some whiskey straight from the bottle.

Excellent.

"I know this looks bad," he says, glancing over at me when I stop next to him and drop my stuff on the floor. I arch a brow.

"You think?"

He nods and takes another swig. "Thing is, I was already too tipsy to safely drive so this seemed like the best thing I could do."

Sighing, I decide not to argue with him about it when we clearly have much bigger things to worry about. The move is dumb as hell and unreasonable but if he was already well on his way to drunk before shit hit the fan, which he was, I can't expect him to think rationally. He offers me some and I shake my head. He may not be able to drive but I can and it's going to stay that way.

"Any idea where we're going to go?"

He shrugs. "Someone suggested Emma and Nix's house since it's fucking massive and already secured."

"Why is it secured?" I ask and he takes another drink before slamming the bottle back down on the bar with a wince. His eyes look glassy and I sigh. Jesus, he's so far gone already.

"We use their house sometimes to keep the girls we rescue safe until we can move them so Blaze ordered that we make it as safe as we can for them," he says before grabbing the bottle again. "They have cameras, perimeter fences, motion detectors… the works."

I nod, turning to gaze out over the clubhouse as people frantically try to pack everything we could possibly need and my heart climbs into my throat when I hear the sound of glass breaking again. This clubhouse, which has felt so safe since the moment I got here, now feels as dangerous as the other side of the fence and I don't want to be here another second longer than we have to. After a few more minutes, Blaze steps into the room and whistles again.

"Okay, Rodriguez will be here momentarily with the fire department so let's get all this shit packed into cars and get out of here."

I turn to Travis and hold out my hand. "Give me your keys."

"Yes, ma'am," he answers, digging them out of his pocket and dropping them into my hand before he stands up with his bottle and stumbles. My muscles tense, ready to react if I have to but he catches himself and takes a deep breath as he stands up straight.

"Do we really need to bring that?" I ask, pointing to the bottle as I grab my bags and he glances down at it before nodding.

"Yeah, we do. I'm being run out of my home by a psychopath. He brought these people here and made them hate us so this is all his fault... you know?"

I nod, my heart breaking for him as I wrap my arm around his waist. "Yeah, I know, baby."

"You need help with anything, Row?" Lincoln asks, stopping next to me and glaring at Travis as he leans against me. I sigh and nod.

"Could you grab his bags?"

He narrows his eyes. "Is he fucking drunk?"

"He is," Travis answers, holding up the bottle of booze. "Because, fuck you, Warren. That's why."

"Jesus Christ. Just get him to his car and I'll get the bags," Lincoln mutters, flashing Travis a look of disappointment but I don't hang around long enough for him to start berating him, not that it would do any good

343

at this point. Since I've been here, I've noticed that, as time passed, there was this edge to Travis's demeanor and I know he's been so stressed trying to save all of us from Warren but it feels like more than that. The problem is, I've been too afraid to ask, too afraid to upset the good thing he and I have going.

When we get out to the Impala, I open the passenger door and help him inside before running around the hood and slipping behind the wheel and starting it. Glancing down the lot, I see Lincoln loading all of our bags into his truck and nod, checking one thing off of my list before rolling my window down to listen to instructions. Red and blue lights bounce off of the clubhouse followed by the "whoop" of a siren and I glance down as four police cruisers pull to a stop outside of the gate and the officers jump out. As they begin to push the crowd back, I scan the area and frown. Where the hell did the other officers go? The ones that have been posted out there day and night since this all started to keep everyone safe.

Two officers jump back into their squad cars and flip a U-turn in opposite directions to act as a barrier between us and the crowd as Blaze stands in front of us and motions for us to move out. He runs over to his bike and as the deep rumble of the engine fills the air, Rodriguez punches the code into the lock and slides the gate open. We move out, one by one, and when it's my turn, I slip behind Fuzz and Piper's Bronco as Travis sighs from the passenger seat. I glance over at him.

"What?"

Peeking over at me, he takes a sip of his whiskey before turning away from me and shaking his head. "You're amazing, you know?"

"No, I didn't know," I answer, fighting back a smile as I eye the bottle in his hand. He's really fucking going for broke tonight and my gaze flicks back up to his face, trying to understand the emotion that flickers through his eyes.

"You're fire, baby... like, for real."

I arch a brow. "Thank you... I think."

"This isn't coming out right," he growls, scrubbing his hand down his face and I glance out of my window to hide my smile. Fuck. I want to be mad at him for getting drunk when shit was seriously going to hell but he's just so damn cute right now that I can't. Turning back to him, I flash a pointed look at the whiskey bottle.

"Maybe we should just have this conversation when you're sober."

"No," he growls. "I'm just trying to say that... there is all of this shit around me... like a fucking hurricane of bad shit but then there's you and with you... it's all calm and I can breathe. I think... I... fuck, I don't know..."

My mind races, replaying everything he just said to me again and again as I try to sort it all out into something intelligible and figure out what he's really trying to say but I don't want to read into anything. Not when I have too much on the line. The Impala slips out onto the street and the screaming of the protestors floods the cab as my heart climbs into my throat. Just before we turn, I glance over and meet Warren's eyes as he stands on the edge of the crowd, watching us leave. The stupid white mask is completely covering his face, like always, but I swear he's smiling at me and it chills me to the bone as my heart thunders in my chest.

"Rowan, I need to tell you something..."

I peek over at Travis again. "Okay."

"He's been calling me... calling me and torturing me. He said I couldn't tell anyone but it's killing me and I don't want to die... but I can't lose you either. Oh, fuck, I shouldn't have said anything," he whispers, an ache in his voice so potent that tears sting my eyes as I glance between his tortured face and the road. Groaning, he scrubs his hand down his face and shakes his head, clearly wrestling with what he just said. It breaks my fucking heart.

"What do you mean you don't want to lose me, Travis?"

He rolls his head to the side and meets my eyes. "He's going to kill us all... he told me and he's going to take you from me. He said you caught his eye... but I won't let him have you because you're mine, right? You said you were mine last night."

"Yeah," I whisper, nodding as my heart hammers in my chest and I grip the wheel tighter as my hands shake. "I'm yours, Travis."

Just when I think I've reached the bottom of the "what the fuck" barrel when it comes to Warren, I manage to find a new low and I can't help but worry how much more we could all lose before this is over. But then, there is another part that wonders if there is no end to this. Maybe this hell is just our lives now and there is no escape.

Chapter Twenty-Nine
Warren

"Yes," I hiss, my chest feeling light as air as the roar of a bike engine fills the air. A wide smile stretches across my face and my body vibrates as I punch my fist into the air. Rain splatters against my face but I don't even give a shit anymore. I'm soaking wet but it doesn't matter when everything is falling into place exactly the way I wanted it to and it's especially fortunate since this is the one part of my plan where things could have gone epically wrong.

But it didn't.

Clearly, fate, God, or the universe is on my side in this mission and I laugh to myself as I think about how I put all of this together. For years, I've been working on making very realistic looking fake profiles all over the internet so after I posted the fake videos of the guys on the website I made for them, all I had to do was comment that we should protest the club and, voila , people showed up outside the clubhouse in droves, ready to fight for their city. Once I started standing out there with them, it was easy enough to stoke the flames and spread fear through the crowd about how dangerous the club is and once that fear was behind the wheel, a well-timed joke about Molotov cocktails inspired a few of them to take action. It's gorgeous the way it all pieced together, actually, and I'm pretty damn proud of myself for what I've already been able to accomplish.

I gotta say, watching the brothers and their old ladies slowly go mad from being cooped up in that building with each other while the protest raged on outside was the best part of my day. Fuck, they still don't even know about the first time I broke into the club a little over a year ago and planted hidden cameras all over the place, hidden cameras that have allowed me to keep an eye on everything they're doing without the risk of getting caught. Chuckling, I shake my head. It's actually surprising just how easy it is to get your hands on tiny little cameras hidden in all sorts of things like clocks, tissue boxes, water bottles, picture frames, smoke detectors, and so much more. And when I couldn't find a replacement item online, it was easy enough to modify the things already in the clubhouse so that I could hide a camera in it. I've been watching their every move for so goddamn long and they didn't have a fucking clue. Not until I insinuated as much to Streak and even that gave me endless entertainment as I watched him try to figure out how I was watching them. He must have run diagnostic checks on his computer and the security system every day for a week and I laughed my ass off each time with a bowl of popcorn in my lap.

The growl of the bike creeps closer, snapping me out of my thoughts and I slip behind a tree as Blaze leads the caravan of vehicles into the driveway of Emma and Nix's plantation house. I despise this place but I'm glad they chose to come here because this is another point where my whole plan could have gone up in smoke. Emma and Nix's house is pretty well secured but I was able to scope it out weeks ago when Blaze ordered everyone to the clubhouse, in the hopes that they would come here when shit went down, and I know my way around their security system. It's honestly almost perfect but there are a few blind spots that will allow me to move around the property without being detected which is good since I don't have cameras inside. Sure, the best-case scenario would have been to keep them at the clubhouse where I had unlimited access to them with my cameras. The thing is, I was actually growing bored with how easy this has all been so having them here will present new challenges.

But I'm up to the task.

"Let's move, y'all!" Blaze hollers as he swings his leg over his bike and scans the area. Everyone else files out of their cars, their eyes wide and their faces pale. I can't help but smile. Fuck. I love seeing the mayhem I've caused in their lives and the fear pumping through their veins as they think of me. Blaze lets out a shrill whistle to gain everyone's attention, his shoulders tight and his eyes narrowed into a glare as he continues scanning the yard. "Let's move, people. I don't want to be standing out here for too long."

They all nod in agreement and he points to Storm, Kodiak, and Moose.

"Grab guns and do a perimeter check. Make sure we're truly safe here."

Storm nods, pulling a pistol from the waistband of his jeans. "On it, boss."

Shit.

That means it's time for me to go.

349

Everyone springs into action, bustling around the driveway to get all of their things hauled into the house as I watch from my hiding spot. Storm, Kodiak, and Moose start off for the other side of the property to start their sweep, giving me a few more precious moments as I soak in the chaos. The voice in my head that demands justice, the one that is constantly screaming at me to take immediate action is silent tonight. Maybe it's because he's temporarily satisfied with their suffering or maybe it's because he knows this next part is going to destroy them and he's just as excited to watch it all fall apart as I am. Finally, after all of this time and all of this work, I'm going to get the justice we deserve and I'm downright fucking giddy.

Rowan steps out of Streak's Impala and my gaze snaps to hers in an instant as my cock springs to life with just one look at her. Shit. She looks damn good tonight in her tight little jeans and fitted hoodie but it's the pink mesh bra and panty set I know she's wearing underneath that is making me crazy. So many nights, I've laid in bed and watched her with Streak, giving him everything I want from her as fantasies of gutting him and fucking her on top of the remains filled my mind. She was never part of the plan and another instance where this whole thing could have been derailed if I wasn't so damn good but I managed to make it all work and when this is all over, I won't be satisfied unless I have her under my arm as we watch the Devils burn. As she looks around the property, I swear she can feel me here with her – that ache in her chest and the current that races over her skin giving me away – and I glance over at the guys doing a sweep before whispering a curse. They are getting close to my hiding spot and it's time to go. Taking one last look at my girl, I smile and blow her a kiss.

"Soon, baby girl," I whisper before turning and creeping back through the forest, away from her, without a sound. It's time for act two and if they think everything up until now has been bad, they aren't ready for what is coming next. I'm going to dig my claws into this club, feel the blood seep over my skin, and tear it apart.

Chapter Thirty
Rowan

Birds sing sweetly somewhere off in the distance and early morning sunlight streams in through the windows, the cheeriness of it all such a stark contrast from the nightmares that tormented me all night long, as I pad down the stairs in desperate need of coffee.

"Morning," Tate calls as I step into the kitchen and I nod, rubbing at my tired eyes. She takes one look at my face and snorts out a laugh as she points to the coffee pot. "Coffee?"

I nod. "You're an angel."

"Well, if that's all it takes." She laughs, turning back to the counter as she fiddles with the pen in her hand. There is a notepad laid on the counter in front of her and I scowl as I grab a mug from the shelf above the coffee pot and fill it up with sweet, sweet caffeine.

"How did you sleep?" Emma asks and I glance over my shoulder at her, nodding as I think back over the last twelve hours. After we got here last night, everyone made quick work of bringing all of the luggage inside and making sure the house and surrounding property were secure before Emma started handing out room assignments. She put Travis and me together in the room at the top of the stairs with white shiplap walls and a giant king-sized bed with a black metal bedframe that felt so homey. Lincoln wasn't too pleased about the sleeping arrangements and with just one look at my big brother, I could see that it's taking every ounce of restraint he has to keep his promise to me and not tell Travis the truth about my feelings for him but he's worried about me.

"Good."

She smiles. "Good. Streak still sleeping?"

"Yeah," I scoff, carrying my mug with two hands as I shuffle over to the massive island in the middle of the room and sit next to Tate. "He finished off one and a half bottles of whiskey last night so he's probably going to be out for a while."

"He okay?" Tate asks, arching a brow and I sigh, remembering the way he stumbled into our room last night with the second bottle of liquor in his hand and collapsed onto the bed. He didn't pass out for a while, though. Instead, we just laid there for hours talking. He told about the three phone calls he received from Warren but he kept it pretty vague when I asked what Warren had said to him - just telling me that he usually spent his time taunting Travis with his inability to find him and threatening to start killing people if he told anyone about the calls. He also mentioned that Warren had taken a liking to me. When I balked, he assured me that Warren's interest was nothing more than another side game to get at him but I can't help but be worried. "Rowan?"

I blink up at Tate, remembering her question. "Oh... yeah... I think he's okay."

I don't.

Travis is clearly not okay and tears sting my eyes as I think about everything he's been going through, silently, these past few weeks. He's been in hell and my chest aches for him. On top of the stress every other member of this club was feeling from the situation, he also had to listen to Warren mock him and threaten the people he cares about. As I laid in bed and watched him sleep for a few minutes this morning, I promised him that I was going to be there for him unconditionally no matter how much it hurt me in the long run because it's clear to me now that he needs me. My mind drifts back to the words he said in the car about me being the calm in this storm for him and the one place where he can breathe as I stare down into my coffee cup. If I'm his harbor, his shelter as this fight rages around us, then that's what I'll be no matter how much it hurts me when he walks away.

No more running.

No more keeping him at a distance because I can't. It hurts me, it hurts him, and I love him too much to watch him suffer like this all alone.

"You two work things out then?" Tate asks, drawing my attention back to her as she chews on one end of the pen and I nod, deciding to keep the truth to myself. I know Tate has good intentions but all it's going to take to set my brother off is one misplaced comment and I can't have him telling Travis the truth about my feelings. I'm not ready for this to end yet.

"More or less… we're figuring it out."

She flashes me a grin. "I knew you would. The two of you were freaking made for each other."

"I don't know about that." I laugh, trying to keep my tone light as a stake pierces my chest and pain floods my body. I so wish her words were true that Travis and I were made for one another but pretending like this could ever be anything more than the casual relationship we agreed to is asking for heartache. Glancing down at the notepad in front of her to distract myself, I nod to it. "What's that?"

"We're making a grocery list," Emma says and Tate nods.

"This poor girl does not have near enough food to feed twenty fucking people for however long we're going to stay here for."

Emma laughs. "To be fair, I wasn't expecting company."

"You guys heading out soon?" I ask and they both nod. "Mind if I join you?"

"Of course not," Tate says, dropping the pen on the counter and wrapping her arm around my shoulders. Someone clears their throat from behind us and we glance back as Blaze arches a brow.

"Sure hope you ladies weren't planning on going out by yourself."

Tate flashes him a sweet smile. "'Course not, Blaze. We were just about to go ask you if you wanted to go, too."

"Mm-hmm," he hums, grabbing a mug from the shelf and pouring himself a cup of coffee. He takes a sip and closes his eyes, sighing, as he swallows and I study his face, noticing the new wrinkles around his eyes from all of the stress we've been enduring lately. This whole situation, it's hell on each and every member of this club, hell on the family of the members, and we need to find a way to end it. I have no freaking idea how but we have to find a way. Blaze sighs again and takes another sip of coffee as he opens his eyes and nods to us. "Let me know when you ladies are ready to go."

I nod as I stand up and grab my coffee. "I'm going to get get ready."

"Ten minutes," Tate calls and I nod in response before walking over to the stairs and dragging my tired body up them. I slip into the room and smile when I see Travis sprawled out in the middle of the giant bed, one leg hooked out of the covers as they ride low on his hips and his hand splayed out on his stomach. His full lips are parted as a gentle sawing noise fills the room. I've never heard him snore before but maybe that's because I usually fall asleep first or it could be the fact that he was *gone* last night. Unable to stop myself, I sit on the edge of the bed and turn to him, studying his handsome face as he sleeps and the pain in his eyes when he told me about Warren last night rushes back to me. Sinking my teeth into my bottom lip, tears sting my eyes as I reach up and brush his dark hair off of his forehead. He looks so peaceful in his sleep, so serene and I shake my head, trying to imagine the hell he's been dealing with over these past few weeks as my chest swells. He lets out a small groan and I can't help but smile.

God, I love him.

Groaning again, he rolls toward me onto his side and sighs as reaches out, feeling along the bed for something as his eyes open.

"Morning," I whisper and he looks up at me, flashing me a sleepy grin as he grabs my hand and gives it a tug.

"Mmm… come back to bed, Princess."

I shake my head, my smile widening. He's so damn cute in the morning and I don't know how I'm ever going to get enough. "I can't. I'm running to the store to get provisions with Tate and Emma."

"I don't fucking think so," he growls, his smile falling away as he narrows his eyes at me and sits up, scooting across the bed and wrapping his arms around my waist. "I'll come, too. You're not fucking going anywhere alone."

"You don't have to…"

His hand slips into my hair, holding the back of my head as he slams his lips to mine, silencing my protests and I sigh, melting into him just like I always do as tears sting my eyes. How is it that after being together for weeks, each kiss still manages to rock me to the core? I've been in love before but I've never fucking felt like this and despite how happy he makes me, each good moment is tinged with the reality of our situation no matter how hard I try to ignore it. Pulling back, he meets my eyes and frowns when he sees the moisture gathering there, brushing his thumb across my cheek with such care that it's hard to hold the tears back.

"What's wrong?"

I shake my head and paste a smile on my face, choosing to focus on the happy as hard as I can. "Absolutely nothing."

"Then, what's with the water works, babe?"

"I don't know," I lie before letting out a humorless chuckle. "Maybe that we literally ran from a mad man again last night or the fact that he wants me or maybe it's just because you're so damn sweet to me."

He nods in understanding and presses his forehead to mine, closing his eyes as he takes a deep breath. "Hey, when this is all over, what do you say we do something so fucking normal it hurts?"

"Like what?" I laugh and he shrugs.

"Dunno… dinner and a movie?"

I nod. "It's a date."

"Good," he whispers, his smile shy as he leans in and presses his lips to mine. His kiss is gentle this time and it melts me on the spot as my chest aches with my love for him. When he pulls·back, he flashes me a grin and gives me playful shove out of the bed. "Now, get ready so we can go shopping."

"Hey, you know... grocery shopping together is a perfectly normal, boring thing to do," I tell him as I stand up and shove my little sleep shorts down my thighs and step out of them. His eyes rake down my bare legs and he licks his lip as he nods.

"You're right."

I snap my fingers. "My eyes are up here."

"I know," he answers, grinning as he meets my gaze. "But I'm busy looking at your gorgeous fucking legs right now, babe. Give me a minute."

"Get dressed." I shake my head as I turn and walk away from him to grab my jeans off of the floor in the corner of the room. Aware of his eyes burning into my backside, I bend over slowly to grab them, smiling when he groans.

"You're a dirty fucking temptress."

I peek over my shoulder and grin. "The sooner you get ready, the quicker we can get back here so you can do something about it."

His eyes widen a second before he flashes me a wide grin and jumps out of bed faster than I've ever seen and I laugh as he scoops his jeans off of the floor and begins pulling them on, almost tripping over his own feet. Once he manages to get them buttoned, he grabs a t-shirt and yanks it over his head as he marches across the room. I button my jeans and when he reaches me, he leans in, kissing my cheek before he picks me up and throws me over his shoulder, smacking my ass.

"Let's go."

Something between a squeal and a laugh slips out of my mouth as I smack his back. "Put me down, Travis."

Laughing, he sets me back on my feet before taking my hand and pulling me into another kiss. My body floats up off the floor as warmth rushes through me and I can't help but smile against his lips as I lean into his body, needing to be closer to him. Lacing his fingers through mine, he plants a few more kisses against my lips before pulling away and tugging me toward the door of our room.

"Come on. I already can't wait to get back here."

Heat rushes to my cheeks and I can't wipe the smile off of my face as we walk down the stairs together, hand in hand and my heart is pounding like crazy in my chest. We meet up with Emma, Tate, and Blaze in the living room and Blaze nods in approval at Travis before slipping a gun in the holster at his waist.

"You armed?" he asks, his gaze bouncing between Travis and Tate. Tate scoffs and reaches behind her back to pull out her pistol as she nods.

"Always."

Travis shakes his head. "I didn't grab mine but I can real quick."

"No," Blaze says, looking around at our little group before shaking his head. "I think two should cover it."

"Three," Tate calls as she turns toward the door, lifting up her pants leg to reveal a second gun hidden there and Blaze laughs.

"Sorry, I forgot that you never have just one," he tells her and she glances back over her shoulder, shooting him a look of disappointment.

"How careless."

They continue giving each other a hard time as we step outside and make our way to the big, black SUV at the end of the driveway. When we pulled up last night and I got my first look at Emma and Nix's home, I was blown away. It's a proper southern plantation house set on two acres of land with huge oak trees dripping in Spanish moss scattered around the property, and a large lake in the back with their own personal dock. Once we all got settled, Emma told us how Nix had purchased the house after it had been foreclosed on and fixed it all up himself. It's honestly so peaceful out here that it's easier to relax and forget the danger we're all in for a moment and I think it will be just what we all need. Not that I want us to get careless but each and every person here needs to chill a bit or things will only get worse.

We pile into the SUV with Blaze behind the wheel, Emma in the passenger seat, and Tate in the back with us. Travis is glued to my side, my hand firmly in his as everyone else makes small talk, a lightness settling over the group that is so refreshing after all of the dark we've endured lately. I sigh. After the drama of last night, which honestly seems like a dream now in the light of day, today feels so free and peaceful and I'm so thankful for it. We need, at least, a day to relax and decompress before we hit this Warren situation head on again. Peeking over at Travis, I vow to find a way to help him sort this whole thing out and find answers as his comment about going out on a normal date drifts through my mind. I shake my head. I'm honestly so confused by what's going on between us and I'm working so hard to keep my expectations non-existent but then he says something like he did in the bedroom that makes me think he sees a future in this.

No.

Don't do that to yourself.

Sucking in a breath, I push all of my thoughts away and focus in on the conversation around me again as they all chat about putting together a big family dinner tonight and my mind drifts to the night after the last time we did that. Travis peeks over at me and we both smile. God, that was a damn good night. He gives my hand a squeeze and I lay my head on his shoulder, unable to wipe the smile off of my face as the city of Baton Rouge comes into view.

The grocery store parking lot is fairly empty when we pull in and Blaze parks the SUV near the back, his eyes scanning the areas around us for any possible danger. Travis's body tenses, on alert just like Blaze as he nods to me and kisses the back of my hand before ushering me out of the SUV. Adrenaline floods my system, making my muscles feel twitchy as I gaze around the lot and Blaze orders us all to stay together. We don't even get ten feet from the SUV when a high-pitched whining sound fills the air, pulling all of our attention to a man in all black sitting on a bright red crotch rocket six feet to our right. His face is covered by his full helmet but even through the dark tint of the visor, I swear I can feel his gaze on me and my stomach drops.

It's him.

He revs his engine, looking straight at us and my heart climbs into my throat as his bike jumps forward, taunting us. I try to retreat to the SUV as Blaze pulls his gun out of its holster and holds it at his side, never taking his eyes off of the man on the bike but Travis grabs me and pulls me firmly into his side as he leans down and presses his lips to the top of my head.

"I've got you, baby."

Time seems to stall as we stand frozen in the lot, watching the man on the bike as he just sits there, revving his engine and teasing us with the possibility of an attack. My heart hammers in my ears and I struggle to draw air into my lungs as tears sting my eyes. We can't just keep standing here, waiting for his next move. We're too out in the open, too exposed, and too far from any help we could get in the store. Standing here, in the middle of an empty lot with this psycho is going to get us killed.

"Go back to the SUV," Blaze orders, his voice hard as he keeps his gaze fixed on the man on the bike, his shoulders tight and posture imposing. We all turn, ready to rush back to the safety of our vehicle. Another sound joins the whining of the bike, similar but deeper, as we all stop in our tracks and turn to the other side. A man, also dressed in all black with his face covered by a helmet, races toward us on a dirt bike. Emma is standing off to the side, a little ways away from the rest of the group and his gaze is focused on her as he twists the handle, accelerating across the lot.

I can't take my eyes off of him, my legs shaking like crazy and my heart thunders in my chest as bolts of pain stab into me. Squeezing Travis's hand, I watch in slow motion as he releases one of the handlebars and lets his arm hang at his side, revealing a blade. He gets closer and closer, closing in on us but none of us move, the fear thick in the air around us and all we can do is watch. Images race through my mind, horrific images that I don't want to see, and a tear slips down my face as a tiny little voice inside screams at me that I need to do something but I can't.

I can't move.

I can't breathe.

I can't speak.

All I can do is watch as the cold claws of dread wrap around my heart, crushing it as he closes in on Emma, fear filling her eyes as she stumbles back a few steps and a gun shot rings out. The dirt bike swerves out of the way before he corrects his course, just mere feet from Emma.

Oh, God.

"No!" Blaze yells, pulling her back and jumping in front of her to shield her with his body just as the man on the dirt bike passes us, lifting his arm up to slice through the air and my breath catches in my throat as everything around us blurs and time stands still. A pained groan drifts through the air as Blaze clutches his stomach and crumples to the ground. Emma screams, her eyes wide as she rushes over to his side and drops to her knees. Blood pours out of his stomach and my stomach churns, my chest aching as I shake my head, turning to the man on the dirt bike as he stops next to the other man and lifts the visor of his helmet, revealing his face to me.

Warren.

For so long, I've wondered what he looked like, what I would see in the face of the man tormenting this club and I guess I always assumed it would be pure evil shining in his gaze but instead, his brown eyes are burning with rage and pain as he stares at me. Travis was right about his appearance – completely average, the kind of man you would walk straight past on the street and not even spare a second glance. I study him, trying to commit his every feature to my memory for later as his gaze bores through me. Slowly, a smile stretches across his face and ice seeps into my bones. He winks, sending a shiver twisting down my spine and tears gather in my eyes but I can't look away.

Another gunshot rings out and my gaze snaps to the side. Tate is holding her pistol in her shaking hand, her phone pressed to her ear as she glares daggers at Warren but when I turn back, the visor is down again and he turns with his partner, racing out of the parking lot as the roar of their bikes fill the air. My stomach rolls and I turn back to the others, hoping one of them saw what just happened but Emma is frantically pressing her sweater to Blaze's stomach, blood all over her and Tate is relaying his condition to the nine-one-one operator, her gun at her side again. Travis is staring down at the whole scene with wide, blank eyes, his hand gripping mine so tightly that I don't know how it hasn't broken.

Ow.

"Rowan!" Emma screams and my head snaps to her. "Help me, please!"

I nod, yanking my hand from Travis's and it seems to snap him out of his daze as he looks around the lot, noticing that our friends are gone for the first time as I rush to Blaze's side, opposite of Emma and place my hands on the sweater, applying pressure to his wound.

"Blaze," Emma whispers, tears streaming down her face as she grits her teeth. "Don't you dare leave us, you hear? You do not get to die today."

He nods weakly.

Blood pools on the ground around him and I glance up at his pale face, trying to make sure he's still breathing as I press my shaking hands harder against his stomach. He groans and winces as he tries to move but Emma shoves his shoulders back to the ground, instructing him to stay down. When he's still again, I lift up part of the sweater, gasping at the sight below. There is a gash all the way across his stomach and blood pours from the wound. It's too much. The cut is too deep and he's losing too much blood. My stomach drops and tears fill my eyes.

We're going to lose him.

"Where is the ambulance?" Emma screams, her tears growing more frantic as she glances up at Tate. If Tate replies to her, I don't hear her as I watch Blaze's chest, begging him every second to take his next breath but it seems like the time between each breath keeps getting longer and my mind screams, begging for help. I know I haven't known Blaze for very long but in the short time I've been here, I've seen the kind of man he is and I've felt his kindness and warmth. He's too good, too important to every member of this club to die.

"Emma," he whispers, his hand weakly rising off the ground. She grabs it in both of her blood stained hands as I use my whole arm to apply pressure to his abdomen, picking up her slack and praying that the paramedics get here soon. "Need you to do something for me, Darlin'."

She shakes her head, a sob bubbling out of her lips. "Don't you dare say your good-byes. You hear me, Malcolm. You still have too much life to live to give up right now."

"Just in case," he murmurs, his voice growing weaker and my heart hammers in my chest as I shake my head, the image of my mom lying on a hospital gurney filling my mind. "Tell my boy how sorry I am, will ya? Tell him I only wanted to protect him and that I love him more than anything else in the fucking world."

"Blaze," she wails, shaking her head but he ignores her.

"Tell him that I'm so fucking proud of the man he's become and the family he's built with you. This is going to hurt him but I'm not worried because I know he has you and you're the best thing that has ever happened to him."

She presses a hand to his face and his eyes open slightly. "We still need you, Blaze - this family and this club needs you. You can't go leavin' us."

He doesn't respond and my breath catches in my throat as I stare at his chest, willing him to breathe.

Oh, God, no.

No.

No.

No.

Emma sobs, shaking him a little and he sucks in a ragged breath, dragging his eyes open again as a ghost of a smile dances across his lips.

"I see her…"

"Who?" Emma asks him, jostling him again to keep him talking. "Who do you see, Blaze?"

His smile widens, happiness filling his eyes as he looks up at the sky. "Sarah… my Sarah. She's waiting for me. I have to go to her."

A sob rips through the air and I peek over my shoulder at Tate as tears streak down her face and she gasps for a breath, her phone hovering in the air next to her ear and her eyes wide. Sarah was her mom and Blaze's one true love but for a bunch of reasons, they had been a secret for a lot of their relationship. When she died last year in a car accident, the truth came out and it brought Tate and Lincoln together but I know she's still grieving the loss. She wobbles on her feet and spots dance in my vision as the babies pop into my head.

She needs help.

"Travis!" I yell and his head whips up, his haunted eyes meeting mine. My heart aches for him but I can't do anything to help him right now so I nod to Tate. "Help her."

He blinks, staring at Tate for a second before he nods and moves to her side, wrapping his arm around her to keep her from collapsing as I turn back to Blaze. Emma shakes him again and he takes another breath.

This can't be happening.

I don't know what to do, how to help him, and my mind spins so I do the only thing I can think of which is to press down harder on Blaze's wound but it works. He gasps in pain and takes another ragged breath as his eyes open. Looking up at Emma, he smiles again and wipes the tears from her face.

"Don't cry…baby girl… it'll be okay…I'm so lucky…to call you my daughter… and I've lived an amazing life… don't be sad."

She shakes her head, sobbing loudly as she buries her face in his shoulder. "You can't leave us, Blaze… you can't…"

"Have to… darlin'… Sarah's waiting for me… miss her so much…"

Her sobs get louder, joining the wail of sirens as she sits back up and shakes his hand. This time he doesn't open his eyes again but he does take a labored breath and I will the ambulance to move faster as I stare at his chest, tears dripping down my face as pain tears through me - old and new twisting together and fueling each other as I think about everyone I've already lost and all of the people I could still lose. I may have only been around this club for a month but Blaze was right, we're a family and I love all of them. Emma shakes him again, screaming at him to breathe as I continue focusing on his chest.

Come on, Blaze.
Breathe.
Fucking breathe.
Please...

Wicked Games

Chapter Thirty-One
Rowan

Dark, ominous clouds loom over our heads, threatening rain, and the wind whips through the cemetery, indicative of our collective shit mood as we stand huddled together, watching the casket slowly being lowered into the ground. A clap of thunder makes me jump as the tears drip down my cheeks and I cling to Travis as the scene from four days ago plays in my mind over and over again – the whine of the bikes, Emma's screams as she tried to keep Blaze talking, and the racing of my heart as I tried to process it all. At the time, everything seemed to move in slow motion but looking back, it all happened so fucking fast that it's getting difficult to keep the details straight but that hasn't stopped Warren from haunting my dreams for the past few nights. Or erased the image of Blaze lying dead on the pavement from flashing through my mind every time I close my eyes.

Sighing, I glance up at Travis as he stares at the casket, his eyes vacant and his lips pressed together in a thin line. I give his hand a squeeze and grip his bicep with my free hand as I cuddle into his side, hoping I can bring him even a sliver of comfort but I'm not holding out hope since nothing else I've tried to ease his suffering has worked yet. Today is the first time since Blaze was murdered that he didn't wake up and immediately start drinking but that's only because he had to drive his bike to the funeral and Storm chewed his ass out last night about not being drunk during the funeral but I have no doubt that as soon as we get back to Emma and Nix's house, he will go straight for a bottle again. My throat feels tight as I watch him but he never takes his eyes off of the casket, swimming with so much pain and anger that I suck in a breath and drag his arm over my shoulder so I can cuddle into his side. He clings to me, holding me tight to his body as a single tear falls down his cheek and he quickly wipes it away, gritting his teeth. The pain in my chest is so potent, so overpowering that I want to wrap my arms around him and tell him how much I love him, tell him that he has me but that little voice in the back of my head stops me, reminding me that doing that will only end in even more heartbreak for me.

The casket comes to a stop, deep in the ground, and Travis holds me tighter, pressing a kiss to my head as two men who work at the cemetery step forward with shovels and behind piling dirt on top. Sniffles surround us as everyone else turns away and starts making their way over to the bikes parked on the street but Travis doesn't move. Peeking up at him, my heart breaks all over again, just like it does every single day as I watch him try to come to grips with his loss. He's so sad and so angry and so lost but I know better than anyone that there is no shortcut wen it comes to grief. As awful as it is, he just has to wade through it but he won't be doing it alone.

Gripping the front of his black button up shirt, I give it a tug, prompting him to glance down at me.

"You ready to go, baby?"

He sighs, glancing back at the grave before nodding. "Yeah."

With a furrowed brow, he sucks in a breath and grabs my hand but before we can turn toward the street, a man steps out from behind a tree about twenty feet away from us and I gasp, stumbling back as my knees buckle but Travis doesn't let me fall. My whole body trembles and tears sting my eyes as I stare at the man, dressed in black with that damn white mask on his face. Travis looks down at me before following my line of sight and he takes off before I can stop him, running at Warren at full speed, his face contorted with rage.

Shit.

"Lincoln!" I scream, glancing back at the rest of the club and my brother's head jerks up, scowling at me before he notices Travis chasing Warren back into the trees.

"Fuck," he hisses, dropping the keys to his bike on the seat as he takes off running toward me. All of the guys turn and without a second thought follow behind him as they chase after Travis and Warren, determination on their faces. Warren cuts to the right and books it back toward me, evading capture, and I stumble back as my heart hammers in my chest. The way he looked at me in the parking lot as Blaze lay dying at my feet pops into my mind and tears sting my eyes.

Is he here for me?

I remember the comment Travis made about Warren taking a liking to me and black dots dance in my vision as I stumble back, running from him, before I trip over something and fall to the ground. He closes in on me, getting closer and closer as my heart beats so fast and so hard, I'm certain it's going to give out and just when I think it's over, Tate steps in front of me, her gun drawn and pointing straight at Warren's chest. He skids to a stop and it gives Travis the valuable seconds he needs to tackle him from behind, taking him down to the ground. In rapid succession, he flips Warren over onto his back, straddles his body, rips his mask off, and begins smashing his fist into his face repeatedly as I watch, bile rising up in my throat.

Glancing over the man's body, I flash back to the memory of Warren in the parking lot and the way his brown hair fell into his eyes, and I scream as my gaze locks onto the man's blond locks. "Stop. Travis, stop! It's not Warren."

"What?" he snaps, his chest heaving as he gasps for air from the exertion and I point to the man's hair, forcing Travis to glance down and really take a good look at him for the first time. Groaning, he throws himself off of the man and scrubs his hand down his face as the rest of the guys reach us.

"What's going on?" Storm growls, striding to the front of the group. Since Blaze's death, he has really taken on the role of acting President, stepping up and being the rock we all needed, and it makes perfect sense to me why Blaze made him his VP.

"I-I'm sorry…" the guy chokes out, turning on his side and coughing before spitting out a mouthful of blood. "This g-guy just paid me to come h-here and wear the mask. I d-didn't know… p-please don't hurt me."

Lincoln sighs, running his hand through his hair. "Do you know his name? The guy who paid you?"

"W-Warren… he said his name was Warren and he gave me five hundred dollars… s-said it was a practical joke."

"At a fucking funeral?" Travis snaps, leveling a glare at the man and he lifts his shaking hands in surrender as he shakes his head.

"He didn't say it was a funeral." He looks down at the ground and shakes his head again. "I'm so s-sorry. Truly."

Storm sighs, studying him for a second before nodding to the exit. "Get the fuck out of here before I set my friend loose on you again."

The man doesn't need to be told twice, jumping up and scurrying away from us as fast as he can. We all watch him go for a second before Lincoln steps up in front of me and holds his hand out to help me off the ground. When I'm back on my feet, he grabs my arms and holds me steady.

"You okay?"

I nod. "Yeah."

"Let's get the fuck out of here before anything else happens," Storm orders, curling his hand above his head in a signal to roll out and I walk across the grass to Travis as he glances back at Blaze's grave. As soon as I'm close, he grabs me and pulls me into his arms, releasing a sigh and I know better than to ask him if he's okay because it's clear that none of us are and I'm not even sure if we ever will be again. Dropping my head back, I meet his eyes and his brows knit together as pain splashes across his face but before I can say anything, he smashes his lips to mine. His kiss is desperate in a way I've never felt before and tears gather in my eyes as he pours his agony into me, clinging to me like I'm the last shred of hope in his battered heart. I want to be that for him. Hell, at this point, I would be anything he needed me to be but he doesn't know that and I can never tell him.

"Let's go," he whispers against my lips before pressing one last quick kiss there. When he pulls back, he throws his arm over my shoulder and we walk down to his bike together and climb on. The engine rumbles to life and I wrap my arms around his waist, laying my head against his back, my mind working in overdrive as he pulls into line behind his brothers.

The last four days have probably been the weirdest four days of my entire life - filled with brief snippets of confusion, fear, pain, and worry but most of the time, I'm just numb. That day in the parking lot doesn't feel real yet and I keep thinking that I'll catch Blaze in the hallway or find him getting coffee in the kitchen every morning. No one has even talked about the case or Warren, all of us just too lost in our pain to think about it but it's clear after the incident at the cemetery that we need to refocus on him and his plan for us.

The wind whips through my hair and as we fly through Baton Rouge, the scene from the parking lot pops into my mind again and tears sting my eyes. By the time the ambulance finally showed up, Blaze was already gone and everything else kind of happened in a blur. I do remember Detective Rodriguez showing up at some point and taking our statements. I gave him the description of Warren but I know it wasn't helpful. He informed us that another detective had been assigned to the case given his relationship with the club but that he'd be around to help as much as possible. Oh, and apparently, Sergeant Williams is doubling down on her investigation into us, convinced that we had something to do with the deaths of all three girls Warren killed as well as Tawny's death and Veronica's kidnapping. It's ridiculous but as far as I'm concerned, it's a problem for another day.

Pulling into the driveway of Emma and Nix's house, the guys line their bikes up along one side before they all jump off and amble inside, everyone lost in their own thoughts. As soon as we get inside, Travis heads straight for the booze, the tortured look on his face hitting me straight in the chest quickly followed by the ache I'm becoming all too familiar with. He snags a bottle of whiskey before walking back into the living room and throwing himself into one of the chairs in the corner. I walk across the space, closing the distance between us, and sit in the chair next to his, eyeing him as he spins the top off of the bottle and raises it to his lips, tipping it back and letting the liquor pour down his throat.

Everyone mills around us, getting drinks of their own as conversation slowly starts to fill the aching silence and Emma pulls out trays of food she prepared for the wake, setting them out on the counter so folks can pick at it when they get hungry. Someone turns on Blaze's favorite music, classic eighties rock, before turning it down a bit so we can all still talk to each other. With the threat from Warren still looming, it won't be much of a party but Blaze and our love for him deserves to be acknowledged, even if it isn't a total rager. Peeking over at Travis again, I sigh. He turns to look at me and holds out the bottle, asking if I want some, and I shake my head. I'm pretty sure he's drinking enough for the both of us and if tonight is anything like the last four nights, I'll have to take care of him and make sure he gets up to our bed. I watch him as he presses the bottle to his lips and tips it back again, chugging the liquor inside for a second before pulling it away with a wince.

"Hey," I whisper and he turns to look at me again as I reach out and grab his hand. A ghost of a smile stretches across his face as he looks down at our joined hands before meeting my eyes again. "You know I'm here for you, right?"

He nods, his eyes clear for a brief moment but his smile falls away. "I know, Princess."

I want to say more, tell him how worried I am about him as he raises the bottle to his lips again but our relationship has become such a balancing act, leaving me frozen on a tightrope because I'm too scared to move. What I want to do is pull him up to our room and confess my love for him, hoping that it'll be enough to make him feel like he has someone to cling to as everything else rages around us but I'm not some naive little girl who thinks love can fix everything. And I'm certain that telling him the truth would only drive him away. Sighing, I squeeze his hand and turn to watch everyone else as Storm clears his throat and holds his drink in the air.

"To Blaze. He's the reason this club exists, the reason we have this incredible family, and I know we'll do whatever we can to honor him every single day we're on this earth."

A chorus of cheers rise up around us as everyone else lifts their glasses before taking a sip and I glance over at Travis as he chugs more of the whiskey, my brows knitting together as my stomach churns.

"To Storm," someone else calls and I glance up as everyone raises their glasses again. Chance takes a step forward. "Our new president. It's a hell of a job and you're not taking over under ideal circumstances but we know you'll kill it."

Storm holds his hand up, shaking his head. "Hold up. We haven't even fucking voted yet."

"Well, let's do it now then," Chance says, turning to look at everyone as they nod in agreement. "If you want Storm as our new President, say yay and if you don't, say nay."

All of the brothers raise their glasses in the air and shout, "yay!" Storm shakes his head, looking around the room at all of them as Chance walks up to him and hands him something, whispering something only meant for Storm's ears before he claps his shoulder. Storm stares down at the thing in his hand for a few seconds before looking up and clearing his throat, lifting his glass in another toast. Nix steps forward.

"Well, hell... if y'all are voting now, there's something I'd like you to take into consideration."

Storm nods. "What?"

"I, uh... I've been thinking a lot over the past four days... about family and legacy and I'd like to join... if y'all will have me," he answers, wrapping his arm around Emma as she walks over to him and everyone stares at him in shock. One night about a week back, I asked Travis about the relationship between Nix and Blaze because there was some tension and it was impossible to miss. He informed me that they were thick as thieves when Nix was a kid but when Nix didn't want to join the MC, a rift formed between them and they didn't speak for years. Emma was actually the one that brought them back together and things were good until all of the stuff about Sarah, Tate's mom, came out last year and they had been struggling to rebuild their relationship a second time.

"You sure about this?" Storm asks. "You've never wanted to be part of the club before."

Nix nods. "Yeah, I am. Back then, the club was so different than it is now and this legacy, the one y'all have built in the last seven years, feels like something I'd be proud to carry on in my dad's memory."

"I suppose you'll want the president patch," Storm replies, shooting Nix a wry smile and he laughs, shaking his head as he takes a step back.

"Uh, no. I've already got plenty of kids to wrangle. Besides, Pops chose you for his VP, knowing that someday you'd take over for him. That's the way it should be."

Storm nods, running his hand through his hair as he looks out at his brothers. "This is highly unusual but let's fucking vote, I guess. If you want to patch in Nix as a full member, say "yay" and if you don't, say "nay"."

"Yay!" Eight voices ring out together, all approving Nix's entry into the club and people raise their glasses in a toast as Nix thanks them, looking proud as hell to be part of the club his dad built. When I think about all he's lost in the last four days, he might be the one my heart hurts the most for. To lose your parent is horrendous, a soul-changing experience, but to lose your dad when you weren't on good terms yet and knowing that you'll never get a chance to make it right, it has to be so fucking hard. I turn to Travis again but the chair next to me is empty and I sigh as I look up, scanning the room. Finding him in the kitchen, I watch him slip out of the back door with the bottle of whiskey in his hand and sigh again as I stand up and go after him. Thankfully, no one stops me to talk as I work through the crowd and when I step outside, I cross my arms over my chest to ward off the chill that seems to settle into my bones.

Travis walks over to the chairs under the big oak tree in the middle of the yard before I take off after him, trying to think of something I could say to get him to open up to me. There is this distance between us right now that kills me and as much as I want to help him, I also miss him like fucking crazy. I want *my* Travis back. He hears me approaching and looks up, warmth in his gaze for just a second before it's snuffed out by pain and he sighs, shaking his head as he takes another gulp of alcohol.

"Just go back inside, Rowan," he slurs, his eyes glassy and I shake my head as I stop in front of him, step between his legs, and run my fingers through his hair.

"I'm not going anywhere."

He sighs. "You shouldn't be out here."

"Neither should you," I argue and he sighs again before grabbing my hand and pulling me down onto his lap. He wraps his arm around my waist, pulling me closer as he takes another sip of whiskey and I lay my head on his shoulder, looking out at the water with a sigh.

"Will you please talk to me?"

He shrugs. "What is there to say?"

"Come on," I snap as I sit up and meet his eyes. "Don't fucking give me that. You're going through hell and everyone can see it so please talk to me."

"What the fuck do you want me to tell you, Rowan? That it's my fault Blaze is dead? That I should have done more to help him instead of just staring at him as he fucking died in front of me? That I'm motherfucking cursed?"

My brow furrows and my heart breaks. "What do you mean you're cursed?"

"Just drop it," he growls, lifting the bottle to his lips again but I yank it away before he can spill another drop of liquor down his throat. His lip curls back as his gaze snaps to mine and he reaches for the bottle again. "Give that to me."

"No. What do you mean you're cursed?"

His eyes meet mine, fierce and determined as I glare down at him, demanding an answer to my question but he refuses to give in. But I won't either. Not when I know how much he needs me and he can get as angry as he fucking wants, he's not going to drive me away, now or ever. He holds my glare and reaches for the bottle again but I keep it away from his grasp as I arch a brow, silently telling him to start talking but before he can, a scream rips through the air. It came from the direction of the house and we both jerk up, looking up at the back door. My heart jumps into my throat as possibilities run through my mind, possibilities of what fresh hell Warren has gifted us with for a second time today as Travis jumps up and sets me on my feet.

He glances back at me, grabs my hand and nods, letting me know that we're going to run before he takes off toward the house, dragging me along behind him. My mind spins with horrid thoughts that I desperately wish I could push from my brain and my heart pounds against my ribs, a mixture of fear and exertion, as we reach the house. Travis rips the back door open and we step inside as every head snaps up to look at us.

"What is it?" Storm asks a sobbing Emma and she drops a card on the counter, her hands shaking, and that same haunted look in her eyes I saw on the day Blaze died. Lowering my gaze, I suck in a breath when I see the sympathy card sitting on the counter with a photo of all of us that day, surrounding Blaze as he slipped away and tears sting my eyes.

"What did it say, Em?" Moose asks and she shakes her head, gasping for air as she turns into her husband's chest and he wraps his arms around her. I turn back to Storm as he drops the card back down on the counter and clenches his fists, looking up at all of us.

"Two down, three to go."

Wicked Games

Chapter Thirty-Two
Rowan

"Morning, Princess," Travis says as he steps out of the bathroom with a towel around his waist and I open my eyes, yawning as they burn and my head throbs relentlessly. I managed to catch about two hours of sleep last night but I spent most of it tossing and turning, tormented by horrific images every time I closed my eyes. And when I wasn't reliving Blaze's death or seeing Warren's face in my mind, I was making myself sick with worry over the man standing in front of me. "Sleep okay?"

I shake my head. "No."

"Baby," he sighs, his brows knitting together as he studies me for a second before sighing and pulling the towel away from his waist. He crawls back into bed and pulls me into his side, wrapping his arms around me as he kisses my forehead. His hand cradles the back of my head, massaging his fingers into my scalp as he takes a deep breath, breathing me in before he kisses my forehead again. "Go back to sleep, okay? I've got you."

My heart cracks wide open at the gesture and I bury my face in his chest as tears sting my eyes. The last few days have just been hell and it's all catching up with me... with all of us. Travis sighs and pulls one hand away from my body. I peek up in time to see him reaching for the bottle of booze on the bedside table. Sinking my teeth into my bottom lip, I choke back a sob and reach out, laying my hand on his arm as he wraps his fingers around the neck of the bottle and he looks back at me, his brow shooting up as I shake my head.

"Not today, baby. Let me be your whiskey," I whisper, pressing a kiss to his chest and he stares down at me, his eyes blazing, and his nostrils flaring. I hold my breath, waiting for his answer and finally, he nods, releasing the bottle. I swing my leg over his body and straddle his waist as he grips my hips in both hands and rises up off of the bed to press his lips to mine as his arms wrap around me, holding me tightly against his body. There is a desperation in his kiss, an intensity that was never there before and every ounce of his pain is on display as his tongue flicks at my lips, demanding entrance and I give it to him. I'll do anything, say anything, give him whatever his heart desires if it means I can ease just a fraction of his suffering.

With his arms locked around me, he scoots back along the mattress until his back hits the headboard and he relaxes, thrusting a hand into my hair as his tongue tangles with mine, stroking and teasing me to the brink of madness. Moaning into his kiss, I rock my hips against him, annoyed that the lace of my panties separates us. I want to ... no, I need to feel him against me. He reaches down and grabs my tit, twisting my nipple between his fingers as he nips at my bottom lip and my pussy clenches.

386

"Travis," I breathe and he growls, his head falling back for a second before his lips are back on mine. He grabs my panties and I jerk away from him as he grabs his pocketknife off the table with his other hand, flicking it open. My heart pounds in my chest as he lowers the knife to my waist and effortlessly slices it through one side of my panties before moving to the other side and doing the same. As he tosses the blade back on the table, he pulls the scrap of lace away from my body and flings it across the room, groaning as my bare sex rubs against his cock.

"Fuck, baby," he groans, his fingers kneading my hips as his head drops back again. I fucking love when he does that, loses himself in the pleasure of being with me and I crave more of it so I slip out of his grasp, kissing a line down his chest as I lower myself on the bed. When I peek up at him again, his eyes are focused on me, blazing with need and he lifts his hips slightly, encouraging me to suck his length into my mouth as he drags his teeth over his bottom lip.

Wrapping my hand around his cock, I watch his face as he fights to keep his eyes open and each breath punches past his lips, reveling in the power I have over him in these moments before I lean down and wrap my lips around the tip. His hand immediately slips into my hair and he releases a soft groan that sounds something like a prayer as his head falls back and his eyes close. The hand in my hair slips down my back, dragging over my skin with reverence as I take all of him, letting him hit the back of my throat as he releases another groan.

"You're so perfect, Row. So fucking perfect," he murmurs and my skin tingles with need as his hands roam over my body, touching me everywhere but it's still not enough. Pulling back, I trail the tip of my tongue up the underside of his cock, teasing him as my fingers wrap around the base and I begin pumping him. He groans again, reaching down to play with my nipples and as soon as he grazes them, they tighten with need.

"Oh, God."

He shakes his head and grabs my arm, pulling me back into his lap with a feral look on his face as he leans in and peppers my face with kisses. "I need you, Princess."

"Yes," I whisper, reaching behind me to grab his cock and line it up with my entrance as every cell in my body shakes with anticipation. He presses against me and I glance back at his handsome face as I slowly sink onto his length, inch by glorious inch. A groan slips past his parted lips as his eyes bore into mine and his hands grip my hips. When he's buried inside me fully, he holds me in his lap and I grab his face in my hands, pressing my lips to his as I circle my hips, loving the way he fills me completely. He drags his lips down my neck to my shoulder and I arch my back as he kisses down to my tit and gently smacks my ass.

"Move, baby."

I do as instructed, lifting up and slowly sinking back down as he catches my nipple with his teeth and sucks it into his mouth, flicking the little bud with his tongue. I shudder, leaning back and bracing my hands on his thighs as I set a slow, seductive pace with my hips. He releases me with a pop and leans back against the headboard as he grips my waist, watching me ride his cock with fire in his eyes. I can't stop watching him as he stares down at where we're joined, skating his tongue over his bottom lip like he wants to taste me and I moan, fighting to keep my eyes open.

His gaze snaps to mine and he growls, reaching forward and hooking a hand around the back of my neck as he drags me back to him and claims my lips. The kiss is fierce, protective, demanding, and possessive like he's branding me with his lips and everything inside me crumbles at the thought. It's what I want more than anything - to be truly his and even though I know it will never happen, I let myself dream for a moment. Dream that he and I have a future together, that we could be happy and tears sting my eyes. With a groan, he rips his lips from mine and tucks my head into his neck as he braces his feet on the bed and begins thrusting up into me, wringing every drop of pleasure from my body as I shake in his arms, an orgasm quickly building in my belly.

"Travis," I cry and he groans, his fingers digging into my hips as he flips me over onto my back and looms above my body, sinking his cock into me again. I cling to him, my nails digging into his back as I wrap my legs around his waist and throw my head back with a moan. He slams into me mercilessly and my pussy throbs, demanding more as I spiral out of control. I'm desperate, frantic, needy as I cling to his body and beg for my release. Each time the word "please" passes my lips, Travis groans in my ear, panting and grunting as he fucks me within an inch of my life as sweat pours down our bodies. He pulls back and I meet his eyes.

"Please, baby," I beg, grabbing the sheet underneath me in one hand as I lift my hips off of the bed to meet him as I reach down with the other hand and circle my clit. "I need to come."

He groans again, unable to take his eyes off of me as I circle the sensitive little bundle of nerves and my body jerks, so close to the release I'm craving. Reaching up, he wraps a hand around my throat and it is exactly what I need. With a scream, my body erupts and convulses beneath him as waves of pleasure slam into me, again and again, rendering me paralyzed as I coast through them. Travis leans down and presses his lips to mine, the hand around my throat tightening as he thrusts into me two more times and stills above me with a guttural roar before his body relaxes. He drops his forehead to mine and releases my throat as we both gasp for air, drifting down slowly from the intense pleasure and after a few seconds, he sighs and slips out of my body.

I open my eyes and meet his gaze. There is something different shining down at me, something I don't recognize, and I cock my head to the side as I study him but he doesn't say anything, just shakes his head and presses his lips to mine again before lying next to me and pulling me into his arms.

"Pretty sure we probably woke up the whole house," Travis says and I laugh as I cuddle into him. Maybe I should care but I just don't - especially when I know our time is limited. Sighing, I drag my fingertips over his chest.

"What's the plan for today?"

He shrugs. "I figure it's about time I get back into the case and try to figure out who the fuck Warren is."

"I saw him, you know."

"What?" he snaps, jumping up and caging me in between his arms as he stares down at me. "What do you mean you saw him?"

I suck in a breath and shudder at the memory. "After he rode by with the knife, you all were distracted by Blaze and he lifted his visor and let me see his face. He smiled and winked at me... it was fucking terrifying but you were right about him, he's completely unmemorable."

"Shit, baby," he whispers, falling to my side and staring up at the ceiling as his jaw ticks. "I'm so fucking sorry I didn't do a better job of protecting you."

I prop myself up on my elbow. "It's not your fault, Travis. The whole thing was… no one was thinking clearly, okay? Hell, even Tate wasn't acting like herself."

"I've fucking let Blaze and this whole club down, Rowan. I should have…" Tears shine in his eyes. "I should have found something sooner, worked harder, and maybe he would still be here with us."

"Baby…"

He shakes his head. "Don't. I don't want to hear you fucking say this isn't my fault because everyone knows it is. This is my *thing*. This is what I do and I failed this time."

"What do you mean this is what you do?" I ask, scowling down at him and he meets my eyes as a tear glides down the side of his face.

"I catch the bad guys… it's what I've always done, what I've always known."

There's a deeper meaning behind his words, I know there is, but I can't see it and I know there is no way he'll tell me. Not with that look on his face. His walls are up, high as hell, and completely unbreachable right now. Laying my hand on his chest, I set my chin on top of it and look up at him.

"Want some help going over the cases?"

He glances down and forces a smile to his face. "From you? Always."

I smile as he climbs out of bed and goes over to his bag, pulling the files out as I scoop one of his shirts up off of the floor and pull it over my head. He glances back at me and nods in approval as he carries the stack of files back over and plops them on the bed. Grabbing the first one, I flip it open and stare down at all of the information Travis has been able to find on Warren but it's not much. As I stare at the name, I keep being drawn to the unusually spelled last name and I glance up at Travis as he flicks through another file.

"Have you ever gotten anywhere with Warren's name?"

His head jerks up. "You mean besides the fact that it's fake as shit? No."

"Right," I say, pursing my lips as I glance back down at the name. "But he had to get it from somewhere, right? And it might mean something to him so why this name?"

Travis stares at me, his brows furrowed, and I can see the wheels turning in his head as he slowly nods. "Okay… so what are you thinking?"

"Well… the easiest would be an anagram, right? And it would explain why his last name is spelled so weird."

"You think there is another name hidden in Warren's name?" he asks and I nod. He studies me for a second before jumping up and grabbing a notebook and a pen. When he climbs back into bed, he flashes me an expectant look.

"Okay, what do you have?"

I stare at the name, running through the letters as I try to find another name hidden there. "There's Ren… which could be spelled with a "w" or without one."

"I don't think we know anyone named Ren or Wren," he answers and I continue studying the letters laid out in front of me as I chew on my lip.

Come on.

There has to be another name here…

"Oh, wait! I've got Ryan," I say as I run through the letters and make sure they work. When he doesn't answer me, I look up and meet his wide eyes. "What?"

He shakes his head. "We knew a Ryan... but..."

"But what, Travis?" I ask, my heart climbing into my throat. He blows out a breath.

"He's dead... Storm killed him in this very fucking house."

My stomach drops. "What do you mean Storm killed him in this house?"

"He was a police officer and he was dating Emma before she met Nix... he was a bad fucking dude and the shit he did to her... it was fucking awful, babe. After Emma met Nix, Ryan lost his fucking mind and started stalking her - that's how we actually met her cause Nix called his dad for help. He broke in here one night and held Emma and Nix at gun point but Storm snuck in the back door and shot him."

"Okay," I whisper, trying to process everything he just told me as I look down at the name again. "So clearly, it's not him but... someone that he was important to?"

Travis shrugs. "I have no fucking clue."

"We should go ask Emma." I'm sure if anyone could help us crack this whole thing wide open, it will be her now that we know more. Travis nods and as we climb out of bed and get dressed, I try to imagine what Emma went through back then and Travis's comment about Emma bringing Nix and Blaze back together pops into my head. It all makes more sense now.

Once I've thrown on a pair of jeans and Travis is dressed, he grabs my hand and we walk downstairs in search of Emma but the house is empty.

"What the hell?" he whispers, pulling a gun from the waistband of his jeans as he pulls me closer. Voices drift in from outside and we follow them to the front door where everyone is standing, watching as a man with blond hair steps out of a sleek sedan. Emma gasps, taking a step forward.

"Zane?"

Nix steps in front of his wife, blocking her with his body. "What the fuck are you doing here?"

"Who is Zane?" I ask Travis and he glances over at me, shrugging his shoulders before we both turn back to watch the scene unfold. Storm steps forward, a gun in his hand as well as he glances between Zane and Emma.

"Em?" he asks. "You know him?"

She nods. "He is Ryan's brother."

All of the guys jerk to attention, turning to Zane with guns raised and he holds his hands up in front of his body, shaking his head as he looks over all of us with wide eyes.

"Don't shoot me. I'm not Warren."

Travis growls and takes a step forward. "How the fuck do you know that name?"

"Because I know who he is… who he really is," he says, glancing up at us and something about him makes me think he's telling the truth. Unlike when Warren revealed his face to me, I don't sense anger or pain when I look at Zane. In fact, he just looks tired.

"You'd better start talking, Wheeler," Storm snarls, taking a step forward with his gun aimed at Zane's chest. He nods and sighs.

"My brothers, Caleb and Jake… they've been working with Ryan's best friend, Evan Nelson, to get revenge on y'all for Ryan's death. He came to me, too, about two years ago to ask me to join them but I didn't want any part of it."

Chance lowers his gun and steps forward, eyeing him skeptically. "Why the fuck would you come tell us this if your brothers are involved?"

"Because," he sighs, running a hand through his hair. "They are involved but Evan is the one running the show and I don't want to see them get hurt because of him. He's... he's fucking unhinged and after he was released from prison, all he talked about was making y'all pay."

"Do you know what they are planning?" Travis asks and Zane shakes his head.

"No. I washed my hands of the whole damn thing but I do know he has specific targets in mind, four people that he blames the most for killing Ryan - Blaze, Storm, Emma, and Streak."

Sucking in a breath, my gaze snaps to Travis and he meets my eyes, his lips pressed into a thin line as all of the hell he's gone through trying to track down Warren fills my mind. It was all designed to drive him crazy because he's one of the targets.

"Speaking of which..." Zane says, scanning the group with a scowl. "Where is Blaze?"

A wave of grief washes through all of us, it's palpable even that even Zane takes notice. Storm sucks in a breath and lowers his gun slightly as he shakes his head.

"Warren... no, *Evan* killed him five days ago."

"Oh, fuck," he whispers, running a hand through his blond hair. "I really hoped I would get here before... fuck!"

Travis tucks his gun back into the waistband of his jeans and grabs my hand before walking to the front of the group and stopping in front of Zane. "Do you know anything else? Anything that can help us find him before he comes after us again?"

"Why don't we take this inside?" Storm says, scanning the tree line around the property and Zane studies us all for a second before nodding as everyone else lowers their weapons. As Travis turns back to the house with my hand in his, I pray that we can finally get some answers and end this before anyone else gets hurt.

Chapter Thirty-Three
Warren

"My brothers, Caleb and Jake… they've been working with Ryan's best friend, Evan Nelson, to get revenge on y'all for Ryan's death. He came to me, too, about two years ago to ask me to join them but I didn't want any part of it."

Fuck.

Fuck.

Fuck.

What the hell have you fucking done, you moron?

"Zane," I growl under my breath, watching him from the safety of the trees as he spills everything to these fuckers, everything I've built for the last two years, everything I've fucking worked for, and everything that was almost mine. My plan was fucking brilliant, flawless, and now I have to change it. I mean, I have always had several back-up plans lined up but I was attached to this one, the one that inflicted the most pain, the most suffering. For days, I've been watching them cope with Blaze's death, happy as a pig in shit because I could see the pain and horror in their eyes. I loved that I did that to them and I've been fantasizing about the next step endlessly but now it's going to have to change.

"Fuck you," I hiss as I watch Zane fucking Wheeler follow the Devils back into Emma and Nix's house, my heart pounding in my ears as I think about what I'll do to him when I manage to get my hands on him. He fucking ruined everything and now, he has to pay, too. Caleb and Jake won't be happy about that but they'll just have to deal with it. As his betrayal dances through my mind, I turn and slam my fist into a nearby tree trunk, unable to quell the boiling of my blood as I think about everything I just lost.

Turning, I begin walking back to my car, clenching and unclenching my fist as thoughts of my best friend play through my head. Ryan and I met when we were just kids and from that moment on, we were joined at the fucking hip. He wasn't just my best friend, he was my brother, and when he decided he wanted to become a police officer just like his pops, I followed him. We worked our way up through the ranks and then he met Emma. Ryan was fucking crazy about her, loved her more than a man should, more than was sane, but that was just who he was and what did she do? She fucking treated him like shit and left him broken hearted. When she met Phoenix West a year later, Ryan lost his goddamn mind. He was still holding out hope that she would come back to him eventually but when he saw them together, he knew it was over. The way he acted, it wasn't rational but he was my best friend and he had always been there for me so I helped him get her back and it got us both arrested. The stupid fucker, though... as soon as he made bail, he came after her again and it got him killed, shot in the back of the head like a goddamn dog by Storm. I spent years in prison, thinking of everyone this club had taken from me and how I would take revenge on them if I ever got the chance and there is no way in hell I'm going to let fucking Zane ruin that for me.

Ripping my phone from my pocket, I press one on the speed dial and hold it to my ear as it rings.

"'Sup?" Caleb answers and I resist the urge to growl.

"Get your brother back to the apartment now. Shit is going down and we need to regroup."

He scoffs. "What the hell does that mean?"

"I'll explain everything when I get there but tell Jake, we strike tonight."

Wicked Games

Chapter Thirty-Four
Rowan

The stars are out in full force tonight, twinkling down at me as I sit curled up in the chair next to the window, staring up at them as I run through everything we learned today... and everything we didn't.

Zane Wheeler stayed with us until well after dinner time, trying to help us figure out Evan's next move but in the end, we came up with a whole lot of nothing. He didn't stick around long enough in the beginning to learn any part of the plan and his brothers had been hush-hush about their dealings with Evan ever since. Emma also told the full story of her relationship with Ryan for those of us who had never heard it before and Travis was right, it was a doozy. But when I wasn't absorbed in everything she had been through, I couldn't help peeking over at Zane's face, intrigued by his reaction as he listened to all of the horrible things his brother had put Emma through. Every time I did, my heart hurt for him. It became very clear to me in the time that he was here that his brother's actions weigh heavily on him and he feels a crazy amount of guilt for not noticing what was going on all those years ago and stepping in to help Emma. She doesn't hold any ill will toward him, though. That became clear when she hugged him by the front door as he was getting ready to leave and told him that Ryan's actions were his alone and I think it made an impact on him. Or, at least, I hope it did.

He also filled us in on Ryan and Evan's whole story - how they met in school, became best friends instantly, and went to the police academy together - and he also told us about the years since Ryan's death. Apparently, Evan was hit the hardest by the news and he went so crazy that he had to be sedated so he didn't hurt himself or anyone else. He was put on a seventy-two hour hold at the hospital where they decided his actions were just a product of grief and released him. After that, he had to go on trial for assisting in the kidnapping of Emma and he pled guilty for a reduced sentence. Zane said he served his time without incident and after being released two years ago, immediately put his plan into motion. Thinking back to the day Blaze died, I remember all of the pain and anger I saw in Evan's eyes and it all makes sense to me in a way. Clearly, he's taken this all too far and held on too tight to the memory of his best friend when he should have tried to move on but his actions make sense to me now and I understand why he's doing all of this. It's still scary and makes me incredibly uneasy but it no longer feels chaotic.

Sighing, I turn away from the window and glance over at the bed as I yawn. Travis has been down in the study at the back of the house, drinking and talking over the cases with the guys for hours and I'm pretty sure all of the girls are passed out by now but he asked me to wait for him. It's especially frustrating since I feel like I might actually be able to get some sleep tonight and I'm beyond exhausted. Turning back to the window, I stare up at the stars, hoping this will all come to an end soon. The boys called Detective Rodriguez over, who was floored to learn that Evan was behind all of this. Apparently, they used to be partners when Evan made detective and he said he knew Evan was messed up but he never guessed he would go this far. Before he left, he called the station and put a BOLO out for him. He said sometime in the next few days we should be able to track him down and put this mess to bed. I'm excited about the idea but also terrified since I have no idea what that means for Travis and me. My mind drifts back to when he asked me to go on a regular date with him when this is all over and I smile. I don't want to get my hopes up but he's not sick of me yet so I suppose there is still a chance. It's slim and could be compared to a ball of ice in hell but it's there.

A piercing screech cuts through the peaceful silence around me and I jerk in my chair, whipping my head toward the door as my brows furrow. My heart races and the smoke detector in my room joins in, wailing so loudly that it is hard to even think. Jumping up, I grab a sweater and pull it over my head before clamping my hands over my ears and walking over to the door. I yank it open and stumble back as a cloud of smoke rushes toward me.

Holy shit.

Smoke is filling the entire hallway, obscuring my vision, and my stomach drops as a shot of adrenaline rushes through my body. There is a dull roar from somewhere else in the house and my skin prickles as tears sting my eyes.

"Rowan!"

I gasp, turning toward the sound of Tate's voice coming up the stairs but I can't see her. "Tate?"

"Just stay right there and keep talking to me. I'm coming to you."

I nod despite the fact that she can't see me. "Where is everyone else?"

"I'm not sure about the boys but all of the girls and kids are out in the yard. I came back in here to find you once we realized you were still up here."

"Where were you guys?" I ask, scowling. I thought everyone else had come up to bed but I guess not.

"Down in Emma and Nix's room talking. The whole front of the house is on fire and we saw the smoke before the alarms went off."

"Oh my God," I whisper as she reaches my room and flashes me a smile but her eyes are full of fear as she reaches down and grabs my hand.

"Ready to get out of here, sweet cheeks?"

I nod. "Most definitely."

"Do not let go of my hand and try not to breathe in too much smoke, okay? We're heading for the back door."

"Okay," I whisper as we step out of my room and turn toward the stairs. I squint, trying desperately to see through the thickening smoke but it's no use so I press my other hand to the wall, feeling my way along the hallway. Once we reach the top of the stairs, Tate begins leading us down and a wave of heat smacks into me as I cough as we wade through the smoke. My heart races as my mind runs through all of the ways this could go wrong, all of the ways we could die in this house tonight and tears sting my eyes.

Travis.

Where are you?

The thought of never getting to see him again makes me want to scream and I push the thought from my mind as we reach the bottom of the stairs and turn in the direction of the kitchen. Tate's hand is firm in mine, guiding me toward safety but I can't help looking back to where I think the study is as I entertain the idea of going in search of Travis. The only problem is Tate would, without a doubt, follow me and I can't do that to my brother. As we round the corner, I suck in a breath and stop, staring at the entire front wall of the house which is engulfed in flames, the roar of the fire louder than before as I watch it consume everything in its path.

"Rowan, keep moving," Tate snaps, tugging on my hand as she coughs. The smoke is so thick down here that it's impossible to take a breath and I cover my mouth with the sleeve of my sweater as we start moving again. Just when I think I'm going to pass out if I don't take a breath, we step outside into fresh air and I stop, releasing Tate's hand to bend over and brace my hands on my knees as I cough and try to catch my breath.

"You all right?" Tate asks and I nod, peeking up at her as my chest aches.

"Yeah, you?"

She nods and points to the rest of the group under the large oak tree in the middle of the yard. "I'm going to go check on everyone else."

"You see the guys yet?" I ask and she shakes her head, scanning the yard.

"No, but Emma said that the study has its own door so they should have gotten out safely," she answers and I nod, straightening and taking a full breath to try and clear my lungs as Storm walks around the side of the house and she points to him. "Look, there they are."

405

Pop!

Pop!

Pop!

Time seems to grind to a halt as I look around the yard, trying to find the source of the noise as everyone drops to the ground. Another pop rips through the air and it finally dawns on me that it's gunshots.

Someone is shooting at us?

I still can't process what's happening around me as Storm stands up and yells, "Get to the trees and stay low!"

Everyone begins running, all of us heading in different directions as another pop fills the air. My heart thunders in my ears as I turn to the forest behind me and start running, my feet working with no instruction from my brain which is still trying to fit all the pieces of the last five minutes together.

Pop!

A searing hot pain slices through my arm and I cry out as I slap my hand over it and glance down. Blood trickles over my fingers before falling to the ground. The pain is unbearable and when I try to move my arm, it radiates up to my shoulder and I release a sob as tears drip down my face.

Oh my God.

I've been shot.

A part of me wants to freeze, crumple to the ground, and cry but I know staying out here in the open is the worst place to be so I push myself to keep running, my heart thundering in my chest as tears sting my eyes and I tuck my arm into my side with my other hand. When I finally make it to the safety of the tress, I slip behind one and lean back against it as I clench my teeth to get through the pain. My breath rings in my ears as I gasp for air and I turn, peeking out into the yard again, searching for danger but it's empty now. Everyone else has scattered into the forest just like me and I turn away, squeezing my eyes shut as I try to think of what to do.

I have no idea where anyone went and the threat could be anywhere. A twig snaps from somewhere off to my left and my eyes snap open, searching the darkness but I still can't see anything and I shake my head as my chest aches.

Okay...

I have to make a decision. If someone is out there, watching me right now, it's stupid to stay here in this spot and wait for him to find me but if there is no one there, if my mind is playing tricks on me and I run, it could get me killed. My whole body shakes as my mind spins but when another twig snaps, this one closer than before, my instincts make the decision for me. Turning to the right, I sprint off in that direction and as I run through the forest, twigs and branches smack me all over my body, scratching up my face but I don't care. I just have to keep running until I'm safe. Just keep running...

Glancing back over my shoulder, my feet stutter. Behind me, too close for my comfort, is Warren. He's running after me with that white mask of his covering his face but it doesn't matter because I can still see it in my mind, it haunts me every time I close my eyes. Chills blanket my skin and I will my legs to move faster, pump harder because I know I'm running out of time. His boots crunch fallen leaves and twigs, reminding me of his progress as he creeps closer and I look around for a place to hide or a way to escape him but there is nothing.

Oh, God.

Run, my mind screams at me and tears streak down my cheeks.

Glancing back again, I scream.

He's too close.

The breath is knocked from my lungs as he tackles me from behind and I scream again, pain shooting through me as we tumble to the ground and his large body covers mine. He slips me to my back and I fight against him, my entire body trembling violently but I don't care. I strike out with my uninjured arm, hitting and fighting him off as best I can but he manages to grab it and pin it to the forest floor above my head as he rips his mask off of his face.

"Hey, baby," he whispers, flashing me a grin that sends ice cold dread washing through me as I struggle to free myself from his hold. It only seems to amuse him more and the wild look in his brown eyes makes me want to cry as my stomach churns. He shakes his head. "You're not going anywhere, sweetheart. You're mine now."

I grit my teeth and shake my head as I try to buck him off of me. "I'll never be yours."

"Now, that's just not true, Rowan." He tosses his mask aside, finally done with the façade, and leans down, dragging the tip of his finger down my cheek as his hot breath blankets my face. It smells like tobacco and stale beer and I gag but he misses it… or ignores it as he traces my lips with his thumb. "See, when I first started all of this, it was all about making the club pay for what they did to me. I never had women or love on my mind but as soon as I saw Streak fucking you up against his window on your first night in Baton Rouge, I was hooked."

"You watched us?" I spit and he laughs quietly.

"Of course I fucking watched. Have you seen yourself, Princess? You're a goddamn smoke show."

I wince at his use of Travis's nickname for me before steeling my gaze and meeting his eyes. "You're fucking sick."

"Naw, baby. That's just you. I stood outside of the clubhouse, watching you and I couldn't look away even if I tried. You put me under your spell."

"Go fuck yourself," I hiss. The thought of him watching us that night makes me shudder as I close my eyes and jerk my face away from him.

"That's no way to talk to your man," he growls, gripping my face in his hand, turning me back to him and squeezing until I'm certain he's going to crack my jaw. Seeing the fear in my eyes, he smiles. "We'll just have to teach you the proper way to behave, won't we?"

"Fuck off," I snarl, meeting his stare and he sighs as he pulls his hand back and backhands me. My head jerks to the side as pain rocks through my head but I won't give him the satisfaction of seeing me cry anymore. Turning back to him, I narrow my eyes into a glare and he laughs.

"Oh, I can see why Streak is so whipped by you, baby. You've got fucking fire." He leans down and grabs my face again, holding me still as he brushes his lips over mine. This time, I can't hold the cry back as I struggle to free myself, thoughts of Travis cementing themselves in my mind. When I refuse to give him what he wants, he releases me and jumps to his feet. As soon as I'm free, I roll to my belly and try to scramble away from him but he grabs my ankle and pulls me back across the ground before lifting me to my feet.

"That's enough of that. Besides, we've got to get going if we don't want to miss our flight."

My heart jumps into my throat. "Flight? To where?"

"You'll see," he answers, flashing me a wide smile. My stomach drops and I struggle against him, pulling a sigh from his lips. "But I promise you're going to love it, baby."

"Rowan?" Travis's panicked voice is my salvation and I look up, opening my mouth to scream to him for help but before I can, something round is shoved between my teeth. My head jerks back and I try to spit it out but Evan chuckles, holding it firmly in place, as he spins me around and secures it with straps behind my head.

A fucking ball gag?

Turning me back to face him, he grins. "Knew that might come in handy."

"Rowan! Please, baby, where are you?" Travis screams, his voice closer than before and I spin around, my eyes wide and my heart climbing into my throat. Evan wraps his arms around my body, holding me back as I try to get away from him, screaming despite the gag in my mouth.

I won't give up.

I won't relent to Evan.

I won't stop fighting to get to Travis unless I'm dead.

I turn to glare at Evan, hoping he can see that shining in my eyes. He studies me, a smile stretching across his face and I flash him a glare before I drop my head back and scream again.

"Rowan?!" His voice is closer again and a wave of calm washes over me. He's almost here and he's going to save me, I just know it.

"Son of a bitch," Evan hisses, grabbing me around the legs and hoisting me up over his shoulder as I scream again. He takes off running in the opposite direction and the feeling of calm is quickly dashed out. My throat is sore from the smoke and all of the screaming I've already done but I keep going, hoping like hell Travis will hear it and be able to find me. The idea of never seeing him again pops into my mind and tears gather in my eyes as I watch as the forest floor races past my vision.

I should have told him I loved him.

Damn the consequences because if I die tonight or Evan manages to get me away from here, that will be my greatest regret.

After what feels like forever, Evan skids to a stop next to a giant oak tree, bigger than the one in the middle of Emma and Nix's yard, and sets me back on my feet. My knees buckle and he catches me as he clenches his teeth and studies me, his chest heaving. Staring back at him, I see the moment something changes and all of the life drains from his eyes until all I'm left with are the cold, dead eyes of a mad man.

"You know what? I really wanted to keep you for myself... I dreamt of the life we could have had together but this is quickly turning into a no win situation."

"Then go," I try to say against the gag but I know it just sounds like gibberish. Evan glances back at the way we came, chewing on his bottom lip, deep in thought, before turning to me with a grin that makes my heart jump into my throat and my stomach churn. I stumble back when he steps toward me but he grabs me, pulling me back into his body.

411

"Guess I'll just have to settle for second best, won't I?"

I have no idea what that means, no idea what to say to him so I just watch him as he bends down and pulls a knife out of his boot. As the blade glints in the moonlight, I scream into the gag and struggle against his hold, desperate to get away from him but it's no use.

"Shh, Princess," he coos, gripping the back of my neck with one hand as I struggle against him. "I wish I could say that this will be over quickly but if I can't have you, if I can't keep this sweet little pussy for myself, then I want Streak to watch you die. I want him to see the life leave your eyes and know it's all his fucking fault."

He sinks the blade into my abdomen, just below my belly button and my eyes widen but I don't feel a thing except for the punch of the handle hitting my skin and he pulls back before doing it again as I crumple in on myself.

What is happening?

Why can't I feel it?

"There, there," he whispers, taking the knife out of my body and tossing it to the ground as he holds me up and pets my hair with his blood-stained hand. He leans in and presses a kiss to my cheek before laying me on my back underneath the tree. "If I can't have you, then the next best thing is to make sure Travis can't either."

Tears pour down my face and I struggle to breathe as pain begins radiating from the wound, white hot, and each second it seems to grow in intensity until I'm certain I'm going to pass out as I stare up at the stars peeking out of the tree branches above me. There is a tug on my wrist and I turn my head to watch Evan as he ties my good hand to the tree, pulling the rope tight so I can't even move it an inch before he turns back to me and flashes me a sad smile.

"Oh, Rowan, it didn't have to be like this."

My brows furrow and more tears fall as I stare up at him, wondering what I ever did to deserve this. He kneels beside me and brushes the hair out of my face, combing his fingers through the long dark strands before he drags the back of his fingers down my cheek.

"Rowan!" Travis's voice cuts through the fog and I cry out, begging the universe that he hears me. Evan glances over his shoulder and sighs.

"It's time for me to go, sweetheart." His smile turns wicked. "Make sure you bleed out nice and slow for me, okay? I want this to hurt him."

And then he's gone.

Turning my head, I stare up at the branches above me. The pain is overwhelming and I can't make my mind work as I wonder if anyone is ever going to find me or if I'm going to die right here as darkness creeps in around the edges of my vision and my body jerks to attention.

No.

Stay awake.

Relaxing back into the ground, I call for Travis in my mind even though I know it's useless. My strength is waning and despite what I want to tell myself, I know I don't have long. The darkness ebbs and flows around the corners of my vision and the sky above me begins to tilt as I suck in a breath and close my eyes.

"Rowan!" Travis screams, closer than before and my eyes snap open. I must have passed out at some point but there is no telling how long I've been unconscious. Gritting my teeth, I use my injured arm to reach down to my stomach and feel the wound there, wincing. "Fuck. Rowan!"

His voice is even closer and I suck in a breath, calling out for him against the gag but it's too quiet for him to hear and I can't muster the strength to scream any louder.

"Rowan, baby, please! Where the hell are you?" The pain in each word he speaks rips a sob from my throat and I look down at my injured hand, the one Evan left unrestrained before peeking down at the ground next to my body. There is a large stick not too far from me and if I get it, I can smash it against the tree trunk to get his attention. But, fuck… it's going to hurt like hell. Sucking in a breath, I lift my arm from my belly and scream, squeezing my eyes shut as pain swamps my body and tears fall down my face into the grass below me.

It's too much.

I can't do this.

"Rowan!" Travis bellows, tears in his voice, and he sounds even closer this time. God, he's right there…It spurs me on and I scream through the pain as I lower my arm and grab the stick before struggling to raise it back up again.

Come on.

Fucking do it.

"If you're out here, baby, I need you to make a noise."

The world spins around me as I use the last of my strength to lift the stick into the air and smack it into the tree again and again, sobbing as I pray to everything I can think of that he'll hear me. Travis bursts through the brush and I cry out in relief as I drop the stick to the ground and close my eyes.

"Jesus," he hisses, kneeling next to me and quickly removing the ball gag from my mouth. I flex my aching jaw as he pulls it away before turning to look at him as he works on untying my arm. When he's finished, he scoots closer to me and runs his hands over my body. "Are you hurt anywhere else besides your arm?"

"Stomach," I whisper, my voice rough from all of the screaming and he glances down, lifting up my sweatshirt as his eyes widen and he turns to look at me. His heart is breaking in his eyes, I can see it clear as day, as he pulls out his cell phone and tries to reassure me with a smile.

"I've got you, baby. I've always fucking got you."

"Travis," I breathe, reaching up and cupping his cheek as he presses the phone to his ear, calling for help but darkness creeps in around my vision again and I know this could be it. This could be the last time I see his handsome face, his green mesmerizing eyes, and his cocky grin and I don't want to die without telling him the truth. His gaze locks on mine as the darkness grows, pulling me under.

"Stay with me, Princess."

"I love you, Travis," I whisper, unable to hold back anymore as I'm swallowed up by shadows once again and if this is death, at least I died with a smile on my face and the love of my life by my side.

Wicked Games

Chapter Thirty-Five
Travis

"Sir, you can't come with us," the paramedic says, placing her hand on my chest to stop me from climbing in there with Rowan. It's not going to fucking work though. There is not a damn thing on this earth that could keep me from her right now and I turn to stare at the paramedic, making that damn clear as I shake my head.

"I'm going with her."

She sighs. "No, you're not, sir. You can follow behind us in your own car."

"Absolutely fucking not. That is my woman in there and she fucking needs me so I'm going."

"Just let him come," the other paramedic calls from inside the ambulance where she's treating Rowan and Justine, the one holding me back, sighs as her hands falls away.

"You best not give me any damn problems."

I hold up three fingers. "Scout's honor."

She hums in agreement and moves out of my way, mumbling something about me never being a scout as she walks to the driver's door and slips behind the wheel.

I jump in the back and grab the doors to close them as Tate and Kodiak come running up.

"You got her, brother?" he asks and I nod, meeting his gaze. After a second, he nods and Tate grabs his hand as she turns back to their cars.

"We'll follow behind you."

Nodding, I slam the doors shut before turning to look down at my girl as she lies in the middle of the stretcher, her skin too fucking pale. She's passed out fucking cold and I watch her chest to make sure she's still breathing for a second before sighing in relief. Laura, the other paramedic, points to the bench behind me and arches a brow.

"Sit there and stay out of my way. She's the patient and I don't have the time or patience to put up with any shit from you, ya hear?"

I nod and sit down, grabbing Rowan's hand in both of mine and bringing it to my lips. "You just keep her breathing."

She gets to work, moving around the back and grabbing things out of cubbies before focusing back on Rowan. The ambulance starts moving and I press my lips to her hand, begging her to come back to me.

"I love you, Travis." Her voice whispers in my head again and again. They keep playing on a loop, repeating endlessly as I try to wrap my mind around everything that just happened. When I heard that first shot go off, I ran around the house so fucking fast, not a goddamn care in the world that I was running straight toward the danger but she was already gone. It took me a minute to find Tate, who told me the last place she saw my girl and I just went from there. Most of the fucking time, I was certain I was going in the wrong direction but something, deep down in my gut, told me to keep going so I did. I searched those woods for what felt like an eternity, screaming her name and begging every deity I could think of that she would call back to me. The relief I felt when I heard that stupid fucking stick banging against the tree almost made me pass out but it was nothing compared to the sight of her, gagged, shot, stabbed, and tied to a tree.

Staring down at her, I shake my head.

She loves me?

Thinking back over the past month, a riot of emotions rocks through me and as I run through the past ten days, everything snaps into place and smacks me in the chest. If I wasn't already sitting, I would have fallen on my ass.

Fuck.

She loves me.

I don't know how to feel about her admission because it's all so much more complicated than she realizes but as I try to think of my life without her, I know I can't fucking walk away. Let's just hope she feels the same way once she knows the truth about me.

The ambulance stops and the front door opens as Laura stands up and begins tucking things into the stretcher and making sure it's safe to move again. When the back door opens, Justine points to me and orders me to stay until they get the gurney out and I nod, releasing Rowan's hand and setting it on her body. They wheel her out and I jump down after her, my hands shaking as I follow them into the emergency room. A team of doctors and nurses rush up to her, taking over for the paramedics and one of the nurses directs me to wait in the family area off to the side but I can't move. With my feet planted to the floor, I watch them wheel her into a trauma bay and begin checking her over as my heart races.

"Sir."

I glance down at the tiny old woman in blue scrubs as she flashes me a no-nonsense look.

"You need to go sit down in the waiting area and someone will come talk to you when we know more."

I nod, raking my hand through my hair before meeting her gaze again. "Just take good care of her, 'kay?"

"Of course," she answers, her eyes softening, and I take one last look at Rowan before turning to go to the waiting area. It's empty when I walk in and I hope that means no one else is here tonight so that Rowan has the best of the best working on her. Sinking into one of the chairs, my knee shakes like fucking crazy and I look down at my hands, my stomach rolling when I see Rowan's blood all over them.

"Fuck."

"Streak!"

I glance up as Tate and Kodiak run in, looking as fucking frazzled as I feel and I stand up, nodding to them.

"They rushed her back and said they'll come find us when they know something."

Kodiak nods, turning to stare out at the bays lined up across from us as he scrubs his jaw, his eyes fucking haunted as he turns back to me. "What the fuck happened out there?"

"Honestly," I whisper, shaking my head. "I don't even know. It was… insane and felt fucking rushed, unlike all of Evan's other attacks."

He nods, his brow furrowed, as his gaze falls to my hands and his face pales.

"Streak, maybe you should go find a bathroom and wash up," Tate suggests and I shake my head. There is no way in hell I'm leaving my girl. Not happening. She places her hand on my shoulder. "I'll come find you if there is news but you're going to scare people looking like that."

"Fine… but I want to know the fucking second something happens."

She nods. "Of course."

Reluctantly, I leave the waiting room and slip into the hallway, spotting a bathroom right across from us and I breathe a sigh of relief. If I have to be away from her, I don't want to be too far. I stop at the first sink and grip the sides of it as I look up in the mirror and almost fall backward. It's been a long fucking time since I've seen this look on my damn face and I can't say that I missed it. Squeezing my eyes shut, I force those memories back and try to focus on Rowan as I turn on the water and shove my hands under it.

The water runs red and my stomach churns. My chest aches when I think about what could have happened if I hadn't heard the stick banging against the tree, or if she hadn't found the strength to lift it up. I picture her cold and alone as she died out there and it takes everything I have to not put my fist through the mirror.

What fucking game was Evan playing at this time?

What was his end game?

Once my hands are clean, I turn off the water and walk back out of the bathroom, eager to see how my girl is doing. Fuck. I don't even care that there is still blood all over my shirt at this point. I've been gone too long and I need to get back to her. A doctor walks into the room from the other side at the same time I do and walks over to us as I stand next to Tate and Kodiak.

"You the family of Rowan Archer?"

We all nod and he sighs.

"Okay, good news and bad news - the wound to her stomach didn't hit anything major and we have that stitched up already but the gunshot wound to her arm is bad. It broke the bone in three places and she's lost a ton of blood so we are taking her up to surgery now to repair the break but as long as everything goes well during the operation, I expect her to make a full recovery."

My knees give out and I grab the chair next to me to keep myself upright as I release a breath. Tate wraps an arm around my shoulders] and gives them a squeeze as the doctor instructs us to another waiting room where we can sit until Rowan is out of surgery. We watch him leave before Kodiak turns to me.

"I don't know about you, brother, but now that we know she's going to be okay," he says, cracking his knuckles. "I can't wait to get my hands on Evan."

I arch a brow. "We caught him?"

"Yeah," Tate answers, nodding her head as she smiles. "Someone managed to call Rodriguez and he showed up just as Evan was running out of the woods to his car. He grabbed him and Storm instructed him to take Evan to our cabin out by the lake. We've got an old barn on the property where they're keeping him and it's so secluded out there that no one will hear y'all."

"What do you say? Want to go handle some business?" Kodiak asks and I glance over as they wheel Rowan into an elevator, fucking torn. I so badly would love a chance to get a hold of Evan and make him pay for the state of my girl right now but leaving her is like stabbing a hot poker in my chest. Tate nudges me and when I glance over at her, she nods.

"I'll keep an eye on her and call you when there's an update. Go make that son of a bitch regret ever coming after this club."

I study her for a second before glancing back at the closed elevator with a sigh. As much as I want to be glued to Rowan's fucking side, they won't let me in the operating room and I'm not doing any good just sitting here so I turn back to Tate and nod.

"You call me if *anything* happens."

She nods. "I've got her, Streak."

Feeling a tiny fucking bit better about the situation, I turn and walk out of the waiting room with Kodiak, ready to tear into Evan for coming after what's mine. This fucker is going to wish he'd never even thought of taking revenge on us and then I'll get back here, ready to greet my girl when she wakes up from surgery 'cause she and I have shit to work out and for the first time in my life, I'm ready to lay it all on the table for her.

Chapter Thirty-Six
Travis

"Hey," Fuzz says, nodding to Kodiak and me as we join them outside of the barn on Kodiak's property where Tate said they were hiding Evan and I stare at the door for a second, tempted to march in there and exact my revenge but instead, I look around the group.

"Where is Smith and Henn?"

Moose tips his head toward the barn. "Taking their frustrations out on Evan's face. How's Rowan?"

"In surgery but she should be okay," Kodiak answers. "Evan didn't hit anything vital when he stabbed her but her arm is broken and needs to be repaired."

They all sigh in relief as Chance claps my shoulder, nodding. "Good to hear."

"So, what are we going to do with this fucker?" I ask, crossing my arms over my chest as I nod toward the barn. Storm sighs and scrubs his hand down his face before shaking his head.

"Not going to lie, but there is a very big part of me that wants to go in there and fucking break his face before I put a bullet in his skull." He shakes his head again and clenches his fist. "He fucking shot at my wife and baby so it's the least he fucking deserves."

Kodiak nods. "I'm fucking with you, brother. I don't even want to think about how close I was to losing my baby sister."

Glancing around at all of them as they nod in agreement, I blow out a breath. I get it. I really fucking do and each time I think about finding Rowan under that tree, bleeding and on the verge of death, a red haze flashes across my vision. In those moments, all I want to do is grab a knife and make sure he knows how it feels to have it buried in his psychotic body. I want to rip him limb from limb but it isn't us... isn't who I am. The revelation slams into me full force and I shake my head, sucking in a breath.

"Should we really be discussing this in certain company?" Moose asks, tilting his head toward Rodriguez, who scoffs.

"No, y'all definitely should not be talking about this in front of me... except that I'm with you on this one. He killed my girl."

"Hold up... this is not who we are. We don't fucking kill people," I say, my mind spinning as I try to keep up with the conversation. Are they really suggesting that we throw away all the work we've done to change this club and Blaze's vision?

"Times change, Streak," Chance says, glancing back at the barn. "Can we risk letting the justice system handle this? What if it all goes to trial and he's found not guilty? Then he's free to come after us again and this time, he might just succeed in destroying all of us."

"Yeah, that's not fucking happening," Fuzz snaps, shaking his head as he clenches his jaw. Silence descends over us until Storm clears his throat and meets Rodriguez's eye.

"What did the BOLO turn up? Is there anyone that is gonna come looking for this fucker?"

Rodriguez shakes his head. "No. He hasn't checked in with his parole officer in weeks and all of his family is gone. I think everyone has just assumed that he ran off."

"And what are we doing with Caleb and Jake?" Fuzz asks, fidgeting as he waits for an answer. The tension in the air is making me fucking antsy, too, and I just want to get this over with so I can get back to my girl.

"We found an apartment in their name after Zane revealed their involvement to us and we searched it earlier this evening. We found enough evidence of everything to charge them with the five murders and Veronica's kidnapping so they will be arrested shortly."

Fuzz arches a brow. "So, no one will care if Evan just disappears?"

"Hold the fuck up," I seethe. "I can't believe you fuckers are actually considering this. We don't do shit like this and you know it."

"We've never been in this spot before, Streak," Storm says, flashing me a look of understanding before shaking his head. "I think the only thing we can do is put it to a vote."

If this conversation is any indication, I know exactly how this vote will go and my stomach churns, memories that I'd rather keep buried flooding my mind.

"This is fucking insane," I breathe, running my hand through my hair as Storm turns to the rest of the group and nods.

"If you're in favor of ending this fucker here and now, say "yay" and if you want to hand him over to the authorities say "nay".

"Nay," I snap, still shocked that we're even voting on this, as everyone else around me calls out "yay" and I shake my head. Even if Smith and Henn side with me, it won't fucking matter because it will only be three to five. Looking at my brothers, I blow out a breath.

"I can't fucking believe y'all."

Storm claps my shoulder. "I'm sorry, Streak. It has to be done. You're welcome to leave, though, if you want."

"No," I growl, shaking my head. "I don't fucking agree with the decision one bit but the vote was fair and I'll find a fucking way to live with it."

I hate every second of it but I will deal with it.

Storm nods and turns to the barn, squaring his shoulders. "Let's do this then."

We follow him and step into the barn before closing the door behind us and when I glance up, Evan grins at me, blood dripping from his mouth.

"Ah, Travis. I was so hoping you'd be here."

"Shut the fuck up, asshole," Henn snarls, clocking him across the face. My desire to make Evan pay and my need to not become a murderer war inside me as his head snaps to the side. He's tied to a wooden chair in the middle of the room and it looks like Smith and Henn have worked him over pretty well already. One eye is almost swollen shut and his lip is cracked right down the center.

Laughing, Evan spits some blood on the ground before looking back up at us. "Hello, boys. Long time no see."

"Shut the fuck up," Fuzz growls, pulling the gun from his waistband but Evan just laughs again.

"What? No foreplay? Don't y'all want to know about all of the awful things I did? I know it's been driving you crazy," he teases as enjoyment flashes in his eyes.

"Sure. Go on and tell us all about your revenge plan," Storm says, planting his feet in front of Evan and crossing his arms over his chest. Evan laughs again and shakes his head.

"Where's the fun in that?"

"Son of a bitch," Kodiak seethes, stepping forward and slamming his fist into his nose. The chair falls back, taking Evan with him and he hits the floor with a thud but he just keeps laughing. Storm turns back to all of us and shakes his head.

"Fucking demented," he whispers and I nod. This isn't news to me since I've been dealing with Evan for weeks now but this is a whole new level. He has nothing left to lose now and it shows every time he cackles with joy at our frustration.

"Look, if we're going to end this, then let's just fucking end it."

"Oh, boys," Evan calls and we all glance back at him as he lies on the floor, unable to move. "Maybe I'll give you a little hint."

Moose arches a brow. "Yeah? And what's that?"

"I had a part in everything. For the last two years, everything that happened in your lives was controlled by me!" he yells followed by maniacal laughter and we all turn back to face each other with wide eyes.

"We think he's telling the truth."

I shrug. "Who knows? That's the whole point. He's playing a game and fucking loving every second of it. He's never going to tell us the truth."

A scuffle pulls my attention back to Evan and I glance up just in time to see him stand up, the arms of the chair still taped to his arms as he punches Henn, knocking him to the floor. Once Henn is down, he grabs his gun off of the floor and points it at Storm. I react before I even realize what I'm doing, whipping my gun out of the waistband of my jeans and leveling it at Evan, pulling the trigger. His gun goes off, too, as he falls backward, his body hitting the floor with a thud that makes my stomach churn as my breath rings in my ears. I look down at the pistol in my hand.

Oh, fuck.

What the hell did I do?

"Motherfucker," Storm hisses and I glance over at him as he clutches his shoulder and my eyes widen when I see the blood oozing through his fingers. He grits his teeth. "Stupid asshole fucking shot me."

"He's dead," Smith calls, kicking the gun from Evan's hand as he turns and meets my eyes. There is a sour taste in my mouth as I try to swallow past the lump in my throat, my mind swimming. My hands tremble as crime scene photos I've never been able to erase from my memory flash through my mind and my chest aches.

Goddamn it.

I've spent years trying to make things right and make sure I never turned into that monster and I just threw it all away with one bullet and now, I'm just like him…

Kodiak steps up in front of me and grabs my shoulder, shaking me until I meet his eyes. "You had to do it, brother. He was going to kill Storm."

"Yeah," I whisper as I nod, my entire body numb and my mind blank.

"Get him out of here," Storm says through clenched teeth. "And someone clean this shit up. We don't need this coming back on us."

Henn, Smith, Fuzz, and Chance nod in unison as Kodiak grabs my shoulder and leads me out of the barn with Storm and Moose on our heels.

"Someone want to take me to the fucking hospital?" he asks, looking a little pale as he holds his hand firm against his shoulder and Kodiak nods.

"Yeah, ride with us." At the mention of the hospital, my attention shifts back to Rowan and I suck in a breath, every other thought fleeing from my mind as I hand my gun off to Moose. All of this shit, all of the baggage I clearly need to sort through can wait for later. The most important thing is getting back to my girl.

Chapter Thirty-Seven
Rowan

"Hey, Princess," a voice whispers, a voice that reaches into my very soul and pulls me from the darkness and I can't help but smile. I don't know how heaven has the man I love but my heart squeezes at the fact that he's here with me. Someone grabs my hand and my eyes fly open, blinking up at the white ceiling tiles and bright florescent lights above me. My brow furrows and my mind spins.

Where am I?

Pressure on my hand pulls my attention to my left and I suck in a breath, unable to stop my smile as I meet Travis's green eyes. I pull my hand from his and reach up, trailing my fingers over his cheek as he flashes me a relieved smile.

"There you are."

"You're here," I whisper and he nods, grabbing my hand again before bringing it to his lips.

"Of course I'm here, baby. Where else would I be?"

I glance at my hand and notice the tube snaking up my arm. I follow it up to an IV stand behind me and a monitor that shows the steady rhythm of my heartbeat. Turning back to him, I scowl. "Where am I?"

"In the hospital," he answers with a grimace, kissing my hand again. "You lost a lot of blood and you needed surgery to fix your arm."

"My arm?" I whisper, my scowl deepening before I glance down at the bed with a gasp. My eyes widen at the large cast wrapped around my entire arm, all the way to my shoulder and the memories come rushing back – the fire, the gunshots, running through the forest, Evan catching me, and Evan stabbing me. I gently touch my belly as I turn to Travis.

"Evan…"

He nods, running a hand through his hair as he presses his lips together into a thin line and reaches up to rub the back of his neck. I watch him, the hair on my arms standing on end as a wave of unease washes over me.

"What is going on?"

Sucking in a breath, he meets my gaze again. "Evan is dead."

"How?" I whisper as a chill seeps into my bones and Travis sucks in a breath again, his knee bouncing like crazy.

"I killed him…"

I gasp.

"Rodriguez caught him after he left you in the forest and we took him to Kodiak's property in the country. We were deciding on what to do with him when he got free and went after Storm. I didn't have a choice…"

My mind drifts back to my time in the woods with Evan and I nod as I turn back to him. "Okay."

"Are you upset?"

"Travis," I scoff. "The man literally tortured me in the woods so no, I'm not upset… but are you okay?"

He sighs, telling me all I need to know and I pull on his hand, urging him to climb into the bed with me. Glancing up, he shakes his head.

"I don't want to hurt you."

"You're hurting me by being all the way over there," I tell him and he studies me for a second before sighing and climbing into bed with me. He gently maneuvers around all of the wires and tubes all around me as he pulls me into his arms and buries his nose in my hair.

"What else is going on, Travis? I can tell that something is bothering you."

"We, uh…" he whispers, laying his head back against the bed. "We have a lot to talk about, baby."

I remember telling him I love him before I passed out and my stomach drops as I nod. "Right."

This is it.

This is the moment that he ends things and I'm trapped in a hospital bed.

"Um… about what I said… we can just pretend I didn't… I mean, I know this… between us… is casual and…"

He sits up, cutting off my words, and leans over me, pressing a soft, adoring kiss against my lips. I sigh, my eyes closing as I cup his cheek and lose myself in it. If this is going to be the last time, I want to savor every second of it. When he pulls back, he flashes me a smile but it doesn't reach his eyes.

"I love you, too, Rowan… even though I shouldn't."

I balk. "What do you mean you shouldn't?"

"Listen," he sighs, lying back in the bed as his body tenses and he cups my cheek like it brings him some level of comfort. "I haven't been completely honest with you… about me… and I'm not good for you, Row. You deserve so much better than what I can give you."

"What in the hell are you talking about?"

He sighs. "It's kind of a long story…"

"Then start at the beginning," I snap as my mind races and my heart thunders in my chest.

What is happening right now?

Is he breaking up with me?

Does he really love me?

"Okay… the beginning… I guess the beginning is when I was born."

My eyes widen but I don't dare say a word, silently encouraging him to keep talking. His hand shakes against my face and I grip it with my hand, holding him steady. He takes another deep breath.

"My dad… he was never what you would call warm and honestly, he never really even gave me the time of day but I never knew any different so it wasn't that big of a deal."

I open my mouth but he looks down at me and shakes his head.

"Just let me get this out before you ask anything, okay?"

"Okay," I whisper.

"When I was fifteen, my mom picked me up from school one day and all of our shit was in the back seat. She said we were leaving my dad and I didn't ask any questions, you know? I guess I didn't really care because he and I never really had a relationship. Anyway, we got a little apartment in the next town over and we went on living our lives. When I turned eighteen, I wanted answers from my dad about why he was the way he was so I drove over to the house. He wasn't there but I was determined to have it out with him so I sat in my car for hours, waiting for him to return but when he did..." His voice breaks and I glance up at him, my chest aching at the pain all over his face.

"What, Travis?"

He shudders. "When he came back, I watched him pull a woman's body out of the trunk of his car. I was so fucking horrified that I couldn't move and I just sat there, watching him, as he took her into the garage and closed the door."

My chest feels tight as his story plays out in my mind and I look up at him, the man I love with every single cell in my body and a tear streaks down my cheek. He glances down at me and his face crumples as he wipes it away and presses his lips to my forehead.

"I was already pretty good at all of the computer stuff back then," he says, holding me tighter as he continues. "So I started a full-blown investigation into my father and the things I saw... the things he has done... they still haunt me to this day, baby."

I tip my head back and press my hand to his cheek, pulling his gaze down to me. "Tell me."

"I... can't. I've never fucking told anyone about this except the police and you... you are my shelter from all of this shit. I can't put this in your head."

I nod in understanding. "Then tell me what happened next."

"It was all an incredibly slow process but over the next year, I managed to collect enough evidence of his crimes to go to the police. I showed them everything I had, everything that proved my father had started killing women who looked just like my mother two months after she left him, and then I waited for them to make their move and arrest him."

"And did they?" I ask, my stomach churning and he nods.

"Yeah, they did… but not before he came after his true target – my mother."

I gasp, more tears falling down my cheeks. "He killed your mom?"

"Yes," he whispers, his voice barely audible as he nods his head before burying it in my hair again and my heart cracks wide open, breaking for him as I cling to his body, wishing I could provide him with something more.

"Oh, baby… I'm so sorry." I try to move but the stupid arm cast gets in my way and I cry out as pain shoots through my shoulder. Travis's head jerks up, his red rimmed eyes meeting mine and he leans down, claiming my lips in a kiss that screams of his pain. When he pulls back and presses our foreheads together, I close my eyes and release a breath.

"What does all of this have to do with us, though? Why do you think you shouldn't love me?"

He rolls his forehead across mine and tension fills the air as I hold my breath, waiting for him to answer me. I honestly can't see any reason why this would change anything between us but I know this is his issue.

"I used to think I was in danger of becoming just like my dad, you know? Like one day I would just snap and start hurting people but my dad, he enjoyed what he did, and if the way I feel now after killing Evan is any indication, I'm not the same as him."

I jerk back, meeting his gaze as I narrow my eyes. "Of course you're not like him, Travis..."

"I agree but that doesn't mean I'm not still damaged goods, baby. I've seen truly awful shit that would send most people into a corner to rock back and forth and I'm a moody fucking bastard sometimes and I lash out. I'm not the kind of man you deserve."

"I don't give a shit," I seethe, shaking my head as I smack my hand over his heart. "I love you, Travis. All of you, every single piece – moody bastard or not. You've stolen my heart completely and I don't want anyone else. Just you."

His brow furrows. "How can you say that? Knowing who I am, where I come from?"

"Who you are? Travis, that's what made me fall in love with you. You try to hide it but you're so incredibly kind and sweet, you stand up for what is right and people who cannot stand on their own, you make me laugh every single day and you're the one person I want to see when I'm happy, sad, angry, scared, annoyed... how can you think that what you've just told me changes any of that? If anything, I love you more now."

"What?" he whispers, searching my eyes for any dishonesty but he won't find it. This man lying in bed next to me is everything I want and more and there is no way his past is ever going to change any of that. The wariness flashing through his gaze kills me and I press my hand to his cheek again, dragging him down to me until his lips press to mine. He sighs and pulls me closer while being careful not to hurt me as the tension slowly seeps out of his body. When he pulls back, he beams at me, his eyes brighter and clear for the first time in weeks. "You really love me, huh?"

I nod as I laugh. "I really do."

"Fuck me." His voice is full of wonder as he falls back onto the bed and I laugh again, cuddling into his side. He presses a kiss against the top of my head and I close my eyes, reveling in the feeling of peace surrounding us. "So... what now?"

"Huh?"

He props himself up on his elbow and meets my gaze, wiggling his eyebrows. "Well, you love me and I love you so based on my vast experience in this area and what I've witnessed around the clubhouse, I suppose we have to get married now."

"Uh, hold up." I giggle, shaking my head at his playful expression. "I think we start with a nice, normal date. Remember, like we talked about?"

Nodding, he leans down and steals a quick kiss. "Yeah, I remember, Princess, and it sounds like the best fucking thing I've ever heard."

A.M. Myers

Epilogue
One Year Later
Rowan

Pulling the Impala into a parking space outside of our apartment, I put the car in park and sigh, smiling to myself as I reach over into the passenger seat and grab the white gift box I picked up on the way home. My stomach flips as I run my fingers along the blue ribbon wrapped around it, wondering how Travis will react when he sees what's inside. I glance up at our apartment, the one we moved into almost eleven months ago, and I can't help but think about everything that has happened in the past year and how far he and I have come.

After I was released from the hospital, Travis and I spent two days locked in his room as he told me as much as he was willing to share about his dad and my heart still aches when I think about the look on his face as he told me about the twenty-three women his father murdered before he was arrested and sent to jail – including his mother. He shared with me that he was the one who found her body in their apartment after he had spent two days digging through crime scene photos of his father's other victims and how he couldn't believe it was real until he watched them zip her up in the black body bag. After that, I wanted to know more and did my own little internet search into Samson Hornback and the things I read will be burned into my mind forever. Tears sting my eyes and my chest aches. Honestly, Travis been through so damn much and I wish, more than anything, that I could take all of his pain away but I know that I can't. I just hope that I help in some way, that I make the hard times a little bit easier.

Leaning my head back against the seat, I sigh as my mind drifts to Evan. As much as I hate to admit it, he still plays a big part in our relationship and we still feel the impacts of his actions in our lives. After Travis killed him, Jake and Caleb were arrested and charged as accomplices in all of Evan's crimes and the brothers spilled their guts as soon as they got the chance. Apparently, as soon as Evan was released from prison, he came to them and told them of his plan to get revenge against the club but they didn't know how far he intended to go until it was too late and they were already in it. They told the police that Evan had a hand in messing with every single guy in one way or another. For some, all it took was a little suggestion and nudging and in other cases, he played a bigger part but they didn't know all of the details. I think it's still something that haunts Travis but he's trying to let it go. We both also struggle with the night Evan almost killed me and we've had to fight to get where we are now but I can honestly say that Travis is the love of my life and my best friend in the whole entire world so he makes every ounce of struggle worth it.

Glancing up at the apartment, I grin. He and I really did try to take things slow and be a "normal" couple for about three weeks before it became clear that we couldn't stand to be away from each other and we started looking for an apartment. It only took us a little over a week to find this place downtown and we both fell in love with it the moment the landlord told us about the private roof access that was included. We've spent so many nights up there, talking, loving, and looking up at the stars. I smile as I touch the star pendant Travis gave me Christmas Eve as my belly flips again as I think about the news I have to share with him. There is no way to know how he will take it but I'm confident that together, he and I can withstand any obstacle.

I turn off the car and open the door, stepping out with the box in my hand. His bike is parked next to me and I take a deep breath as I press my shaking hand to the top of the box. My mind races as I walk up the stairs to our door, going over in my head how I should start this conversation and what I should say but nothing sounds quite right. When I reach the front door, my steps falter and Travis flashes me a grin. He's standing in front of our door in a black button up shirt and jeans, a red rose in his hand, and his green eyes are staring straight into my soul like they always do.

"Hey, Princess."

My belly flips again and I smile. "Hi, baby. What's this?"

"I have a surprise for you," he answers, closing the distance between us and handing me the rose. My smile grows as I bring it to my nose and breathe in its rich scent, my eyes locked on his. God, I love him.

"What is it?"

He cocks his head to the side and flashes me a look full of challenge. "It wouldn't be much of a fucking surprise if I told you, would it?"

"Fine," I reply, arching a brow. "Where is it then?"

"You have to put this on first." He holds up a blindfold and my eyes widen before I slowly nod.

"Okay."

He grabs for my bag and the box in my hand. "Let me set those inside for you."

"Uh, not the box," I snap, my voice going up an octave as I jerk the box out of his reach. He cocks a brow and I swallow, forcing a smile to my face as I hand him my bag. "It's a present for you."

With a nod, he grabs my bag and turns back to the apartment, trying to hide the shy smile on his face but he can't hide anything from me. And I'm glad because that smile, the one when I catch him off guard and make him feel butterflies that he'll never admit to, is my absolute favorite. Once my bag is securely in the apartment, he walks behind me and presses a kiss to my neck as he ties the blindfold around my eyes.

"Can you see anything?"

I shake my head. "Nope. Total darkness."

"Perfect," he answers, taking my hand in his and lacing our fingers together. "Come with me."

He starts leading me somewhere and I try to visualize where we're going in my mind but after a moment, I realize he's leading me in circles so I can't figure out what he's up to and I sigh. I swear, I can feel his triumphant smile.

"Where the hell are we going, Travis?" I ask, squinting into the blindfold as he drags me along behind him but I can't see anything. His laughter floats through the air and a wave of warmth rushes over me. Despite our struggles in the year since Evan attacked the club, I have seen a total change in my man. The weight he has been carrying for most of his life is not gone but it seems to get lighter each and every day we spend together and when he smiles now, it reaches his eyes. It's truly a breathtaking sight and my love for him back then pales in comparison to the way I feel about him now. Travis is my forever, my one true love, and I know it with every fiber of my being.

"Can't you ever be patient, Princess?"

I arch a brow and turn to him as he falls back to walk next to me. "I can't believe you even have to ask that question. Do you know me at all?"

He laughs and the next thing I know, I'm being lifted into the air as I shriek and cling to him as I hold the box in my other hand. It only makes him laugh harder as he hooks one arm under my knees and the other under my back as he begins walking again.

"I love you," he whispers, his voice full of happiness as he presses a kiss to my forehead and I cuddle into him as my chest expands. I love this man so damn much that it's a wonder my heart doesn't just burst out of my chest sometimes but as my mind drifts back to the news I have to share with him today, my stomach churns.

"Are we almost there yet?" I ask, desperate to focus on something else as I hear a door open and we step outside into the cool night air. Where in the hell is he taking me? His lips press against my cheek and I close my eyes as chills blanket my skin and my heart jumps in my chest. He gently sets me back down on my feet and moves behind me, placing his hands on my shoulders.

"Ready?" he whispers, dragging his fingertips down my arms and I fight back a moan as I lean into him and nod, releasing a heavy breath.

"Yes."

He unties my blindfold and pulls it away from my eyes. My vision blurs as it adjusts and I blink a few times before drinking in the scene in front of me. We're on the roof of our apartment and he has a little round table set up in the middle with two chairs. There are candles all over the roof, casting a warm glow around us and I drop my head back, smiling at the stars twinkling down at us before I turn and wrap my arm around his neck.

"What is all of this for?"

He grins. "For you, Princess."

"Right," I muse, glancing back at the incredibly romantic setting before turning back to him. "But why?"

"Can't I just spoil you?"

Narrowing my eyes, I turn to the table and he grabs my hand lacing our fingers again as I peek up at him. "I'm suspicious, Broussard."

"I know," he answers, laughing as he guides me over to the table and pulls out one of the chairs for me. I sit down and set the box on the ground next to me as he sits across from me and points to it.

"When do I get to open that?"

My stomach churns. "Now. I suppose."

I hand him the box, my hand shaking like crazy and my stomach now doing somersaults inside me as my heart races. With a grin, he takes the box and pulls off the ribbon like an over eager little kid on Christmas morning and I can't help but smile despite my nerves. Pulling the lid off, he tosses it aside and peels back the tissue paper before flicking a confused glance up at me. My teeth sink into my lower lip as I wait for him to get it.

He yanks the tiny little leather jacket out of the box and holds it up in the air.

"Rowan, what the hell am I supposed to do with this?"

"Well," I start, clamping my hands together to keep them from shaking. "Right now, nothing. But in a year or so, you could put it on the baby."

His gaze snaps to mine. "What? What fucking baby?"

"Our baby," I whisper, pressing my hand to my belly and he stares at me, his eyes wide, as he drops the jacket onto the table and blows out a breath. Running his fingers through his hair, he shakes his head.

"Fuck... How..."

"You are not about to ask me how this happened, are you?"

He shakes his head and runs his fingers through his hair again. "Right... Shit... I..."

"I know this is a shock but we've got this, babe," I assure him, reaching across the table and grabbing his hand. He stares down at the jacket, his face pale.

"I'm gonna be a dad... Fuck, babe... I don't know how to be someone's fucking dad... I mean, look at the example I had... I'm gonna fuck this kid up so much... he deserves better...and so do you..."

Shaking my head, I stand up and walk over to him before sitting on his lap and grabbing his face, forcing his gaze to me. "Look at me, Travis. I do not ever want to hear you say something like that again, you understand? You are incredible and I love you so damn much."

"I don't know how to do this," he whispers, his eyes shining with unshed tears and my heart breaks.

447

Leaning down, I press my lips to his and kiss him until I feel his body relax slightly underneath me. When I pull back, I meet his gaze.

"No one knows how to be a parent, Travis. You think I've got everything figured out? Hell no. But, I love you and I love this baby and together, I know we can figure this out."

He shakes his head. "My dad…"

"Is not a factor in this," I snap, cutting him off. "You are not your father, Travis. We've had this conversation so many times and I know you struggle with it but I need you to really hear me this time. You are so incredibly kind and brave and you stand up for what's right and the people you love. When I'm down, you lift me up and all it takes is just being in your presence to feel your warmth. Does that sound like your fucked up father?"

"No."

I nod. "No, it sure as hell doesn't. You are your own man and I have no doubt that you are going to be an amazing father to our baby."

Sucking in a breath, his gaze drops down to my stomach and he stares at it for a second before reaching forward and pressing his hand over my belly button. So many emotions flicker through his eyes but finally, I see a sliver of happiness and I release a sigh as he meets my eyes and smiles.

"You believe in fate, Princess?"

I nod. "You know I do. Why?"

"Because," he answers as he reaches into his pocket and pulls out a pear shaped diamond ring with an interwoven band as he meets my eyes again. "I brought you up here tonight to ask you to marry me, to tell you that I never thought I would find someone that understood me the way you do and accepted all my flaws and quirks but as soon as you walked through the door, I was a goddamn goner. I was going to tell you that I can't imagine spending a single day of my life without you and that marrying you would make me the happiest fucking man to ever walk the earth and then you drop this little bomb on me and it seems like fate is at work, once again, that on the night I was going to ask you to be my wife, you tell me that we're going to be a family."

"Travis," I whisper, tears building in my eyes as I stare down at him, my heart thumping wildly in my chest.

"I fucking love you, Rowan, and it's still so crazy to hear myself say that because I never thought I would utter those words, never thought I would have all of this but I need you to know that I'm grateful each and every fucking day for it. I've always known that you deserve the fucking world but I didn't think I was the guy to give it to you. Hell, maybe I'm still not but I'm willing to spend every day working my ass off to try to be... if you'll have me..."

I nod as tears drip down my cheeks because I've never been more sure of anything else in my entire life. "Always."

Wicked Games

Want to stay up to date on A.M. Myers and all things Bayou Devils MC?

Sign up for my newsletter

https://landing.mailerlite.com/webforms/landing/h6m2q7

Or

Join my reader group

https://www.facebook.com/groups/585884704893900/

Wicked Games

Other Books by A.M. Myers

The Hidden Scars Series

Hidden Scars:
https://www.amazon.com/dp/B014B6KFJE

Collateral Damage:
https://www.amazon.com/gp/product/B01G9FOS20

Evading Fate:
https://www.amazon.com/gp/product/B01L0GKMU0

Bayou Devils MC Series

Hopelessly Devoted:
https://www.amazon.com/dp/B01MY5XQFW

Addicted To Love:
https://www.amazon.com/dp/B07B6RPPPV

Every Breath You Take:
https://www.amazon.com/dp/B07DPNTV2G

It Ends Tonight:
https://www.amazon.com/dp/B07JL4FJ18

Wicked Games

Little Do You Know:
https://www.amazon.com/dp/B07M812N1T

Never Let Me Go:
https://www.amazon.com/dp/B07NWWN2VJ

Every Little Thing:
https://www.amazon.com/dp/B07XFGC82J

Wicked Games:
https://www.amazon.com/dp/B07YL8NFQR

About the Author

A.M. Myers lives in Cody, Wyoming – a little town about an hour away from Yellowstone National Park – with her husband and their two boys. She has been writing for most of her life and even had a poem nationally published in the sixth grade but the idea of writing an entire book always seemed so daunting until a certain story got stuck in her head and wouldn't leave her alone until she started typing. Now, she can't imagine a time when she won't be letting all of the stories in her head spill out onto paper.

A.M. Myers writes emotional, gripping romantic suspense novels that will leave you swooning and hanging off the edge of your seat from start until finish. When she is not writing, you can usually find her up in the mountains with her boys, camping, fishing and taking photos of the beautiful landscape she is lucky enough to call home.

Wicked Games

Made in United States
Orlando, FL
17 June 2023

34235112R10250